MARE NOSTRUM
(*OUR SEA*)

A Novel

BY

VICENTE BLASCO IBAÑEZ

AUTHOR OF "THE FOUR HORSEMEN OF THE APOCALYPSE,"
"THE SHADOW OF THE CATHEDRAL," "BLOOD
AND SAND," "LA BODEGA," ETC.

AUTHORIZED TRANSLATION FROM THE SPANISH BY

CHARLOTTE BREWSTER JORDAN
TRANSLATOR OF "THE FOUR HORSEMEN OF THE APOCALYPSE"

NEW YORK
E. P. DUTTON & COMPANY
681 FIFTH AVENUE

CONTENTS

MARE NOSTRUM

MARE NOSTRUM

CHAPTER I

HIS first gallantries were with an empress. He was ten years old, and the empress six hundred.

His father, Don Esteban Ferragut—third quota of the College of Notaries—had always had a great admiration for the things of the past. He lived near the cathedral, and on Sundays and holy days, instead of following the faithful to witness the pompous ceremonials presided over by the cardinal-archbishop, used to betake himself with his wife and son to hear mass in *San Juan del Hospital,*—a little church sparsely attended the rest of the week.

The notary, who had read Walter Scott in his youth, used to gaze on the old and turreted walls surrounding the church, and feel something of the bard's thrills about his own, his native land. The Middle Ages was the period in which he would have liked to have lived. And as he trod the flagging of *the Hospitalarios,* good Don Esteban, little, chubby, and near-sighted, used to feel within him the soul of a hero born too late. The other churches, huge and rich, appeared to him with their blaze of gleaming gold, their alabaster convolutions and their jasper columns, mere monuments of insipid vulgarity. This one had been erected by the Knights of

I

Saint John, who, united with the Templars, had aided King James in the conquest of Valencia.

Upon crossing the covered passageway leading from the street to the inner court, he was accustomed to salute the Virgin of the Conquest, an image of rough stone in faded colors and dull gold, seated on a bench, brought thither by the knights of the military order. Some sour orange trees spread their branching verdure over the walls of the church,—a blackened, rough stone edifice perforated with long, narrow, window-like niches now closed with mud plaster. From the salient buttresses of its reinforcements jutted forth, in the highest parts, great fabled monsters of weather-beaten, crumbling stone.

In its only nave was now left very little of this romantic exterior. The baroque taste of the seventeenth century had hidden the Gothic arch under another semi-circular one, besides covering the walls with a coat of whitewash. But the medieval reredos, the nobiliary coats of arms, and the tombs of the Knights of Saint John with their Gothic inscriptions still survived the profane restoration, and that in itself was enough to keep up the notary's enthusiasm.

Moreover the quality of the faithful who attended its services had to be taken into consideration. They were few but select, always the same. Some of them would drop into their places, gouty and relaxed, supported by an old servant wearing a shabby lace mantilla as though she were the housekeeper. Others would remain standing during the service holding up proudly their emaciated heads that presented the profile of a fighting cock, and crossing upon the breast their gloved hands,—always in black wool in the winter and in thread in the summer time. Ferragut knew all their names, having read them in the *Trovas* of Mosen Febrer, a metrical composition in Provençal, about the warriors that came to the neighborhood of Valencia from Aragon, Catalunia, the South of France, England and remote Germany.

At the conclusion of the mass, the imposing personages would nod their heads, saluting the faithful nearest them. "Good day!" To these, it was as if the sun had just arisen: the hours before did not count. And the notary with meek voice would enlarge his response: "Good day, Señor Marquis!" "Good day, Señor Baron!" Although his relations never went beyond this salutation, Ferragut used to feel toward these noble personages the sympathy that the customers have for an establishment, looking upon them with affectionate eyes for many years without presuming to exchange more than a greeting with them.

His son Ulysses was exceedingly bored as he followed the monotonous incidents of the chanted mass in the darkened, almost deserted, church. The rays of the sun, oblique beams of gold that filtered in from above, illuminating the spirals of dust, flies and moths, made him think in a homesick way of the lush green of the orchard, the white spots of the hamlets, the black smoke columns of the harbor filled with steamships, and the triple file of bluish convexities crowned with froth that were discharging their contents with a sonorous surge upon the bronze-colored beach.

When the embroidered mantles of the three priests ceased to gleam before the high altar, and another priest in black and white appeared in the pulpit, Ulysses would turn his glance toward a side chapel. The sermon always represented for him a half hour of somnolence, peopled with his own lively imaginings. The first thing that his eyes used to see in the chapel of Santa Barbara was a chest nailed to the wall high above him, a sepulcher of painted wood with no other adornment than the inscription: *"Aqui yace Doña Constanza Augusta, Emperatriz de Grecia,"*—Here lies Constance Augusta, Empress of Greece.

The name of Greece always had the power of exciting the little fellow's imagination. His godfather, the lawyer Labarta, poet-laureate, could not repeat this name without a lively thrill passing across his grizzled beard and a new light in his eyes. Sometimes the mysterious power of such a name evoked a new mystery and a more intense interest,—Byzantium. How could that august lady, sovereign of remote countries of magnificence and vision, have come to leave her remains in a murky chapel of Valencia within a great chest like those that treasured the remnants of old trumpery in the garrets of the notary? . . .

One day after mass Don Esteban had rapidly recounted her history to his little son. She was the daughter of Frederick the Second of Suabia, a Hohenstaufen, an emperor of Germany who esteemed still more his crown of Sicily. In the palaces of Palermo,—veritable enchanted bowers of Oriental gardens,—he had led the life both of pagan and savant, surrounded by poets and men of science (Jews, Mahometans and Christians), by Oriental dancers, alchemists, and ferocious Saracen Guards. He legislated as did the jurisconsults of ancient Rome, at the same time writing the first verses in Italian. His life was one continual combat with the Popes who hurled upon him excommunication upon excommunication. For the sake of peace he had become a crusader and set forth upon the conquest of Jerusalem. But Saladin, another philosopher of the same class, had soon come to an agreement with his Christian colleague. The position of a little city surrounded with untilled land and an empty sepulcher was really not worth the trouble of decapitating mankind through the centuries. The Saracen monarch, therefore, graciously delivered Jerusalem over to him, and the Pope again excommunicated Frederick for having conquered the Holy Land without bloodshed.

"He was a great man," Don Esteban used to murmur. "It must be admitted that he was a great man. . . ."

He would say this timidly, regretting that his enthusiasm for that remote epoch should oblige him to make this concession to an enemy of the Church. He shuddered to think of those sacrilegious books that nobody had seen, but whose paternity Rome was accustomed to attribute to this Sicilian Emperor—especially *Los Tres Impostores* (The Three Imposters), in which Frederick measured Moses, Jesus and Mahomet, by the same standard. This royal author was, moreover, the most ancient journalist of history, the first that in the full thirteenth century had dared to appeal to the judgment of public opinion in his manifestoes against Rome.

His daughter had married an Emperor of Byzantium, Juan Dukas Vatatzés, the famous "Vatacio," when he was fifty and she fourteen. She was a natural daughter soon legitimized like almost all his progeny,—a product of his free harem, in which were mingled Saracen beauties and Italian marchionesses. And the poor young girl married to "Vatacio the heretic," by a father in need of political alliances had lived long years in the Orient as a *basilisa* or empress, arrayed in garments of stiff embroidery representing scenes from the holy books, shod with buskins laced with purple which bore on their soles eagles of gold, —the highest symbol of the majesty of Rome.

At first she had reigned in Nicæa, refuge of the Greek Emperors while Constantinople was in the power of the Crusaders, founders of a Latin dynasty; then, when Vatacio died, the audacious Miguel Paleólogo reconquered Constantinople, and the imperial widow found herself courted by this victorious adventurer. For many years she resisted his pretensions, finally manœuvering that her brother Manfred should return her to her own country, where she arrived just in time to receive news of her brother's death in battle, and to follow the flight of her sister-in-law and nephews. They all took refuge in a castle defended by Saracens in the service of Frederick, the only ones faithful to his memory.

The castle fell into the power of the warriors of the Church, and Manfred's wife was conducted to a prison where her life was shortly after extinguished. Obscurity swallowed up the last remnants of the family accursed by Rome. Death was always hovering around the *basilisa*. They all perished—her brother Manfred, her half-brother, the poetic and lamented Encio, hero of so many songs, and her nephew, the knightly Coradino, who was to die later on under the axe of the executioner upon attempting the defense of his rights. As the Oriental empress did not represent any danger for the dynasty of Anjou, the conquerer let her follow out her destiny, as lonely and forsaken as a Shakesperian Princess.

As the widow of the late Emperor she was supposed to have a rental of three thousand *besantes* of fine gold. But this remote rental never arrived, and almost as a pauper she embarked with her niece, Constanza, in a ship going toward the perfumed shores of the Gulf of Valencia, where she entered the convent of Santa Barbara. In the poverty of this recently founded convent, the poor Empress lived until the following century, recalling the adventures of her melancholy destiny and seeing in imagination the palace of golden mosaics on Lake Nicæa, the gardens where "Vatacio" had wished to die under a purple tent, the gigantic walls of Constantinople, and the arches of Saint Sophia, with its hieratic galaxies of saints and crowned monarchs.

From all her journeys and glittering fortunes she had preserved but one thing—a stone—the sole baggage that accompanied her upon disembarking on the shore of Valencia. It was a fragment from Nicodemia that had miraculously sent forth water for the baptism of Santa Barbara.

The notary used to point out this rough, sacred stone inlaid in a baptismal font of Holy Water. Without ceasing to admire these historic bits of knowledge, Ulysses, nevertheless, used to receive them with a certain ingratitude.

"My godfather could explain things to me in a better way. . . . My godfather knows more."

When surveying the chapel of Santa Barbara during the Mass, he used always to turn his eyes away from the funeral chest. The thought of those bones turned to dust filled him with repugnance. That Doña Constanza did not exist for him. The one who was interesting to him was the other one, a little further on who was painted in a small picture. Doña Constanza had had leprosy—an infirmity that in those days was not permitted to Empresses—so Santa Barbara had miraculously cured her devotee. In order to perpetuate this event, Santa Barbara was depicted on the canvas as a lady dressed in a full skirt and slashed sleeves, and at her feet was the *basilisa* in the dress of a Valencian peasant arrayed in great jewels. In vain Don Esteban affirmed that this picture had been painted centuries after the death of the Empress. The child's imagination vaulted disdainfully over such difficulties. Just as she appeared on the canvas, Doña Constanza must have been—flaxenhaired, with great black eyes, exceedingly handsome and a little inclined to stoutness, perhaps, as was becoming to a woman accustomed to trailing robes of state and who had consented to disguise herself as a country-woman, merely because of her piety.

The image of the Empress obsessed his childish thoughts. At night when he felt afraid in bed, impressed by the enormousness of the room that served as his sleeping chamber, it was enough for him to recall the sovereign of Byzantium to make him forget immediately his disquietude and the thousand queer noises in the old building. "Doña Constanza!" . . . And he would go off to sleep cuddling the pillow, as though it were the head of the *basilisa*, his closed eyes continuing to see the black eyes of the regal Señora, maternal and affectionate.

All womankind, on coming near him, took on something of that other one who had been sleeping for the past six centuries in the upper part of the chapel wall. When his mother, sweet and pallid Doña Cristina, would stop her fancy work for an instant to give him a kiss, he always saw in her smile something of the Empress. When Visenteta, a maid from the country—a brunette, with eyes like blackberries, rosy-cheeked and soft-skinned—would help him to undress, or awaken him to take him to school, Ulysses would always throw his arms around her as though enchanted by the perfume of her vigorous and chaste vitality. "Visenteta! . . . Oh, Visenteta! . . ." And he was thinking of Doña Constanza; Empresses must be just that fragrant. . . . Just like that must be the texture of their skin! . . . And mysterious and incomprehensible thrills would pass over his body like light exhalations, bubbling up from the slime that is sleeping in the depths of all infancy and coming to the surface during adolescence.

His father guessed in part this imaginary life upon seeing his pet plays and readings.

"Ah, comedian! . . . Ah, play-actor! . . . you are like your godfather."

He used to say this with an ambiguous smile in which were equally mingled his contempt for useless idealism and his respect for the artist—a respect similar to the veneration that the Arabs feel for the demented, believing their insanity to be a gift from God.

Doña Cristina was very anxious that this only son, as spoiled and coddled as though he were a Crown Prince, should become a priest. To see him intone his first Mass! . . . Then a canon; then a prelate! Who knew if perhaps when she was no longer living, other women might not admire him when preceded by a cross of gold, trailing the red state robe of a cardinal-archbishop, and surrounded by a robed staff—envying the mother who had given birth to this ecclesiastical magnate! . . .

In order to guide the inclinations of her son she had installed a chapel in one of the empty rooms of the great old house. Ulysses' school companions on free afternoons would hasten thither, doubly attracted by the enchantment of "playing priest" and by the generous refreshment that Doña Cristina used to prepare for all the parish clergy.

This solemnity would begin with the furious pealing of some bells hanging over the parlor door, causing the notary's clients, seated in the vestibule waiting for the papers that the clerks were just scribbling off at full speed, to raise their heads in astonishment. The metallic uproar rocked the edifice whose corners had seemed so full of silence, and even disturbed the calm of the street through which a carriage only occasionally passed.

While some of his chums were lighting the candles on the shrines and unfolding the sacred altar cloths of beautiful lace work made by Doña Cristina, the son and his more intimate friends were arraying themselves before

the faithful, covering themselves with surplices and gold-
worked vestments and putting wonderful caps on their
heads. The mother, who was peeping from behind one
of the doors, had to make a great effort not to rush in
and devour Ulysses with kisses. With what grace he was
imitating the mannerisms and genuflections of the chief
priest! . . .

Up to this point all went perfectly. The three officiat-
ing near the pyramid of lights were singing at the top of
their lungs, and the chorus of the faithful were responding from the end of the room with tremors of impatience.
Suddenly surged forth Protest, Schism and Heresy.
Those at the altar had already done more than enough.
They must now give up their chasubles to those who were
looking on in order that they, in their turn, might exercise the sacred ministry. That was what they had agreed
upon. But the clergy resisted with the haughtiness and
majesty of acquired right, and impious hands began pulling off the garb of the saints, profaning them and even
tearing them. Yells, kicks, images and wax candles on
the floor! . . . Scandal and abominations as though the
Anti-Christ were already born! . . . The prudence of
Ulysses put an end to the struggle: "What if we should
go up in the *pòrche* to play? . . ."

The *pòrche* was the immense garret of the great old
house, so all accepted the plan with enthusiasm. Church
was over! And like a flock of birds they went flying up
the stairs over the landings of multi-colored tiles with
their chipped glaze, disclosing the red brick underneath.
The Valencian potters of the eighteenth century had
adorned these tiles with Berber and Christian galleys,
birds from nearby Albufera, white-wigged hunters offering flowers to a peasant girl, fruits of all kinds, and spir-
ited horsemen on steeds that were half the size of their

bodies parading before houses and trees that scarcely reached to the knees of their prancing coursers.

The noisy group spread themselves over the upper floor as in the most terrible invasions of history. Cats and mice fled together to the far-away corners. The terrified birds sped like arrows through the skylights of the roof.

The poor notary! . . . He had never returned empty-handed when called outside of the city by the confidence of the rich farmers, incapable of believing in any other legal science than his. That was the time when the antique dealers had not yet discovered rich Valencia, where the common people dressed in silks for centuries, and furniture, clothing and pottery seemed always to be impregnated with the light of steady sunshine and with the blue of an always clear atmosphere.

Don Esteban, who believed himself obliged to be an antiquarian by virtue of his membership in various local societies, was continually filling up his house with mementoes of the past picked up in the villages, or that his clients freely gave him. He was not able to find wall space enough for the pictures, nor room in his salons for the furniture. Therefore, the latest acquisitions were provisionally taking their way to the *pòrche* to await definite installation. Years afterward, when he should retire from his profession, he might be able to construct a medieval castle—the most medieval possible on the coasts of the *Marina;* near to the village where he had been born, he would put each object in a place appropriate to its importance.

Whatever the notary deposited in the rooms of the first floor would soon make its appearance in the garret as mysteriously as though it had acquired feet; for Doña Cristina and her servants, obliged to live in a continual struggle with the dust and cobwebs of an edifice that was

slowly dropping to pieces, were beginning to feel a ferocious hatred of everything old.

Up here on the top floor, discords and battles because
of lack of things to dress up in, were not possible among
the boys. They had only to sink their hands into any
one of the great old chests, pulsing with the dull gnawing
of the wood-borers, whose iron fretwork, pierced like
lace, was dropping away from its supports. Some of the
youngsters, brandishing short, small swords with hilts of
mother-of-pearl, or long blades such as the Cid carried,
would then wrap themselves in mantles of crimson silk
darkened by ages. Others would throw over their shoulders damask counterpanes of priceless old brocade, peasant skirts with great flowers of gold, farthingales of rich-
ly woven texture that crackled like paper.

When they grew tired of imitating comedians with
noisy clashing of spades and death-blows, Ulysses and
the other active lads would propose the game of "Bandits
and Bailiffs." But thieves could not go clad in such rich
cloths; their attire ought to be inconspicuous. And so
they overturned some mountains of dull-colored stuffs
that appeared like mere sacking in whose dull woven
designs could be dimly discerned legs, arms, heads, and
branching sprays of metallic green.

Don Esteban had found these fragments already torn
by the farmers into covers for their large earthen jars of
oil or into blankets for the work-mules. They were bits
of tapestry copied from cartoons óf Titian and Rubens
which the notary was keeping only out of historic respect. Tapestry then, like all things that are plentiful,
had no special merit. The old-clothes dealers of Valencia
had in their storehouses dozens of the same kind of remnants and when the festival of *Corpus Christi* approached they used them to cover the natural barricades

formed by the ground, instead of building new ones in the street followed by the processions.

At other times, Ulysses repeated the same game under the name of "Indians and Conquerors." He had found in the mountains of books stored away by his father, a volume that related in double columns, with abundant wood cuts, the navigations of Columbus, the wars of Hernando Cortez, and the exploits of Pizarro.

This book cast a glamor over the rest of his existence. Many times afterwards, when a man, he found this image latent in the background of his likes and desires. He really had read few of its paragraphs, but what interested him most were the engravings—in his estimation more worthy of admiration than all the pictures in the garret.

With the point of his long sword he would trace on the ground, just as Pizarro had done before his discouraged companions, ready on the Island of Gallo to desist from the conquest: "Let every good Castilian pass this line. . . ." And the good Castilians—a dozen little scamps with long capes and ancient swords whose hilts reached up to their mouths—would hasten to group themselves around their chief, who was imitating the heroic gestures of the conqueror. Then was heard the war-cry: "At them! Down with the Indians!"

It was agreed that the Indians should flee and on that account they were modestly clad in scraps of tapestry and cock feathers on their head. But they fled treacherously, and upon finding themselves upon *vargueños,* tables and pyramids of chairs, they began to shy books at their persecutors. Venerable leather volumes decorated with dull gold, and folios of white parchment fell face downward on the floor, their fastenings breaking apart and spreading abroad a rain of printed or manuscript pages and yellowing engravings—as though tired of living, they were letting their life-blood flow from their bodies.

The uproar of these wars of conquest brought Doña Cristina to the rescue. She no longer cared to harbor little imps who preferred the adventurous whoops of the garret to the mystic delights of the abandoned chapel. The Indians were most worthy of execration. In order to make splendor of attire counterbalance the humility of their rôle, they had slashed their sinful scissors into entire tapestries, mutilating vestments so as to arrange upon their breasts the head of a hero or goddess.

Finding himself without playfellows, Ulysses discovered a new enchantment in the garret life. The silence haunted by the creaking of wood and the scampering of invisible animals, the inexplicable fall of a picture or of some piled-up books, used to make him thrill with a sensation of fear and nocturnal mystery, despite the rays of sunlight that came filtering in through the skylights; but he began to enjoy this solitude when he found that he could people it to his fancy. Real beings soon annoyed him like the inopportune sounds that sometimes awoke him from beautiful dreams. The garret was a world several centuries old that now belonged entirely to him and adjusted itself to all his fancies.

Seated in a trunk without a lid, he made it balance itself, imitating with his mouth the roarings of the tempest. It was a caravel, a galleon, a ship such as he had seen in the old books, its sails painted with lions and crucifixes, a castle on the poop and a figure-head carved on the prow that dipped down into the waves, only to reappear dripping with foam.

The trunk, by dint of vigorous pushing, could be made to reach the rugged coast at the corner of the old chest, the triangular gulf made of two chests of drawers, and the smooth beach formed by some bundles of clothes. And the navigator, followed by a crew as numerous as it was imaginary, would leap ashore, sword in hand, scaling some mountains of books that were the Andes, and piercing various volumes with the tip of an old lance in order to plant his standard there. Oh, why had he not been one of the conquerors? . . .

Fragments of a conversation between his godfather and his father, who believed everything was already known regarding the surface of the earth, left him unconvinced. Something must still be left for him to discover! He was the meeting point of two families of sailors. His mother's brothers had ships on the coast of Catalunia. His father's ancestors had been valorous and obscure navigators, and there in the *Marina* was his uncle, the doctor, a genuine man of the sea.

When he grew tired of these imaginative orgies, he used to examine the portraits of different epochs stowed away in the garret. He preferred those of the women— noble dames with short-cropped, curled hair bound by a knot of ribbon on the temple, like those that Velazquez loved to paint, and long faces of the century following, with cherry-colored mouth, two patches on the cheeks, and a tower of white hair. The memory of the Grecian *basilisa* appeared to emanate from these paintings. All the high-born dames seemed to have something in common with her.

Among the portraits of the men there was one of a bishop that irritated him by its absurd childishness. He appeared almost his own age, an adolescent bishop, with imperious and aggressive eyes. These eyes used to inspire the sensitive lad with a certain terror, and he therefore decided to have done with them. "Take that!" and he ran his sword through the old chipped picture, making two gashes replace the challenging eyes. Then he added a few gashes more for good measure. . . . That same evening, his godfather having been invited to supper, the notary spoke of a certain portrait acquired a

few months before in the neighborhood of Játiva, a city
that he had always regarded with interest on account of
the Borgias having been born in one of its suburbs. The
two men were of the same opinion. That almost infantile
prelate could have been no other than Cæsar Borgia,
made Archbishop of Valencia when sixteen years old by
his father, the Pope. On their first free day they would
examine the portrait with particular attention. . . . And
Ulysses, hanging his head, felt every mouthful sticking in
his throat.

For the fanciful lad, a pleasure even more intense and
substantial than his lonely games in the garret was a visit
to his godfather's home; to his childish eyes, this godpar-
ent, the lawyer, Don Carmelo Labarta, was the personi-
fication of the ideal life, of glory, of poesy. The notary
was wont to speak of him with enthusiasm, yet pitying
him at the same time.

"That poor Don Carmelo! . . . The leading authority of the age in civilian matters! By applying himself
he might earn some money, but verses attracted him
more than lawsuits."

Ulysses used to enter his office with keen emotion.
Above rows of multicolored and gilded books that covered the walls, he saw some great plaster heads with towering foreheads and vacant eyes that seemed always to
be contemplating an immense nothingness.

The child could repeat their names like a fragment
from a choir book, from Homer to Victor Hugo. Then
his glance would seek another head equally glorious although less white, with blonde and grizzled beard, rubi-
cund nose and bilious cheeks that in certain moments
scattered bits of scale. The sweet eyes of his godfather—
yellowish eyes spotted with black dots—used to receive
Ulysses with the doting affection of an aging, old bachelor who needs to invent a family. He it was who had

given him at the baptismal font the name which had
awakened so much admiration and ridicule among his
school companions; with the patience of an old grand-
sire narrating saintly stories to his descendants, he would
tell Ulysses over and over the adventures of the navigating King of Ithaca for whom he had been named.

With no less devotion did the lad regard all the souvenirs of glory that adorned his house—wreaths of golden
leaves, silver cups, nude marble statuettes, placques of
different metals upon plush backgrounds on which glistened imperishably the name of the poet Labarta. All
this booty the tireless Knight of Letters had conquered
by means of his verse.

When the Floral Games were announced, the competi-
tors used to tremble lest it might occur to the great Don
Carmelo to hanker after some of the premiums. With
astonishing facility he used to carry off the natural flower
awarded for the heroic ode, the cup of gold for the
amorous romance, the pair of statues dedicated to the
most complete historical study, the marble bust for the
best legend in prose, and even the "art bronze" reward of
philological study. The other aspirants might try for the
left-overs.

Fortunately he had confined himself to local literature,
and his inspiration would not admit any other drapery
than that of Valencian verse. Next to Valencia and its
past glories, Greece claimed his admiration. Once a year
Ulysses beheld him arrayed in his frock coat, his chest
starred with decorations and in his lapel the golden
cicada, badge of the poets of Provence.

He it was who was going to be celebrated in the fiesta
of Provençal literature, in which he always played the
principal rôle; he was the prize bard, lecturer, or simple
idol to whom other poets were dedicating their eulogies—
clerics given to rhyming, personifiers of religious images,

silk-weavers who felt the vulgarity of their existence perturbed by the itchings of inspiration—all the brotherhood
of popular bards of the ingenuous and domestic brand
who recalled the *Meistersingers* of the old German cities.

His godson always imagined him with a crown of laurel
on his brows just like those mysterious blind poets whose
portraits and busts ornamented the library. In real life
he saw perfectly well that his head had no such adornment, but reality lost its value before the firmness of his
conceptions. His godfather certainly must wear a wreath
when he was not present. Undoubtedly he was accustomed to wear it as a house cap when by himself.

Another thing which he greatly admired about the
grand man was his extensive travels. He had lived in
distant Madrid—the scene of almost all the novels read
by Ulysses—and once upon a time he had crossed the
frontier, going courageously into a remote country called
the south of France, in order to visit another poet whom
he was accustomed to call "My friend, Mistral." And
the lad's imagination, hasty and illogical in its decisions,
used to envelop his godfather in a halo of historic interest, similar to that of the conquerors.

At the stroke of the twelve o'clock chimes Labarta,
who never permitted any informality in table matters,
would become very impatient, cutting short the account
of his journeys and triumphs.

"Doña Pepa! . . . We have a guest here."

Doña Pepa was the housekeeper, the great man's companion who for the past fifteen years had been chained to
the chariot of his glory. The portières would part and
through them would advance a huge bosom protruding
above an abdomen cruelly corseted. Afterwards, long
afterwards, would appear a white and radiant countenance, a face like a full moon, and while her smile like a
night star was greeting the little Ulysses, the dorsal com-

plement of her body kept on coming in—forty carnal years, fresh, exuberant, tremendous.

The notary and his wife always spoke of Doña Pepa as of a familiar person, but the child never had seen her in their home. Doña Cristina used to eulogize her care of the poet—but distantly and with no desire to make her acquaintance—while Don Esteban would make excuses for the great man.

"What can you expect! . . . He is an artist, and artists are not able to live as God commands. All of them, however dignified they may appear, are rather carnal at heart. What a pity! such an eminent lawyer! . . . The money that he could make. . . !"

His father's lamentations opened up new horizons to the little fellow's suspicions. Suddenly he grasped the prime motive force of our existence, hitherto only conjectured and enveloped in mystery. His godfather had relations with a woman; he was enamored like the heroes of the novels! And the boy recalled many of his Valencian poems, all rhapsodizing a lady—sometimes singing of her great beauty with the rapture and noble lassitude of a recent possession; at others complaining of her coldness, begging of her that disposition of her soul without which the gift of the body is as naught.

Ulysses imagined to himself a grand señora as beautiful as Doña Constanza. At the very least, she must be a Marchioness. His godfather certainly deserved that much! And he also imagined to himself that their rendezvous must be in the morning, in one of the strawberry gardens near the city, where his parents were accustomed to take him for his breakfast chocolate after hearing the first dawn service on the Sundays of April and May.

Much later, when seated at his godfather's table, he surprised the poet exchanging glances over his head with the housekeeper, and began to suspect that possibly Doña Pepa might be the inspiration of so much lachrymose and enthusiastic verse. But his great loyalty rebelled before such a supposition. No, no, it could not be possible; assuredly there must be another!

The notary, who for long years had been friendly with Labarta, kept trying to direct him with his practical spirit, like the boy who guides a blind man. A modest income inherited from his parents was enough for the poet to live upon. In vain his friend brought him cases that represented enormous fees. The voluminous documents would become covered with dust on his table and Don Esteban would have to saddle himself with the dates in order that the end of the legal procedures should not slip by.

His son, Ulysses would be a very different sort of man, thought the notary. In his mind's eye he could see the lad as a great civilian jurist like his godfather, but with a positive activity inherited from his father. Fortune would enter through his doors on waves of stamped paper.

Furthermore, he would also possess the notarial studio—the dusty office with its ancient furniture and great wardrobes, with its screen doors and green curtains, behind which reposed the volumes of the protocol, covered with yellowing calfskin with initials and numbers on their backs. Don Esteban realized fully all that his study represented.

"There is no orange grove," he would say in his expansive moments; "there are no rice plantations that can produce what this estate does. Here there are no frosts, nor strong sea winds, nor inundations."

The clientele was certain—people from the church, who had the devotees back of them and considered Don Esteban as one of their class, and farmers, many rich farmers. The families of the country folk, whenever they heard any talk about smart men, always thought immediately of the notary from Valencia. With religious veneration they saw him adjust his spectacles in order to read as an expert the bill of sale or dowry contract that his amanuenses had just drawn up. It was written in Castilian and for the better understanding of his listeners he would read it, without the slightest hesitation, in Valencian. What a man! . . .

Afterwards, while the contracting parties were signing it, the notary raising the little glass window at the front, would entertain the assembly with some local legends, always decent, without any illusions to the sins of the flesh, but always those in which the digestive organs figured with every degree of license. The clients would roar with laughter, captivated by this funny eschatalogy, and would haggle less in the matter of fees. Famous Don Esteban! . . . Just for the pleasure of hearing his yarns they would have liked a legal paper drawn up every month.

The future destiny of the notarial crown prince was the object of many after-dinner conversations on the special days when the poet was an invited guest.

"What do you want to be?" Labarta asked his godson.

His mother's supplicating glance seemed desperately to implore the little fellow: "Say Archbishop, my king." For the good señora, her son could not make his début in any other way than in a church career. The notary always used to speak very positively from his own viewpoint, without consulting the interested party. He would be an eminent jurisconsult; thousands of dollars were going to roll toward him as though they were pennies; he was going to figure in university solemnities in a cloak of crimson satin and an academic cap announcing from its multiple sides the tasseled glory of the doctorate. The students in his lecture-room would listen to him most respectfully. Who knew what the government of his country might not have in store for him! . . .

Ulysses interrupted these images of future grandeur: "I want to be a captain."

The poet approved. He felt the unreflective enthusiasm which all pacific and sedentary beings have for the plume and the sword. At the mere sight of a uniform his soul always thrilled with the amorous tenderness of a child's nurse when she finds herself courted by a soldier.

"Fine!" said Labarta. "Captain of what? . . . Of artillery? . . . Of the staff? . . .

A pause.

"No; captain of a ship."

Don Esteban looked up at the roof, raising his hands in horror. He well knew who was guilty of this ridiculous idea, the one who had put such absurd longings in his son's head!

And he was thinking of his brother, the retired doctor, who was living in the paternal home over there in the *Marina:*—an excellent man, but a little crazy, whom the people on the coast called the *Dotor,* and the poet Labarta had nicknamed the *Triton.*

CHAPTER II

WHEN the *Triton* occasionally appeared in Valencia, thrifty Doña Cristina was obliged to modify the dietary of her family. This man ate nothing but fish, and her soul of an economical housewife worried greatly at the thought of the extraordinarily high price that fish brings in a port of exportation.

Life in that house, where everything always jogged along so uniformly, was greatly upset by the presence of the doctor. A little after daybreak, just when its inhabitants were usually enjoying the dessert of their night's sleep, hearing drowsily the rumble of the early morning carts and the bell-ringing of the first Masses, the house would reëcho to the rude banging of doors and heavy footsteps making the stairway creak. It was the *Triton* rushing out on the street, incapable of remaining between four walls after the first streak of light. Following the currents of the early morning life, he would reach the market, stopping before the flower stands where were the most numerous gatherings of women.

The eyes of the women turned toward him instinctively with an expression of interest and fear. Some flushed as he passed by, imagining against their will what an embrace from this hideous and restless Colossus must be.

"He is capable of crushing a flea on his arm," the sailors of his village used to boast when trying to empha-

23

size the hardness of his biceps. His body lacked fat, and
under his swarthy skin bulged great, rigid and protruding muscles—an Herculean texture from which had been
eliminated every element incapable of producing strength.
Labarta found in him a great resemblance to the marine
divinities. He was Neptune before his head had silvered,
or Poseidon as the primitive Greek poets had seen him
with hair black and curly, features tanned by the salt air,
and with a ringleted beard whose two spiral ends seemed
formed by the dripping of the water of the sea. The
nose somewhat flattened by a blow received in his youth
and the little eyes, oblique and tenacious, gave to his
countenance an expression of Asiatic ferocity, but this
impression melted away when his mouth parted in a smile
showing his even, glistening teeth, the teeth of a man
of the sea accustomed to live upon salt food.

During the first few days of his visit he would wander
through the streets wavering and bewildered. He was
afraid of the carriages; the patter of the passers-by on
the pavements annoyed him; he, who had seen the most
important ports of both hemispheres, complained of the
bustle in the capital of a province. Finally he would instinctively take the road from the harbor in search of the
sea, his eternal friend, the first to salute him every morning upon opening the door of his own home down there
on the *Marina*.

On these excursions he would oftentimes be accompanied by his little nephew. The bustle on the docks,—
(the creaking of the cranes, the dull rumble of the carts
the deafening cries of the freighters),—always had for
him a certain music reminiscent of his youth when he was
traveling as a doctor on a transatlantic steamer.

His eyes also received a caress from the past upon
taking in the panorama of the port—steamers smoking
sailboats with their canvas spread out in the sunligh

bulwarks of orange crates, pyramids of onions, walls of
sacks of rice and compact rows of wine casks paunch to
paunch. And coming to meet the outgoing cargo were
long lines of unloaded goods being lined up as they arrived—hills of coal coming from England, sacks of cereal
from the Black Sea, dried codfish from Newfoundland
sounding like parchment skins as they thudded down
on the dock, impregnating the atmosphere with their
salty dust, and yellow lumber from Norway that still
held a perfume of the pine woods.

Oranges and onions fallen from the crates were rot-
ting in the sun, scattering their sweet and acrid juices.
The sparrows were hopping around the mountains of
wheat, flitting timidly away when hearing approaching
footsteps. Over the blue surface of the harbor waters
the sea gulls of the Mediterranean, small, fine and white
as doves, twined in and out in their interminable contra-
dances.

The *Triton* went on enumerating to his nephew the
class and specialty of every kind of vessel; and upon
discovering that Ulysses was capable of confusing a
brigantine with a frigate, he would roar in scandalized
amazement.

"Heavens! Then what in the devil do they teach you
in school? . . ."

Upon passing near the citizens of Valencia seated on
the wharves, fishing rod in hand, he would shoot a glance
of commiseration toward their empty baskets. Over
there by his house on the coast, before the sun would
be up, he would already have covered the bottom of his
boat with enough to eat for a week. The misery of the
cities!

Standing on the last points of the rocky ledge, his
glance would sweep the immense plain, describing to
his nephew the mysteries hidden beyond the horizon. At

their left, beyond the blue mountains of Oropesa, which
bound the Valencian gulf, he could see in imagination
Barcelona, where he had numerous friends, Marseilles,
that prolongation of the Orient fastened on the European
coast, and Genoa with its terraced palaces on hills covered with gardens. Then his vision would lose itself
on the horizon stretching out in front of him. That was
the road of his happy youth.

Straight ahead in a direct line was Naples with its
smoking mountain, its music and its swarthy dancing girls
with hoop earrings; further on, the Isles of Greece; at
the foot of an Aquatic Street, Constantinople; and still
beyond, bordering the great liquid court of the Black
Sea, a series of ports where the Argonauts—sunk in a
seething mass of races, fondled by the felinism of slaves,
the voluptuosity of the Orientals, and the avarice of the
Jews—were fast forgetting their origin.

At their right was Africa; the Egyptian ports with
their traditional corruption that at sunset was beginning
to tremble and steam like a fetid morass; Alexandria in
whose low coffee houses were imitation Oriental dancers
with no more clothes than a pocket handkerchief, every
woman of a different nation and shrieking in chorus all
the languages of the earth. . . .

The doctor withdrew his eyes from the sea in order
to observe his flattened nose. He was recalling a night
of Egyptian heat increased by the fumes of whiskey; the
familiarity of the half-clad public women, the scuffle
with some ruddy Northern sailors, the encounter in the
dark which obliged him to flee with bleeding face to the
ship that, fortunately, was weighing anchor at dawn.
Like all Mediterranean men, he never went ashore without wearing a dagger hidden on his person, and he had
to "sting" with it in order to make way for himself.

"What times those were!" said the *Triton* with more

regret and homesickness than remorse; and then he would add by way of excuse, "Ay, but then I was only twenty-four years old!"

These memories made him turn his eyes toward a huge bluish bulk extending out into the sea and looking to the casual spectator like a great barren island. It was the promontory crowned by the Mongó, the great Ferrarian promontory of the ancient geographers, the furthest-reaching point of the peninsula in the lower Mediterranean that closes the Gulf of Valencia on the south.

It had the form of a hand whose digits were mountains, but lacked the thumb. The other four fingers extended out into the waves, forming the capes of San Antonio, San Martin, La Nao and Almoraira. In one of their coves was the *Triton's* native village, and the home of the Ferraguts—hunters of black pirates in other days, contrabandists at times in modern days, sailors in all ages, appearing originally, perhaps, from those first wooden horses that came leaping over the foam seething around the promontory.

In that home in the *Marina* he wished to live and die, with no further desire of seeing more lands, with that sudden immovability that attacks the vagabonds of the waves and makes them fix themselves upon a ledge of the coast like a mollusk or bunch of seaweed.

Soon the *Triton* grew tired of these strolls to the harbor. The sea of Valencia was not a real sea for him. The waters of the river and of the irrigation canals disturbed him. When it rained in the mountains of Aragon, an earthy liquid always discharged itself into the Gulf, tinting the waves with flesh color and the foam with yellow. Besides, it was impossible to indulge in his daily sport of swimming. One winter morning, when he began to undress himself on the beach, the crowd gathered around

him as though attracted by a phenomenon. Even the fish
of the Gulf had to him an insufferable slimy taste.

"I'm going back home," he would finally say to the
notary and his wife. "I can't understand how in the
world you are able to live here!"

In one of these retreats to the *Marina* he insisted upon
taking Ulysses home with him. The summer season was
beginning, the boy would be free from school for three
months, and the notary, who was not able to go far away
from the city, was going to pass the summer with his
family on the beach at Cabañal checkered by bad-smelling
irrigation canals near a forlorn sea. The little fellow was
looking very pale and weak on account of his studies and
hectoring. His uncle would make him as strong and
agile as a dolphin. And in spite of some very lively disputes, he succeeded in snatching the child away from
Doña Cristina.

The first things that Ulysses admired upon entering
the doctor's home were the three frigates adorning the
ceiling of the dining-room—three marvelous vessels in
which there was not lacking a single sail nor pulley rope,
nor anchor, and which might be made to sail over the sea
at a moment's notice.

They were the work of his grandfather Ferragut.
Wishing to release his two sons from the marine service
which had weighed upon the family for many centuries,
he had sent them to the University of Valencia in order
that they might become inland gentlemen. The older,
Esteban, had scarcely terminated his career before he
obtained a notaryship in Catalunia. The younger one,
Antonio, became a doctor so as not to thwart the old
man's wishes, but as soon as he acquired his degree he
offered his services to a transatlantic steamer. His father
had closed the door of the sea against him and he had
entered by the window.

And so, as Ferragut Senior began to grow old, he lived completely alone. He used to look after his property—a few vineyards scattered along the coast in sight of his home—and was in frequent correspondence with his son, the notary. From time to time there came a letter from the younger one, his favorite, posted in remote countries that the old Mediterranean seaman knew only by hear-say. And during his long, dull hours in the shade of his arbor facing the blue and luminous sea, he used to enter-tain himself constructing these little models of boats. They were all frigates of great tonnage and fearless sail. Thus the old skipper would console himself for having commanded during his lifetime only heavy and clumsy merchant vessels like the ships of other centuries, in which he used to carry wine from Cette or cargo pro-hibited in Gibraltar and the coast of Africa.

Ulysses was not long in recognizing the rare popularity enjoyed by his uncle, the doctor—a popularity composed of the most antagonistic elements. The people used to smile in speaking of him as though he were a little touched, yet they dared to indulge in these smiles only when at a safe distance, for he inspired a certain terror in all of them. At the same time they used to admire him as a local celebrity, for he had traversed all seas, and possessed, besides, a violent and tempestuous strength which was the terror and pride of his neighbors. The husky youths when testing the vigor of their fists, boxing with crews of the English vessels that came there for cargoes of raisins, used to evoke the doctor's name as a consolation in case of defeat. "If only the *Dotor* could have been here! . . . Half a dozen Englishmen are noth-ing to him!"

There was no vigorous undertaking, however absurd it might be, that they would not believe him capable of. He used to inspire the faith of the miracle-working saints and audacious highway captains. On calm, sunshiny winter mornings the people would often go running down to the beach, looking anxiously over the lonely sea. The veterans who were toasting themselves in the sun near the overturned boats, on scanning the broad horizon, would finally discern an almost imperceptible point, a grain of sand dancing capriciously on the waves.

They would all break into shouts and conjectures. It was a buoy, a piece of masthead, the drift from a distant shipwreck. For the women it was somebody drowned, so bloated that it was floating like a leather bottle, after having been many days in the water.

Suddenly the same supposition would arise in every perplexed mind. "I wonder if it could be the *Dotor!*" A long silence. . . . The bit of wood was taking the form of a head; the corpse was moving. Many could now perceive the bubble of foam around his chest that was advancing like the prow of a ship, and the vigorous strokes of his arms. . . . Yes, it surely was the *Dotor!*" . . . The old sea dogs loaned their telescopes to one another in order to recognize his beard sunk in the water and his face, contracted by his efforts or expanded by his snortings.

And the *Dotor* was soon treading the dry beach, naked and as serenely unashamed as a god, giving his hand to the men, while the women shrieked, lifting their aprons in front of one eye—terrified, yet admiring the dripping vision.

All the capes of the promontory challenged him to double them, swimming like a dolphin; he felt impelled to measure all the bays and coves with his arms, like a proprietor who distrusts another's measurements and rectifies them in order to affirm his right of possession. He was a human bark who, with the keel of his breast, cut the foam, whirling through the sunken rocks and the pacific waters in whose depths sparkled fishes among mother-of-pearl twigs and stars moving like flowers.

He used to seat himself to rest on the black rocks with overskirts of seaweed that raised or lowered their fringe at the caprice of the wave, awaiting the night and the chance vessel that might come to dash against them like a piece of bark. Like a marine reptile he had even penetrated certain caves of the coast, drowsy and glacial lakes illuminated by mysterious openings where the atmosphere is black and the water transparent, where the swimmer has a bust of ebony and legs of crystal. In the course of these swimming expeditions he ate all the living beings he encountered fastened to the rocks by antennæ and arms. The friction of the great, terrified fish that fled, bumping against him with the violence of a projectile, used to make him laugh.

In the night hours passed before his grandfather's little ships, Ulysses used to hear the *Triton* speak of the *Peje Nicolao,* a man-fish of the Straits of Messina mentioned by Cervantes and other authors, who lived in the water maintaining himself by the donations from the ships. His uncle must be some relative of this *Peje Nicolao*. At other times this uncle would mention a certain Greek who in order to see his lady-love swam the Hellespont every night. And he, who used to know the Dardanelles, was longing to return there as a simple passenger merely that a poet named Lord Byron might not be the only one to imitate the legendary crossing.

The books that he kept in his home, the nautical charts fastened to the walls, the flasks and jars filled with the animal and vegetable life of the sea, and more than all this, his tastes which were so at variance with the customs of his neighbors, had given the *Triton* the reputation of a mysterious sage, the fame of a wizard.

All those who were well and strong considered him

crazy, but the moment that there was the slightest break
in their health they would share the same faith as the
poor women who oftentimes passed long hours in the
home of the *Dotor,* seeing his bark afar off and patiently
awaiting his return from the sea, in order to show him
the sick children they carried in their arms. He had an
advantage over all other doctors, as he made no charge
for his services; better still, many sick people came away
from his house with money in their hands.

The *Dotor* was rich—the richest man in the countryside; a man who really did not know what to do with
his money. His maid-servant—an old woman who had
known his father and served his mother—used daily to
receive from his hands the fish provided for the two with
a regal generosity. The *Triton,* who had hoisted sail at
daybreak, used to disembark before eleven, and soon the
purpling lobster was crackling on the red coals, sending
forth delicious odors; the stew pot was bubbling away,
thickening its broth with the succulent fat of the sea-scor-
pion; the oil in the frying pan was singing, browning the
flame-colored skin of the salmonettes; and the sea urchins and the mussels opened hissing under his knife,
were emptying their still living pulp into the boiling stew
pan. Furthermore, a cow with full udders was mooing
in the yard, and dozens of chickens with innumerable
broods were cackling incessantly.

The flour kneaded and baked by his servant, and the
coffee thick as mud, was all that the *Triton* purchased
with his money. If he hunted for a bottle of brandy on
his return from a swim, it was only to use it in rubbing
himself down.

Money entered through his doors once a year, when
the girls of the vintage lined up among the trellises of
his vineyards, cutting the bunches of little, close fruit
and spreading them out to dry in some small sheds

called *riurraus*. Thus was produced the small raisin preferred by the English for the making of their puddings.
The sale was a sure thing, the boats always coming from
the north to get the fruit. And the *Triton,* upon finding
five or six thousand pesetas in his hand, would be greatly
perplexed, inwardly asking himself what a man was
ever going to do with so much money.

"All this is yours," he said, showing the house to his
nephew.

His also the boat, the books and the antique furniture in whose drawers the money was so openly hid that
it invited attention.

In spite of seeing himself lord of all that surrounded
him, a rough and affectionate despotism, kept nevertheless, weighing the child down. He was very far from his
mother, that good lady who was always closing the
windows near him and never letting him go out without tying his neckscarf around him with an accompani-
ment of kisses.

Just when he was sleeping soundest, believing that
the night would still be many hours longer, he would feel
himself awakened by a violent tugging at his leg. His
uncle could not touch him in any other way. "Get up,
cabin boy!" In vain he would protest with the profound
sleepiness of youth. . . . Was he, or was he not the
"ship's cat" of the bark of which his uncle was the captain and only crew? . . .

His uncle's paws bared him to the blasts of salt air
that were entering through the windows. The sea was
dark and veiled by a light fog. The last stars were
sparkling with twinkles of surprise, ready to flee. A
crack began to appear on the leaden horizon, growing
redder and redder every minute, like a wound through
which the blood is flowing. The ship's cat was loaded up
with various empty baskets, the skipper marching before

him like a warrior of the waves, carrying the oars on his shoulders, his feet rapidly making hollows on the sand. Behind him the village was beginning to awaken and, over the dark waters, the sails of the fishermen, fleeing the inner sea, were slipping past like ghostly shrouds.

Two vigorous strokes of the oar sent their boat out from the little wharf of stones, and soon he was untying the sails from the gunwales and preparing the ropes. The unfurled canvas whistled and swelled in bellying whiteness. "There we are! Now for a run!"

The water was beginning to sing, slipping past both sides of the prow. Between it and the edge of the sail could be seen a bit of black sea, and coming little by little over its line, a great red streak. The streak soon became a helmet, then a hemisphere, then an Arabian arch confined at the bottom, until finally it shot up out of the liquid mass as though it were a bomb sending forth flashes of flame. The ash-colored clouds became stained with blood and the large rocks of the coast began to sparkle like copper mirrors. As the last stars were extinguished, a swarm of fire-colored fishes came trailing along before the prow, forming a triangle with its point in the horizon. The mist on the mountain tops was taking on a rose color as though its whiteness were reflecting a submarine eruption. *"Bon dia!"* called the doctor to Ulysses, who was occupied in warming his hands stiffened by the wind.

And, moved with childlike joy by the dawn of a new day, the *Triton* sent his bass voice booming across the maritime silence, several times intoning sentimental melodies that in his youth he had heard sung by a vaudeville prima donna dressed as a ship's boy, at other times caroling in Valencian the chanteys of the coast—fishermen's songs invented as they drew in their nets, in which most shameless words were flung together on the chance of making them rhyme. In certain windings of the coast the sail would be lowered, leaving the boat with no other motion than a gentle rocking around its anchor rope.

Upon seeing the space which had been obscured by the shadow of the boat's hulk, Ulysses found the bottom of the sea so near that he almost believed that he could touch it with the point of his oar. The rocks were like glass. In their interstices and hollows the plants were moving like living creatures, and the little animals had the immovability of vegetables and stones. The boat appeared to be floating in the air and athwart the liquid atmosphere that wraps this abysmal world, the fish hooks were dangling, and a swarm of fishes was swimming and wriggling toward its encounter with death.

It was a sparkling effervescence of yellowing flames, of bluish backs and rosy fins. Some came out from the caves silvered and vibrant as lightning flashes of mercury; others swam slowly, big-bellied, almost circular, with a golden coat of mail. Along the slopes, the crustaceans came scrambling along on their double row of claws attracted by this novelty that was changing the mortal calm of the under-sea where all follow and devour, only to be devoured in turn. Near the surface floated the medusæ, living parasols of an opaline whiteness with circular borders of lilac or red bronze. Under their gelatinous domes was the skein of filaments that served them for locomotion, nutrition and reproduction.

The fishermen had only to pull in their lines and a new prisoner would fall into their boat. Their baskets were filling up so fast that the *Triton* and his nephew grew tired of this easy fishing. . . . The sun was now near the height of its curve, and every wavelet was carrying away a bit of the golden band that divided the blue immensity. The wood of the boat appeared to be on fire.

"We've earned our day's pay," said the *Triton*, looking

at the sky and then at the baskets. "Now let's clean up a little bit."

And stripping off his clothing, he threw himself into the sea. Ulysses saw him descend from the center of the ring of foam opened by his body, and could gauge by it the profundity of that fantastic world composed of glassy rocks, animal plants and stone animals. As it went down, the tawny body of the swimmer took on the transparency of porcelain. It appeared of bluish crystal—a statue made of a Venetian mirror composition that was going to break as soon as it touched the bottom.

Like a god he was passing through the deeps, snatching plants out by the roots, pursuing with his hands the flashes of vermilion and gold hidden in the cracks of the rocks. Minutes would pass by; he was going to stay down forever; he would never come up again. And the boy was beginning to think uneasily of the possibility of having to guide the bark back to the coast all alone. Suddenly the body of white crystal began taking on a greenish hue, growing larger and larger, becoming dark and coppery, until above the surface appeared the head of the swimmer, who, spouting and snorting, was holding up all his submarine plunder to the little fellow.

"Now then, your turn!" he ordered in an imperious tone.

All attempts at resistance were useless. His uncle either insulted him with the harshest kind of words or coaxed him with promises of safety. He never knew certainly whether he threw himself into the water or whether a tug from the doctor jerked him from the boat. The first surprise having passed, he had the impression of remembering some long forgotten thing. He was swimming instinctively, divining what he ought to do before his master told him. Within him was awakening the ancestral experience of a race of sailors who had struggled with the sea and, sometimes, had remained forever in its bosom.

Recollection of what was existing beyond his feet suddenly made him lose his serenity,—his lively imagination making him shriek,

"Uncle! . . . Uncle!"

And he clutched convulsively at the hard island of bearded and smiling muscles. His uncle came up immovable, as though his feet of stone were fastened to the bottom of the ocean. He was like the nearby promontory that was darkening and chilling the water with its ebony shadow.

Thus would slip by the mornings devoted to fishing and swimming; then in the afternoons there were tramps over the steep shores of the coast.

The *Dotor* knew the heights of the promontory as well as its depths. Up the pathways of the wild goat they clambered to its peaks in order to get a view of the Island of Ibiza. At sunset the distant Balearic Islands appeared like a rose-colored flame rising out of the waves. At other times the cronies made trips along the water's edge, and the *Triton* would show his nephew hidden caves into which the Mediterranean was working its way with slow undulations. These were like maritime roadsteads where boats might anchor completely concealed from view. There the galleys of the Berbers had often hidden, in order to fall unexpectedly upon a nearby village.

In one of these caves, on a rocky pedestal, Ulysses often saw a heap of bundles.

"Well, now, what of it!" expostulated the doctor. "Every man must gain his living as best he can."

When they stumbled upon a solitary custom house officer resting upon his gun and looking out toward the sea, the doctor would offer him a cigar and give him medical advice if he were sick. "Poor men! so badly paid!" . . .

But his sympathies were always going out to the others—
to the enemies of the law. He was the son of his sea, and
in the make-up of all Mediterranean heroes and sailors
there had always been something of the pirate or smuggler. The Phœnicians, who by their navigation spread
abroad the first works of civilization, instituted this service, reaping their reward by filling their barks with stolen
women, rich merchandise of easy transportation.

Piracy and smuggling had formed the historic past of
all the villages that Ulysses was visiting, some huddled
in the shelter of the promontory crowned with a lighthouse, others opening on the concavity of a bay dotted
with barren islands girdled with foam. The old churches
had turrets on their walls and loopholes in their doors
for shooting with culverins and blunderbusses. The
entire neighborhood used to take refuge in them when the
smoke columns from their watchmen would warn them
of the landing of pirates from Algiers. Following the
curvings of the promontory there was a dotted line of
reddish towers, each one accompanied by a smaller pair
for lookouts. This line extended along the south toward
the Straits of Gibraltar, and on its northern side reached
to France.

The doctor had seen their counterpart in all the
islands of the western Mediterranean, on the coasts of
Naples and in Sicily. They were the fortifications of a
thousand-year war, of a struggle ten centuries long between Moors and Christians for the domination of the
blue sea, a struggle of piracy in which the Mediterranean
men—differentiated by religion, but identical at heart—
had prolonged the adventures of the Odyssey down to the
beginnings of the nineteenth century.

Ferragut gradually became acquainted with many old
men of the village who in their youth had been slaves
in Algiers. On winter evenings the oldest of them were

still singing romances of captivity and speaking with terror of the Berber brigantines. These thieves of the sea must have had a pact with the devil, who notified them of opportune occasions. If in a convent some beautiful novices had just made their profession, the doors would give away at midnight under the hatchet-blows of the bearded demons who were advancing inland from the galleys prepared to receive their cargo of feminine freight. If a girl of the coast, celebrated for her beauty, was going to be married, the infidels, lying in wait, would surround the door of the church, shooting their blunder-busses and knifing the unarmed men as they came out, in order to carry away the women in their festal robes.

On all the coast, the pirates stood in awe only of the navigators from the *Marina,* so fearless and warlike were they. If their villages were ever attacked, it was because their seafaring defenders were on the Mediterranean and, in their turn, had gone to sack and burn some village on the coast of Africa.

The *Triton* and his nephew used to eat their supper under the arbor in the long summer twilights. After the cloth was removed Ulysses would manipulate his grand-father's little frigates, learning the technical parts and names of the different apparatus, and the management of the sets of sails. Sometimes the two would stay out on the rustic porch until a late hour gazing out over the luminous sea sparkling under the splendor of the moon, or streaked with a slender wake of starry light in the murky nights.

All that mankind had ever written or dreamed about the Mediterranean, the doctor had in his library and could repeat to his eager little listener. In Ferragut's estimation the *mare nostrum* [1] was a species of blue beast,

---

[1] "Mare Nostrum" (Our Sea), the classic name for the Mediterranean.

powerful and of great intelligence—a sacred animal like
the dragons and serpents that certain religions adored, believing them to be the source of life. The rivers that
threw themselves impetuously into its bosom in order
to renew it were few and scanty. The Rhone and the
Nile appeared to be pitiful little rivulets compared with
the river courses of other continents that empty into the
oceans.

Losing by evaporation three times more liquid than
the rivers bring to it, this sunburnt sea would soon have
been converted into a great salt desert were not the Atlantic sending it a rapid current of renewal that was pre-
cipitated through the Straits of Gibraltar. Under this
superficial current existed still another, flowing in an
opposite direction, that returned a part of the Mediterranean to the ocean, because the Mediterranean waters
were more salt and dense than those of the Atlantic. The
tide scarcely made itself felt on its strands. Its basin
was mined by subterranean fires that were always seeking extraordinary outlets through Vesuvius and Ætna,
and breathed continually through the mouth of Stromboli. Sometimes these Plutonic ebullitions would come
to the surface, making new islands rise up upon the
waters like tumors of lava.

In its bosom exist still double the quantity of animal
species that abound in other seas, although less numerous.
The tunny fish, playful lambs of the blue pasture lands
were gamboling over its surface or passing in schools
under the furrows of the waves. Men were setting
netted traps for them along the coasts of Spain and
France, in Sardinia, the Straits of Messina and the waters
of the Adriatic. But this wholesale slaughter scarcely
lessened the compact, fishy squadrons. After wandering through the windings of the Grecian Archipelago
they passed the Dardanelles and the Bosphorus, stirring

the two narrow passageways with the violence of their invisible gallopade and making a turn at the bowl of the Black Sea, swimming back, decimated but impetuous, to the depths of the Mediterranean.

Red coral was forming immovable groves on the substrata of the Balearic Islands, and on the coasts of Naples and Africa. Ambergris was constantly being found on the steep shores of Sicily. Sponges were growing in the tranquil waters in the shadow of the great rocks of Mallorca and the Isles of Greece. Naked men without any equipment whatever, holding their breath, were still descending to the bottom as in primitive times, in order to snatch these treasures away.

The doctor gave up his geographic descriptions to discourse on the history of his sea, which had indeed been the history of civilization, and was more fascinating to him. At first miserable and scanty tribes had wandered along its coasts seeking their food from the crustaceans drawn from the waves—a life similar to that of the rudimentary people that Ferragut had seen in the islands of the Pacific. When stone saws had hollowed out the trunks of trees and human arms had ventured to spread the first rawhides to the forces of the atmosphere, the coasts became rapidly populated.

Temples were constructed on the promontories, and maritime cities—the first nuclei of modern civilization—came into existence. On this landlocked sea mankind had learned the art of navigation. Every one looked at the waves before looking at the sky. Over this blue highway had arrived the miracles of life, and out of its depths the gods were born. The Phœnicians—Jews, become navigators—abandoned their cities in the depths of the Mediterranean sack, in order to spread the mysterious knowledge of Egypt and the Asiatic monarchies all along the shores of the interior sea. Afterwards the Greeks of the maritime republics took their places.

In Ferragut's estimation the greatest honor to which Athens could lay claim was that she had been a democracy of sailors, her freemen serving their country as rowers and all her famous men as great marine officials.

"Themistocles and Pericles," he added, "were admirals of fleets, and after commanding ships, governed their country."

On that account Grecian civilization had spread itself everywhere and had become immortal instead of lessening and disappearing without fruit as in the interior lands. Then Rome, terrestrial Rome, in order to hold its own against the superiority of the Semitic navigators of Carthage, had to teach the management of the oar and marine combat to the inhabitants of Latium, to their legionaries with faces hardened by the chin straps of their helmets, who did not know how to adjust their world-dominating iron-shod feet to the slippery planks of a vessel.

The divinities of *mare nostrum* always inspired a most loving devotion in the doctor. He knew that they had not existed, but he, nevertheless, believed in them as poetic phantasms of natural forces.

The ancient world only knew the immense ocean in hypothesis, giving it the form of an aquatic girdle around the earth. Oceanus was an old god with a long beard and horned head who lived in a maritime cavern with his wife, Tethys, and his three hundred daughters, the Oceanides. No Argonaut had ever dared to come in contact with these mysterious divinities. Only the grave Æschylus had dared to portray the Oceanides—virgins fresh and demure, weeping around the rock to which Prometheus was bound.

Other more approachable deities were those of the

eternal sea on whose borders were founded the opulent cities of the Syrian coast; the Egyptian cities that sent sparks of their ritual civilization to Greece; the Hellenic cities, hearths of clear fire that had fused all knowledge, giving it eternal form; Rome, mistress of the world; Carthage, famed for her audacious geographical discoveries, and Marseilles, which had made western Europe share in the civilization of the Greeks, scattering it along the lower coast from settlement to settlement, even to the Straits of Cadiz.

A brother of the Oceanides, the prudent Nereus, used to reign in the depths of the Mediterranean. This son of Oceanus had a blue beard, green eyes, and bunches of sea rushes on his eyebrows and breast. His fifty daughters, the Nereids, bore his orders across the waves or frolicked around the ships, splashing in the faces of the rowers the foam tossed up by their arms. But the sons of Father Time, on conquering the giant, had reapportioned the world, determining its rulers by lot. Zeus remained lord of the land, the obscure Hades, lord of the underworld, reigned in the Plutonic abysses, and Poseidon became master of the blue surfaces.

Nereus, the dispossessed monarch, fled to a cavern of the Hellenic sea in order to live the calm existence of the philosopher-counselor of mankind, and Poseidon installed himself in the mother-of-pearl palaces with his white steeds tossing helmets of bronze and manes of gold.

His amorous eyes were fixed on the fifty Mediterranean princesses, the Nereids, who took their names from the aspect of the waves—the Blue, the Green, the Swift, the Gentle. . . . "Nymphs of the green abysses with faces fresh as a rosebud, fragrant virgins that took the forms of all the monsters of the deep," sang the Orphic hymn on the Grecian shore. And Poseidon singled out among them all the Nereid of the Foam, the white Amphitrite who refused to accept his love.

She knew about this new god. The coasts were peopled with cyclops like Polyphemus, with frightful monsters born of the union of Olympian goddesses and simple mortals; but an obliging dolphin came and went, carrying messages between Poseidon and the Nereid, until, overwhelmed by the eloquence of this restless rover of the wave, Amphitrite agreed to become the wife of the god, and the Mediterranean appeared to take on still greater beauty.

She was the aurora that shows her rosy finger-tips through the immense cleft between sky and sea, the warm hour of midday that makes the waters drowsy under its robe of restless gold, the bifurcated tongue of foam that laps the two faces of the hissing prow, the aroma-laden breeze that like a virgin's breath swells the sail, the compassionate kiss that lulls the drowned to rest, without wrath and without resistance, before sinking forever into the fathomless abyss.

Her husband—Poseidon on the Greek coast and Neptune on the Latin—on mounting his chariot, used to awaken the tempest. The brazen-hoofed horses with their stamping would paw up the huge waves and swallow up the ships. The tritons of his cortege would send forth from their white shells the bellowing blasts that snap off the masts like reeds.

O, mater Amphitrite! . . . and Ferragut would describe her as though she were just passing before his eyes. Sometimes when swimming around the promontories, feeling himself enveloped like primitive man in the blind forces of Nature, he used to believe that he saw the white goddess issuing forth from the rocks with all her smiling train after a rest in some marine cave.

A shell of pearl was her chariot and six dolphins harnessed with purpling coral used to draw it along. The tritons, her sons, handled the reins. The Naiads, their sisters, lashed the sea with their scaly tails, lifting their mermaid bodies wrapped in the magnificence of their sea-green tresses between whose ringlets might be seen their heaving bosoms. White seagulls, cooing like the doves of Aphrodite, fluttered around their nude sea-queen, serenely contemplating them from her movable throne, crowned with pearls and phosphorescent stars drawn from the depths of her dominion. White as the cloud, white as the sail, white as the foam, entirely, dazzlingly white was her fair majesty except where a rosy blush tinted the petal-like skin of her heels or her bosom.

The entire history of European man—forty centuries of wars, emigrations, and racial impact—was due, according to the doctor, to the desire of possessing this harmoniously framed sea, of enjoying the transparency of its atmosphere and the vivacity of its light.

The men from the North who needed the burning log and alcoholic drink in order to defend their life from the clutches of the cold, were always thinking of these Mediterranean shores. All their warlike or pacific movements were with intent to descend from the coasts of the glacial seas to the beaches of the warm *mare nostrum*. They were eager to gain possession of the country where the sacred olive alternates its stiff old age with the joyous vineyard; where the pine rears its cupola and the cypress erects its minaret. They longed to dream under the perfumed snow of the interminable orange groves; to be masters of the sheltered valleys where the myrtle and the jasmine spice the salty air; where the aloe and the cactus grow between the stones of extinct volcanoes; where the mountains of marble extend their white veins down even into the depths of the sea and refract the African heat emitted by the opposite coast. ·

The South had replied to the invasion from the North with defensive wars that had extended even into the center of Europe. And thus history had gone on repeating itself with the same flux and reflux of human waves —mankind struggling for thousands of years to gain or hold the blue vault of Amphitrite.

The Mediterranean peoples were to Ferragut the aristocracy of humanity. Its potent climate had tempered mankind as in no other part of the planet, giving him a dry and resilient power. Tanned and bronzed by the profound absorption of the sun and the energy of the atmosphere, its navigators were transmuted into pure metal. The men from the North were stronger, but less robust, less acclimitable than the Catalan sailor, the Provençal, the Genoese or the Greek. The sailors of the Mediterranean made themselves at home in all parts of the world. Upon their sea man had developed his highest energies. Ancient Greece had converted human flesh into spiritual steel.

Exactly the same landscapes and races bordered the two shores. The mountains and the flowers on both shores were identical. The Catalan, the Provençal and the South Italian were more like the inhabitants of the African coast than their kindred who lived inland back of them. This fraternity had shown itself instinctively in the thousand-year war. The Berber pirates, the Genoese sailors, the Spaniards, and the Knights of Malta used implacably to behead each other on the decks of their galleys and, upon becoming conquerors, would respect the life of their prisoners, treating them like gentlemen. The Admiral Barbarossa, eighty-four years of age, used to call Doria, his eternal rival nearly ninety years old, "my brother." The Grand Master of Malta clasped the hand of the terrible Dragut upon finding him his captive.

The Mediterranean man, fixed on the shores that gave

him birth, was accustomed to accept all the changes of history, as the mollusks fastened to the rocks endure the tempests. For him the only important thing was not to lose sight of his blue sea. The Spaniard used to pull an oar on the Liburnian felucca, the Christian would join the crews of the Saracen ships of the Middle Ages; the subjects of Charles V would pass through the fortunes of war from the galleys of the Cross to those of the Crescent, and would end by becoming rulers of Algiers, rich captains of the sea, or by making their names famous as renegades.

In the eighth century the inhabitants of the Valencian coast united with the Andalusian Moors to carry the war to the ends of the Mediterranean and to the island of Crete, taking possession of it and giving it the name of Candia. This nest of pirates was the terror of Byzantium, taking Salonica by assault and selling as slaves the patricians and most important ladies of the realm. Years afterwards, when dislodged from Candia, the Valencian adventurers returned to their native shores and there established a town in a fertile valley, giving it the name of the distant island which was changed to Gandía.

Every type of human vigor had sprung from the Mediterranean race,—fine, sharp and dry as flint, doing good and evil on a large scale with the exaggeration of an ardent character that discounts halfway measures and leaps from duplicity to the greatest extremes of generosity. Ulysses was the father of them all, a discreet and prudent hero, yet at the same time complex and malicious. So was old Cadmus with his Phœnician miter and curled beard, a great old sea-wolf, scattering by means of his various adventures the art of writing and the first notions of commerce.

In one of the Mediterranean islands Hannibal was born, and twenty centuries after, in another of them, the

son of a lawyer without briefs embarked for France, with
no other outfit than his cadet's uniform, in order to make
famous his name of Napoleon.

Over the Mediterranean waves had sailed Roger de
Lauria, knight-errant of vast tracts of sea, who wished
to clothe even the fishes with the colors of Aragon. A
visionary of obscure origin named Columbus had recognized as his country the republic of Genoa. A smuggler
from the coasts of Laguria came to be Messina, the
marshal beloved by Victory, and the last personage of
this stock of Mediterranean heroes associated with the
heroes of fabulous times was a sailor from Nice, simple
and romantic, a warrior called Garibaldi, an heroic tenor
of all seas and lands who cast over his century the reflection of his red shirt, repeating on the coast of Marseilles the remote epic of the Argonauts.

Then Ferragut summed up the various defects of his
race. Some had been bandits and others saints, but none
mediocre. Their most audacious undertakings had much
about them that was prudent and practical. When they
devoted themselves to business they were at the same
time serving civilization. In them the hero and the trader
were so intermingled that it was impossible to discern
where one ended and the other began. They had been
pirates and cruel men, but the navigators from the foggy
seas when imitating the Mediterranean discoveries in
other continents had not shown themselves any more
gentle or loyal.

After these conversations, Ulysses felt greater esteem
for the old pottery and the shabby little figures that
adorned his uncle's bedroom.

They were objects vomited up by the sea, Grecian
amphoras wrested from the shells of mollusks after a
submarine interment centuries long. The deep waters
had embossed these petrified ornaments with strange ar-

abesques that made one think of the art of another planet, and, twined in with the pottery that had held the wine and water of a shipwrecked Liburnian felucca, were bits of rope hardened by limey deposit and flukes of anchors whose metal was disintegrating into reddish scales. Various little statues corroded by the salt sea inspired in the boy as much admiration as his grandfather's frigates. He laughed and trembled before these *Cabiri* coming from the Phœnician or Carthaginian biremes,—grotesque and terrible gods that contracted their faces with grimaces of lust and ferocity.

Some of these muscular and bearded marine divinities bore a remote resemblance to his uncle. Ulysses had overheard certain strange conversations among the fishermen and had noticed, besides, the precipitation of the women and their uneasy glances when they found the doctor near them in a solitary part of the coast. Only the presence of his nephew had made them recover tranquillity and check their step.

At times the sea seemed to craze him with gusts of amorous fury. He was Poseidon rising up unexpectedly on the banks in order to surprise goddesses and mortals. The women of the *Marina* ran away as terrified as those Greek princesses on the painted vases when surprised, washing their robes, by the apparition of a passionate triton.

Some nights at the hour when the lighthouses were beginning to pierce the coming dusk with their fresh shafts of light, he would become melancholy and, forgetting the difference in their age, would talk with his nephew as though he were a sailor companion.

He regretted never having married. . . . He might have had a son by this time. He had known many women of all colors—white, red, yellow, and bronze—but only once had he really been in love, very far away on the other side of the planet, in the port of Valparaiso.

He could still see in imagination a certain graceful Chilean maiden, wrapped in her great black veil like the ladies of the Calderonian theater, showing only one of her dark and liquid eyes, pale and slender, speaking in a plaintive voice.

She enjoyed love-songs, always provided that they were sung "with great sadness"; and Ferragut would devour her with his eyes while she plucked the guitar, chanting the song of Malek-Adhel and other romances about "Roses, sighs and Moors of Granada," that from childhood the doctor had heard sung by the Berbers of his country. The simple attempt at taking one of her hands always provoked her modest resistance. . . . "That, then. . . ." She was ready to marry him; she wished to see Spain. . . . And the doctor might have fulfilled her wishes had not a good soul informed him that in later hours of the night, others were accustomed to come in turns to hear her romantic solos. . . . Ah, these women! and then, on recalling the finale of his trans-oceanic idyl, Ferragut would become reconciled to his celibacy.

Late in the Fall the notary had to go in person to the *Marina* to make his brother give Ulysses up. The boy held the same opinion as did his uncle. The very idea of losing the winter fishing, the cold sunny morning, the spectacle of the great tempests, just for the silly reason that the Institute had commenced, and he must study for his bachelor's degree! . . .

The following year Doña Cristina tried to prevent the *Triton's* carrying off her son, since he could learn nothing but bad words and boastful bullying in the old home of the Ferraguts. And trumping up the necessity of seeing her own family, she left the notary alone in Valencia, going with her boy to spend the summer on the coast of Catalunia near the French frontier.

This was Ulysses' first important journey. In Barcelona he became acquainted with his uncle, the rich and talented financier of the Blanes family,—one of his mother's brothers, proprietor of a great hardware shop situated in one of the damp, narrow and crowded streets that ran into the Rambla. He soon came to know other maternal uncles in a village near the Cape of Creus. This promontory with its wild coasts reminded him of that other one where the *Triton* lived. The first Hellenic sailors had also founded a city here, and the sea had also cast up amphoras, little statues and petrified bits of iron.

The Blanes family had gone much to sea. They loved it as intensely as did the doctor, but with a cold and silent love, appreciating it less for its beauty than for the profits which it offered to the fortunate. Their trips had been to America, in their own sailing vessels, importing sugar from Havana and corn from Buenos Ayres. The Mediterranean was for them only a port that they crossed carelessly on departure and arrival. None of them knew the white Amphitrite even by name.

Moreover, they did not have the devil-may-care and romantic appearance of the bachelor of the *Marina,* ready to live in the water like an amphibian. They were gentlemen of the coast who, having retired from the sea, were entrusting their barks to captains who had been their pilots,—middle class citizens who never laid aside the cravat and silk cap that were the symbols of their high position in their natal town.

The gathering-place of the rich was the Athenæum,—a society that in spite of its title offered no other reading matter than two Catalunian periodicals. A large telescope mounted on a tripod before the door used to fill the club members with pride. For the uncles of Ulysses, it was

enough merely to put one eyebrow to the glass to be able
to state immediately the class and nationality of the ship
that was slipping along over the distant horizon line.
These veterans of the sea were accustomed to speak only
of the freight cargoes, of the thousands and thousands
of dollars gained in other times with only one round trip,
and of the terrible rivalry of the steamship.

Ulysses kept hoping in vain that sometimes they would
allude to the Nereids and other poetic beings that the
Triton had conjured around his promontory. The Blanes
had never seen these extraordinary creatures. Their seas
contained fish only. They were cold, economical men of
few words, friends of order and social preferment. Their
nephew suspected that they had the courage of men of
the sea but without boasting or aggressiveness; their
heroism was that of traders capable of suffering all kinds
of adventures provided their stock ran no risks, but becoming wild beasts if any one attacked their riches.

The members of the Athenæum were all old, the only
masculine beings in the village. Besides them there were
only the carbineers installed in the barracks and various
calkers making their mallets resound on the hull of a
schooner ordered by the Blanes brothers.

All the active men were on the sea. Some were sailing
to America as crew of the brigs and barks of the Catalunian coast. The more timid and unfortunate ones were
always fishing. Others, more valiant and anxious for
ready money, had become smugglers on the French coast
whose shores began on the other side of the promontory.

In the village there were only women, women of all
kinds:—women seated before their doors, making lace
on great cylindrical pillows on their knees, along whose
length their bobbins wove strips of beautiful openwork,
or grouped on the street corners in front of the lonely sea

where their men were, or speaking with an electric nervousness that oftentimes would break out suddenly in
noisy tempests.

Only the parish priest, whose fishing recreations and
official existence were embittered by their constant quar-
rels, understood the feminine irritability which embroiled
the village. Alone and having to live incessantly in such
close contact, the women had come to hate each other as
do passengers isolated on a boat for many months. Besides, their husbands had accustomed them to the use of
coffee, the seaman's drink, and they tried to beguile their
tedium with strong cups of the thick liquid.

A common interest, nevertheless, united these women
miraculously when living alone. When the carbineers in-
spected the houses in search of contraband goods smug-
gled in by the men, the Amazons worked off their nervous
energy in hiding the illegal merchandise, making it pass
from one place of concealment to another with the cunning of savages.

Whenever the government officers began to suspect that
certain packages had gone to hide themselves in the cemetery, they would find there only some empty graves, and
in the bottom of them a few cigars between skulls that
were mockingly stuck up in the ground. The chief of
the barracks did not dare to inspect the church, but he
looked contemptuously upon Mosen Jòrdi, the priest, as a
simpleton quite capable of permitting tobacco to be hidden behind the altars in exchange for the privilege of
fishing in peace.

The rich people lived with their backs turned on the
village, contemplating the blue expanse upon which were
erected the wooden houses that represented all their fortune. In the summer-time the sight of the smooth and
brilliant Mediterranean made them recall the dangers of
the winter. They spoke with religious terror of the

land breeze, the wind from the Pyrenees, the *Tramon-tana* that oftentimes snatched edifices from their bases and had overturned entire trains in the nearby station. Furthermore, on the other side of the promontory began the terrible Gulf of Lyons. Upon its surface, not more than ninety yards in extent, the waters driven by the strong sea winds often became so rough, and raised up waves so high and so solid that upon clashing together and finding no intermediate space upon which to fall, they piled one upon another, forming regular towers.

This gulf was the most terrible of the Mediterranean. The transatlantic liners returning from a good voyage to the other hemisphere used here to tremble with a premonition of danger and sometimes even turned back. The captains who had just crossed the great Atlantic would here furrow their brows with uneasiness.

From the door of the Athenæum the experts used to point out the Latin sailboats that were about to double the promontory. They were merchant vessels such as the elder Ferragut had commanded, embarkations from Valencia that were bringing wine to Cette and fruits to Marseilles. Upon seeing the blue surface of the Gulf on the other side of the Cape with no other roughness than that of a long and infinitely heavy swell, the Valencians would exclaim happily :

"Let us cross quickly, while the lion sleeps."

Ulysses had one friend, the secretary of the city-hall, and the only inhabitant that had any books in his house. Treated by the rich with a certain contempt, the official used to seek the boy's company because he was the only creature who would listen to him attentively.

He adored the *mare nostrum* as much as Doctor Ferragut, but his enthusiasm was not concerned with the Phœnician and Egyptian ships whose keels had first plowed these waves. He was equally indifferent to Gre-

cian and Carthaginian Triremes, Roman warships, and
the monstrous galleys of the Sicilian tyrants,—palaces
moved by oars, with statues, fountains and gardens. That
which most interested him was the Mediterranean of the
Middle Ages, that of the kings of Aragon, the Catalunian
Sea. And the poor secretary would give long daily dis-
sertations about them in order to pique the local pride
of his juvenile listener.

One day after dilating at length on Roger de Lauria
and the Catalan navy, he wound up his tedious history
by telling the little fellow how Alfonso V, his brother the
King of Navarre, and all his cortège of magnates, had
remained prisoners of the Republic of Genoa, which, terrified by the importance of its royal prey, had entrusted
the captives to the guard of the Duke of Milan. . . . But
the monarchs easily came to an understanding in order
to deceive the democratic governments, and the Milanese
sovereign released the King of Aragon with all his suite.
Thereupon he immediately blockaded Genoa with an
enormous fleet. The Provençal navy came promptly to
the relief of its neighbors, and the Aragonese King
forced the port of Marseilles, bearing away as trophy
the chains that closed its entrance.

Ulysses nodded affirmatively. The sailor king had deposited these chains in the cathedral of Valencia. His
godfather, the poet, had pointed them out to him in a
Gothic chapel, forming a garland of iron over the black
hewn stones.

The Catalan navy still continued to dominate the Mediterranean commercially, adding to its ancient vessels great
galleons, lighter galleys, caravels, cattle boats, and other
ships of the period.

"But Christopher Columbus," concluded the Catalan
sadly, "discovered the Indies, thereby giving a death blow
to the maritime riches of the Mediterranean. Besides,

Aragon and Castile became united and their life and power were then concentrated in the center of the Peninsula, far from the sea."

Had Barcelona been the capital of Spain, Catalunia would have preserved the Mediterranean domination. Had Lisbon been the capital, the Spanish colonial realm would have developed into something organic and solid with a robust life. But what could you expect of a nation which had stuck its head into a pillow of yellow interior steppes, the furthest possible from the world's highways, showing only its feet to the waves! . . .

The Catalan would always end by speaking sadly of the decadence of the Mediterranean marine. Everything that was pleasing to his tastes made him hark back to the good old time of the domination of the Mediterranean by the Catalan marine. One day he offered Ulysses a sweet and perfumed wine.

"It is Malvasian, the first stock the Almogavars brought here from Greece."

Then he said in order to flatter the boy:

"It was a citizen of Valencia, Ramon Muntaner, who wrote of the expeditions of the Catalans and Aragonese against Constantinople."

The mere recollection of this novel-like adventure, the most unheard-of in history, used to fill him with enthusiasm, and, in passing, he paid highest tribute to the Almogavar chronicler, a rude Homer in song, Ulysses and Nestor in council, and Achilles in hard action.

Doña Cristina's impatience to rejoin her husband and to return to the comforts of her well-regulated household finally carried Ulysses away from this life by the coast.

For many years thereafter he saw no other sea than the Gulf of Valencia. The notary, under various pretexts, contrived to prevent the doctor's again carrying off his nephew; and the *Triton* made his trips to Valencia less frequently, rebelling against all the inconveniences and dangers of these terrestrial adventures.

And Labarta, when occupied with the future of Ulysses, used to take on a certain air of a good-natured regent charged with the guardianship of a little prince. The boy appeared to belong to them more than to his own father; his studies and his future destiny filled completely their after-dinner conversations when the doctor was in town.

Don Esteban felt a certain satisfaction in annoying his brother by eulogizing the sedentary and prosperous life.

Over there on the coasts of Catalunia lived his brothers-in-law, the Blanes, genuine wolves of the sea. The doctor would not be able to contradict that. Very well, then,—their sons were in Barcelona, some as business clerks, others making a name for themselves in the office of their rich uncle. They were all sailors' sons and yet they had completely freed themselves from the sea. Their business was entirely on *terra firma*. Only crazyheads could think of ships and adventures.

The *Triton* used to smile humbly before such pointed allusions, and exchange glances with his nephew.

A secret existed between the two. Ulysses, who was finishing his studies for a bachelor's degree, was at the same time taking the courses of pilotage at the institute. Two years would be sufficient for the completion of these latter studies. The uncle had provided the matriculation fees and the books, besides recommending the boy to a former sailor comrade.

CHAPTER III

WHEN Don Esteban died very suddenly, his eighteen-year-old son was still studying in the university.

In his latter days the notary had begun to suspect that Ulysses was not going to be the celebrated jurist that he had dreamed. He had a way of cutting classes in order to pass the morning in the harbor, exercising with the oars. If he entered the university, the beadles were on their guard fearing his long-reaching hands: for he already fancied himself a sailor and liked to imitate the men of the sea who, accustomed to contend with the elements, considered a quarrel with a man as a very slight affair. Alternating violently between study and laziness, he was laboriously approaching the end of his course when neuralgia of the heart carried off the notary.

Upon coming out from the stupefaction of her grief, Doña Cristina looked around her with aversion. Why should she linger on in Valencia? Since she could no longer be with the man who had brought her to this country, she wanted to return to her own people. The poet Labarta would look after her properties that were not so valuable nor numerous as the income of the notary had led them to suppose. Don Esteban had suffered great losses in extravagant business speculations good-naturedly accepted, but there was still left a fortune sufficient to enable his wife to live as an independent widow among her relatives in Barcelona.

In arranging her new existence, the poor lady en-

countered no opposition except the rebelliousness of
Ulysses. He refused to continue his college course and
he wished to go to sea, saying that for that reason he had
studied to become a pilot. In vain Doña Cristina entreated the aid of relatives and friends, excluding the
Triton, whose response she could easily guess. The rich
brother from Barcelona was brief and affirmative, "But
wouldn't that bring him in the money?" . . . The Blanes
of the coast showed a gloomy fatalism. It would be
useless to oppose the lad if he felt that to be his voca-
tion. The sea had a tight clutch upon those who followed
it, and there was no power on earth that could dissuade
him. On that account they who were already old were
not listening to their sons who were trying to tempt them
with the convenience of life in the capital. They needed
to live near the coast in agreeable contact with the
dark and ponderous monster which had rocked them so
maternally when it might just as easily have dashed them
to pieces.

The only one who protested was Labarta. A sailor?
. . . that might be a very good thing, but a warlike
sailor, an official of the Royal Armada. And in his mind's
eye the poet could see his godson clad in all the splendors of naval elegance,—a blue jacket with gold buttons
for every day, and for holiday attire a coat trimmed with
galloon and red trappings, a pointed hat, a sword. . . .

Ulysses shrugged his shoulders before such grandeur.
He was too old now to enter the naval school. Besides
he wanted to sail over all oceans, and the officers of the
navy only had occasion to cruise from one port to another
like the people of the coast trade, or even passed years
seated in the cabinet of the naval executive. If he had
to grow old in an office, he would rather take up his
father's profession of notary.

After seeing Doña Cristina well established in Barce-

lona, surrounded with a cortège of nephews fawning
upon the rich aunt from Valencia, her son embarked as
apprentice on a transatlantic boat which was making
regular trips to Cuba and the United States. Thus began the seafaring life of Ulysses Ferragut, which terminated only with his death.

The pride of the family placed him on a luxurious
steamer, a mail-packet full of passengers, a floating hotel
on which the officials were something like the managers
of the Palace Hotel, while the real responsibility de-
volved upon the engineers, who were always going below,
and upon returning to the light, invariably remained modestly in a second place, according to a hieratical law anterior to the progress of mechanics.

He crossed the ocean several times, as do those making a land journey at the full speed of an express train.
The august calm of the sea was lost in the throb of the
screws and in the deafening roar of the machinery.
However blue the sky might be, it was always darkened
by the floating crêpe band from the smokestacks. He
envied the leisurely sailboats that the liner was always
leaving behind. They were like reflective wayfarers
who saturate themselves with the country atmosphere and
commune deeply with its soul. The people of the steamer
lived like terrestrial travelers who sleepily survey from
the car-windows a succession of indefinite and dizzying
views streaked by telegraph wires.

When his novitiate was ended he became second mate
on a sailing vessel bound for Argentina for a cargo
of wheat. The slow day's run with little wind and
the long equatorial calms permitted him to penetrate a
little into the mysteries of the oceanic immensity, severe
and dark, that for ancient peoples had been "the night
of the abyss," "the sea of utter darkness," "the blue
dragon that daily swallows the sun."

He no longer regarded Father Ocean as the capricious and tyrannical god of the poets. Everything in his depths was working with a vital regularity, subject to the general laws of existence. Even the tempests roared within prescribed and charted quadrangles.

The fresh trade-winds pushed the bark toward the Southeast, maintaining a heavenly serenity in sky and sea. Before the prow hissed the silken wings of flying fish, spreading out in swarms, like little squadrons of diminutive aeroplanes.

Over the masts and yards covered with canvas, the albatross, eagles of the Atlantic desert, traced their long, sweeping circles, flashing across the purest blue their great, sail-like wings. From time to time the boat would meet floating prairies, great fields of seaweed dislodged from the Sargasso Sea. Enormous tortoises drowsed in the midst of these clumps of gulf-weed, serving as islands of repose to the seagulls perched on their shells. Some of the seaweeds were green, nourished by the luminous water of the surface; others had the reddish color of the deep where enters only the deadly chill of the last rays of the sun. Like fruits of the oceanic prairies, there floated past close bunches of dark grapes, leathery capsules filled with brackish water.

As they approached the equator, the breeze kept falling and falling, and the atmosphere became suffocating in the extreme. It was the zone of calms, the ocean of dark, oily waters, in which boats remained for entire weeks with sails limp, without the slightest breath rippling the atmosphere.

Clouds the color of pit coal reflected the ship's slow progress over the sea; showers of rain like whipcord occasionally lashed the deck, followed by a flaming sun that was soon blotted out by a new downpour. These clouds, pregnant with cataracts, this night descending upon the

full daylight of the Atlantic, had been the terror of the
ancients, and yet, thanks to just such phenomena, the
sailors could pass from one hemisphere to another without the light wounding them to death, or the sea scorching
them like a burning glass. The heat of the equator, raising up the water in steam, had formed a band of shade
around the earth. From other worlds it must appear like
a girdle of clouds almost similar to the sidereal rings.

In this gloomy, hot sea was the heart of the ocean,
the center of the circulatory life of the planet. The sky
was a regulator that, absorbing and returning, restored
the evaporation to equilibrium. From this place were
sent forth the rains and dews to all the rest of the
earth, modifying its temperatures favorably for the development of animal and vegetable life. There were exchanged the exhalations of the two worlds; and, converted into clouds, the water of the southern hemisphere
—the hemisphere of the great seas with no other points
of relief than the triangular extremities of Africa and
America, and the humps of the oceanic archipelagoes—
was always reinforcing the rills and rivers of the northern
hemisphere with its inhabited lands.

From this equatorial zone, the heart of the globe, come
forth two rivers of tepid water that heat the coasts of
the north. They are the two currents that issue from
the Gulf of Mexico and the Java Sea. Their enormous
liquid masses, fleeing ceaselessly from the equator, govern a vast assemblage of water from the poles that comes
to occupy their space, and these chilled and fresher currents are constantly precipitating themselves on the electric hearth of the equator that warms and salts them
anew, renewing with its systole and diastole the life
of the world. The ocean struggles vainly to condense
these two warm currents without ever succeeding in
mingling itself with them. They are torrents of a deep

blue, almost black, that flow across the cold and green waters.

The Atlantic current, upon reaching Newfoundland, divides its arms, sending one of them to the North Pole. With the other, weak and exhausted by its long journey, it modifies the temperature of the British Isles, tempering refreshingly the coasts of Norway. The Indian current that the Japanese call, because of its color, "the black river," circulates between the islands, maintaining for a longer time than the other its prodigious powers of creation and agitation which enable it to trail over the planet an enormous tail of life.

Its center is the apogee of terrestrial energy in the vegetable and animal creations, in monsters and in fish. One of its arms, escaping toward the south, goes on forming the mysterious world of the coral sea. In a space as large as four continents, the polyps, strengthened by the lukewarm water, are building up thousands of atolls, ring-shaped islands, reefs and submarine pillars that, when united together by the work of a thousand years, are going to create a new land, an exchange continent in case the human species should lose its present base in some cataclysm of Nature.

The pulse of the blue god is the tides. The earth turns towards the moon and the stars with a sympathetic rotation like that of the flowers that turn towards the sun. Its most movable part—the fluid mass of the atmosphere—dilates twice daily, swelling its cavities; and this atmospheric suction, the work of universal attraction, is reflected in the tidal waters. Closed seas, like the Mediterranean, scarcely feel its effects, the tides stopping at their door. But on the oceanic coast the marine pulsation vexes the army of the waves, hurrying them daily to their assault of the steep cliffs, making them roar with fury among the islands, promontories and straits, and impelling them to swallow up extensive lands which they return hours afterward.

This salty sea, like our body, that has a heart, a pulse and a circulation of two different bloods incessantly renewed and transformed, becomes as furious as an organic creature when the horizontal currents of its interior come to unite themselves with the vertical currents descending from the atmosphere. The violent passage of the winds, the crises of evaporation, and the obscure electrical forces produce the tempests.

These are no more than cutaneous shudderings. The storms, so deadly for mankind, merely contract the marine epidermis while the profound mass of its waters remains in murky calm, fulfilling its great function of nourishing and renewing life. Father Ocean completely ignores the existence of the human insects that dare to slip across his surface in microscopic cockle-shells. He does not inform himself as to the incidents that may be taking place upon the roof of his dwelling. His life continues on,—balanced, calm, infinite, engendering millions upon millions of beings in the thousandth part of a second.

The majesty of the Atlantic on tropical nights made Ulysses forget the wrathful storms of its black days. In the moonlight it was an immense plane of vivid silver streaked with serpentine shadows. Its soft doughlike undulations, replete with microscopic life, illuminated the nights. The infusoria, a-tremble with love, glowed with a bluish phosphorescence. The sea was like luminous milk. The foam breaking against the prow sparkled like broken fragments of electric globes.

When it was absolutely tranquil and the ship remained immovable with drooping sail, the stars passing slowly from one side of the mast to the other, the delicate medusæ, that the slightest wave was able to crush, would come to the surface floating on the waters, around the island of wood. There were thousands of these umbrellas filing slowly by, green, blue, rose, with a vague coloring similar to oil-lights,—a Japanese procession seen from above, that on one side was lost in the mystery of the black waters and incessantly reappeared on the other side.

The young pilot loved navigation in a sailing ship,—the struggle with the wind, the solitude of its calms. He was far nearer the ocean here than on the bridge of a transatlantic liner. The bark did not beat the sea into such rabid foam. It slipped discreetly along as in the maritime silence of the first millennium of the new-born earth. The oceanic inhabitants approached it confidently upon seeing it rolling like a mute and inoffensive whale.

In six years Ulysses changed his boat many times. He had learned English, the universal language of the blue dominions, and was refreshing himself with a study of Maury's charts—the sailors' Bible—the patient work of an obscure genius who first snatched from ocean and atmosphere the secret of their laws.

Desirous of exploring new seas and new lands, he did not stop in the usual travel zones or ports, and the British, Norwegian, and North American captains received cordially this good-mannered official so little exacting as to salary. So Ulysses wandered over the oceans as had the king of Ithaca over the Mediterranean, guided by a fatality which impelled him with a rude push far from his country every time that he proposed to return to it. The sight of a boat anchored near by and ready to set sail for some distant port was a temptation that invariably made him forget to return to Spain.

He traveled in filthy, old, happy-go-lucky sea-tramps, in which the crews used to spread all the sails to the tempest, get drunk and fall asleep, confident that the

devil, friend of the brave, would awaken them on the
following morning. He lived in white boats as silent
and scrupulously clean as a Dutch home, whose captains
were taking wife and children with them, and where
white-aproned stewardesses took care of the galley and
the cleaning of the floating hearthside, sharing the dangers of the ruddy and tranquil sailors exempt from the
temptation that contact with women provokes. On Sundays, under the tropic sun or in the ash-colored light of
the northern heavens, the boatswain would read the Bible.
The men would listen thoughtfully with uncovered heads.
The women had dressed themselves in black with lace
headdress and mittened hands.

He went to Newfoundland to load codfish. There is
where the warm current from the Gulf of Mexico meets
that from the Poles. In the meeting of these two marine
rivers the infinitesimal little beings that the gulf stream
drags thither die, suddenly frozen to death, and a rain
of minute corpses descends across the waters. The
cod gather there to gorge themselves on this manna which
is so abundant that a great part of it, freed from their
greedy jaws, drops to the bottom like a snowstorm of
lime.

In Iceland (the *Ultima Thule* of the ancients), they
showed Ulysses bits of wood that the equatorial current
had brought thither from the Antilles. On the coasts of
Norway, as he watched the herring during the spawning
season, he marveled at the formidable fertility of the sea.

From their refuge in the shadowy depths, these fish
mount to the surface moved by the message of the spring,
desirous of taking their part in the joy of the world.
They swim one against another, close, compact, forming
strata that subdivide and float out to sea. They look
like an island just coming to the surface, or a continent
beginning to sink. In the narrow passages the shoals

are so numerous that the waters become solidified, making almost impossible the advance of a row boat. Their number is beyond the possibilities of calculation, like the sands and the stars.

Men and carnivorous fish fall upon them, opening great furrows of destruction in their midst: but the breaches are closed instantly and the living bank continues on its way, growing denser every moment, as though defying death. The more their enemies destroy them, the more numerous they become. The thick and close columns ceaselessly reproduce themselves *en route*. At sunrise the waves are greasy and viscous,—replete with life that is fermenting rapidly. For a space of hundreds of leagues the salt ocean around them is like milk.

The fecundity of these fishy masses was placing the world in danger. Each individual could produce up to seventy thousand eggs. In a few generations there would be enough to fill the ocean, to make it solid, to make it rot, extinguishing other beings, depopulating the globe. . . . But death was charged with saving universal life. The cetaceans bore down upon this living density and with their insatiable mouths devoured the nourishment by ton loads. Infinitely little fish seconded the efforts of the marine giants, stuffing themselves with the eggs of the herring. The most gluttonous fish, the cod and the hake, pursued these prairies of meat, pushing them toward the coasts and finally dispersing them.

The cod increases its species most prodigiously, surfeiting itself upon hake, until the world is again menaced. The ocean might be converted into a mass of cod, for each one can produce as many as nine million eggs. . . . Mankind might be overwhelmed under the onslaught of the more fertile fishes, and the cod might maintain immense fleets, creating, besides, colonies and cities. Human generations might become exhausted

without succeeding in conquering this monstrous reproduction. The great marine devourers, therefore, are
those that reëstablish equilibrium and order. The stur-
geon, insatiable stomach, intervenes in the oceanic ban-
quet, relishing in the cod the concentrated substance of
armies of herring. But this oviparous devourer of such
great reproductive power would, in turn, continue the
world danger were it not that another monster as avid
in appetite as it is weak in procreation, intervenes and
cuts down with one blow the ever-increasing fecundity of
the ocean.

The superior glutton is the shark,—that mouth with
fins, that natatory intestine which swallows with equal indifference the dead and the living, flesh and wood,
cleanses the waters of life and leaves a desert behind its
wriggling tail; but this destroyer brings forth only one
shark that is born armed and ferocious ready from the
very first moment to continue the paternal exploits, like a
feudal heir.

Ferragut's wandering life as a pilot abounded in dramatic adventures,—a few always standing out clearly
from his many confused recollections of exotic lands
and interminable seas.

In Glasgow he embarked as second mate on an old
sailing tramp that was bound for Chile, to unload coal in
Valparaiso and take on saltpeter in Iquique. The crossing of the Atlantic was good, but upon leaving the Malvina Islands the boat had to go out in the teeth of a torrid, furious blast that closed the passage to the Pacific.
The Straits of Magellan are for ships that are able to
avail themselves at will of a propelling force. The sailboat needs a wide sea and a favorable wind in order to
double Cape Horn,—the utmost point of the earth, the
place of interminable and gigantic tempests.

While summer was burning in the other hemisphere,

ιe terrible southern winter came to meet the navigators.
'he boat had to turn its course to the west, just as the
·inds were blowing from the west, barring its route.

Eight weeks passed and it was still contending with
:a and tempest. The wind carried off a complete set
f sails. The wooden ship, somewhat strained by this
ιterminable struggle, commenced to leak, and the crew
ιad to work the hand-pumps night and day. Nobody
·as able to sleep for many hours running. All were
ck from exhaustion. The rough voice and the oaths of
ιe captain could hardly maintain discipline. Some of
ιe seamen lay down wishing to die, and had to be roused
y blows.

Ulysses knew for the first time what waves really
·ere. He saw mountains of water, literally mountains,
ɔuring over the hull of the boat, their very immensity
ιaking them form great slopes on both sides of it.
Vhen the crest of one broke upon the vessel Ferragut
·as able to realize the monstrous weight of salt water.
'either stone nor iron had the brutal blow of this liquid
ɔrce that, upon breaking, fled in torrents or dashed up
ι spray. They had to make openings in the bulwarks
ι order to provide a vent for the crushing mass.

The southern day was a livid and foggy eclipse, re-
:ating itself for weeks and weeks without the slightest
·reak of clearing, as though the sun had departed from
ιe earth forever. Not a glimmer of white existed in this
:mpestuous outline; always gray,—the sky, the foam, the
:agulls, the snows. . . . From time to time the leaden
:ils of the tempest were torn asunder, leaving visible a
·rrifying apparition. Once it was black mountains with
lacial winding sheets from the Straits of Beagle. And
ιe boat tacked, fleeing away from this narrow aquatic
ιssageway full of perilous ledges. Another time the
:aks of Diego Ramirez, the most extreme point of the

cape, loomed up before the prow, and the bark again
tacked, fleeing from this cemetery of ships. The wind
shifting, then brought their first icebergs into view and
at the same time forced them to turn back on their
course in order not to be lost in the deserts of the South
Pole.

Ferragut came to believe that they would never double
the Cape, remaining forever in full tempest, like the accursed ship of the legend of the Flying Dutchman. The
captain, a regular savage of the sea, taciturn and superstitious, shook his fist at the promontory, cursing it as
an infernal divinity. He was convinced that they would
never succeed in doubling it until it should be propitiated
with a human offering. This Englishman appeared to
Ulysses like one of those Argonauts who used to placate
the wrath of the marine deities with sacrifices.

One night one of the crew was washed overboard and
lost; the following day a man fell from the topmast
that no one might think salvation impossible. And although the Southern Demon had only been awaiting this
tribute, the gale from the west ceased, the bark no
longer had the impassable barrier of a hostile sea before
its prow, and was able to enter the Pacific, anchoring
twelve days later in Valparaiso.

Ulysses appreciated now the agreeable memory that
this port always leaves in the memory of sailors. It
was a resting-place after the struggle of doubling the
cape; it was the joy of existence, after having felt the
blast of death; it was life again in the cafés and in the
pleasure houses, eating and drinking until surfeited, with
the stomach still suffering from the salty food and the
skin still smarting from boils due to the sea-life.

His admiring gaze followed the graceful step of the
women veiled in black who reminded him of his uncle

the doctor. In the nights of the *remolienda*,[1] his glance was many times distracted from the dark-hued and youthful beauties dancing the *Zamacueca*[2] in the middle of the room, to the matrons swathed in black veils, who were playing the harp and piano, accompanying the dance with languishing songs which interested him greatly. Perhaps one of these sentimental, bearded ladies might have been his aunt.

While his ship finished loading its cargo in Iquique, he came in contact with the crowd of workers from the saltpeter works,—"broken-down"[3] Chileans, laboring men from all countries, who did not know how to spend their day's wages in the monotony of these new settlements. Their intoxication diverted itself with most mistaken magnificence. Some would let the wine run from an entire cask just to fill a single glass. Others used the bottles of champagne lined up on the shelves of the cafés as a target for their revolvers, paying cash for all that they broke.

From this trip Ferragut gained a feeling of pride and confidence that made him scornful of every danger. Afterwards he encountered the tornadoes of the Asiatic seas, those horrible circular tempests that in the northern hemisphere revolve from right to left, and in the south from left to right—rapid incidents of a few hours or days at the most. He had doubled Cape Horn in midwinter after a struggle against the elements that had lasted two months. He had been able to run all risks; the ocean had exhausted for him all its surprises. . . . And yet, nevertheless, the worst of his adventures occurred in a calm sea.

He had been at sea seven years and was thinking of

[1] *Remolienda,*—a popular gathering or festival in Chile.
[2] *Zamacueca,* the national dance of Chile.
[3] *"Rotos chilenos,"* originally a term of contempt is now a complimentary by-name.

returning once more to Spain when, in Hamburg, he
accepted the post of first mate of a swift-sailing ship that
was setting out for Cameroon and German East Africa.
A Norwegian sailor tried to dissuade him from this
trip. It was an old ship, and they had insured it for
four times its value. The captain was in league with the
proprietor, who had been bankrupt many times. . . . And
just because this voyage was so irrational, Ulysses hastened to embark. For him, prudence was merely a vulgarity, and obstacles and dangers but tempted more irresistibly his reckless daring.

One evening in the latitude of Portugal, when they
were far from the regular route of navigation, a column
of smoke and flames suddenly swept the deck, breaking
through the hatchways and devouring the sails. While
Ferragut at the head of a band of negroes was trying
to get control of the fire, the captain and the German
crew were escaping from the ship in two prepared lifeboats. Ferragut felt sure that the fugitives were laughing
at seeing him run about the deck that was beginning to
warp and send up fire through all its cracks.

Without ever knowing exactly how, he found himself
in a boat with some negroes and different objects piled
together with the precipitation of flight,—a half-empty
barrel of biscuits and another that contained only water.

They rowed all one night, having behind them as their
unlucky star the burning boat that was sending its blood-
red gleams across the water. At daybreak they noted
on the sun's disk some light, black, wavy lines. It was
land. . . . but so far away!

For two days they wandered over the moving crests
and gloomy valleys of the blue desert. Several times
Ferragut collapsed in mortal lethargy, with his feet in
the water filling the bottom of the boat. The birds of
the sea were tracing spirals around this floating hearse,

following it with vigorous strokes of the wing, and uttering croakings of death. The waves raised themselves slowly and sluggishly over the boat's edge as though wishing to contemplate with their sea-green eyes this medley of white and dark bodies. The shipwrecked men rowed with nervous desperation; then they lay down inert, recognizing the uselessness of their efforts, lost in the great immensity.

The mate, drowsing on the hard stern, finally smiled with closed eyes. It was all a bad dream. He was sure of awaking in his bed surrounded with the familiar comforts of his stateroom. And when he opened his eyes, the harsh reality made him break forth into desperate orders, which the Africans obeyed as mechanically as though they were still sleeping.

"I do not want to die! . . . I ought not to die!" asserted his inner monitor in a brazen tone.

They shouted and made unavailing signals to distant boats that disappeared from the great watery expanse without ever seeing them. Two negroes died of the cold. Their corpses floated many hours near the boat as if unable to separate themselves from it. Then they were drawn under by an invisible tugging, and some triangular fins passed over the water's surface, cutting it like knives at the same time that its depths were darkened by swift, ebony shadows.

When at last they approached land, Ferragut realized that death was nearer here than on the high sea. The coast rose up before them like an immense wall. Seen from the boat it appeared to cover half the sky. The long oceanic undulation became a ravenous wave upon encountering the outer bulwarks of these barren islands, breaking in the depths of their caves, and forming cascades of foam that rolled around them from top to bot-

tom, raising up furious columns of spray with the report
of a cannonade.

An irresistible hand grasped the keel, making the landing a vertical one. Ferragut shot out like a projectile,
falling in the foaming whirlpools and having the impression, as he sank, that men and casks together were rolling
and raining into the sea.

He saw bubbling streaks of white and black hulks.
He felt himself impelled by contradictory forces. Some
dragged at his head and others at his feet in different
directions, making him revolve like the hands of a clock.
Even his thoughts were working double. "It is useless to
resist," Discouragement was murmuring in his brain,
while his other half was affirming desperately, "I do not
want to die! . . . I must not die!"

Thus he lived through a few seconds that seemed to
him like hours. He felt the brute force of hidden friction, then a blow in the abdomen that arrested his course
between the two waters, and grasping at the irregularities
of a projecting rock, he raised his head and was able to
breathe. The wave was retreating, but another again
overwhelmed him, detaching him from the point with
its foamy churning, making him leave in the stony crevices bits of the skin of his hands, his breast, and his
knees.

The oceanic suction seemed dragging him down in spite
of his desperate strokes. "It's no use! I'm going to die,"
half of his mind was saying and at the same time his
other mental hemisphere was reviewing with lightning
synthesis his entire life. He saw the bearded face of
the *Triton* in this supreme instant. He saw the poet
Labarta just as when he was recounting to his godson
the adventures of the old Ulysses, and his shipwrecked
struggle with the rocky peaks and waves.

Again the marine dilatation tossed him against a rock,

and again he anchored himself to it with an instinctive
clutch of his hands. But before this wave retired it
hurled him desperately upon another ledge, the refluent
water passing back below him. Thus he struggled a long
time, clinging to the rocks when the sea overwhelmed
him, and crawling along upon the jutting points whenever
the retiring water permitted.

Finding himself upon a projecting point of the coast,
free at last from the suction of the waves, his energy
suddenly disappeared. The water that dripped from his
body was red, each time more red, spreading itself in
rivulets over the greenish irregularities of the rock. He
felt intense pain as though all his organism had lost the
protection of its covering,—his raw flesh remaining exposed to the air.

He wished to get somewhere, but over his head the
coast was rearing its stark bulk,—a concave and inaccessible wall. It would be impossible to get away from
this spot. He had saved himself from the sea only to
die stationed in front of it. His corpse would never float
to an inhabited shore. The only ones that were going
to know of his death were the enormous crabs scrambling
over the rocky points, seeking their nourishment in the
surge ; the sea gulls were letting themselves drop vertically
with extended wings from the heights of the steep-sloped
shore. Even the smallest crustaceans had the advantage
of him.

Suddenly he felt all his weakness, all his misery,
while his blood continued crimsoning the little lakes
among the rocks. Closing his eyes to die, he saw in the
darkness a pale face, hands that were deftly weaving
delicate laces, and before night should descend forever
upon his eyelids, he moaned a childish cry:

"*Mamá! . . . Mamá! . . .*"

Three months afterward upon arriving at Barcelona,

he found his mother just as he had seen her during his death-agony on the Portuguese coast. . . . Some fishermen had picked him up just as his life was ebbing away. During his stay in the hospital he wrote many times in a light and confident tone to Doña Cristina, pretending that he was detained by important business in Lisbon.

Upon seeing him enter his home, the good lady dropped her eternal lace-work, turned pale and greeted him with tremulous hands and troubled eyes. She must have known the truth; and if she did not know it, her motherly instinct told her when she saw Ulysses convalescent, emaciated, hovering between courageous effort and physical breakdown, just like the brave who come out of the torture chamber.

"Oh, my son! . . . How much longer! . . ."

It was time that he should bring to an end his madness for adventure, his crazy desire for attempting the impossible, and encountering the most absurd dangers. If he wished to follow the sea, very well. But let it be in respectable vessels in the service of a great company, following a career of regular promotion, and not wandering capriciously over all seas, associated with the international lawlessness that the ports offer for the reinforcement of crews. Remaining quietly at home would be best of all. Oh, what happiness if he would but stay with his mother! . . .

And Ulysses, to the astonishment of Doña Cristina, decided to do so. The good señora was not alone. A niece was living with her as though she were her daughter. The sailor had only to go down in the depths of his memory to recall a little tot of a girl four years old, creeping and frolicking on the shore while he, with the gravity of a man, had been listening to the old secretary of the town, as he related the past grandeurs of the Catalunian navy.

She was the daughter of a Blanes (the only poor one in the family) who had commanded his relatives' ships, and had died of yellow fever in a Central American port. Ferragut had difficulty in reconciling the little creature crawling over the sand with this same slender, olive-colored girl wearing her mass of hair like a helmet of ebony, with two little spirals escaping over the ears. Her eyes appeared to have the changing tints of the sea, some-times black and others blue, or green and deep where the light of the sun was reflected like a point of gold.

He was attracted by her simplicity and by the timid grace of her words and smile. She was an irresistible novelty for this world-rover who had only known coppery maidens with bestial roars of laughter, yellowish Asiatics with feline gestures, or Europeans from the great ports who, at the first words, beg for drink, and sing upon the knees of the one who is treating, wearing his cap as a testimony of love.

Cinta, that was her name, appeared to have known him all his life. He had been the object of her conversations with Doña Cristina when they spent monotonous hours together weaving lace, as was the village custom. Pass-ing her room, Ulysses noticed there some of his own portraits at the time when he was a simple apprentice aboard a transatlantic liner. Cinta had doubtless taken them from her aunt's room, for she had been admiring this adventurous cousin long before knowing him. One evening the sailor told the two women how he had been rescued on the coast of Portugal. The mother listened with averted glance, and with trembling hands moving the bobbins of her lace. Suddenly there was an outcry. It was Cinta who could not listen any longer, and Ulysses felt flattered by her tears, her convulsive la-ments, her eyes widened with an expression of terror.

Ferragut's mother had been greatly concerned regard-

ing the future of this poor niece. Her only salvation was
matrimony, and the good señora had focused her glances
upon a certain relative a little over forty who needed this
young girl to enliven his life of mature bachelorhood. He
was the wise one of the family. Doña Cristina used to
admire him because he was not able to read without the
aid of glasses, and because he interlarded his conversation with Latin, just like the clergy. He was teaching
Latin and rhetoric in the Institute of Manresa and spoke
of being transferred some day to Barcelona,—glorious
end of an illustrious career. Every week he escaped to
the capital in order to make long visits to the notary's
widow.

"He doesn't come on my account," said the good señora, "who would bother about an old woman like me?
. . . I tell you that he is in love with Cinta, and it will
be good luck for the child to marry a man so wise, so
serious. . . ."

As he listened to his mother's matrimonial schemes,
Ulysses began to wonder which of a professor of rhetoric's bones a sailor might break without incurring too
much responsibility.

One day Cinta was looking all over the house for a
dark, worn-out thimble that she had been using for
many years. Suddenly she ceased her search, blushed and
dropped her eyes. Her glance had met an evasive look
on her cousin's face. He had it. In Ulysses' room might
be seen ribbons, skeins of silk, an old fan—all deposited
in books and papers by the same mysterious reflex that
had drawn his portraits from his mother's to his cousin's
room.

The sailor now liked to remain at home passing long
hours meditating with his elbows on the table, but at the
same time attentive to the rustling of light steps that
could be heard from time to time in the near-by hallway.

He knew about everything,—spherical and rectangular trigonometry, cosmography, the laws of the winds and the tempest, the latest oceanographic discoveries—but who could teach him the approved form of addressing a maiden without frightening her? . . . Where the deuce could a body learn the art of proposing to a shy girl? . . .

For him, doubts were never very long nor painful affairs. Forward march! Let every one get out of such matters as best he could. And one evening when Cinta was going from the parlor to her aunt's bedroom in order to bring her a devotional book, she collided with Ulysses in the passageway.

If she had not known him, she might have trembled for her existence. She felt herself grasped by a pair of powerful hands that lifted her up from the floor. Then an avid mouth stamped upon hers two aggressive kisses. "Take that and that!" . . . Ferragut repented on seeing his cousin trembling against the wall, as pale as death, her eyes filled with tears.

"I have hurt you. I am a brute. . . . a brute!"

He almost fell on his knees, imploring her pardon; he clenched his fists as if he were going to strike himself, punishing himself for his audacity. But she would not let him continue. . . . "No, No! . . ." And while she was moaning this protest, her arms were forming a ring around Ulysses' neck. Her head drooped toward his, seeking the shelter of his shoulder. A little mouth united itself modestly to that of the sailor, and at the same time his beard was moistened with a shower of tears.

And they said no more about it.

When, weeks afterward, Doña Cristina heard her son's petition, her first movement was one of protest. A mother listens with benevolent appreciation to any request for the hand of her daughter, but she is ambitious and exacting where her son is concerned. She had dreamed of something so much more brilliant; but her indecision was short. That timid girl was perhaps the best companion for Ulysses, after all. Furthermore the child was well suited to be the wife of a man of the sea, having seen its life from her infancy. . . . Good-by Professor!

They were married. Soon afterwards Ferragut, who was not able to lead an inactive life, returned to the sea, but as first officer of a transatlantic steamer that made regular trips to South America. To him this seemed like being employed in a floating office, visiting the same ports and invariably repeating the same duties. His mother was extremely proud to see him in uniform. Cinta fixed her gaze on the almanac as the wife of a clerk fixes it on the clock. She had the certainty that when three months should have passed by she would see him reappear, coming from the other side of the world laden down with exotic gifts, just as a husband who returns from the office with a bouquet bought in the street.

Upon his return from his first two voyages, she went to meet him on the wharf, her eager glance searching for his blue coat and his cap with its band of gold among the transatlantic passengers fluttering about the decks, rejoicing at their arrival in Europe.

On the following trip, Doña Cristina obliged her to remain at home, fearing that the excitement and the crowds at the harbor might affect her approaching maternity. After that on each of his return trips Ferragut saw a new son, although always the same one; first it was a bundle of batiste and lace carried by a showily-uniformed nurse; then by the time he was captain of the transatlantic liner, a little cherub in short skirts, chubby-cheeked, with a round head covered with a silky down, holding out its little arms to him; finally a boy who was beginning to go to school and at sight of his father would grasp his hard right hand, admiring him with his great eyes, as though he saw in his person the concentrated perfection of all the forces of the universe.

Don Pedro, the professor, continued visiting the house of Doña Cristina, although with less assiduity. He had the resigned and coldly wrathful attitude of the man who believes that he has arrived too late and is convinced that his bad luck was merely the result of his carelessness. . . . If he had only spoken before! His masculine self-importance never permitted him to doubt that the young girl would have accepted him jubilantly.

In spite of this conviction, he was not able to refrain at times from a certain ironical aggressiveness which expressed itself by inventing classic nicknames. The young wife of Ulysses, bending over her lace-making, was Penelope awaiting the return of her wandering husband.

Doña Cristina accepted this nickname because she knew vaguely that Penelope was a queen of good habits. But the day that the professor, by logical deduction, called Cinta's son Telemachus, the grandmother protested.

"He is named Esteban after his grandfather. . . . Telemachus is nothing but a theatrical name."

On one of his voyages Ulysses took advantage of a four-hour stop in the port of Valencia to see his godfather. From time to time he had been receiving letters from the poet,—each one shorter and sadder,—written in a trembling script that announced his age and increasing infirmity.

Upon entering the office Ferragut felt just like the legendary sleepers who believe themselves awaking after a few hours of sleep when they have really been dozing for dozens of years. Everything there was still just as it was in his infancy:—the busts of the great poets on the top of the book-cases, the wreaths in their glass cases, the jewels and statuettes, prizes for successful poems—

were still in their crystal cabinets or resting on the same pedestals; the books in their resplendent bindings formed their customary close battalions the length of the book-cases But the whiteness of the busts had taken on the color of chocolate, the bronzes were reddened by oxidation, the gold had turned greenish, and the wreaths were losing their leaves. It seemed as though ashes might have rained down upon perpetuity.

The occupants of this spell-bound dwelling presented the same aspect of neglect and deterioration. Ulysses found the poet thin and yellow, with a long white beard, with one eye almost closed and the other very widely opened. Upon seeing the young officer, broad-chested, vigorous and bronzed, Labarta, who was huddled in a great arm chair, began to cry with a childish hiccough as though he were weeping over the misery of human illusions, over the brevity of a deceptive life that necessitates continual renovation.

Ferragut found even greater difficulty in recognizing the little and shrunken señora who was near the poet. Her flabby flesh was hanging from her skeleton like the ragged fringe of past splendor; her head was small; her face had the wrinkled surface of a winter apple or plum, or of all the fruits that shrink and wither when they lose their juices. "Doña Pepa! . . ." The two old people were thee-ing and thou-ing each other with the tranquil non-morality of those that realize that they are very near to death, and forget the tremors and scruples of a life crumbling behind them.

The sailor shrewdly suspected that all this physical misery was the sad finale of an absurd, happy-go-lucky and childish dietary,—sweets serving as the basis of nutrition, great heavy rice dishes as a daily course, water-melons and cantaloupes filling in the space between meals,

topped with ices served in enormous glasses and sending
out a perfume of honeyed snow.

The two told him, sighing, of their infirmities, which
they thought incomprehensible, attributing them to the
ignorance of the doctors. It was really the morbid wasting away that suddenly attacks people of the abundant,
food-yielding countries. Their life was one continual
stream of liquid sugar. . . . And yet Ferragut could
easily guess the disobedience of the two old folks to the
discipline of diet, their childish deceptions, their cunning in order to enjoy alone the fruits and syrups which
were the enchantment of their existence.

The interview was a short one. The captain had to
return to the port of Grao where his steamer was awaiting him, ready to weigh anchor for South America.

The poet wept again, kissing his god-son. He never
would see again this Colossus who seemed to repel his
weak embraces with the bellows of his respiration.

"Ulysses, my son! . . . Always think of Valencia. . . .
Do for her all that you can. . . . Keep her ever in mind,
always Valencia!"

He promised all that the poet wished without understanding exactly what it was that Valencia might expect from him, a simple sailor, wandering over all the
seas. Labarta wished to accompany him to the door but
he sank down in his seat, obedient to the affectionate
despotism of his companion who was always fearing the
greatest catastrophes for him.

Poor Doña Pepa! . . . Ferragut felt inclined to laugh
and to weep at the same time upon receiving a kiss from
her withered mouth whose down had turned into pin
points. It was the kiss of an old beauty who remembers the gallantry of a youthful lover, the kiss of a child-
less woman caressing the son she might have had.

"Poor unhappy Carmelo! . . . He no longer writes,

he no longer reads. . . . Ay! what will ever become of me? . . ."

She always spoke of the poet's failing powers with the commiseration of a strong and healthy person, and she became terrified when thinking of the years in which she might survive her lord. Taken up with caring for him, she never even glanced at herself.

A year afterward, on returning from the Philippines, the captain found a letter from his god-father awaiting him at Port Said. Doña Pepa had died, and Labarta, working off the tearful heaviness of his low spirits, bade her farewell in a long canticle. Ulysses ran his eyes over the enclosed newspaper clipping containing the last verses of the poet. The stanzas were in Castilian. A bad sign! . . . After that there could be no doubt that his end must be very near.

Ferragut never again had an opportunity to see his god-father, who died while he was on one of his trips. Upon disembarking at Barcelona, Doña Cristina handed him a letter written by the poet almost in his death-agony. "Valencia, my son! Always Valencia!" And after repeating this recommendation many times, he announced that he had made his god-son his heir.

The books, the statues, all the glorious souvenirs of the poet-laureate, came to Barcelona to adorn the sailor's home. The little Telemachus amused himself pulling apart the old wreaths of the troubador, and tearing out the old prints from his volumes with the inconsequence of a lively child whose father is very far away and who knows that he is idolized by two indulgent ladies. Besides his trophies, the poet left Ulysses an old house in Valencia, some real estate and a certain amount in negotiable securities,—total, thirty thousand dollars.

The other guardian of his infancy, the vigorous *Triton,* seemed to be unaffected by the passing of the years.

Upon his return to Barcelona, Ferragut frequently found
him installed in his home, in mute hostility to Doña Cristina, devoting to Cinta and her son a part of the affection that he had formerly lavished upon Ulysses alone.

He was very desirous that the little Esteban should
know the home of his great grandparents.

"You will let me have him? . . . You know well
enough," he coaxed, "that down in the *Marina* men become as strong as though made of bronze.   Surely you
will let me have him? . . ."

But he quailed before the indignant gesture of the
suave Doña Cristina.   Entrust her grandson to the
Triton, and let him awaken in him the love of maritime
adventure, as he had done with Ulysses? . . . Behind
me, thou blue devil!

The doctor used to wander around bewildered by
the port of Barcelona. . . . Too much noisy bustle, too
much movement!   Walking proudly along by the side of
Ulysses, he loved to recount to him the adventures of
his life as a sailor and cosmopolitan vagabond.   He considered his nephew the greatest of the Ferraguts, a true
man of the sea like his ancestors but with the title of
captain;—an adventurous rover over all oceans, as he
had been, but with a place on the bridge, invested with
the absolute command that responsibility and danger con-
fer.   When Ulysses reëmbarked, the *Triton* would take
himself off to his own dominions.

"It will be next time, sure!" he would say in order
to console himself for having to part with his nephew's
son; and after a few months had passed by, he would
reappear, each time larger, uglier, more tanned, with
a silent smile which broke into words before Ulysses
just as tempestuous clouds break forth in thunder claps.

Upon his return from a trip to the Black Sea, Doña
Cristina announced to her son: "Your uncle has died."

The pious señora lamented as a Christian the departure of her brother-in-law, dedicating a part of her prayers to him; but she insisted with a certain cruelty in giving an account of his sad end, for she had never been able to pardon his fatal intervention in the destiny of Ulysses. He had died as he had lived,—in the sea, a victim of his own rashness, without confession, just like any pagan.

Another legacy thus fell to Ferragut. . . . His uncle had gone out swimming one sunny, winter morning and had never come back. The old folks on the shore had their way of explaining how the accident had happened, —a fainting spell probably, a clash against the rocks. The *Dotor* was still vigorous, but the years do not pass without leaving their footprints. Some believed that he must have had a struggle with a shark or some other of the carnivorous fish that abound in the Mediterranean waters. In vain the fishermen guided their skiffs through all the twisting entrances and exits of the waters around the promontory, exploring the gloomy caves and the lower depths of crystalline transparency. No one was ever able to find the *Triton's* body.

Ferragut recalled the cortege of Aphrodite which the doctor had so often described to him on summer evenings, by the light of the far-away gleam of the lighthouse. Perhaps he had come upon that gay retinue of nereids, joining it forever!

This absurd supposition that Ulysses mentally formulated with a sad and incredulous smile, frequently recurred in the simple thoughts of many of the people of the *Marina.*

They refused to believe in his death. A wizard is never drowned. He must have found down below something very interesting and when he got tired of living in the green depths, he would probably some day come swimming back home.

No: the *Dotor* had not died.

And for many years afterwards the women who were going along the coast at nightfall would quicken their steps, crossing themselves upon distinguishing on the dark waters a bit of wood or a bunch of sea weed. They feared that suddenly would spring forth the *Triton,* bearded, dripping, spouting, returning from his excursion into the mysterious depths of the sea.

CHAPTER IV

THE name of Ulysses Ferragut began to be famous among the captains of the Spanish ports, although the nautical adventures of his early days contributed very little to this popularity. The most of them had encountered greater dangers, but they appreciated him because of the instinctive respect that energetic and simple men have for an intelligence which they consider superior to their own. Reading nothing except what pertained to their career, they used to speak with consternation of the numerous books that filled Ferragut's stateroom, many of them upon matters which appeared to them most mysterious. Some even made inexact statements in order to enlarge the prestige of their comrade.

"He knows much. . . . He is a lawyer as well as a sailor."

Consideration of his fortune also contributed to the general appreciation. He was an important share-holder of the company by which he was employed. His companions loved to calculate with proud exaggeration the riches of his mother, piling it up into millions

He met friends on every ship carrying the Spanish flag, whatever might be its home port or the nationality of its crews.

They all liked him:—the Basque captains, economical in words, rude and sparing in affectionate discourse; the Asturian and Galician captains, self-confident and spend-thrift in strange contrast to their sobriety and avaricious character when ashore; the Andalusian captains, reflecting in their witty talk white Cadiz and its luminous wines; the Valencian captains who talk of politics on the bridge, imagining that they are going to become the navy of a future republic; and the captains from Catalunia and Mallorca as thoroughly acquainted with business affairs as are their ship-owners. Whenever necessity obliged them to defend their rights, they immediately thought of Ulysses. Nobody could write as he could.

The old mates who had worked their way up from the lower ranks, men of the sea who had begun their career on coasting vessels and could only with great difficulty adjust their practical knowledge to the handling of books, used to speak of Ferragut with pride.

"They say that men of the sea are an uncultivated people. . . . Here they have *Don Luis* who is one of us. They may ask him whatever they wish. . . . A real sage!"

The name of Ulysses always made them stammer. They believed it a nickname, and not wishing to show any lack of respect, they had finally transformed it into "Don Luis." For some of them, Ferragut's only defect was his good luck. So far not a single boat of which he had had command had been lost. And every sailor constantly on the sea ought to have at least one of these misfortunes in his history in order to be a real captain. Only landlubbers never lose their boats.

When his mother died, Ulysses was very undecided about the future, not knowing whether to continue his sea life, or undertake something entirely different. His relatives at Barcelona, merchants quick to understand and appraise a fortune, added up what the notary and his wife had left him and put with that what Labarta and the doctor had contributed, until it amounted to a million pesetas. . . . And was a man with as much money

as that to go on living like a poor captain dependent upon
wages to maintain his family! . . .

His cousin, Joaquin Blanes, proprietor of a factory for
knit goods, urged him repeatedly to follow his example.
He ought to remain on shore and invest his capital in
Catalan industry. Ulysses belonged to this country both
on his mother's side and because he was born in the
neighboring land of Valencia. There was great need of
men of fortune and energy to take part in the government. Blanes was entering local politics with the enthusiasm of a middle-class man for novel adventure.

Cinta never said a word to influence her husband. She
was the daughter of a sailor and had accepted the life
of a sailor's wife. Furthermore, she looked upon matrimony in the light of the old familiar traditions:—
the woman absolute mistress of the interior of the
home, but trusting outside affairs to the will of the
lord, the warrior, the head of the hearth, without permitting herself opinions or objections to their acts.

It was Ulysses, therefore, who decided to abandon
the seafaring life. Worked upon by the suggestions of
his cousins, it needed only a little dispute with one of the
directors of the shipping firm to make him hand in his
resignation, and refuse to reconsider it, although urged
by the protests and entreaties of the other stockholders.

In the first months of his existence ashore, he was
amazed at the desperate immovability of everything.
The world was made up of revolting rigidity and solidity.
He felt almost nauseated at seeing all his possessions
remain just where he left them, without the slightest fluc-
tuation, or the least bit of casual caprice.

In the mornings upon opening his eyes, he at first experienced the sweet sensation of irresponsible liberty.
Nothing affected the fate of that house. The lives of
those that were sleeping on the other floors above and be-

low him had not been entrusted to his vigilance. . . . But in a few days he began to feel that there was something lacking, something which had been one of the greatest satisfactions of his existence,—the sensation of power, the enjoyment of command.

Two maids were now always hastening to him with a frightened air at the sound of his voice, or the ringing of his bell. That was all that was left to him who had commanded dozens of men of such ugliness of temper that they struck terror to all beholders when they went ashore in the ports. Nobody consulted him now, while on the sea everybody was seeking his counsel and many times had to interrupt his sleep. The house could go on without his making the rounds daily from the cellars to the roof, overseeing even the slightest spigot. The women who cleaned it in the mornings with their brooms were always obliging him to flee from his office. He was not permitted to make any comment nor could he extend a gold-striped arm as when he used to scold the barefooted, barebreasted deck swabbers, insisting that the deck should be as clean as the saloon. He felt himself belittled, laid to one side. He thought of Hercules dressed as a woman and spinning wool. His love of family life had made him renounce that of a powerful man.

Only the considerate treatment of his wife, who surrounded him with assiduous care as though wishing to compensate for their long separations, made the situation bearable. Furthermore, his conscience was enjoying a certain satisfaction in being a land-father, taking much interest in the life of his son who was beginning to prepare to enter the institute, looking over his books, and aiding him in understanding the notes.

But even these pleasures were not of long duration. The family gatherings in his home or at his relatives' bored him unspeakably; so did the conversations with his cousins and nephews about profits and business deals, or about the defects of centralized tyranny. According to them, all the calamities of heaven and earth were coming from Madrid. The governor of the province was the "Consul of Spain."

These merchants interrupted their criticisms only to listen in religious silence to Wagner's music banged out on the piano by the girls of the family. A friend with a tenor voice used to sing *Lohengrin* in Catalan. Enthusiasm made the most excitable roar, "the hymn! . . . the hymn!" It was not possible to misunderstand. For them there was only one hymn in existence, and in a trilling undertone they would accompany the liturgic music of *Los Segadores* (The Reapers).[1]

Ulysses used to recall with homesickness his life as commander of a transatlantic liner,—a wide, universal life of incessant and varied horizons, and cosmopolitan crowds. He could see himself detained on deck by groups of elegant maidens who would beg him for new dances in the coming week. His footsteps were surrounded with white fluttering skirts, veils that waved like colored clouds, laughter and trills, Spanish chatter that appeared set to music:—all the frolicsome jargon of a cage of tropical birds.

Ex-presidents of the South American republics,—generals or doctors who were going to Europe to rest,—used to relate to him on the bridge, with Napoleonic gravity, the principal events in their history. The business men starting out for America confided to him their stupendous plans:—rivers turned from their courses, railroads built across the virgin forests, monstrous electric forces extracted from huge waterfalls varying in breadth, cities vomited from the desert in a few weeks, all the marvels of

[1] The revolutionary song of Catalunia, originated by a band of reapers in the seventeenth century.

an adolescent world that desires to realize whatever its
youthful imagination may conceive. He was the demi-
urge of this little floating world: he disposed of joy
and love as the spirit moved him.

In the scorching evenings around the equator, it was
enough for him to give an order to rouse things and
beings from their brutish drowsiness. "Let the music
begin, and refreshments be served." And in a few moments dancers would be revolving the whole length of
the deck, and smiling lips and eyes would become brilliantly alight with illusion and desire. Behind him, his
praises were always being sounded. The matrons found
him very distinguished. "It is plain to be seen that he
is an exceptional person." Stewards and crew circulated
exaggerated accounts of his riches and his studies. Some
young girls sailing for Europe with imaginations seething
with romance were very much aghast to learn that the
hero was married and had a son. The solitary ladies
stretched out on a *chaise-longue,* book in hand, upon seeing him would arrange the corolla of their petticoats,
hiding their legs with so much precipitation that it always
left them more uncovered; then fixing upon him a languishing glance, they would begin a dialogue always in
the same way.

"How is it that any one so young as you has already
become a captain? . . ."

Ah, the misery of it! . . . He who had gallantly passed
many years cruising from one extreme of the Atlantic to
the other with a rich, gay, perfumed world, at times re-
sisting feminine caprice through mere prudence, yielding
at others with the secrecy of a discreet sailor, now found
himself with no other admirers than the mediocre tribe
of the Blanes, with no other hallucinations than those
which his cousin the manufacturer might suggest, when

waxing enthusiastic because the great apostles of politics were taking a certain interest in the captain.

Every morning, on awaking, his taste now received a rude shock. The first thing that he contemplated was a room "without personality," a dwelling that was not characteristic of him in any way, arranged by the maids with excessive cleanliness and a lack of logic that was constantly changing the situation of his things.

He recalled with longing his compact and well-ordered stateroom where there was not a piece of furniture that could escape his glance nor a drawer whose contents he did not know down to the slightest detail. His body was accustomed to slip without embarrassment through the spaces of his cabin furnishings. He had adapted himself to all incoming and outgoing angles just as the body of the mollusk adapts itself to the winding curves of its shells. The cabin seemed formed by the secretions of his being. It was a covering, a sheath, that went with him from one extreme of the ocean to the other, heating itself with the high temperature of the tropics, or becoming as cosy as an Esquimo hut on approaching the polar seas.

His love for it was somewhat like that which the friar has for his cell; but this cell was a secular one, and entering it after a tempestuous night on the bridge, or a trip ashore in most curious and foreign ports, he found it always the same, with his papers and books untouched on the table, his clothes hanging from their hooks, his photographs fixed on the walls. The daily spectacle of seas and lands was always changing—the temperature, the course of the stars, and the people that one week were bundled up in winter greatcoats, and were clad in white the week after, hunting the heavens for the new stars of another hemisphere. . . . Yet his cozy little stateroom was always the same, as though it were the corner of a planet apart, unaffected by the variations of this world.

Upon awaking in it, he found himself every morning enwrapped in a greenish and bland atmosphere as though he might have been sleeping in the bottom of an enchanted lake. The sun traced over the whiteness of his ceiling and sheets a restless network of gold whose meshes constantly succeeded each other. This was the reflection of the invisible water. When his ship was immovable in the ports, there always came in through his window the whirling noise of the cranes, the cries of the stevedores and the voices of those who were in the neighboring vessels. On the high sea the cool and murmuring silence of immensity used to fill his sleeping room. A wind of infinite purity that came perhaps from the other side of the planet—slipping past thousands of leagues, over the salty deserts without touching a single bit of corruption—would come stealing into Ferragut's throat like an effervescent wine. His chest always expanded to the impulses of this life-giving draught as his eyes roved over the sparkling, luminous blue of the horizon.

Here in his home, the first thing that he saw through the window upon awaking was a Catalunian edifice, rich and monstrous, like the palaces that the hypnotist evolves in his dreams,—an amalgamation of Persian flowers, Gothic columns, trunks of trees, with quadrupeds, reptiles and snails among the cement foliage. The paving wafted up to him through its drains the fetidity of sewers dry for lack of water; the balconies shed the dust of shaken rugs; the absurd palace appropriated, with the insolence of the new-rich, all the heaven and sun that used to belong to Ferragut.

One night he surprised his relatives by informing them that he was about to return to the sea. Cinta assented to this resolution in painful silence, as though she had foreseen it long before. It was something inevitable and fatal that she must accept. The manufacturer, Blanes, stammered with astonishment. Return to his life of adventures, when the great gentlemen of the district were becoming interested in his personality! . . . Perhaps in the next elections they might have made him a member of the municipal council!

Ferragut laughed at his cousin's simplicity. He wanted to command a vessel again, but one of his own, without being obliged to consider the restrictions of the ship owners. He could permit himself this luxury. It would be like an enormous yacht, ready to set forth according to his tastes and convenience, yet at the same time bringing him in untold profits. Perhaps his son might in time become director of a maritime company, this first ship laying the foundation of an enormous fleet in the years to come.

He knew every port in the world, every highway of traffic, and he would be able to find the places where, lacking transportation facilities, they paid the highest freight rates. Until now he had been a salaried man, brave and care-free. He was going to begin an absolutely independent life as a speculator of the sea.

Two months afterwards he wrote from England saying that he had bought the *Fingal*, a mail packet of three thousand tons that had made trips twice a week between London and a port of Scotland.

Ulysses appeared highly delighted with the cheapness of his acquisition. The *Fingal* had been the property of a Scotch captain who, in spite of his long illness, had never wished to give up command, dying aboard his vessel. His heirs, inland men tired by their long wait, were anxious to get rid of it at any price.

When the new proprietor entered the aft saloon surrounded with staterooms,—the only habitable place in the ship,—memories of the dead came forth to meet him. On

the wall-panels were painted the heroes of the Scotch
Iliad,—the bard Ossian with his harp, Malvina with the
round arms and waving golden tresses, the undaunted
warriors with their winged helmets and protruding biceps, exchanging gashes on their shields while awaking
the echoes of the green lochs.

A deep and spongy arm chair opened its arms before
a stove. There the owner of the ship had passed his last
years, sick at heart and with swollen legs, directing from
his seat a course that was repeated every week across
the foggy winter waves tossing bits of ice snatched from
the icebergs. Near the stove was a piano and upon
its top an orderly collection of musical scores yellowed
by time,—*La Sonnambula, Lucia,* Romances of Tosti,
Neapolitan songs, breezy and graceful melodies that the
old chords of the instrument sent forth with the fragile
and crystalline tinkling of an old music box. The poor
old captain with sick heart and legs of stone had always
turned to the sea of light for distraction. It was music
that made appear in the foggy heavens the peaks of
Sorrento covered with orange and lemon trees, and the
coast of Sicily, perfumed by its flaming flora.

Ferragut manned his boat with friendly people. His
first mate was a pilot who had begun his career in a fishing smack. He came from the same village as Ulysses'
ancestors, and he remembered the *Dotor* with respect and
admiration. He had known this new captain when he
was a little fellow and used to go fishing with his uncle.
In those days Toni was already a sailor on a coast-trad-
ing vessel, and his superiority in years had then justified
his using the familiar thee and thou when talking with
the lad Ulysses.

Finding himself now under his orders, he wished to
change his mode of address, but the captain would not
permit it. Perhaps he and Toni were distant relatives,—

all those living in that village of the *Marina* had become related through long centuries of isolated existence and common danger. The entire crew, from the first engineer to the lowest seaman, showed an equal familiarity in this respect. Some were from the same land as the captain, others had been sailing a long time under his orders.

As shipowner, Ulysses now underwent numberless experiences whose existence he had never before suspected. He went through the anguishing transformation of the actor who becomes a theatrical manager, of the author who branches out into publishing, of the engineer with a hobby for odd inventions who becomes the proprietor of a factory. His romantic love for the sea and its adventures was now overshadowed by the price and consumption of coal, by the maddening competition that lowered freight rates, and by the search for new ports with fast and remunerative freight.

The *Fingal* which had been rebaptized by its new proprietor with the name of *Mare Nostrum,* in memory of his uncle, turned out to be a dubious purchase in spite of its low price. As a navigator Ulysses had been most enthusiastic upon beholding its high and sharp prow disposed to confront the worst seas, the slenderness of the swift craft, its machinery, excessively powerful for a freight steamer,—all the conditions that had made it a mail packet for so many years. It consumed too much fuel to be a profitable investment as a transport of merchandise. The captain during his navigation could now think only of the ravenous appetite of the boilers. It always seemed to him that the *Mare Nostrum* was speeding along with excess steam.

"Half speed!" he would shout down the tube to his first engineer.

But in spite of this and many other precautions, the expense for fuel was enormously disproportioned to the tonnage of the vessel. The boat was eating up all the profits. Its speed was insignificant compared with that of a transatlantic steamer, though absurd compared with that of the merchant vessels of great hulls and little machinery that were going around soliciting cargo at any price, from all points.

A slave of the superiority of his vessel and in continual struggle with it, Ferragut had to make great efforts in order to continue sailing without actual heavy loss. All the waters of the planet now saw the *Mare Nostrum* specializing in the rarest kind of transportation. Thanks to this expedient, the Spanish flag waved in ports that had never seen it before.

Under this banner, he made trips through the solitary seas of Syria and Asia Minor, skirting coasts where the novelty of a ship with a smoke stack made the people of the Arabian villages run together in crowds. He disembarked in Phœnician and Greek ports choked up with sand that had left only a few huts at the foot of mountains of ruins, and where columns of marble were still sticking up like trunks of lopped-off palm trees. He anchored near to the terrible breakers of the western coast of Africa under a sun which scorched the deck, in order to take on board india-rubber, ostrich feathers, and elephants' tusks, brought out in long pirogues by negro oarsmen, from a river filled with crocodiles and hippopotamuses, and bordered by groups of huts with straw cones for roofs.

When there were no more of these extraordinary voyages, the *Mare Nostrum* turned its course towards South America, resigning itself to competition in rates with the English and Scandinavians who are the muleteers of the ocean. His tonnage and draught permitted him to sail up the great rivers of North America, even reaching the cities of the remote interior where rows of factory chimneys smoked on the border of a fresh-water lake converted into a port.

He sailed up the ruddy Paraná to Rosario and Colastiné, in order to load Argentine wheat; he anchored in the amber waters of Uruguay opposite Paysandú and Fray Ventos, taking on board hides destined to Europe and salt for the Antilles. From the Pacific he sailed up the Guayas bordered with an equatorial vegetation, in search of cocoa from Guayaquil. His prow cut the infinite sheet of the Amazon,—dislodging gigantic tree-trunks dragged down by the inundations of the virgin forest—in order to anchor opposite Pará or Manaos, taking on cargoes of tobacco and coffee. He even carried from Germany implements of war for the revolutionists of a little republic.

These trips that in other times would have awakened Ferragut's enthusiasm now resulted disastrously. After having paid all expenses and lived with maddening economy, there was scarcely anything left for the owner. Each time the freight boats were more numerous and the transportation rates cheaper. Ulysses with his elegant *Mare Nostrum* could not compete with the southern captains, drunken and taciturn, eager to accept freight at any price in order to fill their miserable transports crawling across the ocean at the speed of a tortoise.

"I can do no more," he said sadly to his mate. "I shall simply ruin my son. If anybody will buy the *Mare Nostrum*, I'm going to sell it."

On one of his fruitless expeditions, just when he was most discouraged, some unexpected news changed the situation for him. They had just arrived at Teneriffe with maize and bales of dry alfalfa from Argentina.

When Toni returned aboard after having cleared the vessel, he shouted in Valencian, the language of intimacy, "War, *Che!*"

Ulysses, who was pacing the bridge, received the news with indifference. "War? . . . What war is that? . . ." But upon learning that Germany and Austria had begun hostilities with France and Russia, and that England was just intervening in behalf of Belgium, the captain began quickly to calculate the political consequences of this conflagration. He could see nothing else.

Toni, less disinterested, spoke of the future of the vessel. . . . Their misery was at last at an end! Freightage at thirteen shillings a ton was going to be henceforth but a disgraceful memory. They would no longer have to plead for freight from port to port as though begging alms. Now they were on the point of achieving importance, and were going to find themselves solicited by consignors and disdainful merchants. The *Mare Nostrum* was going to be worth its weight in gold.

Such predictions, though Ferragut refused to accept them, began to be fulfilled in a very short time. Ships on the ocean routes suddenly became very scarce. Some of them were taking refuge in the nearest neutral ports, fearing the enemy's cruisers. The greater part were mobilized by their governments for the enormous transportation of material that modern war exacts. The German corsairs, craftily taking advantage of the situation, were increasing with their captures the panic of the merchant marine.

The price of freight leaped from thirteen shillings a ton to fifty, then to seventy, and a few days later to a hundred. It couldn't climb any further, according to Captain Ferragut.

"It will climb higher yet," affirmed the first officer with cruel joy. "We shall see tonnage at a hundred and fifty, at two hundred. . . . We are going to become rich! . . ."

And Toni always used the plural in speaking of the future riches without its ever occurring to him to ask his captain a penny more than the forty-five dollars that he was receiving each month. Ferragut's fortune and that of the ship, he invariably looked upon as his own, considering himself lucky if he was not out of tobacco, and could send his entire wages home to his wife and children living down there in the *Marina*.

His ambition was that of all modest sailors—to buy a plot of land and become an agriculturist in his old age. The Basque pilots used to dream of prairies and apple orchards, a little cottage on a peak and many cows. He pictured to himself a vineyard on the coast, a little white dwelling with an arbor under whose shade he could smoke his pipe while all his family, children and grandchildren, were spreading out the harvest of raisins on the frame-hurdles.

A familiar admiration like that of an ancient squire for his paladin, or of an old subaltern for a superior officer, bound him to Ferragut. The books that filled the captain's stateroom recalled his agonies upon being examined in Cartagena for his license as a pilot. The grave gentlemen of the tribunal had made him turn pale and stutter like a child before the logarithms and formulas of trigonometry. But just let them consult *him* on practical matters and his skill as master of a bark habituated to all the dangers of the sea, and he would reply with the self-possession of a sage!

In the most difficult perils,—days of storm and sinister shoals in the neighborhood of the treacherous coasts, Ferragut could decide to rest only when Toni replaced him on the bridge. With him, he had no fear that, through carelessness, a wave would sweep across the deck and stop the machinery, or that an invisible ledge would drive its stony point into the vitals of the vessel. He held the helm to the course indicated. Silent and immovable he stood, as though sleeping on his feet; but at the right moment he always uttered the brief word of command.

He was very skinny, with the dried up leanness of the bronzed Mediterranean. The salt wind more than his years had tanned his face, wrinkling it with deep crevices. A capricious coloring had darkened the depths of these cracks while the part exposed to the sun appeared washed several shades lighter. His short stiff beard extended over all the furrows and crests of his skin. Furthermore, he had hair in his ears, hair in the nasal passages, coarse and vibrating growths, ready to tremble in moments of wrath or admiration. . . . But this ugliness disappeared under the light of his little eyes with pupils between green and olive color,—mild eyes with a canine expression of resignation, when the captain made fun of his beliefs.

Toni was a "man of ideas." Ferragut only knew of his having four or five, but they were hard, crystallized, tenacious, like the mollusks that stick to the rocks and eventually become a part of the stony excrescence. He had acquired them in twenty-five years of Mediterranean coast service by reading all the periodicals of lyric radicalism that were thrust upon him on entering the harbors. Furthermore, at the end of every journey was Marseilles; and in one of its little side alleys was a red room adorned with symbolic columns where sailors of all races and tongues met together, fraternally understanding each other by means of mysterious signs and ritual words.

Whenever Toni entered a South American port after a long absence, he particularly admired the rapid progress of the new villages,—enormous wharves constructed within the year, interminable streets that were not in existence on his former voyage, shady and elegant parks, replacing old, dried-up lakes.

"That's only natural," he would affirm roundly. "With good reason they are republics!"

Upon entering the Spanish ports, the slightest deviation in the docking, a discussion with the official employees, the lack of space for a good anchorage would make him smile with bitterness. "Unfortunate country! . . . Everything here is the work of the altar and the throne!"

In the Thames, and before the docks of Hamburg Captain Ferragut would chaff his subordinate.

"There's no republic here, Toni! . . . But, nevertheless this is rather worth while."

But Toni never gave in. He would contract his hairy visage, making a mental effort to formulate his vague ideas, clothing them with words. In the very background of these grandeurs existed the confirmation of the idea he was so vainly trying to express. Finally he admitted himself checkmated, but not convinced.

"I don't know how to explain it; I haven't the words for it . . . but . . . it's the *people* who are doing all this."

Upon receiving in Teneriffe the news of war, he summed up all his doctrines with the terseness of a victor.

"In Europe there are too many kings. . . . If all the nations could be republics! . . . This calamity just had to come!"

And this time Ferragut did not venture to ridicule the single-mindedness of his second.

All the people of the *Mare Nostrum* showed great enthusiasm over the new business aspect of things. The seamen who in former voyages were taciturn, as though foreseeing the ruin or exhaustion of their captain, were now working as eagerly as though they were going to participate in the profits.

In the forward mess room many of them set themselves to work on commercial calculations. The first trip of the war would be equal to ten of their former

nes; the second, perhaps, might bring in the profit of
wenty. And recalling their former bad business ven-
ures, they rejoiced for Ferragut, with the same disin-
erestedness as the first officer. The engineers were no
onger called to the captain's cabin in order to contrive
ew economies in fuel. They had to take advantage of
he time and opportunity; and the *Mare Nostrum* was
ow going at full steam, making fourteen knots an hour,
ke a passenger vessel, stopping only when its course
as blocked at the entrance of the Mediterranean by an
nglish destroyer, sending out an officer to make sure
hat they were not carrying on board enemy passengers.

Abundance reigned equally between bridge and fore-
astle where were the sailors' quarters and the galley,—
he space respected by every one on the boat as the incon-
estable realm of Uncle Caragol.

This old man, nicknamed "Caracol" (snail), another
ld friend of Ferragut's, was the ship's cook, and, al-
hough he did not dare to talk as familiarly to the captain
s in former times, the tone of his voice made it under-
tood that mentally he was continuing to use the old,
ffectionate form. He had known Ulysses when he used
o run away from the classrooms to row in the har-
or and, on account of the bad state of his eyes, he
ad finally retired from the navigation of coast vessels,
escending to be a simple bargeman. His gravity and
orpulence had something almost priestly in character.
Ie was the obese type of Mediterranean with a little
ead, voluminous neck and triple chin, seated on the stern
f his fishing skiff like a Roman patrician on the throne of
is trireme.

His culinary talent suffered eclipse whenever rice did
ot figure as the fundamental basis of his compositions.
ll that this food could give of itself, he knew perfectly.
n the tropical ports, the crews surfeited with bananas,

pineapples, and alligator-pears, would greet with e
thusiasm the apparition of a great frying pan of ri
with cod and potatoes, or a casserole of rice from t'
oven with its golden crust perforated by the rud
faces of garbanzos and points of black sausage. At oth
times, under the leaden-colored sky of the northern sea
the cook made them recall their distant native land l
giving them the monastic rice dish with beet roots, or bu
tery rice with turnips and beans.

On Sundays and the fiestas of the Valencian sain
who for Uncle Caragol were the first in heaven,—*S*
Vicente Mártir, San Vicente Ferrer, La Virgin de l
Desamparados and the *Cristo del Grao*—would appea
the smoking *paella,* a vast, circular dish of rice upo
whose surface of white, swollen grains were lying bits o
various fowls. The cook loved to surprise his followir
by distributing rotund, raw onions, with the whiteness o
marble and an acrid surprise that brought tears to tl
eyes. They were a princely gift maintained in secre
One had only to break them with one blow and the
sticky juices would gush forth and lose themselves in th
palate like crisp mouthfuls of a sweet and spicy brea
alternating with knifefuls of rice. The boat was
times near Brazil in sight of Fernando de Noroña,—ye
even while viewing the conical huts of the negroes in
stalled on an island under an equatorial sun, the crew
could almost believe—thanks to Uncle Caragol's magic—
that they were eating in a cabin of the farmland of Va
lencia, as they passed from hand to hand the long-spoute
jug filled with strong wine from Liria.

When they anchored in ports where fish was abundan
he achieved the great work of cooking a rice *abanda*
The cabin boys would bring to the captain's table the po
in which was boiled the rich sea food mixed with lob
sters, mussels, and every kind of shell-fish available, bu

ie *chef* invariably reserved for himself the honor of ffering the accompanying great platter with its pyramid f rice, every grain golden and distinct.

Boiled apart (*abanda*) each grain was full of the suc-ulent broth of the stew-pot. It was a rice dish that con-ained within it the concentration of all the sustenance f the sea. As though he were performing a liturgical eremony, the *chef* would go around delivering half a emon to each one of those seated at the table. The rice hould only be eaten after moistening it with this per-umed dew which called to mind the image of an oriental arden. Only the unfortunate beings who lived inland vere ignorant of this exquisite confection, calling any ness of rice a Valencian rice dish.

Ulysses would humor the cook's notions, carrying the rst spoonful to his mouth with a questioning glance. . . . Then he would smile, giving himself up to gastric in-oxication. "Magnificent, Uncle Caragol!" His good umor made him affirm that only the gods should be ourished with rice *abanda* in their abodes on Mount Olympus. He had read that in books. And Caragol, living great praise in all this, would gravely reply, 'That is so, my captain." Toni and the other officers by his time would be chewing away with heads down, only nterrupting their feast to regret that the old Ganymede hould have skimped them when measuring the ambrosia.

In his estimation, oil was as precious as rice. In the ime of their money-losing navigation, when the captain vas making special efforts at economy, Caragol used to keep an especially sharp eye on the great oil bottles in his galley, for he suspected that the cabin boys and the young seamen appropriated it to dress their hair when hey wanted to play the dandy, using the oil as a pomade. Every head that put itself within reach of his disturbed glance he grasped between his arms, raising it to his

nose. The slightest perfume of olive oil would arouse hi
wrath. "Ah, you thief!" . . . And down would fall hi
enormous hand, soft and heavy as a fencing gauntlet.

Ulysses believed him quite capable of climbing th
bridge, and declaring that navigation could not go on be
cause of his having exhausted the leathern bottles o
amethyst-colored liquid proceeding from the Sierra d
Espadán.

In the ports, his short-sighted eyes recognized imme
diately the nationality of the boats anchored on both side
of the *Mare Nostrum*. His nose would sniff the ai
sadly. "Nothing! . . ." They were unsavory barks
barks from the North that prepared their dinner witl
lard or butter,—Protestant barks, perhaps.

Sometimes he would sneak along the gunwale, follow
ing an intoxicating trail until he planted himself in fron
of the galley of the neighboring boat, breathing in its ricl
perfume. "Hello, brothers!" Impossible to fool him
they were probably Spaniards and, if not, they wer
from Genoa or Naples,—in short, were compatriots ac
customed to live and eat in all latitudes just as thougl
they were in their own little inland sea. Soon the
would begin a speech in the Mediterranean idiom, a
mixture of Spanish, Provençal and Italian, invented b
the hybrid peoples of the African coast from Egypt t
Morocco. Sometimes they would send each other pres
ents, like those that are exchanged between tribes,—
fruits from distant countries. At other times, suddenly
inimical, without knowing why, they would shake thei
fists over the railing, yelling insults at each other in
which, between every two or three words, would appear
the names of the Virgin and her holy Son.

This was the signal for Uncle Caragol, religious soul
to return in haughty silence to his galley. Toni, the
mate, used to make fun of his devout enthusiasm. On

he other hand, the foremast hands, materialistic and gluttonous, used to listen to him with deference, because he was the one who doled out the wine and the choicest tid-bits. The old man used to speak to them of the *Cristo del Grao,* whose pictures occupied the most prominent site in the kitchen, and they would all listen as to a new tale, to the story of the arrival by sea of the sacred image, mounted upon a ladder in a boat that had dissolved in smoke after discharging its miraculous cargo.

This had been when the *Grao* was no more than a group of huts far from the walls of Valencia and threatened by the raids of the Moorish pirates. For many years Caragol, barefooted, had carried this sacred ladder on his shoulder on the day of the fiesta. Now other men of the sea were enjoying such honor and he, old and half-blind, would be waiting among the public for the procession to pass in order that he might throw himself upon the enormous relic, touching his clothes to the wood.

All his outer garments were sanctified by this contact. In reality they weren't very many, since he usually strolled about the boat very lightly clad, with the immodesty of a man who sees poorly and considers himself above human preoccupations.

A shirt with the tail always floating, and a pair of pantaloons of dirty cotton or yellow flannel, according to the season, constituted his entire outfit. The bosom of the shirt was open on all occasions, leaving visible a thatch of white hair. The pantaloons were fastened together with a single button. A palm leaf hat always covered his head even when he was working among his cooking pots.

The *Mare Nostrum* could not be shipwrecked nor suffer any harm while it carried him aboard. In the days of tempest, when waves were sweeping the deck

from prow to poop, and the sailors were treading warily
fearing that a heavy sea might carry them overboard
Caragol would stick his head out through the door o
the galley, scorning a danger which he could not see.

The great water-spouts would pass over him, eve
putting out his fires, but only increasing his faith
"Courage, boys! Courage, lads!" The *Cristo del Gra*
had special charge of them and nothing bad could happe
to the ship. . . . Some of the seamen were silent, whil
others said this and that about the image without arous
ing the indignation of the old devotee. God, who send
dangers to the men of the sea, knows that their bad word
lack malice.

His religiosity extended to the very deeps. He di
not wish to say anything about the ocean fish, for the
inspired him with the same indifference as those col
and unperfumed boats that were ignorant of olive oil
and all that was cooked with "pomade." They must b
heretics.

He was better acquainted with the fish of the Mediter
ranean and even came to believe that they must be goo
Catholics, since in their own way they proclaimed th
glory of God. Standing near the taffrail on torrid even
ings in the tropics, he would recount, in honor of th
inhabitants of his distant sea, the portentous miracl
which had taken place in the glen of Alboraya.

A priest was one day fording on horseback the mouth
of a river in order to carry the eucharist to a dying
person, when his beast stumbled and the ciborium, fall
ing open, the Hosts fell out and were carried off by th
current. From that time on, mysterious lights glowed
every night on the water, and at sunrise a swarm o
little fishes would come to range themselves opposit
the glen, their heads emerging from the water, in order
to show the Host which each one of them was carrying

ı his mouth. In vain the fishermen wished to take
ıem away from them. They fled to the inland sea with
ıeir treasures. Only when the clergy, with cross erect
ınd with the same priest, fell on their knees in the glen
ıid they decide to approach; and one after the other deposited his Host in the ciborium, retiring then from
vave to wave, gracefully waggling their little tails.

In spite of the vague hope for a jug of choice wine
that was animating most of his hearers, a murmur of in-
redulity always arose at the end of this tale. The de-
out Caragol then became as wrathful and foul-mouthed
s a prophet of old when he considered his faith in dan-
er. "Who was that son of a flea? . . . Who *was* that
on of a flea daring to doubt what I myself have
een? . . ." And what he had seen was the fiesta of the
Peixet that was celebrated every year, simply listening to
nost learned men discoursing about the miracle in a com-
memorative chapel built on the banks of the glen.

This prodigy of the little fishes was almost always
ollowed with what he called the miracle of the *Peixōt*,
ndeavoring with the weight of such a marvelous fish
ale to crush the doubts of the impious.

The galley of Alphonso V of Aragon (the only sailor
:ing of Spain), upon coming out of the Gulf of Naples,
nce struck a hidden rock near the island of Capri which
ook away a side of the ship without making it leak; and
he vessel continued on with all sails spread, carrying
he king, the ladies of his court, and the retinue of mail-
lad barons. Twenty days afterward they arrived at
Valencia safe and sound like all sailors who in moments
f danger ask aid of the *Virgen del Puig*. Upon inspect-
ng the hull of the galley, the master calkers beheld a
nonstrous fish detach itself from its bottom with the
ranquillity of an upright person who has fulfilled his
luty. It was a dolphin sent by the most holy Señora in

order that his side might stop up the open breach. And
thus, like a plug, it had sailed from Naples to Valencia
without allowing a drop of water to pass in.

The *chef* would not admit any criticisms nor protests.
This miracle was undeniable. He had seen it with his
own eyes, and they were good. He had seen it in an
ancient picture in the monastery of Puig, everything
appearing on the tablet with the realism of truth,—the
galley, the king, the *peixòt* and the Virgin above giving
the order.

At this juncture the breeze would flap the narrator's
shirt tail, disclosing his abdomen divided into hemispheres
by the tyranny of its only pantaloon button.

"Uncle Caragol, look out!" warned a teasing voice.

The holy man would smile with the seraphic calm
of one who sees beyond the pomps and vanities of ex
istence, and would begin the relation of a new miracle.

Ferragut used to attribute his cook's periods of ex
altation to the lightness of his clothing in all weathers.
Within him was burning a fire incessantly renewed.
On foggy days he would climb to the bridge with some
glasses of a smoking drink that he used to call *calentets*.
Nothing better for men that had to pass long hours
in the inclement weather in motionless vigilance! It
was coffee mixed with rum, but in unequal proportions,
having more alcohol than black liquid. Toni would drink
rapidly all the glasses offered. The captain would re
fuse them, asking for clear coffee.

His sobriety was that of the ancient sailor,—the
sobriety of Father Ulysses who used to mix wine with
water in all his libations. The divinities of the old sea
did not love alcoholic drinks. The white *Amphitrite* and
the Nereids only accepted on their altars the fruits of
the earth, sacrifices of doves, libations of milk. Perhaps
because of this the seafaring men of the Mediterranean

following an hereditary tendency, looked upon intoxication as the vilest of degradations. Even those who were not temperate avoided getting frankly drunk like the sailors of other seas, dissimulating the strength of their alcoholic beverage with coffee and sugar.

Caragol was the understudy charged with drinking all which the captain refused, together with certain others which he dedicated to himself in the mystery of the galley. On warm days he manufactured *refresquets,* and these refreshments were enormous glasses, half of water and half of rum upon a great bed of sugar,—a mixture that made one pass like a lightning flash, without any gradations, from vulgar serenity to most angelic intoxication.

The captain would scold him upon seeing his inflamed and reddened eyes. He was going to make himself blind. . . . But the guilty one was not moved by this threat. He had to celebrate the prosperity of the vessel in his own way. And of this prosperity the most interesting thing for him was his ability to use oil and brandy lavishly without any fear of recriminations when the accounts were settled. *Cristo del Grao!* . . . would that the war would last forever! . . .

The *Mare Nostrum's* third voyage from South America to Europe came suddenly to an end in Naples, where they were unloading wheat and hides. A collision at the entrance of the port, with an English hospital ship that was going to the Dardanelles, injured her stern, carrying away a part of the screw.

Toni roared with impatience upon learning that they would have to remain nearly a month in enforced idleness. Italy had not yet intervened in the war, but her defensive precautions were monopolizing all naval industries. It was not possible to make the repairs sooner, although Ferragut well knew what this loss of time

would represent in his business. Valuable freight was
waiting for him in Marseilles and Barcelona, but, wishing to tranquillize himself and to pacify his mate, he
would say repeatedly:

"England will indemnify us. . . . The English are
just."

And in order to soothe his impatience he went ashore.

Compared with other celebrated Italian cities, Naples
did not appear to him of much importance. Its true
beauty was its immense gulf between hills of orange trees
and pines, with a second frame of mountains one of
which outlined upon the azure heavens its eternal crest
of volcanic vapors.

The town did not abound in famous edifices. The
monarchs of Naples had generally been foreigners who
had resided far away and had governed through their
delegates. The best streets, the palaces, the monumental
fountain, had come from the Spanish viceroys. A sovereign of mixed origin, Charles the III, Castilian by birth
and Neapolitan at heart, had done the most for the city.
His building enthusiasm had embellished the ancient
districts with works similar to those that he erected years
afterward, upon occupying the throne of Spain.

After admiring the Grecian statuary in the museum,
and the excavated objects that revealed the intimate life
of the ancients, Ulysses threaded the tortuous and often
gloomy arteries of the popular districts.

There were streets clinging to the slopes forming
landings flanked with narrow and very high houses.
Every vacant space had its balconies, and from every
railing to its opposite were extended lines spread with
clothes of different colors, hung out to dry. Neapolitan
fertility made these little alleys seethe with people.
Around the open-air kitchens there crowded patrons,

eating, while standing, their boiled macaroni or bits of meat.

The hucksters were hawking their goods with melodious, song-like cries, and cords to which little baskets were fastened were lowered down to them from balconies. The bargaining and purchases reached from the depth of the street gutters to the top of the seventh floor, but the flocks of goats climbed the winding steps with their customary agility in order to be milked at the various stair landings.

The wharves of the Marinela attracted the captain because of the local color of this Mediterranean port. Italian unity had torn down and reconstructed much of it, but there still remained standing various rows of little low-roofed houses with white or pink façades, green doors, and lower floors further forward than the upper ones, serving as props for galleries with wooden balustrades. Everything there that was not of brick was of clumsy carpentry resembling the work of ship calkers. Iron did not exist in these terrestrial constructions suggestive of the sailboat whose rooms were as dark as staterooms. Through the windows could be seen great conch-shells upon the chests of drawers, harsh and childish oil paintings representing frigates, and multi-colored shells from distant seas.

These dwellings repeated themselves in all the ports of the Mediterranean just as though they were the work of the same hand. As a child, Ferragut had seen them in the *Grao* of Valencia and continually ran across them in Barcelona, in the suburbs of Marseilles, in old Nice, in the ports of the western islands, and in the sections of the African coast occupied by Maltese and Sicilians.

Over the town, lined up along the Marinela, the churches of Naples reared their domes and towers with glazed roofs, green and yellow, which appeared more like pinnacles of Oriental baths than the roofs of Christian temples.

The barefooted *lazzarone* with his red cap no longer existed, but the crowd,—clad like the workmen of all ports—still gathered around the daubed poster that represented a crime, a miracle or a prodigious specific, listening in silence to the harangue of the narrator or charlatan. The old popular comedians were declaiming with heroic gesticulations the epic octavos of Tasso, and harps and violins were sounding accompaniments to the latest melody that Naples had made fashionable throughout the entire world. The stands of the oyster-men constantly sent forth an organic perfume from the spent wave, and all around them empty shells scattered their disks of pearly lime over the mud.

Near to the ancient Captaincy of the port, the palace of Charles III,—blue and white, with an image of the immaculate conception,—were assembled the unloading trucks, whose teams still preserved their ancient hybrid originality. In some instances the shafts were occupied by a white ox, sleek with enormous and widely branching horns, an animal similar to those that used to figure in the religious ceremonies of the ancients. At his right would be hooked a horse, at his left, a great raw-boned mule, and this triple and discordant team appeared in all the carts, standing immovable before the ships the length of the docks, or dragging their heavy wheels up the slopes leading to the upper city.

In a few days the captain grew tired of Naples and its bustle. In the cafés of the Street of Toledo and the Gallery of Humbert I, he had to defend himself from some noisy youths with low-cut vests, butterfly neckties and little felt hats perched upon their manes, who, in low voices, proposed to him unheard-of spectacles organized for the diversion of foreigners.

He had also seen enough of the paintings and domestic objects excavated from the ancient cities. The lewdness of the secret cabinets finally irritated him. It appeared to him the reverse of recreation to contemplate so many childish fantasies of sculpture and painting having the antique symbol of masculinity as its principal motif.

One morning he boarded a train and, after skirting the smoking mountain of Vesuvius, passing between rose-colored villages surrounded with vineyards, he stopped at the station of Pompeii.

From the funereal solitudes of hotels and restaurants, the guides came forth like a suddenly awakened swarm of wasps, lamenting that the war had cut off the tourist trade. Perhaps he would be the only one who would come that day. *"Signor,* at your service, at any price whatever! . . ." But the sailor continued on alone. Always, in recalling Pompeii, he had wished to see it again alone, absolutely alone, so as to get a more direct impression of the ancient life.

His first view of it had been seventeen years ago when, as a mate of a Catalan sailing vessel anchored in the port of Naples, he had taken advantage of the cheapness of Sunday rates and had seen everything as one of a crowd that was pushing and treading on everybody's feet so as to listen to the nearest guide.

At the head of the expedition had been a priest, young and elegant, a Roman *Monsignor,* clad in silk, and with him two showy foreign women, who were always climbing up in the highest places, raising their skirts rather high for fear of the star lizards that were writhing in and out of the ruins. Ferragut, in humble admiration, always remained below, glimpsing the country from behind their legs. "Ay! Twenty-two years! . . ." Afterwards when he heard Pompeii spoken of, it always evoked in his memory several strata of images. "Very

beautiful! Very interesting!" And in his mind's eye
he saw again the palaces and temples, but as a secondary
consideration, like a shrouded background, while in the
forefront were four magnificent legs standing forth,—a
human colonnade of slender shafts swathed in transparent black silk.

The solitude so long desired for his second visit was
now aggressively in evidence. In this deserted, dead
city there were to-day no other sounds than the whir-
ring of insect wings over the plants beginning to clothe
themselves with springtime verdure, and the invisible
scampering of reptiles under the layers of ivy.

At the gate of Herculaneum, the guardian of the little
museum left Ferragut to examine in peace the excavations of the various corpses, petrified Pompeiians of
plaster still in the attitudes of terror in which death
had surprised them. He did not abandon his post in
order to trouble the captain with his explanations; he
scarcely raised his eyes from the newspaper that he
had before him. The news from Rome,—the intrigues
of the German diplomats, the possibility that Italy might
enter the war,—were absorbing his entire attention.

Afterwards on the solitary streets the sailor found
everywhere the same preoccupation. His footsteps resounded in the sunlight as though treading the depths of
the hollow tombs. The moment he stopped, silence again
enveloped him,—"A silence of two thousand years,"
thought Ferragut to himself, and in the midst of this
primeval silence sounded far-away voices in the violence
of a sharp discussion. They were the guardians and
the employees of the excavations who, lacking work,
were gesticulating and insulting each other in these
strongholds twenty centuries old so profoundly isolated
from patriotic enthusiasm or fear of the horrors of war.

Ferragut, map in hand, passed among these groups

without annoyance from insistent guides. For two hours
he fancied himself an inhabitant of ancient Pompeii who
had remained alone in the city on a holiday devoted to
the rural divinities. His glance could reach to the very
end of the straight streets without encountering persons
or things recalling modern times.

Pompeii appeared to him smaller than ever in this
solitude,—an intersection of narrow roads with high
sidewalks paved with polygonal blocks of blue lava. In
its interstices Spring was forming green grass plots
dotted with flowers. Carriages,—of whose owners not
even the dust was left,—had with their deep wheels
opened up ridges in the pavement more than a thousand
years ago. In every crossway was a public fountain
with a grotesque mask which had spouted water through
its mouth.

Certain red letters on the walls were announcements
of elections to be held in the beginning of that era,—
candidates for ædile or duumvir who were recommended
to the Pompeiian voters. Some doors showed above,
the *phallus* for conjuring the evil eyes; others, a pair of
serpents intertwined, emblem of family life. In the
corners of the alleyways, a Latin verse engraved on the
walls asked the passerby to observe the laws of sanita-
tion, and there still could be seen on the stuccoed walls
caricatures and scribbling, handiwork of the little street
gamins of Cæsar's day.

The houses were lightly constructed upon floors
cracked by minor earthquakes before the arrival of the
final catastrophe. The lower floors were of bricks or
concrete and the others, of wood, had been devoured by
the volcanic fire, only the stairways remaining.

In this gracious city of amiable and easy-going life,
more Greek than Roman, all the lower floors of the ple-
beian houses had been occupied by petty traders. They

were shops with doors the same size as the establishment, four-sided caves like the Arabian *zocos* whose furthermost corners were visible to the buyer stopping in the street. Many still had their stone counters and their large earthen jars for the sale of wine and oil. The private dwellings had no façades, and their outer walls were smooth and unapproachable, but with an interior court providing the surrounding chambers with light as in the palaces of the Orient. The doors were merely half-doors of escape, parts of larger ones. All life was concentrated around the interior, the central patio, rich and magnificent, adorned with fish ponds, statues and flower-bordered beds.

Marble was rare. The columns constructed of bricks were covered with a stucco that offered a fine surface for painting. Pompeii had been a polychrome city. All the columns, red or yellow, had capitals of divers colors. The center of the walls was generally occupied with a little picture, usually erotic, painted on black varnished walls varied with red and amber hues. On the friezes were processions of cupids and tritons, between rustic and maritime emblems.

Tired of his excursion through the dead city, Ferragut seated himself on a stone bench among the ruins of the temple, and looked over the map spread out on his knees, enjoying the titles with which the most interesting constructions had been designated because of a mosaic or a painting,—Villa of Diomedes, the House of Meleager, of the wounded Adonis, of the Labryinth, of the Faun, of the Black Wall. The names of the streets were not less interesting: The Road of the Hot Baths, the Road of the Tombs, the Road of Abundance, the Road of the Theaters.

The sound of footsteps made the sailor raise his head. Two ladies were passing, preceded by a guide. One was tall, with a firm tread. They were wearing face-veils and still another larger veil crossing behind and coming over the arms like a shawl. Ferragut surmised a great difference in the ages of the two. The stout one was moving along with an assumed gravity. Her step was quick, but with a certain authority she planted on the ground her large feet, loosely shod and with low heels. The younger one, taller and more slender, tripping onwards with little steps like a bird that only knows how to fly, was teetering along on high heels.

The two looked uneasily at this man appearing so unexpectedly among the ruins. They had the preoccupied and timorous air of those going to a forbidden place or meditating a bad action. Their first movement was an impulse to go back, but the guide continued on his way so imperturbably that they followed on.

Ferragut smiled. He knew where they were going. The little cross street of the *Lupanares* was near. The guard would open a door, remaining on watch with dramatic anxiety as though he were endangering his job by this favor in exchange for a tip. And the two ladies were about to see some tarnished, clumsy paintings showing nothing new or original in the world,—nude, yellowish figures, just alike at first glance with no other novelty than an exaggerated emphasis on sex distinction.

Half an hour afterwards Ulysses abandoned his bench, for his eyes had tired of the severe monotony of the ruins. In the street of the Hot Baths (*Thermae*), he again visited the house of the tragic poet. Then he admired that of Pansa, the largest and most luxurious in the city. This Pansa had undoubtedly been the most pretentious citizen of Pompeii. His dwelling occupied an entire block. The *xystus,* or garden, adjoining the house had been laid out like a Grecian landscape with cypresses and laurels between squares of roses and violets.

Following along the exterior wall of the garden, Ferragut again met the two ladies. They were looking at the flowers across the bars of the door. The younger one was expressing in English her admiration for some roses that were flinging their royal color around the pedestal of an old faun.

Ulysses felt an irresistible desire to show off in a gallant and intrepid fashion. He wished to pay the two foreign ladies some theatrical homage. He felt that necessity of attracting attention in some gay and dashing way that characterizes Spaniards far from home.

With the agility of a mast-climber, he leaped the garden wall in one bound. The two ladies gave a cry of surprise, as though they had witnessed some impossible maneuver. This audacity appeared to upset the ideas of the older one, accustomed to life in disciplined towns that rigidly respect every established prohibition. Her first movement was of flight, so as not to be mixed up in the escapade of this stranger. But after a few steps she paused. The younger one was smiling, looking at the wall, and as the captain reappeared upon it she almost clapped with enthusiasm as though applauding a dangerous acrobatic feat.

Believing them to be English, the sailor spoke in that language when presenting to them the two roses that he carried in his hand. They were merely flowers, like all others, grown in a land like other lands, but the frame of the thousand-year-old wall, the propinquity of the alcoves and drinking shops of a house built by Pansa in the time of the first Cæsars, gave them the interest of roses two thousand years old, miraculously preserved.

The largest and most luxuriant he gave to the young woman, and she accepted it smilingly as her natural right. Her companion as soon as she acknowledged the gift, appeared impatient to get away from the stranger. "Thanks! . . . Thanks!" And she pushed along the other one, who had not yet finished smiling,—the two going hurriedly away. A corner adorned with a fountain soon hid their steps.

When Ulysses, after a light lunch in the restaurant of Diomedes, came running to the station, the train was just about to start. He was planning to see Salerno, celebrated in the Middle Ages for its physicians and navigators, and then the ruined temples of Pæstum. As he climbed into the nearest coach, he fancied that he spied the veils of the two ladies vanishing behind a little door that was just closing.

In the station of Salerno he again caught sight of them in a distant hack disappearing in a neighboring street, and during the afternoon he frequently ran across them as travelers will in a small city. They met one another in the harbor, so fatally threatened with bars of moving sand; they saw each other in the gardens bordering the sea, near the monument of Carlo Pisacana, the romantic duke of San Juan, a precursor of Garibaldi, who died in extreme youth for the liberty of Italy.

The young woman smiled whenever she met him. Her companion passed on with a casual glance, trying to ignore his presence.

At night they saw more of each other, as they were stopping at the same hotel, a lodging house like all those in the small ports with excellent meals and dirty rooms. They had adjoining tables, and after a coldly acknowledged greeting, Ferragut had a good look at the two ladies who were speaking very little and in a low tone, fearing to be overheard by their neighbor.

Upon looking at the older one without her veils, he found his original impression confirmed. In other times, perhaps, she might have destroyed the peace of male admirers, but she could now continue her hostile and distant attitude with impunity. The captain was not at all affected by it.

She must have been over forty. Her excessive flesh still had a certain freshness, the result of hygienic care and gymnastic exercise. On the other hand, her white complexion showed underneath it a yellowish subcutaneous, granular condition that looked as though made up of particles of bran. Upon her ancient switch, reddish in tone, were piled artificial curls hiding bald spots and gray hairs. Her green pupils, when freed from their near-sighted glasses, had the tranquil opacity of ox-eyes; but the minute these gold-mounted crystals were placed between her and the outer world, the two glaucous drops took on a sharpness which fairly perforated persons and objects. At other times they appeared a glacial and haughty void, like the circle that a sword traces.

The young woman was less intractable. She appeared to be smiling out of the corners of her eyes, while her back was half turned to Ferragut, acknowledging his mute and scrutinizing admiration. She had her hair loosely arranged like a woman who is not afraid of naturalness in her coiffure, and lets her waving locks peep out under her hat in all their original willfulness.

She was a dainty ash-blonde with a high color in striking contrast to her general delicacy of tone. Her great, almond-shaped, black eyes appeared like those of an Oriental dancer, and were yet further prolonged by skillful retouching of shadows that augmented the seductive contrast with her dull gold hair.

The whiteness of her skin became very evident when her arm showed outside her sleeve and at the opening of her low-necked dress. But this whiteness was now, temporarily effaced by a ruddy mask. Her vigorous beauty had been fearlessly exposed to the sun and the breath of the sea, and a scarlet triangle emphasized the sweet curve of her bosom, accentuating the low cut of her gown. Upon her sunburned throat a necklace of pearls hung in moonlight drops. Further up, in a face tanned by the inclemency of the weather, the mouth parted its two scarlet, bow-shaped lips with an audacious and serene smile, showing the reflection of her strong and handsome teeth.

Ferragut reviewed his past without finding a single woman that could be exactly compared with her. The distant perfume of her person and her genteel elegance reminded him of certain dubious ladies who were always traveling alone when he was captain of the transatlantic liners. But these acquaintances had been so rapid and were so far away! . . . Never in his history as a world-rover had he had the good luck to chance upon a woman just like this one.

Again exchanging glances with her, he felt that throb in the heart and flash in the brain which accompany a lightning-like and unexpected discovery. . . . He had known that woman: he could not recall where he had seen her, but he was sure that he must have known her.

Her face told his memory nothing, but those eyes had exchanged glances with his on other occasions. In vain he reflected, concentrating his thoughts. . . . And the queer thing about it all was that, by some mysterious perception, he became absolutely certain that she was doing the same thing at the very same moment. She also had recognized him, and was evidently making great effort to give him a name and place in her memory. He had only to notice the frequency with which she turned her eyes toward him and her new smile, more

confident and spontaneous, such as she would give to an
old friend.

Had her dragon not been present, they would have
talked together enthusiastically, instinctively, like two
restless, curious beings wishing to clear up the mystery; but the gold-rimmed glasses were always gleaming
authoritatively and inimically, coming between the two.
Several times the fat lady spoke in a language that
reached Ferragut confusedly and which was not English, and their dinner was hardly finished before they
disappeared just as they had done in the streets of Pompeii,—the older one evidently influencing the other with
her iron will.

The following morning they all met again in a first-
class coach in the station of Salerno. Undoubtedly they
had the same destination. As Ferragut began to greet
them, the hostile dame deigned to return his salutation,
looking then at her companion with a questioning expression. The sailor guessed that during the night they had
been discussing him while he, under the same roof, had
been struggling uselessly, before falling asleep, to concentrate his recollections.

He never knew with certainty just how the conversation began. He found himself suddenly talking in English with the younger one, just as on the preceding
morning. She, with the audacity that quickly makes
the best of a dubious situation, asked him if he was a
sailor. And upon receiving an affirmative response, she
then asked if he was Spanish.

"Yes, Spanish."

Ferragut's answer was followed by a triumphant
glance toward the chaperone, who seemed to relax a little and lose her hostile attitude. And for the first time
she smiled upon the captain with her mouth of bluish-

rose color, her white skin sprinkled with yellow, and her glasses of phosphorescent splendor.

Meanwhile, the young woman was talking on and on, verifying her extraordinary powers of memory.

She had traveled all over the world without forgetting a single one of the places which she had seen. She was able to repeat the titles of the eighty great hotels in which those who make the world's circuit may stay. Upon meeting with an old traveling companion, she always recognized his face immediately, no matter how short a time she had seen him, and oftentimes she could even recall his name. This last was what she had been puzzling over, wrinkling her brows with the mental effort.

"You are a captain? . . . Your name is? . . ."

And she smiled suddenly as her doubts came to an end.

"Your name is," she said positively, "Captain Ulysses Ferragut."

In long and agreeable silence she relished the sailor's astonishment. Then, as though she pitied his stupefaction, she made further explanations. She had made a trip from Buenos Ayres to Barcelona in a steamship which he had commanded.

"That was six years ago," she added. "No; seven years ago."

Ferragut, who had been the first to suspect a former acquaintance, could not recall this woman's name and place among the innumerable passengers that filled his memory. He thought, nevertheless, that he must lie for gallantry's sake, insisting that he remembered her well.

"No, Captain; you do not remember me. I was accompanied by my husband and you never looked at me. . . . All your attentions on that trip were devoted to a very handsome widow from Brazil."

She said this in Spanish, a smooth, sing-song Spanish learned in South America, to which her foreign accent contributed a certain childish charm. Then she added coquettishly:

"I know you, Captain. Always the same! . . . That affair of the rose at Pompeii was very well done. . . . It was just like you."

The grave lady of the glasses, finding herself forgotten, and unable to understand a word of the new language employed in the conversation, now spoke aloud, rolling her eyes in her enthusiasm.

"Oh, Spain! . . ." she said in English. "The land of knightly gentlemen. . . . Cervantes . . . Lope! . . . The Cid! . . ."

She stopped hunting for more celebrities. Suddenly she seized the sailor's arm, exclaiming as energetically as though she had just made a discovery through the little door of the coach. "Calderon de la Barca!" Ferragut saluted her. "Yes, Señora." After that the younger woman thought that it was necessary to present her companion.

"Doctor Fedelmann. . . . A very wise woman distinguished in philology and literature."

After clasping the doctor's hand, Ferragut indiscreetly set himself to work to gather information.

"The Señora is German?" he said in Spanish to the younger one.

The gold-rimmed spectacles appeared to guess the question and shot a restless gleam at her companion.

"No," she replied. "My friend is a Russian, or rather a Pole."

"And you, are you Polish, too?" continued the sailor.

"No, I am Italian."

In spite of the assurance with which she said this, Ferragut felt tempted to exclaim, "You little liar!"

Then, as he gazed upon the full, black, audacious eyes fixed upon him, he began to doubt. . . . Perhaps she was telling the truth.

Again he found himself interrupted by the wordiness of the doctor. She was now speaking in French, repeating her eulogies on Ferragut's country. She could read Castilian in the classic works, but she would not venture to speak it. "Ah, Spain! Country of noble traditions. . . ." And then, seeking to relieve these eulogies by some strong contrast, she twisted her face into a wrathful expression.

The train was running along the coast, having on one side the blue desert of the Gulf of Salerno, and on the other the red and green mountains dotted with white villages and hamlets. The doctor took it all in with her gleaming glasses.

"A country of bandits," she said, clenching her fists. "Country of mandolin-twangers, without honor and without gratitude! . . ."

The girl laughed at this outburst with that hilarity of light-heartedness in which no impressions are durable, considering as of no importance anything which does not bear directly upon its own egoism.

From a few words that the two ladies let fall, Ulysses inferred that they had been living in Rome and had only been in Naples a short time, perhaps against their will. The younger one was well acquainted with the country, and her companion was taking advantage of this enforced journey in order to see what she had so many times admired in books.

The three alighted in the station of Battipaglia in order to take the train for Pæstum. It was a rather long wait, and the sailor invited them to go into the restaurant, a little wooden shanty impregnated with the double odor of resin and wine.

This shack reminded both Ferragut and the young woman of the houses improvised on the South American deserts; and again they began to speak of their oceanic voyage. She finally consented to satisfy the captain's curiosity.

"My husband was a professor, a scholar like the doctor. . . . We were a year in Patagonia, making scientific explorations."

She had made the dangerous journey through an ocean of desert plains that had spread themselves out before them as the expedition advanced; she had slept in ranch houses whose roofs shed bloodthirsty insects; she had traveled on horseback through whirlwinds of sand that had shaken her from the saddle; she had suffered the tortures of hunger and thirst when losing the way, and she had passed nights in intemperate weather with no other bed than her poncho and the trappings of the horses. Thus they had explored those lakes of the Andes between Argentina and Chile that guard in their pure and untouched desert solitude the mystery of the earliest days of creation.

Rovers over these virgin lands, shepherds and bandits, used to talk of glimpses of gigantic animals at nightfall on the shores of the lakes devouring entire meadows with one gulp; and the doctor, like many other sages, had believed in the possibility of finding a surviving prehistoric animal, a beast of the monstrous herds anterior to the coming of man, still dwelling in this unexplored section of the planet.

They saw skeletons dozens of yards long in the foothills of the Cordilleras so frequently agitated by volcanic cataclysms. In the neighborhood of the lakes the guides pointed out to them the hides of devoured herds, and enormous mountains of dried material that appeared to have been deposited by some monster. But no matter how far they penetrated into the solitude, they were always unable to find any living descendant of prehistoric fauna.

The sailor listened absent-mindedly, thinking of something else that was quickening his curiosity.

"And you, what is your name?" he said suddenly.

The two women laughed at this question, amusing because so unexpected.

"Call me Freya. It is a Wagnerian name. It means the earth, and at the same time liberty. . . . Do you like Wagner?"

And before he could reply she added in Spanish, with a Creole accent and flashing eyes:

"Call me, if you wish, 'the merry widow.' The poor doctor died as soon as we returned to Europe."

The three had to run to catch the train ready to start for Pæstum. The landscape was changing on both sides of the way, as now they were crossing over marshy portions of land. On the soft meadows flocks of buffaloes, rude animals that appeared carved out in hatchet strokes, were wading and grazing.

The doctor spoke of Pæstum, the ancient Poseidonia, the city of Neptune, founded by the Greeks of Sybaris six centures before Christ.

Commercial prosperity once dominated the entire coast. The gulf of Salerno was called by the Romans the Gulf of Pæstum. And this city with mountains like those of Athens had suddenly become extinguished without being swallowed up by the sea, and with no volcano to cover it with ashes.

Fever, the miasma of the fens, had been the deadly lava for this Pompeii. The poisonous air had caused the inhabitants to flee, and the few who insisted upon living within the shadow of the ancient temples had had to escape from the Saracen invasions, founding in the

neighboring mountains a new country—the humble town
of Capaccio Vecchio. Then the Norman kings, fore-
runners of Frederick II (the father of Doña Constanza,
the empress beloved by Ferragut), had plundered the
entire deserted city, carrying off with them its columns
and sculpture.

All the medieval constructions of the kingdom of
Naples were the spoils of Pæstum. The doctor recalled
the cathedral of Salerno, seen the afternoon before,
where Hildebrand, the most tenacious and ambitious of
the popes, was buried. Its columns, its sarcophagi, its
bas-reliefs had come from this Grecian city, forgotten for
centuries and centuries and only in modern times—thanks
to the antiquarians and artists—recovering its fame.

In the station of Pæstum, the wife of the only employee
looked curiously at this group arriving after the war had
blocked off the trail of tourists.

Freya spoke to her, interested in her malarial and resigned aspect. They were yet in good time. The spring
sun was warming up these lowlands just as in midsum-
mer, but she was still able to resist it. Later, during the
summer, the guards of the ruins and the workmen in the
excavations would have to flee to their homes in the
mountains, handing the country over to the reptiles and
insects of the marshy fields.

The lodging keeper and his wife in the little station
were the only evidences of humankind still able to exist
in this solitude, trembling with fever, trying to endure
the corrupt air, the poisonous sting of the mosquito, and
the solar fire that was sucking from the mud the vapors
of death. Every two years this humble stopping place
through which passed the lucky ones of the earth,—the
millionaires of two hemispheres, beautiful and curious
dames, rulers of nations, and great artists,—was obliged
to change its station-master.

The three tourists passed near the remains of an aqueduct and an antique pavement. Then they went through the *Porta della Sirena,* an entrance arch into a forgotten quarter of the city, and continued along a road bordered on one side by marshy lands of exuberant vegetation and on the other by the long mud wall of a grange, through whose mortar were sticking out fragments of stones or columns. On turning the last corner, the imposing spectacle of the dead city, still surviving in the magnificent proportions of its temples, presented itself to view.

There were three of these temples, and their colonnades stood forth like mast heads of ships becalmed in a sea of verdure. The doctor, guide-book in hand, was pointing them out with masterly authority—that was Neptune's, that Ceres', and that was called the Basilica without any special reason.

Their grandeur, their solidity, their elegance made the edifices of Rome sink into insignificance. Athens alone could compare the monuments of her Acropolis with these temples of the most severe Doric style. That of Neptune had well preserved its lofty and massive columns,—as close together as the trees of a nursery,—enormous trunks of stone that still sustained the high entablature, the jutting cornice and the two triangular walls of its façades. The stone had taken on the mellow color of the cloudless countries where the sun toasts readily and the rain does not deposit a grimy coating.

The doctor recalled the departed beauties and the old covering of these colossal skeletons,—the fine and compact coating of stucco which had closed the pores of the stone, giving it a superficial smoothness like marble,—the vivid colors of its flutings and walls making the antique city a mass of polychrome monuments. This gay decoration had become volatilized through the centuries and its colors, borne away by the wind, had fallen like a rain of dust upon a land in ruins.

Following an old guard, they climbed the blue, tiled steps of the temple of Neptune. Above, within four rows of columns, was the real sanctuary, the *cella*. Their footsteps on the tiled flags, separated by deep cracks filled with grass, awoke all the animal world that was drowsing there in the sun.

These actual inhabitants of the city,—enormous lizards with green backs covered with black warts,—ran in all directions. In their flight they scurried blindly over the feet of the visitors. The doctor raised her skirts in order to avoid them, at the same time breaking into nervous laughter to hide her terror.

Suddenly Freya gave a cry, pointing to the base of the ancient altar. An ebony-hued snake, his sides dotted with red spots, was slowly and solemnly uncoiling his circles upon the stones. The sailor raised his cane, but before he could strike he felt his arm grasped by two nervous hands. Freya was throwing herself upon him with a pallid face and eyes dilated with fear and entreaty.

"No, Captain! . . . Leave it alone!"

Ulysses thrilled upon feeling the contact of her firm, curving bosom and noting her respiration, her warm breath charged with distant perfume. It would have suited him if she had remained in this position a long time, but Freya freed herself in order to advance toward the reptile, coaxing it and holding out her hands to it as though she were trying to caress a domestic animal. The black tail of the serpent was just slipping away and disappearing between two square tiles. The doctor who had fled down the steps at this apparition, by her repeated calls, obliged Freya also to descend.

The captain's aggressive attitude awoke in his companion a nervous animosity. She believed she knew this reptile. It was undoubtedly the divinity of the dead temple that had changed its form in order to live among the ruins. This serpent must be twenty centuries old. If it had not been for Ferragut she would have been able to have taken it up in her hands. . . . She would have spoken to it. . . . She was accustomed to converse with others. . . .

Ulysses was about to express his doubts rudely as to the mental equilibrium of the exasperated widow when the doctor interrupted them. She was contemplating the swampy plains of acanthus and ferns trembling under the shrill chirping of the cicadas, and this spectacle of green desolation made her recall the roses of Pæstum of which the poets of ancient Rome had sung. She even recited some Latin verses, translating them to her hearers so as to make them understand that the rose bushes of this land used to bloom twice a year. Freya smoothed out her brow and began to smile again. She forgot her recent ill humor and expressed a great longing for one of the marvelous rose bushes: and at this caprice of child-ish vehemence, Ferragut spoke to the custodian with authority. He had to have at once a rose bush from Pæstum, cost what it might.

The old fellow made a bored gesture. Everybody asked the same thing, and he who belonged to that country had never seen a rose of Pæstum. . . . Some-times, just in order to satisfy the whim of tourists, he would bring rose bushes from Capaccio Vecchio and other mountain villages,—rose bushes just like others with no difference except in price. . . . But he didn't wish to take advantage of anybody. He was sad and greatly troubled over the possibility of war.

"I have eight sons," he said to the doctor, because she seemed to be the most suitable one to receive his confidences. "If they mobilize the army, six of them will leave me."

And he added with resignation:

"That's the way it ought to be if we would end forever, in one blow, our eternal enmity with the Goth. My sons will battle against them, just as my father fought."

The doctor stalked haughtily away, and then said in a low voice to her companions that the old guard was an imbecile.

They wandered for two hours through the ancient district of the city,—exploring the network of its streets, the ruins of the amphitheater and the *Porta Aurea* which opened upon a road flanked with tombs. By the *Porta di Mare* they climbed to the walls, ramparts of great limestone blocks, extending a distance of five kilometers. The sea, which from the lowlands had looked like a narrow blue band, now appeared immense and luminous, —a solitary sea with a feather-like crest of smoke, without a sail, given completely over to the sea-gulls.

The doctor walked stiffly ahead of them, still ill-humored about the guide's remark and consulting the pages of her guide book. Behind her Ulysses came close up to Freya, recalling their former contact.

He thought that it would be an easy matter now to get possession of this capricious and free-mannered woman. "Sure thing, Captain!" The rapid triumphs that he had always had in his journeys assured him that there was not the slightest doubt of success. It was enough for him to see the widow's smile, her passionate eyes, and the little tricks of malicious coquetry with which she responded to his gallant advances. "Forward, sea-wolf!" . . . He took her hand while she was speaking of the beauty of the solitary sea, and the hand yielded without protest to his caressing fingers. The doctor was far away and, sighing hypocritically, he encircled

Freya's waist with his other arm while he inclined his
head upon her open throat as though he were going to
kiss her pearls.

In spite of his strength, he found himself energetically
repulsed and saw Freya freed from his arms, two steps
away, looking upon him with hostile eyes that he had
not noticed before.

"None of your child's play, Captain! . . . It is useless
with me. . . . You are just wasting time."

And she said no more. Her stiffness and her silence
during the rest of the walk made the sailor understand
the enormity of his mistake. In vain he tried to keep
beside the widow. She always maneuvered that the doctor should come between the two.

Upon returning to the station they took refuge from
the heat in a little waiting room with dusty velvet divans.
In order to beguile the time while waiting for the train,
Freya took from her handbag a gold cigarette-case and
the light smoke of Egyptian tobacco charged with opium
whirled among the shafts of sunlight from the partly-
opened windows.

Ferragut, who had gone out in order to ascertain the
exact hour of the arrival of the train, on returning
stopped near the door, amazed at the animation with
which the two ladies were speaking in a new language.
Recollections of Hamburg and Bremen came surging up
in his memory. His companions were talking German
with the ease of a familiar idiom. At sight of the sailor,
they instantly continued their conversation in English.

Wishing to take part in the dialogue, he asked Freya
how many languages she spoke.

"Very few,—no more than eight. The doctor, perhaps, knows twenty. She knows the languages of people who passed away many centuries ago.

And the young woman said this with gravity, without

looking at him, as though she had lost forever that smile
of a light woman which had so deceived Ferragut.

In the train she became more like a human being, even
losing her offended manner. They were soon going to
separate. The doctor grew less and less approachable
as the cars rolled towards Salerno. It was the chilliness
that appears among companions of a day, when the hour
of separation approaches and each one draws into himself, not to be seen any more.

Words fell flat, like bits of ice, without finding any
echo in their fall. At each turn of the wheel, the imposing lady became more reserved and silent. Everything had been said. They, too, were going to remain
in Salerno in order to take a carriage-trip along the gulf.
They were going to Amalfi and would pass the night on
the Alpine peak of Ravello, a medieval city where Wagner had passed the last months of his life, before dying
in Venice. Then, passing over to the Gulf of Naples,
they would rest in Sorrento and perhaps might go to the
island of Capri.

Ulysses wished to say that his line of march was exactly the same, but he was afraid of the doctor. Furthermore, their trip was to be in a vehicle which they
had already rented and they would not offer him a seat.

Freya appeared to surmise his sadness and wished to
console him.

"It is a short trip. No more than three days. . . .
Soon we shall be in Naples."

The farewell in Salerno was brief. The doctor was
careful not to mention their stopping-place. For her,
the friendship was ending then and there.

"It is probable that we shall run across each other
again," she said laconically. "It is only the mountains
that never meet."

Her young companion was more explicit, mentioning

the hotel on the shores of S. Lucia in which she lodged.

Standing by the step of the carriage, he saw them take their departure, just as he had seen them appear in a street of Pompeii. The doctor was lost behind a screen of glass, talking with the coachman who had come to meet them. Freya, before disappearing, turned to give him a faint smile and then raised her gloved hand with a stiff forefinger, threatening him just as though he were a mischievous and bold child.

Finding himself alone in the compartment that was carrying toward Naples the traces and perfumes of the absent one, Ulysses felt as downcast as though he were returning from a burial, as if he had just lost one of the props of his life.

His appearance on board the *Mare Nostrum* was regarded as a calamity. He was capricious and intractable, complaining of Toni and the other two officials because they were not hastening repairs on the vessel. In the same breath he said it would be better not to hurry things too much, so that the job would be better done. Even Caragol was the victim of his bad humor which flamed forth in the form of cruel sermons against those addicted to the poison of alcohol.

"When men need to be cheered up, they have to have something better than wine. That which brings greater ecstasy than drink . . . is woman, Uncle Caragol. Don't forget this counsel!"

Through mere force of habit the cook replied, "That is so, my captain. . . ." But down in his heart he was pitying the ignorance of those men who concentrate all their happiness on the whims and grimaces of this most frivolous of toys.

Two days afterwards those on board drew a long breath when they saw the captain taken ashore. The ship was moored in a very uncomfortable place,—near some that were discharging coal,—with the stern shored up so that the screw of the steamer might be repaired. The workmen were replacing the damaged and broken plates with ceaseless hammering. Since they would undoubtedly have to wait nearly a month, it would be much more convenient for the owner to go to a hotel; so he sent his baggage to the *Albergo Partenope,* on the ancient shore of S. Lucia,—the very one that Freya had mentioned.

Upon installing himself in an upper room, with a view of the blue circle of the gulf framed by the outlines of the balcony, Ferragut's first move was to change a bill for five liras into coppers, preparatory to asking various questions. The jaundiced and mustached steward listened to him attentively with the complacency of a go-between, and at last was able to formulate a complete personality with all its data. The lady for whom he was inquiring was the *Signora* Talberg. She was at present away on an excursion, but she might return at any moment.

Ulysses passed an entire day with the tranquillity of one who awaits at a sure place, gazing at the gulf from the balcony. Below him was the *Castello dell' Ovo* connected with the land by a bridge.

The *bersaglieri* were occupying their ancient castle, work of the viceroy, Pedro of Toledo. Many turrets of dark rose color were crowded together upon this narrow, egg-shaped island, where, in other days, the pusillanimous Spanish garrison was locked in the fortress for the purpose of aiming bombards and culverins at the Neapolitans when they no longer wished to pay taxes and imposts. Its walls had been raised upon the ruins of another castle in which Frederick II had guarded his treasures, and whose chapel Giotto had painted. And the medieval castle of which only the memory now remained had, in its turn, been erected upon the remnants of the Palace of Lucullus, who had located the center of his celebrated gardens in this little island, then called *Megaris*.

The cornets of the *bersaglieri* rejoiced the captain like the announcement of a triumphal entry. "She's going to come! She's going to come at any moment! . . ." And he would look across the double mountain of the island of Capri, black in the distance, closing the gulf like a promontory, and the coast of Sorrento as rectilinear as a wall. "There she is. . . ." Then he would lovingly follow the course of the little steamboats plowing across the immense blue surface, opening a triangle of foam. In some of these Freya must be coming.

The first day was golden and full of hope. The sun was sparkling in a cloudless sky, and the gulf was foaming with bubbles of light under an atmosphere so calm that not the slightest zephyr was rippling its surface. The smoke plume of Vesuvius was upright and slender, expanding upon the horizon like a pine tree of white vapor. At the foot of the balcony the strolling musicians kept succeeding each other from time to time, singing voluptuous barcarolles and love serenades. . . . And— she did not come!

The second day was silvery and desperate. There was fog on the gulf; the sun was no more than a reddish disk such as one sees in the northern countries; the mountains were clothed with lead; the clouds were hiding the cone of the volcano; the sea appeared to be made of tin, and a chilly wind was distending sails, skirts, and overcoats, making the people scurry along the promenade and the shore. The musicians continued their singing but with melancholy sighs in the shelter of a corner, to keep out of the furious blasts from the sea. "To die. . . . To die for thee!" a baritone voice groaned between the harps and violins. And—she came!

Upon learning from the waiter that the *signora* Talberg was in her room on the floor below, Ulysses thrilled with restlessness. What would she say upon finding him installed in her hotel? . . .

The luncheon hour was at hand, and he impatiently awaited the usual signals before going down to the dining room. First an explosion would be heard behind the *albergo* making the walls and roofs tremble, swelling out into the immensity of the gulf. That was the midday cannonade from the high castle of S. Elmo. Then cornets from the *Castello dell' Ovo* would respond with their joyous call to the smoking *olla,* and up the stairway of the hotel would come the beating of the Chinese gong, announcing that luncheon was served.

Ulysses went down to take his place at table, looking in vain at the other guests who had preceded him. Freya perhaps was going to come in with the delay of a traveler who has just arrived and has been occupied in freshening her toilet.

He lunched badly, looking continually at a great glass doorway decorated with pictures of boats, fishes, and sea gulls, and every time its polychromatic leaves parted, his food seemed to stick in his throat. Finally came the end of the lunch, and he slowly sipped his coffee. She did not appear.

On returning to his room, he sent the whiskered steward in search of news. . . . The *signora* had not lunched in the hotel; the *signora* had gone out while he was in the dining-room. Surely she would show herself in the evening.

At dinner time he had the same unpleasant experience, believing that Freya was going to appear every time that an unknown hand or a vague silhouette of a woman pushed the door open from the other side of the opaque glass.

He strolled up and down the vestibule a long time, chewing rabidly on a cigar, and finally decided to accost the porter, an astute brunette whose blue lapels embroidered with keys of gold were peeping over the edge of his writing desk, taking in everything, informing himself of everything, while he appeared to be asleep.

The approach of Ulysses made him spring up as though he heard the rustling of paper money. His information was very precise. The *signora* Talberg very seldom ate at the hotel. She had some friends who were occupying a furnished flat in the district of Chiaja, with whom she usually passed almost the entire day. Sometimes she did not even return to sleep. . . . And he again sat down, his hand closing tightly upon the bill which his imagination had foreseen.

After a bad night Ulysses arose, resolved to await the widow at the entrance to the hotel. He took his breakfast at a little table in the vestibule, read the newspaper, had to go to the door in order to avoid the morning cleaning, pursued by the dust of brooms and shaken rugs. And once there, he pretended to take great interest in the wandering musicians, who dedicated their love songs and serenades to him, rolling up the whites of their eyes upon presenting their hats for coins.

Some one came to keep him company. It was the porter who now appeared very familiar and confidential, as though since the preceding night a firm friendship, based upon their secret, had sprung up between the two.

He spoke of the beauties of the country, counseling the Spaniard to take divers excursions. . . . A smile, an encouraging word from Ferragut, and he would have immediately proposed other recreations whose announcement appeared to be fluttering around his lips. But the sailor repelled all such amiability, glowering with displeasure. This vulgar fellow was going to spoil with his presence the longed-for meeting. Perhaps he was hanging around just to see and to know. . . . And taking advantage of one of his brief absences, Ulysses went off down the long *Via Partenope,* following the parapet that extends along the coast, pretending to be interested in everything that he met, but without losing sight of the door of the hotel.

He stopped before the oystermen's stands, examining the valves of pearly shells piled up on the shelves, the baskets of oysters from Fusaro and the enormous conchshells in whose hollow throats, according to the peddlers, the distant roll of the sea was echoing like a haunting memory. One by one he looked at all the motor launches, the little regatta skiffs, the fishing barks, and the coast schooners anchored in the quiet harbor of the island *dell' Ovo.* He stood a long time quietly watching the gentle waves that were combing their foam on the rocks of the dikes under the horizontal fishing rods of various fishermen.

Suddenly he saw Freya following the avenue beside the houses. She recognized him at once and this discovery made her stop near a street-opening, hesitating whether to continue on or to flee toward the interior of Naples. Then she came over to the seaside pavement, approaching Ferragut with a placid smile, greeting him afar off, like a friend whose presence is only to be expected.

Such assurance rather disconcerted the captain. They shook hands and she asked him calmly what he was doing there looking at the waves, and if the repairs of his boat were progressing satisfactorily.

"But admit that my presence has surprised you!"

said Ulysses, rather irritated by this tranquillity. "Confess that you were not expecting to find me here."

Freya repeated her smiles with an expression of sweet compassion.

"It is natural that I should find you here. You are in your district, within sight of a hotel. . . . We are neighbors."

In order more thoroughly to amuse herself with the captain's astonishment, she made a long pause. Then she added:

"I saw your name on the list of arrivals yesterday, on my return to the hotel. I always look them over. It pleases me to know who my neighbors are."

"And for that reason you did not come down to the dining-room? . . ."

Ulysses asked this question hoping that she would respond negatively. She could not answer it in any other way, if only for good manners' sake.

"Yes, for that reason," Freya replied simply. "I guessed that you were waiting to meet me and I did not wish to go into the dining-room. . . . I give you fair warning that I shall always do the same."

Ulysses uttered an "Ah!" of amazement. . . . No woman had ever spoken to him with such frankness.

"Neither has your presence here surprised me," she continued. "I was expecting it. I know the innocent wiles of you men. 'Since he did not find me in the hotel, he will wait for me to-day in the street,' I said to myself, upon arising this morning. . . . Before coming out, I was following your footsteps from the window of my room. . . ."

Ferragut looked at her in surprise and dismay. What a woman! . . .

"I might have escaped through any cross street while your back was turned. I saw you before you saw me.

. . . But these false situations stretching along indefinitely are distasteful to me. It is better to speak the entire truth face to face. . . . And therefore I have come to meet you. . . ."

Instinct made him turn his head toward the hotel. The porter was standing at the entrance looking out over the sea, but with his eyes undoubtedly turned toward them.

"Let us go on," said Freya. "Accompany me a little ways. We shall talk together and then you can leave me. . . . Perhaps we shall separate greater friends than ever."

They strolled in silence all the length of the *Via Partenope* until they reached the gardens along the beach of Chiaja, losing sight of the hotel. Ferragut wished to renew the conversation, but could not begin it. He feared to appear ridiculous. This woman was making him timid.

Looking at her with admiring eyes, he noted the great changes that had been made in the adornment of her person. She was no longer clad in the dark tailor-made in which he had first seen her. She was wearing a blue and white silk gown with a handsome fur over her shoulders and a cluster of purple heron feathers on top of her wide hat.

The black hand-bag that had always accompanied her on her journeys had been replaced by a gold-meshed one of showy richness,—Australian gold of a greenish tone like an overlay of Florentine bronze. In her ears were two great, thick emeralds, and on her fingers a half dozen diamonds whose facets twinkled in the sunlight. The pearl necklace was still on her neck peeping out through the V-shaped opening of her gown. It was the magnificent toilet of a rich actress who puts everything on herself,—of one so enamored with jewels that she

is not able to live without their contact, adorning herself
with them the minute she is out of bed, regardless of the
hour and the rules of good taste.

But Ferragut did not take into consideration the un-
suitableness of all this luxury. Everything about her
appeared to him admirable.

Without knowing just how, he began to talk. He was
astonished at hearing his own voice, saying always the
same thing in different words. His thoughts were inco-
herent, but they were all clustered around an incessantly
repeated statement,—his love, his immense love for
Freya.

And Freya continued marching on in silence with a
compassionate expression in her eyes and in the corners
of her mouth. It pleased her pride as a woman to contemplate this strong man stuttering in childish confusion.
At the same time she grew impatient at the monotony
of his words.

"Don't say any more, Captain," she finally interrupted.
"I can guess all that you are going to say, and I've heard
many times what you have said,—You do not sleep—
you do not eat—you do not live because of me. Your
existence is impossible if I do not love you. A little
more conversation and you will threaten me with shooting yourself, if I am not yours. . . . Same old song!
They all say the same thing. There are no creatures
with less originality than you men when you wish something. . . ."

They were in one of the avenues of the promenade.
Through the palm trees and glossy magnolias the luminous gulf could be seen on one side, and on the other
the handsome edifices of the beach of Chiaja. Some
ragged urchins kept running around them and following
them, until they took refuge in an ornamental little white
temple at the end of the avenue.

"Very well, then, enamored sea-wolf," continued
Freya; "you need not sleep, you need not eat, you may
kill yourself if the fancy strikes you; but I am not able
to love you; I shall never love you. You may give up
all hope; life is not mere diversion and I have other
more serious occupations that absorb all my time."

In spite of the playful smile with which she accompanied these words, Ferragut surmised a very firm will.

"Then," he said in despair, "it will all be useless? . . .
Even though I make the greatest sacrifices? . . . Even
though I give proofs of love greater than you have ever
known? . . ."

"All useless," she replied roundly, without a sign of a
smile.

They paused before the ornamental little temple-shaped
building, with its dome supported by white columns and
a railing around it. The bust of Virgil adorned the center,—an enormous head of somewhat feminine beauty.

The poet had died in Naples in "Sweet Parthenope,"
on his return from Greece and his body, turned to dust,
was perhaps mingled with the soil of this garden. The
Neapolitan people of the Middle Ages had attributed to
him all kinds of wonderful things, even transforming the
poet into a powerful magician. The wizard Virgil in one
night had constructed the *Castello dell' Ovo,* placing it
with his own hands upon a great egg (*Ovo*) that was
floating in the sea. He also had opened with his magic
blasts the tunnel of Posilipo near which are a vineyard
and a tomb visited for centuries as the last resting place
of the poet. Little scamps, playing around the railing,
used to hurl papers and stones inside the temple. The
white head of the powerful sorcerer attracted them and
at the same time filled them with admiration and fear.

"Thus far and no further," ordered Freya. "You will
continue on your way. I am going to the high part of

Chiaja. . . . But before separating as good friends, you are going to give me your word not to follow me, not to importune me with your amorous attentions, not to mix yourself in my life."

Ulysses did not reply, hanging his head in genuine dismay. To his disillusion was added the sting of wounded pride. He who had imagined such very different things when they should see each other again together, alone! . . .

Freya pitied his sadness.

"Don't be a baby! . . . This will soon pass. Think of your business affairs, and of your family waiting for you over there in Spain. . . . Besides, the world is full of women; I'm not the only one."

But Ferragut interrupted her. "Yes, she was the only one! . . . The only one! . . ." And he said it with a conviction that awakened another one of her compassionate smiles.

This man's tenacity was beginning to irritate her.

"Captain, I know your type very well. You are an egoist, like all other men. Your boat is tied up in the harbor because of an accident; you've got to remain ashore a month; you meet on one of your trips a woman who is idiot enough to admit that she remembers meeting you at other times, and you say to yourself, 'Magnificent occasion to while away agreeably a tedious period of waiting! . . .' If I should yield to your desire, within a few weeks, as soon as your boat was ready, the hero of my love, the knight of my dreams, would betake himself to the sea, saying as a parting salute: 'Adieu, simpleton!' "

Ulysses protested with energy. No: he wished that his boat might never be repaired. He was computing with agony the days that remained. If it were necessary, he would abandon it, remaining forever in Naples.

"And what have I to do in Naples?" interrupted Freya. "I am a mere bird of passage here, just as you are. We knew each other on the seas of another hemisphere, and we have just happened to run across each other here in Italy. Next time, if we ever meet again, it will be in Japan or Canada or the Cape. . . . Go on your way, you enamored old shark, and let me go mine. Imagine to yourself that we are two boats that have met when becalmed, have signaled each other, have exchanged greetings, have wished each other good luck, and afterwards have continued on our way, perhaps never to see each other again."

Ferragut shook his head negatively. Such a thing could not be, he could not resign himself to losing sight of her forever.

"These men!" she continued, each time a little more irritated. "You all imagine that things must be arranged entirely according to your caprices. 'Because I desire thee, thou must be mine. . . .' And what if I don't want to? . . . And if I don't feel any necessity of being loved? . . . If I wish only to live in liberty, with no other love than that which I feel for myself? . . ."

She considered it a great misfortune to be a woman. She always envied men for their independence. They could hold themselves aloof, abstaining from the passions that waste life, without anybody's coming to importune them in their retreat. They were at liberty to go wherever they wanted to, to travel the wide world over, without leaving behind their footsteps a wake of solicitors.

"You appear to me, Captain, a very charming man. The other day I was delighted to meet you; it was an apparition from the past; I saw in you the joy of my youth that is beginning to fade away, and the melancholy of certain recollections. . . . And nevertheless, I am

going to end by hating you. Do you hear me, you tedious
old Argonaut? . . . I shall loathe you because you will
not be a mere friend; because you know only how to
talk everlastingly about the same thing; because you are
a person out of a novel, a Latin, very interesting, perhaps, to other women,—but insufferable to me."

Her face contracted with a gesture of scorn and pity.
"Ah, those Latins! . . ."

"They're all the same,—Spaniards, Italians, Frenchmen. . . . They were born for the same thing. They
hardly meet an attractive woman but they believe that
they are evading their obligations if they do not beg for
her love and what comes afterward. . . . Cannot a man
and woman simply be friends? Couldn't you be just a
good comrade and treat me as a companion?"

Ferragut protested energetically. No; no, he couldn't.
He loved her and, after being repelled with such cruelty,
his love would simply go on increasing. He was sure of
that.

A nervous tremor made Freya's voice sharp and cutting, and her eyes took on a dangerous gleam. She
looked at her companion as though he were an enemy
whose death she longed for.

"Very well, then, if you must know it. I abominate
all men; I abominate them, because I know them so well.
I would like the death of all of them, of every one! . . .
The evil that they have wrought in my life! . . . I would
like to be immensely beautiful, the handsomest woman on
earth, and to possess the intellect of all the sages concentrated in my brain, to be rich and to be a queen, in
order that all the men of the world, crazy with desire,
would come to prostrate themselves before me. . . . And
I would lift up my feet with their iron heels, and I
would go trampling over them, crushing their heads . . .
so . . . and so . . . and so! . . ."

She struck the sands of the garden with the soles of her little shoes. An hysterical sneer distorted her mouth.

"Perhaps I might make an exception of you. . . . You who, with all your braggart arrogance, are, after all, out-right and simple-hearted. I believe you capable of assuring a woman of all kinds of love-lies . . . believing them yourself most of all. But the others! . . . *Ay, the others!* . . . How I hate them! . . ."

She looked over toward the palace of the Aquarium, glistening white between the colonnade of trees.

"I would like to be," she continued pensively, "one of those animals of the sea that can cut with their claws, that have arms like scissors, saws, pincers . . . that devour their own kind, and absorb everything around them."

Then she looked at the branch of a tree from which were hanging several silver threads, sustaining insects with active tentacles.

"I would like to be a spider, an enormous spider, that all men might be drawn to my web as irresistibly as flies. With what satisfaction would I crunch them between my claws! How I would fasten my mouth against their hearts! . . . And I would suck them. . . . I would suck them until there wasn't a drop of blood left, tossing away then their empty carcasses! . . ."

Ulysses began to wonder if he had fallen in love with a crazy woman. His disquietude, his surprise and questioning eyes gradually restored Freya's serenity.

She passed one hand across her forehead, as though awakening from a nightmare and wishing to banish remembrance with this gesture. Her glance became calmer.

"Good-by, Ferragut; do not make me talk any more. You will soon doubt my reason. . . . You are doing so already. We shall be friends, just friends and nothing

more. It is useless to think of anything else. . . . Do
not follow me. . . . We shall see each other. . . . I shall
hunt you up. . . . Good-by! . . . Good-by!"

And although Ferragut felt tempted to follow her,
he remained motionless, seeing her hurry rapidly away,
as though fleeing from the words that she had just let
fall before the little temple of the poet.

CHAPTER V

In spite of her promise, Freya made no effort to meet the sailor. "We shall see each other. . . . I shall hunt you up." But it was Ferragut who did the hunting, stationing himself around the hotel.

"How crazy I was the other morning! . . . I wonder what you could have thought of me!" she said the first time that she spoke to him again.

Not every day did Ulysses have the pleasure of a conversation which invariably developed from the *Via Partenope* to Virgil's monument. The most of the mornings he used to wait in vain opposite the oyster stands, listening to the musicians who were bombarding the closed windows of the hotel with their sentimental romances and mandolins. Freya would not appear.

His impatience usually dragged Ulysses back to the hotel in order to beg information of the porter. Animated by the hope of a new bill, the flunkey would go to the telephone and inquire of the servants on the upper floor. And then with a sad and obsequious smile, as though lamenting his own words: "The *signora* is not in. The *signora* has passed the night outside of the *albergo*." And Ferragut would go away furious.

Sometimes he would go to see how the repairs were getting on in his boat,—an excellent pretext for venting his wrath on somebody. On other mornings he would go to the garden of the beach of Chiaja,—to the very same places through which he had strolled with Freya. He

154

was always looking for her to appear from one moment to another. Everything 'round about suggested some reminder of her. Trees and benches, pavements and electric lights knew her perfectly because of having formed a part of her regular walk.

Becoming convinced that he was waiting in vain, a last hope made him glance toward the white building of the Aquarium. Freya had frequently mentioned it. She was accustomed to amuse herself, oftentimes passing entire hours there, contemplating the life of the inhabitants of the sea. And Ferragut blinked involuntarily as he passed rapidly from the garden boiling under the sun into the shadow of the damp galleries with no other illumination than that of the daylight which penetrated to the interior of the Aquarium,—a light that, seen through the water and the glass, took on a mysterious tone, the green and diffused tint of the subsea depths.

This visit enabled him to kill time more placidly. There came to his mind old readings confirmed now by direct vision. He was not the kind of sailor that sails along regardless of what exists under his keel. He wanted to know the mysteries of the immense blue palace over whose roof he was usually navigating, devoting himself to the study of oceanography, the most recent of sciences.

Upon taking his first steps in the Aquarium, he immediately pictured the marine depths which exploration had divided and charted so unequally. Near the shores, in the zone called "the littoral" where the rivers empty, the materials of nourishment were accumulated by the impulse of the tides and currents, and there flourished subaquatic vegetation. This was the zone of the great fish and reached down to within two hundred fathoms of the bottom,—a depth to which the sun's rays never penetrate.

Beyond that there was no light; plant life disappeared and with it the herbivorous animals.

The submarine grade, a gentle one down to this point, now becomes very steep, descending rapidly to the oceanic abysses,—that immense mass of water (almost the entire ocean), without light, without waves, without tides, without currents, without oscillations of temperature, which is called the "abyssal" zone.

In the littoral, the waters, healthfully agitated, vary in saltiness according to the proximity of the rivers. The rocks and deeps are covered with a vegetation which is green near the surface, becoming darker and darker, even turning to a dark red and brassy yellow as it gets further from the light. In this oceanic paradise of nutritive and luminous waters charged with bacteria and microscopic nourishment, life is developed in exuberance. In spite of the continual traps of the fishermen, the marine herds keep themselves intact because of their infinite powers of reproduction.

The fauna of the abyssal depths where the lack of light makes all vegetation impossible, is largely carnivorous, the weak inhabitants usually devouring the residuum and dead animals that come down from the surface. The strong ones, in their turn, nourish themselves on the concentrated sustenance of the little cannibals.

The bottom of the ocean, a monotonous desert of mud and sand, the accumulated sediment of hundreds of centuries, has occasional oases of strange vegetation. These grove-like growths spring up like spots of light just where the meeting of the surface currents rain down a manna of diminutive dead bodies. The twisted limestone plants, hard as stone, are really not plants at all, but animals. Their leaves are simply inert and treacherous tentacles which contract very suddenly, and their flowers, avid mouths, which bend over their prey, and suck it in through their gluttonous openings.

A fantastic light streaks this world of darkness with multicolored shafts, animal light produced by living organisms. In the lowest abysses sightless creatures are very scarce, contrary to the common opinion, which imagines that almost all of them lack eyes because of their distance from the sun. The filaments of the carnivorous trees are garlands of lamps; the eyes of the hunting animals, electric globes; the insignificant bacteria, light-producing little glands all of which open or close with phosphorescent switches according to the necessity of the moment,—sometimes in order to persecute and devour, and at others in order to keep themselves hidden in the shadows.

The animal-plants, motionless as stars, surround their ferocious mouths with a circle of flashing lights, and immediately their diminutive prey feel themselves as irresistibly drawn toward them as do the moths that fly toward the lamp, and the birds of the sea that beat against the lighthouse.

None of the lights of the earth can compare with those of this abyssal world. All artificial fires pale before the varieties of its organic brilliance.

The living branches of polyps, the eyes of the animals, even the mud sown with brilliant points, emit phosphoric shafts like sparks whose splendors incessantly vanish and reappear. And these lights pass through many gradations of colors:—violet, purple, orange, blue, and especially green. On perceiving a victim nearby, the gigantic cuttle-fishes become illuminated like livid suns, moving their arms with death-dealing strokes.

All the abyssal beings have their organs of sight enormously developed in order to catch even the weakest rays of light. Many have enormous, protruding eyes.

Others have them detached from the body at the end of two cylindrical tentacles like telescopes.

Those that are blind and do not throw out any radiance are compensated for this inferiority by the development of the tactile organs. Their antennæ and swimming organs are immeasurably prolonged in the darkness. The filaments of their body, long hairs rich in nerve terminals, can distinguish instantaneously the appetizing prey, or the enemy lying in wait.

The abyssal deeps have two floors or roofs. In the highest, is the so-called neritic zone,—the oceanic surface, diaphanous and luminous, far from any coast. Next is seen the pelagic zone, much deeper, in which reside the fishes of incessant motion, capable of living without reposing on the bottom.

The corpses of the neritic animals and of those that swim between the two waters are the direct or indirect sustenance of the abyssal fauna. These beings with weak dental equipment and sluggish speed, badly armed for the conquest of living prey, nourish themselves with the dropping of this rain of alimentary material. The great swimmers, supplied with formidable mandibles and immense and elastic stomachs, prefer the fortunes of war, the pursuit of living prey, and devour,—as the carnivorous devour the herbivorous on land,—all the little feeders on débris and *plancton*. This word of recent scientific invention presented to Captain Ferragut's mind the most humble and interesting of the oceanic inhabitants. The *plancton* is the life that floats in loose clusters or forming cloud-like groups across the neritic surface, even descending to the abyssal depths.

Wherever the *plancton* goes, there is living animation, grouping itself in closely packed colonies. The purest and most translucent salt water shows under certain luminous rays a multitude of little bodies as restless as the dust motes that dance in shafts of sunlight. These transparent beings mingled with microscopic algæ and embryonic mucosities are the *plancton*. In its dense mass, scarcely visible to the human eye, float the *siphonoforas*, garlands of entities united by a transparent thread as fragile, delicate and luminous as Bohemian crystal. Other equally subtle organisms have the form of little glass torpedoes. The sum of all the albuminous materials floating on the sea are condensed in these nutrient clouds to which are added the secretions of living animals, the remnants of cadavers, the bodies brought down by the rivers, and the nourishing fragments from the meadows of algæ.

When the *plancton*, either by chance or following some mysterious attraction, accumulates on some determined point of the shore, the waters boil with fishes of an astonishing fertility. The seaside towns increase in number, the sea is filled with sails, the tables are more opulent, industries are established, factories are opened and money circulates along the coast, attracted thither from the interior by the commerce in fresh and dried fish.

If the *plancton* capriciously withdraws itself, floating toward another shore, the marine herds emigrate behind these living meadows, and the blue plain remains as empty as a desert accursed. The fleets of fishing boats are placed high and dry on the beach, the shops are closed, the stewpot is no longer steaming, the horses of the gendarmerie charge against protesting and famine-stricken crowds, the Opposition howls in the Chambers, and the newspapers make the Government responsible for everything.

This animal and vegetable dust nourishes the most numerous species which, in their turn, serve as pasture for the great swimmers armed with teeth.

The whales, most bulky of all the oceanic inhabitants,

close this destructive cycle, since they devour each other in order to live. The Pacific giant, without teeth, supplies his organism with *plancton* alone, absorbing it by the ton; that imperceptible and crystalline manna nourishes his body (looking like an overturned belfry), and makes purple, fatty rivers of warm blood circulate under its oily skin.

The transparency of the beings in the *plancton* recalled to Ferragut's memory the marvelous colorings of the inhabitants of the sea, adjusted exactly to their needs of preservation. The species that live on the surface have, as a general rule, a blue back and silver belly. In this way it is possible for them to escape the sight of their enemies; seen from the shadows of the depths, they are confounded with the white and luminous color of the surface. The sardines that swim in shoals are able to pass unnoticed, thanks to their backs blue as the water, thus escaping the fish and the birds which are hunting them.

Living in the abysses where the light never penetrates, the pelagic animals are not obliged to be transparent or blue like the neritic beings on the surface. Some are opaque and colorless, others, bronzed and black; most of them are clad in somber hues, whose splendor is the despair of the artist's brush, incapable of imitating them. A magnificent red seems to be the base of this color scheme, fading gradually to pale pink, violet, amber, even losing itself in the milky iris of the pearls and in the opalescence of the mother-of-pearl of the mollusks. The eyes of certain fish placed at the end of jaw bones separated from the body, sparkle like diamonds in the ends of a double pin. The protruding glands, the warts, the curving backs, take on the colorings of jewelry.

But the precious stones of earth are dead minerals

that need rays of light in order to emit the slightest flash. The animated gems of the ocean—fishes and corals—sparkle with their own colors that are a reflex of their vitality. Their green, their rose color, their intense yellow, their metallic iridescence, all their liquid tints are eternally glazed by a moist varnish which cannot exist in the atmospheric world.

Some of these beings are capable of a marvelous power of mimicry that makes them identify themselves with inanimate objects, or in a few moments run through every gamut of color. Some of great nervous activity, make themselves absolutely immovable and contract, filling themselves with wrinkles, taking on the dark tone of the rocks. Others in moments of irritation or amorous fever, cover themselves with streaks of light and tremulous spots, different colored clouds passing over their epidermis with every thrill. The cuttlefish and ink fish, upon perceiving that they are pursued, enwrap themselves in a cloud of invisibility, just as did the enchanters of old in the books of chivalry, darkening the water with the ink stored in their glands.

Ferragut continued to pass slowly along the Aquarium between the two rows of vertical tanks,—stone cases with thick glass that permitted full view of the interior. The clear and shining walls that received the fire of the sun through their upper part, spread a green reflection over the shadows of the corridors. As they made the rounds, the visitors took on a livid paleness, as though they were marching through a submarine defile.

The tranquil water within the tanks was scarcely visible. Behind the thick glass there appeared to exist only a marvelous atmosphere, an air of dreamland in which drifted up and down various floating beings of many colors. The bubbles of their respiration was the only thing that announced the presence of the liquid. In the upper part of these aquatic cages, the luminous atmosphere vibrated under a continual spray of transparent dust,—the sea water with air injected into it that was renewing the conditions of existence for these guests of the Aquarium.

Seeing these revivifying streams, the captain admired the nourishing force of the blue water upon which he had passed almost all his life.

Earth lost its pride when compared with the aquatic immensity. In the ocean had appeared the first manifestations of life, continuing then its evolutionary cycle over the mountains which had also come up from its depths. If the earth was the mother of man, the sea was his grandmother.

The number of terrestrial animals is most insignificant compared with the maritime ones. Upon the earth's surface (much smaller than the ocean) the beings occupy only the surface of the soil, and an atmospheric canopy of a certain number of meters. The birds and insects seldom go beyond this in their flights. In the sea, the animals are dispersed over all its levels, through many miles of depth multiplied by thousands and thousands of longitudinal leagues. Infinite quantities of creatures, whose number it is impossible to calculate, swim incessantly in all the strata of its waters. Land is a surface, a plane; the sea is a volume.

The immense aquatic mass, three times more salty than at the beginning of the planet, because of a millennarian evaporation that has diminished the liquid without absorbing its components, retains mixed with its chlorides, copper, nickel, iron, zinc, lead, and even gold, from the metallic veins that planetary upheaval deposits upon the oceanic bottom; compared with this mass, the veins of mountains with their golden sands deposited by the rivers are but insignificant tentacles.

Silver also is dissolved in its waters. Ferragut knew by certain calculations that with the silver floating in the ocean could be erected pyramids more enormous than those in Egypt.

The men who once had thought of exploiting these mineral riches had given up the visionary idea because the minerals were too diluted and it would be impossible to make use of them. The oceanic beings know better how to recognize their presence, letting them filter through their bodies for the renovation and coloration of their organs. The copper accumulates in their blood; the gold and silver are discovered in the texture of the animal-plants; the phosphorus is absorbed by the sponges; the lead and the zinc by species of algæ.

Every oceanic creature is able to extract from the water the residuum from certain metals dissolved into particles so incalculably tiny that no chemical process could ever capture them. The carbonates of lime deposited by the rivers or dragged from the coast serve innumerable species for the construction of their coverings, skeletons, and spiral shells. The corals, filtering the water across their flabby and mucous bodies, solidify their hard skeletons so that they may finally be converted into habitable islands.

The beings of disconcerting diversity that were floating, diving, or wiggling around Ferragut were no more than oceanic water. The fish were water made into flesh; the slimy, mucilaginous animals were water in a gelatinous state; the crustaceans and the polypi were water turned to stone.

In one of the tanks he saw a landscape which appeared like that of another planet, grandiose yet at the same time reduced, like a woods seen in a diorama. It was a palm grove, surging up between the rocks, but the rocks were only pebbles, and the palm trees,—annelides of the sea,—were simply worms holding themselves in up-right immovability.

They kept their ringed bodies within a leathern tube that formed their protective case, and from this rec-tilinear, marble-colored trunk sent forth, like a spout of branches, the constantly moving tentacles which served them as organs for breathing and eating.

Endowed with rare sensitiveness, it was enough for a cloud to pass before the sun to make them shrink quickly within these tubes, deprived of their showy capi-tals, like beheaded palm trees. Then, slowly and pru-dently the animated pincers would come protruding again through the opening of their cylindrical scabbards, float-ing in the water with anxious hope. All these trees and flower-animals developed a mechanical voracity when-ever a microscopic victim fell under the power of their tentacles; then the soft clusters of branches would con-tract, close, drawing in their prey, and the worm, with-drawing into the lowest part of the slender tower se-creted by himself, would digest his conquest.

The other tanks then attracted the attention of the sailor.

Slipping over the stones, introducing themselves into their caverns, drowsing, half buried in the sand,—all the varied and tumultuous species of crustaceans were moving their cutting and tentacular grinders and making their Japanese armor gleam: some of their frames were red—almost black—as though guarding the dry blood of a remote combat; others were of a scarlet freshness as though reflecting the first fires of the flaming dawn.

The largest of the lobsters (the *homard,* the sover-eign of the tables of the rich) was resting upon the scissors of its front claws, as powerful as an arm, or a double battle-axe. The spiny lobster was leaping with agility over the peaks, by means of the hooks on its claws, its weapons of war and nutrition. Its nearest relative, the cricket of the sea, a dull and heavy animal, was sulking in the corners covered with mire and with sea weed, in an immovability that made it easily confounded with the stones. Around these giants, like a democracy accustomed to endure from time to time the attack of the strong, crayfish and shrimps were swimming in shoals. Their movements were free and graceful, and their sensitiveness so acute that the slightest agitation made them start, taking tremendous springs.

Ulysses kept thinking of the slavery that Nature had imposed upon these animals, giving them their beautiful, defensive envelopment.

They were born armored and their development obliged them repeatedly to change their form of arms. They sloughed their skins like reptiles, but on account of their cylindrical shape were able to perform this operation with the facility of a leg that abandons its stocking. When it begins to crack, the crustaceans have to withdraw from out their cuirass the multiple mechanism of their members and appendages,—claws, antennæ and the great pincers,—a slow and dangerous operation in which many perish, lacerated by their own efforts. Then, naked and disarmed, they have to wait until a new skin forms that in time is also converted into a coat of mail,—all this in the midst of a hostile environment, surrounded with greedy beasts, large and small, attracted by their rich flesh,—and with no other defense than that of keeping themselves in hiding.

Among the swarm of small crustaceans moving around on the sandy bottom, hunting, eating, or fighting with a ferocious entanglement of claws, the onlookers always search for a bizarre and extravagant little creature, the *paguro,* nicknamed "Bernard, the Hermit." It is a snail

that advances upright as a tower, upon crab claws, yet
having as a crown the long hair of a sea-anemone.

This comical apparition is composed of three distinct
animals one upon the other—or, rather, of two living
beings carrying a bier between them. The *paguro* crab
is born with the lower part of his case unprotected,—a
most excellent tid-bit, tender and savory for hungry
fishes. The necessity for defending himself makes him
seek a snail shell in order to protect the weak part of
his organism. If he encounters an empty dwelling of
this class, he appropriates it. If not, he eats the inhabitant, introducing his posterior armed with two hooked
claws into its mother-of-pearl refuge.

But these defensive precautions are not sufficient for
the weak *paguro*. In order to live he needs rather to put
himself on the offensive, to inspire respect in devouring
monsters, especially in the octopi that are seeking as
prey his trunk and hairy claws, exposed to locomotion
outside his tower.

In course of time a sea-anemone comes along and
attaches itself to the calcareous peak, the number often
amounting to five or six, although there is no bodily relation between the *paguro* and the organisms on top. They
are simply partners with a reciprocal interest. The animal-plants sting like nettles; all the monsters without a
shell flee from the poison of their tingling organs, and
the fragments of their hair burns like pins of fire. In
this manner the humble *paguro*, carrying upon his back
his tower crowned with formidable batteries, inspires
terror in the gigantic beasts of the deep. The anemones
on their part are grateful to him for being thus able to
pass incessantly from one side to the other, coming in
contact with every class of animals. In this way, they
can eat with greater facility than their sisters fixed on
the rocks; for they do not have to wait, as the others

must, until food drifts casually to their tentacles. Besides this, there is always floating on top some of the remains of the booty that the crafty crab in his wandering impunity has gathered below.

Ferragut, on passing from one tank to the other, mentally established the gradation of the fauna from the primitive protoplast to the perfect organism.

The sponges of the Mediterranean swam as soon as they were born, when they were like pin-heads, with vibratory movements. Then they remained immovable, the water filtering through the cracks and crannies of their texture, protecting their delicate flesh with a bristling of spikes,—sharp limestone needles with which they pierced the passing fishes and rendered them immovable, availing themselves of the nourishment of their putrefying remains.

The nettles of the sea spread out their stinging threads by the thousands, discharging a venom that stupefies the victim and makes him fall into their corolla. With unlimited voracity, and fastened to the rocks, they overpower fish much larger than they, and at the first hint of danger shrink together in such a way that it is very difficult to see them. The sea-plumes lie flabby and dark as dead animals, until absorbing water, they suddenly rear themselves up, transparent and full of leaves. Thus they go from one side to the other, with the lightness of a feather, or, burrowing in the sand, send forth a phosphoric glow. The belles of the sea, the elegant Medusæ, open out the floating circle of their fragile beauty. They are transparent fungi, open umbrellas of glass that advance by means of their contractions. From the inner center of their dome hangs a tube equally transparent and gelatinous,—the mouth of the animal. Long filaments depend from the edges of their circular forms,

sensitive tentacles that at the same time maintain their
floating equilibrium.

These fragile beings, that appear to belong to an
enchanted fauna, white as rock crystal with soft borders of rose color or violet, sting like nettles and defend
themselves by their fiery touch. Some subtle and colorless parasols were living here in the tank under the protection of a second enclosure of crystal, and their mucous
mistiness scarcely showed itself within this bell-shaped
glass except as a pale line of blue vapor.

Below these transparent and ethereal forms that burn
whatever they touch, venturing to capture prey much
larger than themselves, were grouped as in gardens the
so-called "flower of blood," the red coral, and especially
the star-fish, forming with their corolla an orange-col-
ored ring.

The captain had seen these stony vegetations, like submerged groves, in the depths of the Dead Sea and also in
the southern seas. He had sailed over them under the
illusion that through the bluish depths of the ocean were
circulating broad rivers of blood.

The *oseznos* (bear-cubs) and the star-fish were slowly
waving the forms that had given rise to their names,
secreting poisons in order to paralyze their victims, contracting themselves until they formed a ball of lances
that grasped their prey in a deadly embrace or cut it
with the bony knives of their radiating body. The iris
of the sea balanced themselves on end, moving their
members as though they were petals.

Upon the fine sandy depths or attached to the rocks,
the mollusks lived in the protection of their shells.

The necessity of giving themselves up to sleep with
relative security, without fear of the general rapacity
which is the oceanic law, is a matter of concern to all
of these marine beings, making them constructive and

inventive. The crustaceans live within their shells or take advantage of ready-made refuges of limestone, expelling their former owners; the animal-plants exhale toxins; the *planctonic* beings, transparent and gelatinous, burn like a crystal exposed to fire; some organisms apparently weak and flabby, have in their tails the force of a carpenter's bit, perforating the rock sufficiently to create a cavern of refuge in its hard interior. . . . And the timid mollusks, trembling and succulent pulp, have fabricated for their protection the strong shields of their valves,—two concave walls that on opening form their door, and on closing, their house.

A bit of flesh protrudes outside these shells, like a white tongue. In some it takes the form of a sole, and serves as a foot, the mollusk marching with his dwelling upon the back of this unique support. In others it is a swimmer, and the shell, opening and shutting its valves like a propelling mouth, ascends in a straight line to the surface, falling afterwards with the two shields closed.

These herbivorous fresh-water animals live by drinking in the light,—feeling the necessity of the surface waters or the shallow depths with their limpid glades— and this light, spreading over the white interior of their dwelling, decorates it with all the fleeting colors of the iris, giving to the limestone the mysterious shimmer of mother-of-pearl.

Ulysses admired the odd forms of their winding passageways. They were like the palaces of the Orient, dark and forbidding on the outside, glistening within like a lake of pearl. Some received their terrestrial names because of the special form of their shell—the rabbit, the helmet, triton's horn, the cask, the Mediterranean parasol.

They were grazing with bucolic tranquillity on the maritime pasture lands, contemplated from afar by the

mussels, the oysters, and other bi-valves, attached to the
rocks by a hard and horny hank of silk that enwrapped
their enclosures. Some of these shells, called hams,—
clams of great size, with valves in the form of a club,—
had fixed themselves upright in the mire, giving the appearance of a submerged Celtic camp, with a succession
of obelisks swallowed up by the depths of the sea.

The one called the date-shell can, assisted by its
liquid acid, pierce the hardest stone with its cylindrical
gimlet. The columns of Hellenic temples, submerged
in the Gulf of Naples and brought to light by an earth-
quake, are bored from one end to the other by this
diminutive perforator.

Cries of surprise and nervous laughter suddenly
reached Ferragut. They came from that part of the
Aquarium where the fish tanks were. In the corridor
was a little trough of water and at the bottom a kind of
rag, flabby and gray, with black rings on the back. This
animal always attracted the immediate curiosity of the
visitors. Everybody would ask for it.

Groups of countrymen, city families preceded by their
offspring, pairs of soldiers, all might be seen consulting
before it and experimenting, advancing their hands over
the trough with a certain hesitation. Finally they would
touch the living rag at the bottom,—the gelatinous flesh
of the fish-torpedo,—receiving a series of electric shocks
which quickly made them loosen their prey, laughing and
raising the other hand to their jerking arms.

Ulysses on reaching the fish tanks had the sensation
of a traveler who, after having lived among inferior
humanity, encounters beings that are almost of his own
race.

There was the oceanic aristocracy, the fish free as
the sea, swift, undulating and slippery, like the waves.
They all had accompanied him for many years, appear-

ing in the transparencies opened by the prow of his vessel.

They were vigorous and therefore had no neck,—the most fragile and delicate portion of terrestrial organism,—making them more like the bull, the elephant and all the battering animals. They needed to be light, and in order to be so had dispensed with the rigid and hard shell of the crustacean that prevents motion, preferring the coat of mail covered with scales, which expands and contracts, yields to the blow but is not injured. They wished to be free, and their body, like that of the ancient wrestlers, was covered with a slippery oil, the oceanic mucus that becomes volatilized at the slightest pressure.

The freest animals on earth cannot be compared with them. The birds need to perch and to rest during their sleep, but the fish continue floating around and moving from place to place while asleep. The entire world belongs to them. Wherever there is a mass of water,—ocean, river or lake, in whatever altitude or latitude, a mountain peak lost in the clouds, a valley boiling like a whirlpool, a sparkling and tropical sea with a forest of colors in its bosoms, or a polar sea encrusted with ice and people, with sea-lions and white bears,—there the fish always appears.

The public of the Aquarium, seeing the flat heads of the swimming animals near the glass, would scream and wave their arms as though they could be seen by the fishy eyes of stupid fixity. Then they would experience a certain dismay upon perceiving that the fish continued their course with indifference.

Ferragut smiled before this deception. The crystal that separated the water from the atmosphere had the density of millions of leagues,—an insuperable obstacle

interposed between two worlds that do not know each
other.

The sailor recalled the imperfect vision of the ocean
inhabitants. In spite of their bulging and movable eyes
that enable them to see before and behind them, their
visual power extends but a short distance. The splendors with which Nature clothes the butterfly cannot be
appreciated by them. Absolutely color-blind, they can
appreciate only the difference between light and darkness.

Complete silence accompanies their incomplete vision.
All the aquatic animals are deaf, or rather they completely lack the organs of hearing, because they are
unnecessary to them. Atmospheric agitations, thunder-
bolts and hurricanes do not penetrate the water. Only
the cracking shell of certain crabs and the dolorous
moaning near the surface of certain fishes, called snor-
ers, alter this silence.

Since the ocean lacks acoustic waves, their inhabitants
have never needed to form the organs that transform
them into sound. They feel impetuously the primal necessities of animal life,—hunger and love. They suffer
madly the cruelty of sickness and pain; among themselves they fight to the death for a meal or a mate.
But all in absolute silence, without the howl of triumph
or agony with which terrestrial animals accompany the
same manifestations of their existence.

Their principal sense is that of smell, as is that of sight
in the bird. In the twilight world of the ocean, streaked
with phosphorescent and deceptive splendors, the big
fish trust only to their sense of smell and at times to
that of touch.

Sometimes buried in the mud, they will ascend hundreds of yards, attracted by the odor of the fish that
are swimming on the surface. This prodigious faculty

renders useless, in part, the colors in which the timid
species clothe themselves in order to confound themselves
with lights or shadows.   The greatest flesh-eaters see
badly, but they scrape the bottom with a divining touch
and scent their prey at astonishing distances.

Only the Mediterranean fishes, especially those of
the Gulf of Naples, were living in the tanks of this
Aquarium.   Some were lacking,—the dolphin, of nervous
movement, and the tunny, so impetuous in its career.
The captain smiled upon thinking of the mischievous
pranks of these ungovernable guests whose presence had
been declined.

The voracious shark (*cabeza de olla*), the persecuting
wolf of the Mediterranean herds, was not here either.
In his place were swimming other animals of the same
species, whitish and long, with great fins, with eyes always open for lack of movable eyelids, and a mouth split
like a half-moon, under the head at the beginning of the
stomach.

Ferragut sought on the bottom of the tanks the fishes
of the deep,—flattened animals that pass the greater part
of their time sunk in the sand under a coverlet of algæ.
The dark *uranoscopo,* with its eyes almost united on
the peak of its enormous head and its body in the form
of a club, leaves visible only a long thread coming from
its lower jaw, waving it in all directions in order to attract its prey.   Believing it a worm, the victims usually
chase the moving bait until pounced upon by the teeth
of the hunter who then springs from his bed, floats
around for a few moments, and falls heavily to the bottom, opening a new pit with his pectoral, shovel-shaped
swimming bladders.

The toad fish, the most hideous animal of the Mediterranean, goes hunting in the same way.   Three-fourths
of his flattened body is made up of head, mostly mouth,

armed with hooks and curved knives. Guided by his yellowish eyes fixed on top, he waves his pointed little beard, cut like leaves, and a pair of dorsal appendages like feathers. This false bait attracts the unwary ones and soon the cavernous mandibles close upon them.

The plane fishes swim quickly over these monsters of the mire, that are always horizontally flat resting upon their bellies, whilst the flatness of the soles and others of the same species is vertical. The two sides of the bodies of the soles, compressed laterally, have different colorings. In this way, when lying down, they are able to merge themselves at the same time with the light of the surface and the shadow of the bottom, thus getting rid of their persecutors.

All the infinite varieties of the Mediterranean fauna were moving in the other tanks.

There passed by the greenish plates of glass the gilt-heads, the cackerels, and the sea roaches, clad in vivid silver with bands of gold on their sides. There also flashed past the purple of the salmonoids, the brilliant majesty of the gold fish, the bluish belly of the sea bream, the striped back of the sheep's head, the trumpet-mouthed marine sun-fish, the immovable sneer of the so-called "joker," the dorsal pinnacle of the peacock-fish which appears made of feathers, the restless and deeply bifurcated tail of the horse mackerel, the fluttering of the mullet with its triple wings, the grotesque rotundity of the boar-fish and the pig-fish, the dark smoothness of the sting-ray, floating like a fringe, the long snout of the woodcock-fish, the slenderness of the haddock, agile and swift as a torpedo, the red gurnard all thorns, the angel of the sea with its fleshy wings, the gudgeon, bristling with swimming angularities, the notary, red and white, with black bands similar to the flourishes on signatures, the modest *esmarrido,* the little

sand fish, the superb turbot almost round with fan tail
and a swimming fringe spotted with circles, and the
gloomy conger-eel whose skin is as bluish black as that
of the ravens.

Hidden between two rocks like the hunting crustaceans was the *rascaza*,—the scorpion of the Valencian
sea that Ferragut had known in his childhood, the animal beloved by his uncle, the *Triton,* because of its substantial flesh which thickened the seamen's soup, the
precious component sought by Uncle Caragol for the
broth of his succulent rice dishes. The enormous head
had a pair of eyes entirely red. Its great swimming
bladders stung venomously. The heavy body with its
dark bands and stripes was covered with singular appendages in the form of leaves and could easily take
the color of the deep where, in the semi-obscurity, it
looked like a stone covered with plants. With this
mimicry it was accustomed to escape its enemies and
could better detect its prey.

A gloomy creature, in Ferragut's opinion like a beadle
of the Holy Office, was parading through the upper part
of the tanks, passing from glass to glass, reflected like a
double animal when it approached the surface. It was
the ray-fish with a flat head, ferocious eyes, and thong-
like tail, moving the black mantle of its fleshy wings
with a deliberation that rippled the edges.

From the sandy bottom was struggling forth a convex
shield that, when floating, showed its lower face smooth
and yellow. The four wrinkled paws and the serpent-
like head of the turtle were emerging from its cuirass
of tortoise-shell. The little sea horses, slender and graceful as chess-pieces, were rising and descending in the
bluish environment, wiggling their tails and twisting
themselves in the form of interrogation points.

When the captain approached the end of the four

galleries of the Aquarium without having seen more
than the maritime animals behind the glistening glasses
and a few uninteresting people in the greenish semi-light,
he felt all the discouragement of a day lost.

"She won't come now! . . ."

In passing from this damp, cellar-like atmosphere to
the sunlit garden, the report of the midday gun struck
him like an atmospheric blow. Lunch hour! . . . And
surely Freya was not going to lunch in the hotel!

During the afternoon his footsteps strayed instinctively
toward the hill streets of the district of Chiaja. All
old buildings of manorial aspect invariably attracted his
attention. These were great, reddish houses of the
time of the Spanish viceroys, or palaces of the reign of
Charles III. Their broad staircases were adorned with
polychrome busts brought from the first excavations in
Herculaneum and Pompeii.

Ulysses had faint hopes of running across the widow
while passing in front of one of these mansions, now
rented in floors and displaying little metal door-plates
indicative of office and warehouse. In one of these undoubtedly must be living the family that was so friendly
to Freya.

Then, noticing the whiteness of the showy constructions rising up around the old districts, he became dubious. The doctor would dwell only in a modern and
hygienic edifice. But not daring to ask questions, he
passed on, fearing to be seen from a window.

Finally he gave it up. Chiaja had many streets and
he was wandering aimlessly, since the concierge of the
hotel had not been able to give him any precise directions. The *signora* Talberg was evidently bent on out-
witting all his finesse, trying to keep from him the address of her friends.

The following morning the captain took up his usual

watch in the promenade near the white Virgil. It was all in vain. After ten o'clock he again wandered into the Aquarium, animated by a vague hope.

"Perhaps she may come to-day. . . ."

With the superstition of the enamored and all those who wait, he kept hunting certain places preferred by the widow, believing that in this way he would attract her from her distant preoccupation, obliging her to come to him.

The tanks of the molluscas had always been especially interesting to her. He recalled that Freya had several times spoken to him of this section.

Among its aquatic cases she always preferred the one marked number fifteen, the exclusive dominion of the polypi (cuttlefish). A vague presentiment warned him that something very important in his life was going to be unrolled in that particular spot. Whenever Freya visited the Aquarium, it was to see these repulsive and gluttonous animals eat. There was nothing to do but to await her before this cavern of horrors.

And while she was making her way thither, the captain had to amuse himself like any landlubber, contemplating the ferocious chase and laborious digestion of these monsters.

He had seen them much larger in the deep-sea fishing grounds; but by curtailing his imaginative powers he could pretend that the blue sheet of the tank was the entire mass of the ocean—the rough bits of stone on the bottom its submarine mountains, and by contracting his own personality, he could reduce himself to the same scale as the little victims that were falling under the devouring tentacles. In this manner he could fancy of gigantic dimensions these cuttlefish of the Aquarium, just as the monstrous oceanic octopi must be that, thousands of yards down, were illuminating the gloom of the waters with the greenish star of their phosphorescent nuclei.

From prehistoric times the men of the sea had known this great, ropy beast of the abysses. The geographers of antiquity used to speak of it, giving the measurement of its terrible arms.

Pliny used to recount the destruction accomplished by a gigantic octopus in the vivarium of the Mediterranean. When some sailors succeeded in killing it they carried it to the epicure, Lucullus,—the head as big as a barrel, and some of its tentacles so huge that one person could hardly reach around them. The chroniclers of the Middle Ages had also spoken of the gigantic cuttlefish that on more than one occasion had, with its serpentine arms, snatched men from the decks of the ships.

The Scandinavian navigators, who had never encountered it in their fjords, nicknamed it the *kraken*, exaggerating its proportions and even converting it into a fabulous being. If it came to the surface, they confounded it with an island; if it remained between the two waters, the captains, on making their soundings, became confused in their calculations, finding the depth less than that marked on their charts. In such cases they had to escape before the *kraken* should awake and sink the vessel as though it were a fragile skiff among its whirlpools of foam.

During many long years Science had laughed at the gigantic polypus and at the sea serpent, another prehistoric animal many times encountered, supposing them to be merely the inventions of an imaginative sailor, stories of the forecastle made up to pass the night-watch. Wise men can only believe what they can study directly and then catalogue in their museums. . . .

And Ferragut laughed in his turn at poor Science,

ignorant and defenseless before the mysterious immensity of the ocean, and having scarcely achieved the measurement of its great depth. The apparatus of the diver could go down but a few meters; their only instrument of exploration was the metal diving-bell, less important than a spider-web thread that might try to explore the earth by floating across its atmosphere.

The great cuttlefish living in the tremendous depths do not deign to come to the surface in order to become acquainted with mankind. Sickness and oceanic war are the only agents that from time to time announce their existence in a casual way, as they float over the waves with members relaxed, snatched at by the iron jaws of the flesh-eating fish. The great danger for them is that a chance current might place this plunder of the immense marine desert before the prow of a slow-going sailboat.

A corvette of the French navy once encountered near the Canary Isles a complete specimen of one of these monsters floating upon the sea, sick or wounded. The officials sketched its form and noted its phosphorescence and changes of color, but after a two-hour struggle with its indomitable force and its slippery mucosity constantly escaping the pressure of blows and harpoons, they had to let it slip back into the ocean.

It was the Prince of Monaco, supreme pontiff of oceanographic science, who established forever the existence of the fabulous *kraken*. In one of his intelligent excursions across oceanic solitudes he fished up an arm of a cuttlefish eight yards long. Furthermore the stomachs of sharks, upon being opened, had revealed to him the gigantic fragments of the adversary.

Short and terrible battles used to agitate the black and phosphorescent water, thousands of fathoms from the surface, with whirlwinds of death.

The shark would descend, attracted by the appetizing prospect of a boneless animal,—all flesh and weighing several tons. He would make his hostile invasion in all haste so as not to be obliged to endure for a long time the formidable pressure of the abyss. The struggle between the two ferocious warriors disputing oceanic dominion was usually brief and deadly,—the mandible battling with the sucker; the solid and cutting equipment of teeth with the phosphorescent mucosity incessantly slipping by and opposing the blow of the demolishing head like a battering ram, with the lashing blow of tentacles thicker and heavier than an elephant's trunk. Sometimes the shark would remain down forever, enmeshed in a skein of soft snakes absorbing it with gluttonous deliberation; at other times it would come to the surface with its skin bristling with black tumors,—open mouths and slashes big as plates,—but with its stomach full of gelatinous meat.

These cuttlefish in the Aquarium were nothing more than the seaside inhabitants of the Mediterranean coast, —poor relations of the gigantic octopus that lighten the black gloom of the oceanic night with their bluish gleam of burned-out planets. But in spite of their relative smallness, they are animated by the same destructive iniquity as the others. They are rabid stomachs that cleanse the waters of all animal life, digesting it in a vacuum of death. Even the bacteria and infusoria appear to flee from the liquid that envelops these ferocious solitudes.

Ferragut passed many mornings contemplating their treacherous immovability, followed by deadly unfoldings the moment that their prey came down into the tank. He began to hate these monsters for no other reason than because they were so interesting to Freya. Their stupid cruelty appeared to him but a reflex of that incomprehensible woman's character that was repulsing him by fleeing from him and yet, at the same time, by her smiles and her signals, was sending out a wireless in order to keep him prisoner.

Masculine wrath convulsed the sailor after each futile daily trip in pursuit of her invisible personality.

"She's just doing it to lead me on! . . . ." he exclaimed. "It's got to come to an end! I won't stand any more bull-baiting. . . . I'll just show her that I'm able to live without her!"

He swore not to seek her any more. It was an agreeable diversion for the weeks that he had to spend in Naples, but why keep it up when she was fatiguing him in such an insufferable way? . . .

"All is ended," he said again, clenching his hands.

And the following day he was waiting outside of the hotel just as on other days. Then he would go for his customary stroll, afterwards entering the Aquarium in the same, old hope of seeing her before the tanks of the cuttlefish.

He finally met her there one morning, about midday. He had been over to his boat and on returning entered, through force of habit, sure that at this hour he would find nobody but the employees feeding the fishes.

His dazzled eyes were affected with almost instantaneous blindness before becoming accustomed to the shadows of the greenish galleries. . . . And when the first images began to be vaguely outlined on his retina, he stepped hastily backward, so great was his surprise.

He couldn't believe it and raised his hand to his eyes as though wishing to clarify his vision with an energetic rubbing. Was that really Freya? . . . Yes, it was she, dressed in white, leaning on the bar of iron that separated the tanks from the public, looking fixedly at the glass which covered the rocky cavern like a transparent

door. She had just opened her hand-bag, giving some
coins to the guardian who was disappearing at the end
of the gallery.

"Oh, is that you?" she said, on seeing Ferragut,
without any surprise, as if she had left him but a short
time before.

Then she explained her presence at this late hour.
She had not visited the Aquarium for a long time. The
tank of cuttlefish was to her like a cage of tropical
birds, full of colors and cries that enlivened the solitude
of a melancholy matron.

She always adored the monsters living on the other
side of these crystals, and before going to lunch she had
felt an irresistible desire to see them. She feared that
the guard had not been taking good care of them during
her absence.

"Just see how beautiful they are! . . ."
And she pointed to a tank that appeared empty.
Neither in its quiet still waters nor on the floor of the
oily sand could be seen the slightest animal motion.
Ferragut followed the direction of her eyes and after
long contemplation discovered there three occupants.
With the amazing mimicry of their species, they had
changed themselves to appear like minerals. Only a
pair of expert eyes would have been able to discover
them, heaped together, each one huddled in a crack of
the rocks, voluntarily raising his smooth skin into stone-
like protuberances and ridges. Their faculty of changing color permitted them to take on that of their hard
base and, disguised in this way like three rocky excrescences, they were treacherously awaiting the passing of
their victim, just as though they were in the open sea.

"Soon we shall see them in all their majesty," continued Freya as though she were speaking of something
belonging to her. "The guardian is going to feed them.

. . . Poor things! Nobody pays any attention to them; everybody detests them. To me they owe whatever they get between meals."

As if scenting the proximity of food, one of the three stones suddenly shuddered with a polychromatic chill. Its elastic covering began swelling. There passed over its surface stripes of color, reddish clouds changing from crimson to green, circular spots that became inflated in the swelling, forming tremulous excrescences. Between two cracks there appeared a yellowish eye of ferocious and stupid fixity; a darkened and malignant globe like that of serpents, was now looking toward the crystal as though seeing far beyond that diamond wall.

"They know me!" exclaimed Freya joyously. "I'm sure that they know me! . . ."

And she enumerated the clever traits of these monsters to whom she attributed great intelligence. They were the ones that, like astute builders, had dappled the stones piled up on the bottom, forming bulwarks in whose shelter they had disguised themselves in order to pounce upon their victims. In the sea, when wishing to surprise a meaty, toothsome oyster, they waited in hiding until the two valves should open to feed upon the water and the light, and had often introduced a pebble between the shells and then inserted their tentacles in the crevice.

Their love of liberty was another thing which aroused Freya's enthusiasm. If they should have to endure more than a year of enclosure in the Aquarium, they would become sick with sadness and would gnaw their claws until they killed themselves.

"Ah, the charming and vigorous bandits!" she continued in hysterical enthusiasm. "I adore them. I should like to have them in my home, as they have gold-fishes in a globe, to feed them every hour, to see how they would devour. . . ."

Ferragut felt a recurrence of the same uneasiness that he had experienced one morning in the temple of Virgil.

"She's crazy!" he said to himself.

But in spite of her craziness, he greatly enjoyed the faint perfume that exhaled through the opening at her throat.

He no longer saw the silent world that, sparkling with color, was swimming or paddling behind the crystal. She was now the only creature who existed for him. And he listened to her voice as though it were distant music as it continued explaining briefly all the particulars about those stones that were really animals, about those globes that, on distending themselves, showed their organs and again hid themselves under a gelatinous succession of waves.

They were a sac, a pocket, an elastic mask, in whose interior existed only water or air. Between their armpits was their mouth, armed with long jaw bones, like a parrot's beak. When breathing, a crack of their skin would open and close alternately. From one of their sides came forth a tube in the form of a tunnel that swallowed equally the respirable water and drew it through both entrances into its branching cavity. Their multiple arms, fitted out with cupping glasses, functioned like high-pressure apparatus for grasping and holding prey, for paddling and for running.

The glassy eye of one of the monsters appearing and disappearing among its soft folds, stirred Freya's memories. She began speaking in a low tone as if to herself, without paying any attention to Ferragut who was perplexed at the incoherence of her words. The appear-

ance of this octopus brought to her mind "the eye of
the morning."

The sailor asked: "What is the 'eye of the morning'?"
... And he again told himself that Freya was crazy
when he learned that this was the name of a tame serpent, a reptile of checkered sides that she wore as necklace or bracelet over there in her home in the island
of Java,—an island where groves exhaled an irresistible
perfume, covered in the sunlight with trembling and
monstrous flowers like animals, peopled at night with
phosphorescent stars that leaped from tree to tree.

"I used to dance naked, with a transparent veil tied
around my hips and another floating from my head. . . .
I would dance for hours and hours, just like a Brahman
priestess before the image of the terrible Siva, and the
'eye of the morning' would follow my dances with elegant undulations. . . . I believe in the divine Siva. Don't
you know who Siva is? . . ."

Ferragut uttered an impatient aside to the gloomy
god. What he wanted to know was the reason that had
taken her to Java, the paradisiacal and mysterious island.

"My husband was a Dutch commandant," she said.
"We were married in Amsterdam and I followed him
to Asia."

Ulysses protested at this piece of news. Had not her
husband been a great student? . . . Had he not taken
her to the Andes in search of prehistoric beasts? . . .

Freya hesitated a moment in order to be sure, but her
doubts were short.

"So he was," she said as a matter of course. "That
professor was my second husband. I have been married
twice."

The captain had not time to express his surprise. Over
the top of the tank, on the crystalline surface silvered
by the sun, passed a human shadow. It was the silhou-

ette of the keeper. Down below, the three shapeless
bags began to move. Freya was trembling with emotion
like an enthusiastic and impatient spectator.

Something fell into the water, descending little by little,
a bit of dead sardine that was scattering filaments of
meat and yellow scales. An odd community interest
appeared to exist among these monsters: only the one
nearest the prey bestirred himself to eat. Perhaps they
voluntarily took turns; perhaps their glance only reached
a little beyond their tentacles.

The one nearest to the glass suddenly unfolded itself with the violence of a spring escaping from an explosive projectile. He gave a bound, remaining fastened
to the ground by one of his radiants, and raised the others
like a bundle of reptiles. Suddenly he converted himself
into a monstrous star, filling almost the entire glassy
tank, swollen with rage, and coloring his outer covering
with green, blue, and red.

His tentacles clutched the miserable prey, doubling it
inward in order to bear it to his mouth. The beast
then contracted, and flattened himself out so as to rest
on the ground. His armed feet disappeared and there
only remained visible a trembling bag through which was
passing like a succession of waves, from one extreme to
the other, the digestive swollen mass which became a
bubbling, mucous pulpiness in a dye-pot that colored and
discolored itself with contortions of assimilative fury;
from time to time the agglomeration showed its stupid
and ferocious eyes.

New victims continued falling down through the waters and other monsters leaped in their turn, spreading
out their stars, then shrinking together in order to grind
their prey in their entrails with the assimilation of a
tiger.

Freya gazed upon this horrifying digestive process

with thrills of rapture. Ulysses felt her resting instinctively upon him with a contact growing more intimate
every moment. From shoulder to ankle the captain could
see the sweet reliefs of her soft flesh whose warmth
made itself perceptible through her clothing and filled
him with nervous tremors.

Frequently she turned her eyes away from the cruel
spectacle, glancing at him quickly with an odd expression. Her pupils appeared enlarged, and the whites
of her eyes had a wateriness of morbid reflection. Ferragut felt that thus the insane must look in their great
crises.

She was speaking between her teeth, with emotional
pauses, admiring the ferocity of the cuttlefish, griev-
ing that she did not possess their vigor and their cruelty.
"If I could only be like them! . . . To be able to go
through the streets . . . through the world, stretching
out my talons! . . . To devour! . . . to devour! They
would struggle uselessly to free themselves from the
winding of my tentacles. . . . To absorb them! . . . To
eat them! . . . To cause them to disappear! . . ."

Ulysses beheld her as on that first day near the temple
of the poet, possessed with a fierce wrath against men,
longing extravagantly for their extermination

Their digestion finished, the polypi had begun to swim
around, and were now horizontal skeins, fluting the tank
with elegance. They appeared like torpedo boats with a
conical prow, dragging along the heavy, thick and long
hair of their tentacles. Their excited appetite made them
glide through the water in all directions, seeking new
victims.

Freya protested. The guard had only brought them
dead bodies. What she wanted was the struggle, the
sacrifice, the death. The bits of sardine were a meal

without substance for these bandits that had zest only for food seasoned with assassination.

As though the pulps had understood her complaints, they had fallen on the sandy bottom, flaccid, inert, breathing through their funnels.

A little crab began to descend at the end of a thread desperately moving its claws.

Freya pressed still closer to Ulysses, excited at the thought of the approaching spectacle. One of the bags, transformed into a star, suddenly leaped forward. Its arms writhed like serpents seeking the recent arrival. In vain the guard pulled the thread up, wishing to prolong the chase. The tentacles clamped their irresistible openings upon the body of the victim, pulling upon the line with such force that it broke, the octopus falling on the bottom with his prey.

Freya clapped her hands in applause.

"Bravo! . . ." She was exceedingly pale, though a feverish heat was coursing through her body.

She leaned toward the crystal in order to see better the devouring activity of that pyramidal stomach which had on its sharp point a diminutive parrot head with two ferocious eyes and around its base the twisted skeins of its arms full of projecting disks. With these it pressed the crab against its mouth, injecting under its shell the venomous output of its salivary glands, paralyzing thus every movement of existence. Then it swallowed its prey slowly with the deglutition of a boa constrictor.

"How beautiful it is!" she said.

The other beasts also seized their live victims, paralyzed and devoured them, moving their flabby bodies in order to permit the passage of their swelling nutritive waves and clouds of various colors.

Then the guard tossed in a crab, but one without any string whatever. Freya screamed with enthusiasm.

This was the kind of hunt that takes place in the ferocious mystery of the sea, a race with death, a destruction preceded with emotional agony and hazards. The poor crustacean, divining its danger, was swimming towards the rocks hoping to take refuge in the nearest crevice. A polypus came up behind it, whilst the others continued their digestion.

"It's escaping! . . . It's escaping!" cried Freya, palpitating with interest.

The crab scrambled through the stones, sheltering itself in their windings. The polypus was no longer swimming; it was running like a terrestrial animal, climbing over the rocks by its armed extremities, which were now serving as apparatus of locomotion. It was the struggle of a tiger with a mouse. When the crab had half of its body already hidden within the green lichens of a hole, one of the heavy serpents fell upon its back clutching it with the irresistible suction of his air-holes, and causing it to disappear within his skein of tentacles.

"Ah!" sighed Freya, throwing herself back as though she were going to faint on Ulysses' breast.

He shuddered, feeling that a serpentine band of tremulous pressure had encircled his body. The acts of that unbalanced creature were fraying his nerves.

He felt as though a monster of the same class as those in the tank but much larger—a gigantic octopus from the oceanic depths—must have slipped treacherously behind him and was clutching him in one of its tentacles. He could feel the pressure of its feelers around his waist, growing closer and more ferocious.

Freya was holding him captive with one of her arms. She had wound herself tightly around him and was clasping his waist with all her force, as though trying to break his vigorous body in two.

Then he saw the head of this woman approaching him

with an aggressive swiftness as if she were going to bite him. . . . Her enlarged eyes, tearful and misty, appeared to be far off, very far off. Perhaps she was not even looking at him. . . . Her trembling mouth, bluish with emotion, a round and protruding mouth like an absorbing duct, was seeking the sailor's mouth, taking possession of it and devouring it with her lips.

It was the kiss of a cupping-glass, long, dominating, painful. Ulysses realized that he had never before been kissed in this way. The water from that mouth surging across her row of teeth, discharged itself in his like swift poison. A shudder unfamiliar until then ran the entire length of his back, making him close his eyes.

He felt as if all his interior had turned to liquid. He had a presentiment that his life was going to date from this kiss, that with it was going to begin a new existence, that he never would be able to free himself from these deadly and caressing lips with their faint savor of cinnamon, of incense, of Asiatic forests haunted with sensuousness and intrigue.

And he let himself be dragged down by the caress of this wild beast, with thought lost and body inert and resigned, like a castaway who descends and descends the infinite strata of the abyss without ever reaching bottom.

CHAPTER VI

THE WILES OF CIRCE

AFTER that kiss, the lover believed that all his desires were about to be immediately realized. The most difficult part of the road was already passed. But with Freya one always had to expect something absurd and inconceivable.

The midday gun aroused them from a rapture that had lasted but a few seconds as long as years. The steps of the guard, growing nearer all the time, finally separated the two and unlocked their arms.

Freya was the first to calm herself. Only a slight haze flitted across her pupils now, like the vapor from a recently extinguished fire.

"Good-by. . . . They are waiting for me."

And she went out from the Aquarium followed by Ferragut, still stammering and tremulous. The questions and petitions with which he pursued her while crossing the promenade were of no avail.

"So far and no further," she said at one of the cross streets of Chiaja. "We shall see one another. . . . I formally promise you that. . . . Now leave me."

And she disappeared with the firm step of a handsome huntress, as serene of countenance as though not recalling the slightest recollection of her primitive, passional paroxysm.

This time she fulfilled her promise. Ferragut saw her every day.

They met in the mornings near the hotel, and some-

times she came down into the dining-room, exchanging
smiles and glances with the sailor, who fortunately
was sitting at a distant table.   Then they took strolls
and chatted together, Freya laughing good-naturedly at
the amorous vows of the captain. . . . And that was all.

With a woman's skilfulness in sounding a man's depth
and penetrating into his secrets,—keeping fast-locked
and unapproachable her own,—she gradually informed
herself of the incidents and adventures in the life of
Ulysses.   Vainly he spoke, in a natural reciprocity, of
the island of Java, of the mysterious dances before Siva,
of the journeys through the lakes of the Andes.   Freya
had to make an effort to recall them.   "Ah! . . . Yes!"
And after giving this distracted exclamation for every
answer, she would continue the process of delving eagerly
into the former life of her lover.   Ulysses sometimes began to wonder if that embrace in the Aquarium could
have occurred in his dreams.

One morning the captain managed to bring about the
realization of one of his ambitions.   He was jealous of
the unknown friends that were lunching with Freya.   In
vain she affirmed that the doctor was the only companion
of the hours that she passed outside of the hotel.   In
order to tranquillize himself, the sailor insisted that the
widow should accept his invitations.   They ought to
extend their strolls; they ought to visit the beautiful
outskirts of Naples, lunching in their gay little *trattorias*
or eating-houses.

They ascended together the funicular road of Monte
Vomero to the heights crowned by the castle of S. Elmo
and the monastery of S. Martino.   After admiring in
the museum of the abbey the artistic souvenirs of the
Bourbon domination and that of Murat, they entered into
a nearby *trattoria* with tables placed on an esplanade
from whose balconies they could take in the unforget-

able spectacle of the gulf, seeing Vesuvius in the distance and the chain of mountains smoking on the horizon like an immovable succession of dark rose-colored waves.

Naples was extended in horseshoe form on the bow-shaped border of the sea tossing up from its enormous white mass, as though they were bits of foam, the clusters of houses in the suburbs.

A swarthy oysterman, slender, with eyes like live coals, and enormous mustaches, had his stand at the door of the restaurant, offering cockles and shell fish of strong odor that had been half a week perhaps in ascending from the city to the heights of Vomero. Freya jested about the oysterman's typical good looks and the languishing glances that he was forever casting toward all the ladies that entered the establishment . . . a prime discovery for a tourist anxious for adventures in local color.

In the background a small orchestra was accompanying a tenor voice or was playing alone, enlarging upon the melodies and amplifying the measures with Neapolitan exaggeration.

Freya felt a childish hilarity upon seating herself at the table, seeing over the cloth the luminous summit. Bisected in the foreground by a crystal vase full of flowers, the distant panorama of the city, the gulf, and its capes spread itself before her eager eyes. The air on this peak enchanted her after two weeks passed without stirring outside of Naples. The harps and violins gave the situation a pathetic thrill and served as a background for conversation, just as the vague murmurs of a hidden orchestra give the effect in the theater of psalmody or of melancholy verses moving the listener to tears.

They ate with the nervousness which joy supplies. At some tables further on a young man and woman were forgetting the courses in order to clasp hands underneath the cloth and place knee against knee with frenzied pressure. The two were smiling, looking at the landscape and then at each other. Perhaps they were foreigners recently married, perhaps fugitive lovers, realizing in this picturesque spot the billing and cooing so many times anticipated in their distant courtship.

Two English doctors from a hospital ship, white haired and uniformed, were disregarding their repast in order to paint directly in their albums, with a childish painstaking crudeness, the same panorama that was portrayed on the postal cards offered for sale at the door of the restaurant.

A fat-bellied bottle with a petticoat of straw and a long neck attracted Freya's hands to the table. She ridiculed the sobriety of Ferragut, who was diluting with water the reddish blackness of the Italian wine.

"Thus your ancestors, the Argonauts, must have drunk," she said gayly. "Thus your grandfather, Ulysses, undoubtedly drank."

And herself filling the captain's glass with an exaggeratedly careful division of the parts of water and wine, she added gayly:

"We are going to make a libation to the gods."

These libations were very frequent. Freya's peals of laughter made the Englishmen, interrupted in their conscientious work, turn their glances toward her. The sailor felt himself overcome by a warm feeling of well-being, by a sensation of repose and confidence, as though this woman were unquestionably his already.

Seeing that the two lovers, terminating their luncheon hastily, were arising with blushing precipitation as though overpowered by some sudden desire, his glance became tender and fraternal. . . . Adieu, adieu, companions!

The voice of the widow recalled him to reality.

"Ulysses, make love to me. . . . You haven't yet told me this whole day long that you love me."

In spite of the smiling and mocking tone of this order, he obeyed her, repeating once more his promises and his desires. Wine was giving to his words a thrill of emotion; the musical moaning of the orchestra was exciting his sensibilities and he was so touched with his own eloquence that his eyes slightly filled with tears.

The high voice of the tenor, as though it were an echo of Ferragut's thought, was singing a romance of the fiesta of Piedigrotta, a lamentation of melancholy love, a canticle of death, the final mother of hopeless lovers.

"All a lie!" said Freya, laughing. "These Mediterraneans. . . . What comedians they are for love! . . ."

Ulysses was uncertain as to whether she was referring to him or to the singer. She continued talking, placid and disdainful at the same time, because of their surroundings.

"Love, . . . love! In these countries they can't talk of anything else. It is almost an industry, somewhat scrupulously prepared for the credulous and simple people from the North. They all harp on love: this howling singer, you . . . even the oysterman. . . ."

Then she added maliciously:

"I ought to warn you that you have a rival. Be very careful, Ferragut!"

She turned her head in order to look at the oysterman. He was occupied in the contemplation of a fat lady with grisled hair and abundant jewels, a lady escorted by her husband, who was looking with astonishment at the vendor's killing glances without being able to understand them.

The lady-killer was stroking his mustache affectedly, looking from time to time at his cloth suit in order to

smooth out the wrinkles and brush off the specks of dust.
He was a handsome pirate disguised as a gentleman.
Upon noticing Freya's interest, he changed the course
of his glances, poised his fine figure and replied to her
questioning eyes with the smile of a bad angel, making
her understand his discretion and skillfulness in ingratiat-
ing himself behind husbands and escorts.

"There he is!" cried Freya with peals of laughter. "I
already have a new admirer! . . ."

The swarthy charmer was restrained by the scandalous publicity with which this lady was receiving his
mysterious insinuations. Ferragut spoke of knocking
the scamp down on his oyster shells with a good pair
of blows.

"Now don't be ridiculous," she protested. "Poor man!
Perhaps he has a wife and many children. . . . He is
the father of a family and wants to take money
home."

There was a long silence between the two. Ulysses
appeared offended by the lightness and cruelty of his
companion.

"Now don't you be cross," she said. "See here, my
shark! Smile a bit. Show me your teeth. . . . The
libations to the gods are to blame. Are you offended
because I wished to compare you with that clown? . . .
What if you are the only man that I appreciate at all!
. . . Ulysses, I am speaking to you seriously,—with all
the frankness that wine gives. I ought not to tell you
so, but I admit it. . . . If I should ever love a man,
that man would be you."

Ferragut instantly forgot all his irritation in order to
listen to her and envelop her in the adoring light of his
eyes. Freya averted her glance while speaking, not wishing to meet his eye, as though she were weighing what

she was saying while her glance wandered over the wide-spread landscape.

Ulysses' origin was what interested her most. She who had traveled over almost the entire world, had trodden the soil of Spain only a few hours, when disembarking in Barcelona from the transatlantic liner which he had commanded. The Spaniards inspired her both with fear and attraction. A noble gravity reposed in the depths of their ardent hyperbole.

"You are an exaggerated being, a meridional who enlarges everything and lies about everything, believing all his own lies. But I am sure that if you should ever be really in love with me, without fine phrases or passionate fictions, your affection would be more sane and deep than that of other men. . . . My friend, the doctor, says that you are a crude people and that you have only simulated the nervousness, unbalanced behavior, and intrigues that accompany love in other civilized countries even to refinement."

Freya looked at the sailor, making a long pause.

"Therefore you strike," she continued, "therefore you kill when you feel love and jealousy. You are brutes but not mediocre. You do not abandon a woman intentionally; you do not exploit her. . . You are a new species of man for me, who has known so many. If I were able to believe in love, I would have you at my side all my life. . . . All my life long!"

A light, gentle music, like the vibration of fragile and delicate crystal, spread itself over the terrace. Freya followed its rhythm with a light motion of the head. She was accustomed to this cloying music, this *Serenata* of Toselli,—a passionate lament that always touches the soul of the tourist in the halls of the grand hotels. She, who at other times had ridiculed this artificial and refined little music, now felt tears welling up in her eyes.

"Not to be able to love anybody!" she murmured. "To wander alone through the world! . . . And love is such a beautiful thing!"

She guessed what Ferragut was going to say,—his protest of eternal passion, his offer to unite his life to hers forever, and she cut his words short with an energetic gesture.

"No, Ulysses, you do not know me; you do not know who I am. . . . Go far from me. Some days ago it was a matter of indifference to me. I hate men and do not mind injuring them, but now you inspire me with a certain interest because I believe you are good and frank in spite of your haughty exterior. . . . Go! Do not seek me. This is the best proof of affection that I can give you."

She said this vehemently, as if she saw Ferragut running toward danger and was crying out in order to ward him from it.

"On the stage," she continued, "there is a rôle that they call 'The Fatal Woman,' and certain artists are not able to play any other part. They were born to represent this personage. . . . I am a 'Fatal Woman,' but really and truly. . . . If you could know my life! . . . It is better that you do not know it; even I wish to ignore it. I am happy only when I forget it. . . . Ferragut, my friend, bid me farewell, and do not cross my path again."

But Ferragut protested as though she were proposing a cowardly thing to him. Flee? Loving her so much? If she had enemies, she could rely upon him for her defense; if she wanted wealth, he wasn't a millionaire, but. . . .

"Captain," interrupted Freya, "go back to your own people. I was not meant for you. Think of your wife and son; follow your own life. I am not the conquest that is cherished for a few weeks, no more. Nobody can trust me with impunity. I have suckers just like the animals that we saw the other day; I burn and sting just like those transparent parasols in the Aquarium. Flee, Ferragut! . . . Leave me alone. . . . Alone!"

And the image of the immense barrenness of her lonely future made the tears gush from her eyes.

The music had ceased. A motionless waiter was pretending to look far away, while really listening to their conversation. The two Englishmen had interrupted their painting in order to glare at this *gentleman* who was making a lady weep. The sailor began to feel the nervous disquietude which a difficult situation creates.

"Ferragut, pay and let us go," she said, divining his state of mind.

While Ulysses was giving money to the waiters and musicians, she dried her eyes and repaired the ravages to her complexion, drawing from her gold-mesh bag a powder puff and little mirror in whose oval she contemplated herself for a long time.

As they passed out, the oysterman turned his back, pretending to be very much occupied in the arrangement of the lemons that were adorning his stand. She could not see his face, but she guessed, nevertheless, that he was muttering a bad word,—the most terrible that can be said of a woman.

They went slowly toward the station of the funicular road, through solitary streets and between garden walls one side of which was yellow in the golden sunlight and the other blue in the shade. She it was who sought Ulysses' arm, supporting herself on it with a childish abandon as if fatigue had overcome her after the first few steps.

Ferragut pressed this arm close against his body, feeling at once the stimulus of contact. Nobody could see them; their footsteps resounded on the pavements with the echo of an abandoned place. The fermented ardor of those libations to the gods was giving the captain a new audacity.

"My poor little darling! . . . Dear little crazy-head! . . ." he murmured, drawing closer to him Freya's head which was resting on one of his shoulders.

He kissed her without her making any resistance. And she in turn kissed him, but with a sad, light, faint-hearted kiss that in no way recalled the hysterical caress of the Aquarium. Her voice, which appeared to be coming from afar off, was repeating what she had counseled him in the *trattoria*.

"Begone, Ulysses! Do not see me any more. I tell you this for your own good. . . . I bring trouble. I should be sorry to have you curse the moment in which you met me."

The sailor took advantage of all the windings of the streets in order to cut these recommendations short with his kisses. She advanced limply as though towed by him with no will power of her own, as though she were walking in her sleep. A voice was singing with diabolic satisfaction in the captain's brain:

"Now it is ripe! . . . Now it is ripe! . . ."

And he continued pulling her along always in a direct line, not knowing whither he was going, but sure of his triumph.

Near the station an old man approached the pair,—a white-haired, respectable gentleman with an old jacket and spectacles. He gave them the card of a hotel which he owned in the neighborhood, boasting of the good qualities of its rooms. "Every modern comfort. . . . Hot water." Ferragut spoke to her familiarly:

"Would you like? . . . Would you like? . . . ."

She appeared to wake up, dropping his arm brusquely.

"Don't be crazy, Ulysses. . . . That will never be.
. . . Never!"

And drawing herself up magnificently, she entered the
station with a haughty step, without looking around,
without noticing whether Ferragut was following her
or abandoning her.

During the long wait and the descent to the city Freya
appeared as ironical and frivolous as though she had
no recollection of her recent indignation. The sailor,
under the weight of his failure and the unusual libations,
relapsed into sulky silence.

In the district of Chiaja they separated. Ferragut,
finding himself alone, felt more strongly than ever the
effects of the intoxication that was dominating him,
the intoxication of a temperate man overcome by the
intense surprise of novelty.

For a moment he had a forlorn idea of going to his
boat. He needed to give orders, to contend with somebody; but the weakness of his knees pushed him toward
his hotel and he flung himself face downward on the
bed,—whilst his hat rolled on the floor,—content with
the sobriety with which he had reached his room without
attracting the attention of the servants.

He fell asleep immediately, but scarcely had night
fallen before his eyes opened again, or at least he believed that they opened, seeing everything under a light
which was not that of the sun.

Some one had entered the room, and was coming on
tiptoe towards his bed. Ulysses, who was not able to
move, saw out of the tail of one eye that what was approaching was a woman and that this woman appeared
to be Freya. Was it really she? . . .

She had the same countenance, the blonde hair, the
black and oriental eyes, the same oval face. It was
Freya and it was not, just as twins exactly alike physi-

cally, nevertheless have an indefinable something which differentiates them.

The vague thoughts which for some time past had been slowly undermining his subconsciousness with dull, subterranean labor, now cleared the air with explosive force. Whenever he had seen the widow this subconsciousness had asserted itself, forewarning him that he had known her long before that transatlantic voyage. Now, under a light of fantastic splendor, these vague thoughts assumed definite shape.

The sleeper thought he was looking at Freya clad in a bodice with flowing sleeves adjusted to the arms with filagree buttons of gold; some rather barbarous gems were adorning her bosom and ears, and a flowered skirt was covering the rest of her person. It was the classic costume of a farmer's wife or daughter of other centuries that he had seen somewhere in a painting. Where? . . . Where? . . .

"Doña Constanza! . . ."

Freya was the counterpart of that august Byzantian queen. Perhaps she was the very same, perpetuated across the centuries, through extraordinary incarnations. In that moment Ulysses would have believed anything possible.

Besides he was very little concerned with the reasonableness of things just now; the important thing to him was that they should exist; and Freya was at his side; Freya and that other one, welded into one and the same woman, clad like the Grecian sovereign.

Again he repeated the sweet name that had illuminated his infancy with romantic splendor. "Doña Constanza! Oh, Doña Constanza! . . ." And night overwhelmed him, cuddling his pillow as when he was a child, and falling asleep enraptured with thoughts of the young widow of "Vatacio the Heretic."

When he met Freya again the next day, he felt attracted by a new force,—the redoubled interest that people in dreams inspire. She might really be the empress resuscitated in a new form as in the books of chivalry, or she might simply be the wandering widow of a learned sage,—for the sailor it was all the same thing. He desired her, and to his carnal desire was added others less material,—the necessity of seeing her for the mere pleasure of seeing her, of hearing her, of suffering her negatives, of being repelled in all his advances.

She had pleasant memories of the expedition to the heights of S. Martino.

"You must have thought me ridiculous because of my sensitiveness and my tears. You, on the other hand, were as you always are, impetuous and daring. . . . The next time we shall drink less."

The "next time" was an invitation that Ferragut repeated daily. He wanted to take her to dine at one of the *trattorias* on the road to Posilipo where they could see spread at their feet the entire gulf, colored with rose by the setting sun.

Freya had accepted his invitation with the enthusiasm of a school girl. These strolls represented for her hours of joy and liberty, as though her long sojourns with the doctor were filled with monotonous service.

One evening Ulysses was waiting for her far from the hotel so as to avoid the porter's curious stares. As soon as they met and glanced toward the neighboring cabstand, four vehicles advanced at the same time—like a row of Roman chariots anxious to win the prize in the circus—with a noisy clattering of hoofs, cracking of whips, wrathful gesticulations and threatening appeals to the Madonna. Listening to their Neapolitan curses, Ferragut believed for an instant that they were going to kill one another. . . . The two climbed into the near-

est vehicle, and immediately the tumult ceased. The
empty coaches returned to occupy their former places
in the line, and the deadly rivals renewed their placid
and laughing conversation.

An enormous upright plume was waving on their
horses' heads. The cabman, in order not to be discourte-
ous to his two clients, would occasionally turn half-way
around, giving them explanations.

"Over there," and he pointed with his whip, "is the
road of Piedigrotta. The gentleman ought to see it on a
day of fiesta in September. Few return from it with a
firm step. *S. Maria di Piedigrotta* enabled Charles III to
put the Austrians to flight in Velletri. . . . *Aooo!*"

He moved his whip like a fishing rod over the upright
plume, increasing the steed's pace with a professional
howl. . . . And as though his cry were among the sweetest of melodies, he continued talking, by association of
ideas:

"At the fiesta of *Piedigrotta,* when I was a boy, were
given out the best songs of the year. There was proclaimed the latest fashionable love song, and long after
we had forgotten it foreigners would come here repeating it as though it was a novelty."

He made a short pause.

"If the lady and gentleman wish," he continued, "I will
take them, on returning, to *Piedigrotta.* Then we'll see
the little church of *S. Vitale.* Many foreign ladies hunt
for it in order to put flowers on the sepulcher of a hunch-
back who made verses,—Giacomo Leopardi."

The silence with which his two clients received these
explanations made him abandon his mechanical oratory
in order to take a good look at them. The gentleman
was taking the lady's hand and was pressing it, speaking in a very low tone. The lady was pretending not

to listen to him, looking at the villas and the gardens at the left of the road sloping down toward the sea.

With noble magnanimity, however, the driver still wished to instruct his indifferent clients, showing them with the point of his whip the beauty and wonders of his repertoire.

"That church is *S. Maria del Parto,* sometimes called by others the *Sannazaro. Sannazaro* was also a noted poet who described the loves of shepherdesses, and Frederick II of Aragon made him the gift of a villa with gardens in order that he might write with greater comfort. . . . Those were other days, sir! His heirs converted it into a church and——"

The voice of the coachman stopped short. Behind him the pair were talking in an incomprehensible language, without paying the slightest attention to him, without acknowledging his erudite explanations. Ignorant foreigners! . . . And he said no more, wrapping himself in offended silence, relieving his Neapolitan verbosity with a series of shouts and grunts to his horse.

The new road from Posilipo, the work of Murat, skirted the gulf, rising along the mountain edge and constantly emphasizing the declivity between the covering of its feet and the border of the sea. On this hanging slope may be seen villas with white or rosy façades midst the splendor of a vegetation that is always green and glossy. Beyond the colonnades of palm trees and parasol pines, appeared the gulf like a blue curtain, its upper edge showing above the murmuring tops of the trees.

An enormous edifice appeared facing the water. It was a palace in ruins, or rather a roofless palace never finished, with thick walls and huge windows. On the lower floor the waves entered gently through doors and windows which served as rooms of refuge for the fishermen's skiffs.

The two travelers were undoubtedly talking about this ruin, and the forgiving coachman forgot his snub in order to come to their aid.

"That is what many people call the Palace of Queen Joanna. . . . A mistake, sir. Ignorance of the uneducated people! That is the *Palazzo di Donn' Anna,* and *Donna Anna Carafa* was a great Neapolitan *signora,* wife of the Duke of Medina, the Spanish viceroy who constructed the palace for her and was not able to finish it." . . .

He was about to say more but stopped himself. Ah, no! By the Madonna! . . . Again they had begun to talk, without listening to him. . . . And he finally took refuge in offended silence, while they chattered continually behind his back.

Ferragut felt an interest in the remote love-affairs of the Neapolitan great lady with the prudent and aristocratic Spanish magnate. His passion had made the grave viceroy commit the folly of constructing a palace in the sea. The sailor was also in love with a woman of another race and felt equal desires to do whimsical things for her.

"I have read the mandates of Nietzsche," he said to her, by way of explaining his enthusiasm,—" 'seek thy wife outside thy country.' That is the best thing."

Freya smiled sadly.

"Who knows? . . . That would complicate love with the prejudices of national antagonism. That would create children with a double country who would end by belonging to none, who would wander through the world like mendicants with no place of refuge. . . . I know something about that."

And again she smiled with sadness and skepticism.

Ferragut was reading the signs of the *trattorias* on both sides of the highway: "The Ledge of the Siren," "The Joy of Parthenope," "The Cluster of Flowers." . . . And meanwhile he was squeezing Freya's hand, putting his fingers upon the inner side of her wrist and caressing her skin that trembled at every touch.

The coachman let the horse slowly ascend the continuous ascent of Posilipo. He was now concerned in not turning around and not being troublesome. He knew well what they were talking about behind him. "Lovers,—people who do not wish to arrive too soon!" And he forgot to be offended, gloating over the probable generosity of a gentleman in such good company.

Ulysses made him stop on the heights of Posilipo. It was there where he had eaten a famous "sailor's soup," and where they sold the best oysters from Fúsaro. At the right of the road, there arose a pretentious and modern edifice with the name of a restaurant in letters of gold. On the opposite side was the annex, a terraced garden that slipped away down to the sea, and on these terraces were tables in the open air or little low roofed cottages whose walls were covered with climbing vines. These latter constructions had discreet windows opening upon the gulf at a great height thus forestalling any outside curiosity.

Upon receiving Ferragut's generous tip, the coachman greeted him with a sly smile, that confidential gesture of comradeship which passes down through all the social strata, uniting them as simple men. He had brought many folk to this discreet garden with its locked dining-rooms overlooking the gulf. "A good appetite to you, *Signore!*"

The old waiter who came to meet them on the little sloping footpath made the identical grimace as soon as he spied Ferragut. "I have whatever the gentleman may need." And crossing a low, embowered terrace with various unoccupied tables, he opened a door and bade them enter a room having only one window.

Freya went instinctively toward it like an insect toward the light, leaving behind her the damp and gloomy room whose paper was hanging loose at intervals. "How beautiful!" The gulf pictured through the window appeared like an unframed canvas,—the original, alive and palpitating,—of the infinite copies throughout the world.

Meanwhile the captain, while informing himself of the available dishes, was secretly following the discreet sign language of the waiter. With one hand he was holding the door half open, his fingers fumbling with an enormous archaic bolt on the under side which had belonged to a much larger door and looked as though it were going to fall from the wood because of its excessive size. . . . Ferragut surmised that this bolt was going to count heavily, with all its weight, in the bill for dinner.

Freya interrupted her contemplation of the panorama on feeling Ferragut's lips trying to caress her neck.

"None of that, Captain! . . . You know well enough what we have agreed. Remember that I have accepted your invitation on the condition that you leave me in peace."

She permitted his kiss to pass across her cheek, even reaching her mouth. This caress was already an accepted thing. As it had the force of custom, she did not resist it, remembering the preceding ones, but fear of his abusing it made her withdraw from the window.

"Let us examine the enchanted palace which my true love has promised me," she said gayly in order to distract Ulysses from his insistence.

In the center there was a table made of planks badly planed and with rough legs. The covers and the dishes would hide this horror. Passing her eyes scrutinizingly over the old seats, the walls with their loose papering and the chromos in greenish frames, she spied something dark, rectangular and deep occupying one corner of the room. She did not know whether it was a divan, a bed or a funeral catafalque. The shabby covers that were spread over it reminded one of the beds of the barracks or of the prison.

"Ah, no! . . ." Freya made one bound toward the door. She would never be able to eat beside that filthy piece of furniture which had come from the scum of Naples. "Ah, no! How loathesome!"

Ulysses was standing near the door, fearing that Freya's discoveries might go further, and hiding with his back that bolt which was the waiter's pride. He stammered excuses but she mistook his insistence, thinking that he was trying to lock her in.

"Captain, let me pass!" she said in an angry voice. "You do not know me. That kind of thing is for others. . . . Back, if you do not wish me to consider you the lowest kind of fellow. . . ."

And she pushed him as she went out, in spite of the fact that Ulysses was letting her pass freely, reiterating his excuses and laying all the responsibility on the stupidity of the servant.

She stopped under the arbor, suddenly tranquillized upon finding herself with her back to the room.

"What a den!" . . . she said. "Come over here, Ferragut. We shall be much more comfortable in the open air looking at the gulf. Come, now, and don't be babyish! . . . All is forgotten. You were not to blame."

The old waiter, who was returning with table-covers and dishes, did not betray the slightest astonishment at seeing the pair installed on the terrace. He was accustomed to these surprises and evaded the lady's eye like

a convicted criminal, looking at the gentleman with the
forlorn air which he always employed when announcing
that there was no more of some dish on the bill of fare.
His gestures of quiet protection were trying to console
Ferragut for his failure. "Patience and tenacity!" . . .
He had seen much greater difficulties overcome by his
clientele.

Before serving dinner he placed upon the table, in
the guise of an aperitive, a fat-bellied bottle of native
wine, a nectar from the slopes of Vesuvius with a slight
taste of sulphur. Freya was thirsty and was suspicious
of the water of the *trattoria*. Ulysses must forget his
recent mortification. . . . And the two made their libations to the gods, with an unmixed drink in which not
a drop of water cut the jeweled transparency of the
precious wine.

A group of singers and dancers now invaded the terrace. A coppery-hued girl, handsome and dirty, with
wavy hair, great gold hoops in her ears and an apron
of many colored stripes, was dancing under the arbor,
waving on high a tambourine that was almost the size
of a parasol. Two bow-legged youngsters, dressed
like ancient lazzarones in red caps, were accompanying
with shouts the agitated dance of the *tarantella*.

The gulf was taking on a pinkish light under the
oblique rays of the sun, as though there were growing
within it immense groves of coral. The blue of the sky
had also turned rosy and the mountain seemed aflame
in the afterglow. The plume of Vesuvius was less white
than in the morning; its nebulous column, streaked with
reddish flutings by the dying light, appeared to be reflecting its interior fire.

Ulysses felt the friendly placidity that a landscape
contemplated in childhood always inspires. Many a
time he had seen this same panorama with its dancing

girls and its volcano there in his old home at Valencia; he had seen it on the fans called "Roman Style" that his father used to collect.

Freya felt as moved as her companion. The blue of the gulf was of an extreme intensity in the parts not reflected by the sun; the coast appeared of ochre; although the houses had tawdry façades, all these discordant elements were now blended and interfused in subdued and exquisite harmony. The shrubbery was trembling rhythmically under the breeze. The very air was musical, as though in its waves were vibrating the strings of invisible harps.

This was for Freya the true Greece imagined by the poets, not the island of burned-out rocks denuded of vegetation that she had seen and heard spoken of in her excursions through the Hellenic archipelago.

"To live here the rest of my life!" she murmured with misty eyes. "To die here, forgotten, alone, happy! . . ."

Ferragut also would like to die in Naples . . . but with her! . . . And his quick and exuberant imagination described the delights of life for the two,—a life of love and mystery in some one of the little villas, with a garden peeping out over the sea on the slopes of Posilipo.

The dancers had passed down to the lower terrace where the crowd was greater. New customers were entering, almost all in pairs, as the day was fading. The waiter had ushered some highly-painted women with enormous hats, followed by some young men, into the locked dining-room. Through the half-open door came the noise of pursuit, collision and rebound with brutal roars of laughter.

Freya turned her back, as if the memory of her passage through that den offended her.

The old waiter now devoted himself to them, beginning

to serve dinner. To the bottle of Vesuvian wine had succeeded another kind, gradually losing its contents.

The two ate little but felt a nervous thirst which made
them frequently reach out their hands toward the glass.
The wine was depressing to Freya. The sweetness of
the twilight seemed to make it ferment, giving it the
acrid perfume of sad memories.

The sailor felt arising within him the aggressive fever
of temperate men when becoming intoxicated. Had he
been with a man he would have started a violent discussion on any pretext whatever. He did not relish the
oysters, the sailor's soup, the lobster, everything that
another time, eaten alone or with a passing friend in the
same site, would have appeared to him as delicacies.

He was looking at Freya with enigmatical eyes while,
in his thought, wrath was beginning to bubble. He almost
hated her on recalling the arrogance with which she had
treated him, fleeing from that room. "Hypocrite! . . ."
She was just amusing herself with him. She was a
playful and ferocious cat prolonging the death-agony
of the mouse caught in her claws. In his brain a brutal
voice was saying, as though counseling a murder: "This
will be her last day! . . . I'll finish her to-day! . . . No
more after to-day! . . ." After several repetitions, he
was disposed to the greatest violence in order to extri-
cate himself from a situation which he thought ridiculous.

And she, ignorant of her companion's thought, deceived by the impassiveness of his countenance, continued chatting with her glance fixed on the horizon,
talking in an undertone as though she were recounting
to herself her illusions.

The momentary suggestion of living in a cottage of
Posilipo, completely alone, an existence of monastic isola-

tion with all the conveniences of modern life, was dominating her like an obsession.

"And yet, after all," she continued, "this atmosphere is
not favorable to solitude; this landscape is for love. To
grow old slowly, two who love each other, before the
eternal beauty of the gulf! . . . What a pity that I have
never been really loved! . . ."

This was an offense against Ulysses who expressed
his annoyance with all the aggressiveness that was seething beneath his bad humor. How about him? . . . Was
he not loving her and disposed to prove it to her by all
manner of sacrifices? . . .

Sacrifices as proof of love always left this woman
cold, accepting them with a skeptical gesture.

"All men have told me the same thing," she added;
"they all promise to kill themselves if I do not love
them. . . . And with the most of them it is nothing
more than a phrase of passionate rhetoric. And what
if they did kill themselves really? What does that prove?
. . . To leave life on the spur of a moment that gives no
opportunity for repentance;—a simple nervous flash, a
posture many times assumed simply for what people will
say, with the frivolous pride of an actor who likes to
pose in graceful attitudes. I know what all that means.
A man once killed himself for me. . . ."

On hearing these last words Ferragut jerked himself
out of his sullen silence. A malicious voice was chanting in his brain, "Now there are three! . . ."

"I saw him dying," she continued, "on a bed of the
hotel. He had a red spot like a star on the bandage
of his forehead,—the hole of the pistol shot. He died
clutching my hands, swearing that he loved me and that
he had killed himself for me . . . a tiresome, horrible
scene. . . . And nevertheless I am sure that he was deceiving himself, that he did not love me. He killed him-

self through wounded vanity on seeing that I would
have nothing to do with him,—just for stubbornness, for
theatrical effect, influenced by his readings. . . . He was
a Roumanian tenor. That was in Russia. . . . I have
been an actress a part of my life. . . ."

The sailor wished to express the astonishment that the
different changes of this mysterious wandering existence,
always showing a new facet, were producing in him; but
he contained himself in order to listen better to the cruel
counsels of the malignant voice speaking within his
thoughts. . . . He was not trying to kill himself
for her. Quite the contrary! His moody aggressiveness
was considering her as the next victim. There was in
his eyes something of the dead *Triton* when in pursuit
of a distant woman's skirt on the coast.

Freya continued speaking.

"To kill one's self is not a proof of love. They all
promise me the sacrifice of their existence from the very
first words. Men don't know any other song. Don't
imitate them, Captain."

She remained pensive a long time. Twilight was
rapidly falling; half the sky was of amber and the
other half of a midnight blue in which the first stars
were beginning to twinkle. The gulf was drowsing
under the leaden coverlet of its water, exhaling a mysterious freshness that was spreading to the mountains
and trees. All the landscape appeared to be acquiring
the fragility of crystal. The silent air was trembling
with exaggerated resonance, repeating the fall of an oar
in the boats that, small as flies, were slipping along under
the sky arching above the gulf, and prolonging the feminine and invisible voices passing through the groves on
the heights.

The waiter went from table to table, distributing candles enclosed in paper shades. The mosquitoes and moths,

revived by the twilight, were buzzing around these red and yellow flowers of light.

Her voice was again sounding in the twilight air with the vagueness of one speaking in a dream.

"There is a sacrifice greater than that of life,—the only one that can convince a woman that she is beloved. What does life signify to a man like you? . . . Your profession puts it in danger every day and I believe you capable of risking your life, when tired of land, for the slightest motive. . . ."

She paused again and then continued.

"Honor is worth more than life for certain men,— respectability, the preservation of the place that they occupy. Only the man that would risk his honor and position for me, who would descend to the lowest depths without losing his will to live, would ever be able to convince me. . . . That indeed would be a sacrifice!"

Ferragut felt alarmed at such words. What kind of sacrifice was this woman about to propose to him? . . . But he grew calmer as he listened to her. It was all a fancy of her disordered imagination. "She is crazy," again affirmed the hidden counselor in his brain.

"I have dreamed many times," she continued, "of a man who would rob for me, who would kill if it was necessary and might have to pass the rest of his years in prison. . . . My poor thief! . . . I would live only for him, spending night and day near the walls of his prison, looking through the bars, working like a woman of the village in order to send a good dinner to my outlaw. . . . That is genuine love and not the cold lies, the theatrical vows of our world."

Ulysses repeated his mental comment, "She certainly is crazy"—and his thought was so clearly reflected in his eyes that she guessed it.

"Don't be afraid, Ferragut," she said, smiling. "I

have no thought of exacting such a sacrifice of you. All this that I am talking about is merely fancy, a whimsy invented to fill the vacancy of my soul. 'Tis the fault of the wine, of our exaggerated libations,—that to-day have been without water,—to the gods. . . . Just look!"

And she pointed with comical gravity to the two empty bottles that were occupying the center of the table.

Night had fallen. In the dark sky twinkled infinite eyes of starry light. The immense bowl of the gulf was reflecting their sparkles like thousands of will o' the wisps. The candle shades in the restaurant were throwing purplish spots upon the table covers, casting upon the faces of those who were eating around them violent contrasts of light and shade. From the locked rooms were escaping sounds of kisses, pursuit and falling furniture.

"Let us go!" ordered Freya.

The noise of this vulgar orgy was annoying her as though it were dishonoring the majesty of the night. She needed to move about, to walk in the darkness, to breathe in the freshness of the mysterious shade.

At the garden gate they hesitated before the appeals of various coachmen. Freya was the one who refused their offers. She wished to return to Naples on foot, following the easy descent of the road of Posilipo after their long inaction in the restaurant. Her face was warm and flushed because of the excess of wine.

Ulysses gave her his arm and they began to move through the shadows, insensibly impelled in their march by the ease of the downward slope. Freya knew just what this trip would mean. At the very first step the sailor advised her with a kiss on the neck. He was going to take advantage of all the windings of the road,

of the hills and terraces cut through in certain places
to show the phosphorescent gulf across the foliage, and
of the long shadowy stretch broken only now and then
by the public echoes or the lanterns of carriages and
tramways. . . .

But these liberties were already an accepted thing.
She had taken the first step in the Aquarium: besides,
she was sure of her ability to keep her lover at whatever distance she might choose to fix. . . . And convinced of her power of checking herself in time, she gave
herself up like a lost woman.

Never had Ferragut had such a propitious occasion.
It was a trysting-place in the mystery of the night with
plenty of time ahead of them. The only trouble was the
necessity of walking on, of accompanying his embraces
and protests of love with the incessant activity of walking. She protested, coming out from her rapture every
time that the enamored man would propose that they
sit down on the side of the road.

Hope made Ulysses very obedient to Freya, desirous
of reaching Naples as soon as possible. Down there in
the curve of the light near the gulf was the hotel, and
the sailor looked upon it as a place of happiness.

"Say yes," he murmured in her ear, punctuating his
words with kisses, "say that it will be to-night! . . ."

She did not reply, leaning on the arm that the captain had passed around her waist, letting herself be
dragged along as if she were half-fainting, rolling her
eyes and offering her lips.

While Ulysses was repeating his pleadings and caresses
the voice in his brain was chanting victoriously, "Here
it is! . . . It's settled now. . . . The thing now is to
get her to the hotel."

They roamed on for nearly an hour, fancying that
only a few minutes had passed by.

Approaching the gardens of the *Villa Nazionale*, near the Aquarium, they stopped an instant. There were fewer people and more life here than in the road to Posilipo. They avoided the electric lights of the *Via Caracciolo* reflected in the sea,—the two instinctively approaching a bench, and seeking the ebony shade of the trees.

Freya had suddenly become very composed. She appeared annoyed at herself for her languor during the walk. Finding herself near the hotel, she recovered her energy as though in the presence of danger.

"Good-by, Ulysses! We shall see each other again to-morrow. . . . I am going to pass the night in the doctor's home."

The sailor withdrew a little in the shock of surprise. "Was it a jest? . . ." But no, he could not think that. The very tone of her words displayed firm resolution.

He entreated her humbly with a thick and threatening voice not to go away. At the same time his mental counselor was rancorously chanting, "She's making a fool of you! . . . It's time to put an end to all this. . . . Make her feel your masculine authority." And this voice had the same ring as that of the dead *Triton*.

Suddenly occurred a violent, brutal, dishonorable thing. Ulysses threw himself upon her as though he were going to kill her, holding her tightly in his arms, and the two fell upon the bench, panting and struggling. But this only lasted an instant.

The vigorous Ferragut, trembling with emotion, was only using half of his powers. He suddenly sprang back, raising his two hands to his shoulders. He felt a sharp pain, as though one of his bones had just broken. She had repelled him with a certain Japanese fencing trick that employs the hands as irresistible weapons.

"Ah! . . . *Tal!* . . ." he roared, hurling upon her the worst of feminine insults.

And he fell upon her again as though he were a man, uniting to his original purpose the desire of maltreating her, of degrading her, of making her his.

Freya awaited him firmly. . . . Seeing the icy glitter of her eyes, Ulysses without knowing why recalled the "eye of the morning," the companionable reptile of her dances.

In this furious onslaught he was stopped by the simple contact on his forehead of a diminutive metal circle, a kind of frozen thimble that was resting on his skin.

He looked. . . . It was a little revolver, a deadly toy of shining nickel. It had appeared in Freya's hand, drawn secretly from her clothes, or perhaps from that gold-mesh bag whose contents seemed inexhaustible.

She was looking at him fixedly with her finger on the trigger. He surmised her familiarity with the weapon that she had in her hand. It could not be the first time that she had had recourse to it.

The sailor's indecision was brief. With a man, he would have taken possession of the threatening hand, twisting it until he broke it, without the slightest fear of the revolver. But he had opposite him a woman . . . and this woman was entirely capable of wounding him, and at the same time placing him in a ridiculous situation.

"Retire, sir!" ordered Freya with a ceremonious and threatening tone as though she were speaking to an utter stranger.

But it was she who retired finally, seeing that Ulysses stepped back, thoughtful and confused. She turned her back on him at the same time that the revolver disappeared from her hand.

Before departing, she murmured some words that Ferragut was not able to understand, looking at him for the last time with contemptuous eyes. They must be terri-

ble insults, and just because she was uttering them in
a mysterious language, he felt her scorn more deeply.

"It cannot be. . . . It is all ended. It is ended forever! . . ."

She said this repeatedly before returning to her hotel.
And he thought of it during all the wakeful night between agonizing attacks of nightmare. When the
morning was well advanced the bugles of the *bersaglieri* awakened him from a heavy sleep.

He paid his bill in the manager's office and gave a last
tip to the porter, telling him that a few hours later
a man from the ship would come for his baggage.

He was happy, with the forced happiness of one
obliged to accommodate himself to circumstances. He
congratulated himself upon his liberty as though he had
gained this liberty of his own free will and it had not
been imposed upon him by her scorn. Since the memory of the preceding day pained him, putting him in a
ridiculous and gross light, it was better not to recall
the past.

He stopped in the street to take a last look at the
hotel. "Adieu, accursed *albergo!* . . . Never will I see
you again. Would that you might burn down with all
your occupants!"

Upon treading the deck of the *Mare Nostrum,* his enforced satisfaction became immeasurably increased.
Here only could he live far from the complications and
illusions of terrestrial life.

All those aboard who in previous weeks had feared
the arrival of the ill-humored captain, now smiled as
though they saw the sun coming out after a tempest.
He distributed kindly words and affectionate grasps of
the hand. The repairs were going to be finished the
following day. . . . Very good! He was entirely content. Soon they would be on the sea again.

In the galley he greeted Uncle Caragol. . . . That man *was* a philosopher. All the women in the world were not in his estimation worth a good dish of rice. Ah, the great man! . . . He surely was going to live to be a hundred! And the cook flattered by such praises, whose origin he did not happen to comprehend, responded as always,—"That is so, my captain."

Toni, silent, disciplined and familiar, inspired him with no less admiration. His life was an upright life, firm and plain, as the road of duty. When the young officials used to talk in his presence of boisterous suppers on shore with women from distant countries, the pilot had always shrugged his shoulders. "Money and pleasure ought to be kept for the home," he would say sententiously.

Ferragut had laughed many times at the virtue of his mate who, timid and torpid, used to pass over a great part of the planet without permitting himself any distraction whatever, but would awake with an overpowering tension whenever the chances of their voyage brought him the opportunity of a few days' stay in his home in the *Marina*.

And with the tranquil grossness of the virtuous stay-at-home, he was accustomed to calculate the dates of his voyages by the age of his eight children. "This one was on returning from the Philippines. . . . This other one after I was in the coast trade in the Gulf of California. . . ."

His methodical serenity, incapable of being perturbed by frivolous adventures, made him guess from the very first the secret of the captain's enthusiasm and wrath. "It must be a woman," he said to himself, upon seeing him installed in a hotel in Naples, and after feeling the effects of his bad humor in the fleeting appearances that he made on board.

Now, listening to Ferragut's jovial comments on his
mate's tranquil life and philosophic sagacity, Toni again
ejaculated mentally, without the captain's suspecting anything from his impassive countenance: "Now he has
quarreled with the woman. He has tired of her. But
better so!"

He was more than ever confirmed in this belief on
hearing Ferragut's plans. As soon as the boat could
be made ready, they were going to anchor in the commercial port. He had been told of a certain cargo for Barcelona,—some cheap freight,—but that was better than going empty. . . . If the cargo should be delayed, they
would set sail merely with ballast. More than anything else, he wished to renew his trips. Boats were
scarcer and more in demand all the time. It was high
time to stop this enforced inertia.

"Yes, it's high time," responded Toni who, during the
entire month, had only gone ashore twice.

The *Mare Nostrum* left the repair dock coming to anchor opposite the commercial wharf, shining and rejuvenated, with no imperfections recalling her recent
injuries.

One morning when the captain and his second were
in the saloon under the poop undecided whether to start
that night—or wait four days longer, as the owners of
the cargo were requesting,—the third officer, a young Andalusian, presented himself greatly excited by the piece
of news of which he was the bearer. A most beautiful
and elegant lady (the young man emphasized his admiration with these details) had just arrived in a launch
and, without asking permission, had climbed the ladder,
entering the vessel as though it were her own dwelling.

Toni felt his heart thump. His swarthy countenance
became ashy pale. *"Cristo!* . . . The woman from

Naples!" He did not really know whether she was from Naples; he had never seen her, but he was certain that she was coming as a fatal impediment, as an unexpected calamity. . . . Just when things were going so well, too! . . .

The captain whirled around in his arm chair, jumped up from the table, and in two bounds was out on deck.

Something extraordinary was perturbing the crew. They, too, were all on deck as though some powerful attraction had drawn them from the orlop, from the depths of the hold, from the metallic corridors of the engine rooms. Even Uncle Caragol was sticking his episcopal face out through the door of the kitchen, holding a hand closed in the form of a telescope to one of his eyes, without being able to distinguish clearly the announced marvel.

Freya was a few steps away in a blue suit somewhat like a sailor's, as though this visit to the ship necessitated the imitative elegance and bearing of the multimillionaires who live on their yachts. The seamen, cleaning brass or polishing wood, were pretending extraordinary occupations in order to get near her. They felt the necessity of being in her atmosphere, of living in the perfumed air that enveloped her, following her steps.

Upon seeing the captain, she simply extended her hand, as though she might have seen him the day before.

"Do not object, Ferragut! . . . As I did not find you in the hotel, I felt obliged to visit you on your ship. I have always wanted to see your floating home. Everything about you interests me."

She appeared an entirely different woman. Ulysses noted the great change that had taken place in her person during the last days. Her eyes were bold, challenging, of a calm seductiveness. She appeared to be sur-

rendering herself entirely. Her smiles, her words, her
manner of crossing the deck toward the staterooms of
the vessel proclaimed her determination to end her long
resistance as quickly as possible, yielding to the sailor's
desires.

In spite of former failures, he felt anew the joy of
triumph. "Now it is going to be! My absence has
conquered her. . . ." And at the same time that he was
foretasting the sweet satisfaction of love and triumphant
pride, there arose in him a vague instinct of suspicion
of this woman so suddenly transformed, perhaps loving
her less than in former days when she resisted and advised him to be gone.

In the forward cabin he presented her to his mate. The
crude Toni experienced the same hallucination that had
perturbed all the others on the boat. What a woman!
. . . At the very first glance he understood and excused
the captain's conduct. Then he fixed his eyes upon her
with an expression of alarm, as though her presence made
him tremble for the fate of the steamer: but finally he
succumbed, dominated by this lady who was examining
the saloon as though she had come to remain in it forever.

For a few moments Freya was interested in the hairy
ugliness of Toni. He was a true Mediterranean, just the
kind she had imagined to herself,—a faun pursuing
nymphs. Ulysses laughed at the eulogies which she
passed on his mate.

"In his shoes," she continued, "he ought to have pretty
little hoofs like a goat's. He must know how to play
the flute. Don't you think so, Captain? . . ."

The faun, wrinkled and wrathful, took himself off,
saluting her stolidly as he went away. Ferragut felt
greatly relieved at his absence, since he was fearful of
some rude speech from Toni.

Finding herself alone with Ulysses, she ran through the great room from one side to the other.

"Is here where you live, my dear shark? . . . Let me see everything. Let me poke around everywhere. Everything of yours interests me. You will not say now that I do not love you. What a boast for Captain Ferragut! The ladies come to seek him on his ship. . . ."

She interrupted her ironic and affectionate chatter in order to defend herself gently from the sailor. He, forgetting the past, and wishing to take advantage of the happiness so suddenly presented to him, was kissing the nape of her neck.

"There, . . . there!" she sighed. "Now let me look around. I feel the curiosity of a child."

She opened the piano,—the poor piano of the Scotch captain—and some thin and plaintive chords, showing many years' lack of tuning, filled the saloon with the melancholy of resuscitated memories.

The melody was like that of the musical boxes that we find forgotten in the depths of a wardrobe among the clothes of some deceased old lady. Freya declared that it smelled of withered roses.

Then, leaving the piano, she opened one after the other, all the doors of the staterooms surrounding the saloon. She stopped at the captain's sleeping room without wishing to pass the threshold, without loosening her hold on the brass doorknob in her right hand. Ferragut behind her, was pushing her with treacherous gentleness, at the same time repeating his caresses on her neck.

"No; here, no," she said. "Not for anything in the world! . . . I will be yours, I promise you; I give you my word of honor. But where I will and when it seems best to me. . . . Very soon, Ulysses!"

He felt complete gratification in all these affirmations

made in a caressing and submissive voice, all possible pride in such spontaneous, affectionate address, equivalent to the first surrender.

The arrival of one of Uncle Caragol's acolytes made them recover their composure. He was bringing two enormous glasses filled with a ruddy and foamy cocktail, —an intoxicating and sweet mixture, a composite of all the knowledge acquired by the *chef* in his intercourse with the drunkards of the principal ports of the world.

She tested the liquid, rolling up her eyes like a greedy tabby. Then she broke forth into praises, lifting up the glass in a solemn manner. She was offering her libation to Eros, the god of Love, the most beautiful of the gods, and Ferragut who always had a certain terror of the infernal and agreeable concoctions of his cook, gulped the glass in one swallow, in order to join in the invocation.

All was arranged between the two. She was giving the orders. Ferragut would return ashore, lodging in the same *albergo*. They would continue their life as before, as though nothing had occurred.

"This evening you will await me in the gardens of the *Villa Nazionale.* . . . Yes, there where you wished to kill me, you highwayman! . . ."

Before he should clearly recall that night of violence, Freya continued her recollections with feminine astuteness. . . . It was Ulysses who had wanted to kill her; she reiterated it without admitting any reply.

"We shall visit the doctor," she continued. "The poor woman wants to see you and has asked me to bring you. She is very much interested in you because she knows that I love you, my pirate!"

After having arranged the hour of meeting, Freya wished to depart. But before returning to her launch, she felt curious to inspect the boat, just as she had examined the saloon and the staterooms.

With the air of a reigning princess, preceded by the captain and followed by the officials, she went over the two decks, entered the galleries of the engine room and the four-sided abyss of the hatchways, sniffing the musty odor of the hold. On the bridge she touched with childish enthusiasm the large brass hood of the binnacle and other steering instruments glistening as though made of gold.

She wished to see the galley and invaded Uncle Caragol's dominions, putting his formal lines of casseroles into lamentable disorder, and poking the tip of her rosy little nose into the steam arising from the great stew in which was boiling the crew's mess.

The old man was able to see her close with his half-blind eyes. "Yes, indeed, she was pretty!" The frou-frou of her skirts and the frequent little clashes that he had with her in her comings and goings, perturbed the apostle. His *chef*-like sense of smell made him feel annoyed by the perfume of this lady. "Pretty, but with the smell of . . ." he repeated mentally. For him all feminine perfume merited this scandalous title. Good women smelled of fish and kitchen pots; he was sure of that. . . . In his faraway youth, the knowledge of poor Caragol had never gone beyond that.

As soon as he was alone, he snatched up a rag, waving it violently around, as though he were driving away flies. He wished to clear the atmosphere of bad odors. He felt as scandalized as though she had let a cake of soap fall into one of his delicious rice compounds.

The men of the crew crowded to the railings in order to follow the course of the little launch that was making toward shore.

Toni, standing on the bridge, also contemplated her
with enigmatic eyes.

"You are handsome, but may the sea swallow you up
before you come back!"

A handkerchief was waving from the stern of the
little boat. "Good-by, Captain!" And the captain
nodded his head, smiling and gratified by the feminine
greeting while the sailors were envying him his good
luck.

Again one of the men of the crew carried Ferragut's
baggage to the *albergo* on the shore of *S. Lucia*. The
porter, as though foreseeing the chance of getting an
easy fee from his client, took it upon himself to select
a room for him, an apartment on a floor lower than
on his former stay, near that which the *signora* Talberg
was occupying.

They met in mid-afternoon in the *Villa Nazionale*, and
began their walk together through the streets of Chiaja.
At last Ulysses was going to know where the doctor was
hiding her majestic personality. He anticipated something extraordinary in this dwelling-place, but was disposed to hide his impressions for fear of losing the affection and support of the wise lady who seemed to be
exercising so great a power over Freya.

They entered into the vestibule of an ancient palace.
Many times the sailor had stopped before this door, but
had gone on, misled by the little metal door plates announcing the offices and counting-houses installed on the
different floors.

He beheld an arcaded court paved with great tiled
slabs upon which opened the curving balconies of the
four interior sides of the palace. They climbed up a
stairway of resounding echoes, as large as one of the hill-
side streets, with broad turnings which in former time
permitted the passage of the litters and chairmen. As

souvenirs of the white-wigged personages and ladies of voluminous farthingales who had passed through this palace, there were still some classic busts on the landing places, a hand-wrought iron railing, and various huge lanterns of dull gold and blurred glass.

They stopped on the first floor before a row of doors rather weather-beaten by the years.

"Here it is," said Freya.

And thereupon she pointed to the only door that was covered with a screen of green leather displaying a commercial sign,—enormous, gilded and pretentious. The doctor was lodging in an office. . . . How could he ever have found it!

The first room really was an office, a merchant's room with files for papers, maps, a safe for stocks, and various tables. One employee only was working here,—a man of uncertain age with a childish face and a clipped beard. His obsequious and smiling attitude was in striking contrast to his evasive glance,—a glance of alarm and distrust.

Upon seeing Freya he arose from his seat. She greeted him, calling him Karl, and passed on as though he were a mere porter. Ulysses upon following her, surmised that the suspicious glance of the writer was fixed upon his back.

"Is he a Pole, too?" he asked.

"Yes, a Pole. . . . He is a protégé of the doctor's."

They entered a salon evidently furnished in great haste, with the happy-go-lucky and individual knack of those accustomed to traveling and improvising a dwelling place;—divans with cheap and showy chintzes, skins of the American llama, glaring imitation-Oriental rugs, and on the walls, prints from the periodicals between gilt moldings. On a table were displayed their marble ornaments and silver things, a great dressing-case with a

cover of cut leather, and a few little Neapolitan statuettes which had been bought at the last moment in order
to give a certain air of sedentary respectability to this
room which could be dismantled suddenly and whose
most valuable adornments were acquired *en route*.

Through a half-drawn portière they descried the doctor writing in the nearby room. She was bending over
an American desk, but she saw them immediately in
a mirror which she kept always in front of her in order
to spy on all that was passing behind her.

Ulysses surmised that the imposing dame had made
certain additions to her toilette in order to receive him.
A gown as close as a sheath molded the exuberance of
her figure. The narrow skirt drawn tightly over the edge
of her knees appeared like the handle of an enormous
club. Over the green sea of her dress she was wearing a spangled white tulle draped like a shawl. The
captain, in spite of his respect for this wise lady, could
not help comparing her to a well-nourished mother-mer-
maid in the oceanic pasture lands.

With outstretched hands and a joyous expression on
her countenance irradiating even her glasses, she advanced toward Ferragut. Her meeting was almost an
embrace. . . . "My dear Captain! Such a long time
since I have seen you! . . ." She had heard of him frequently through her young friend, but even so, she could
not but consider it a misfortune that the sailor had
never come to see her.

She appeared to have forgotten her coldness when bidding him farewell in Salerno and the care which she
had taken to hide from him her home address.

Neither did Ferragut recall this fact now that he was
so agreeably touched by the doctor's amiability. She had
seated herself between the two as though wishing to protect them with all the majesty of her person and the af-

fection of her eyes. She was a real mother for her young friend. While speaking, she was patting Freya's great locks of hair, which had just escaped from underneath her hat, and Freya, adapting herself to the tenderness of the situation, cuddled down against the doctor, assuming the air of a timid and devoted child while she fixed on Ulysses her eyes of sweet promise.

"You must love her very much, Captain," continued the matron. "Freya speaks only of you. She has been so unfortunate! . . . Life has been so cruel to her! . . ."

The sailor felt as though he were in the placid bosom of a family. That lady was discreetly taking everything for granted, speaking to him as to a son-in-law. Her kindly glance was somewhat melancholy. It was the sweet sadness of mature people who find the present monotonous, the future circumscribed, and taking refuge in memories of the past, envy the young who enjoy the reality of what they can taste only in memory.

"Happy you! . . . You love each other so much! . . . Life is worth living only because of love."

And Freya, as though irresistibly affected by these counsels, threw one arm around the doctor's globular, corseted figure, while convulsively clasping Ulysses' right hand.

The gold-rimmed spectacles, with their protecting gleam, appeared to incite them to even greater intimacy. "You may kiss each other. . . ." And the imposing dame, trumping up an insignificant pretext, so as to facilitate their love-making was about to go out when the drapery of the door between the salon and office was raised.

There entered a man of Ferragut's age, but shorter, with a weather-beaten face. He was dressed in the English style with scrupulous correctness. It was plain to be seen that he was accustomed to take the most exces-

sive and childish interest in everything referring to the
adornment of his person. The suit of gray wool appeared to have achieved its finishing touch in the harmony of cravat, socks, and handkerchief sticking out
of his pocket,—all in the same tone. The three pieces
were blue, without the slightest variation in shade, chosen
with the exactitude of a man who would undoubtedly
suffer cruel discomfort if obliged to go out into the
street with his cravat of one color and his socks of another. His gloves had the same dark tan tone as his
shoes.

Ferragut thought that this dandy, in order to be absolutely perfect, ought to be clean shaved. And yet, he
was wearing a beard, close clipped on the cheeks and
forming over the chin a short, sharp point. The captain suspected that he was a sailor. In the German
fleet, in the Russian, in all the navies of the North where
they are not shaved in the English style, they use this
traditional little beard.

The newcomer bowed, or, more properly speaking,
doubled himself over at right angles, with a brusque
stiffness, upon kissing the hands of the two ladies. Then
he raised his impertinent monocle and fixed it in one
of his eyes while the doctor made the introduction.

"Count Kaledine . . . Captain Ferragut."

The count gave the sailor his hand, a hard hand, well-
cared for and vigorous, which for a long time enclosed
that of Ulysses, wishing to dominate it with an ineffectual pressure.

The conversation continued in English which was the
language employed by the doctor in her relations with
Ulysses.

"The gentleman is a sailor?" asked Ferragut in order
to clarify his doubts.

The monocle did not move from its orbit, but a light

ripple of surprise appeared to cross its luminous convexity. The doctor hastened to reply.

"The count is an illustrious diplomat who is now on leave, regaining his health. He has traveled a great deal, but he is not a sailor."

And she continued her explanations.

The Kaledines were of a Russian family ennobled in the days of Catherine the Great. The doctor, being a Polish woman, had been connected with them for many years. . . . And she ceased speaking, giving Kaledine his cue in the conversation.

At the beginning the count appeared cold and rather disdainful in his words, as though he could not possibly lay aside his diplomatic haughtiness. But this hauteur gradually melted away.

Through his "distinguished friend,—Madame Talberg," he had heard of many of Ferragut's nautical adventures. Men of action, the heroes of the ocean, were always exceedingly interesting to him.

Ulysses suddenly noticed in his noble interlocutor a warm affection, a desire to make himself agreeable, just like the doctor's. What a lovely home this was in which everybody was making an effort to be gracious to Captain Ferragut!

The count, smiling amiably, ceased to avail himself of his English, and soon began talking to him in Spanish, as though he had reserved this final touch in order to captivate Ulysses' affection with this most irresistible of flatteries.

"I have lived in Mexico," he said, in order to explain his knowledge of the language. "I made a long trip through the Philippines when I was living in Japan."

The seas of the extreme Far East were those least frequented by Ulysses. Only twice had he entered the Chinese and Nipponese harbors, but he knew them sufficiently to keep up his end of the conversation with this traveler who was displaying in his tastes a certain artistic refinement. For half an hour, there filed through the vulgar atmosphere of this salon, images of enormous pagodas with superimposed roofs whose strings of bells vibrated in the breeze like an Æolian harp, monstrous idols—carved in gold, in bronze, or in marble-houses made of paper, thrones of bamboo, furniture with mother-of-pearl inlay, screens with flocks of flying storks.

The doctor disappeared, bored by a dialogue of which she could only understand a few words. Freya, motionless, with drowsy eyes, and a knee between her crossed hands, held herself aloof, understanding the conversation, but without taking any part in it, as though she were offended at the forgetfulness in which the two men were leaving her. Finally she slipped discreetly away, responding to the call of a hand peeping through the portières. The doctor was preparing tea and needed help.

The conversation continued on in no way affected by their absence. Kaledine had abandoned the Asiatic waters in order to pass to the Mediterranean, and there he anchored himself with admirable insistence. Another sign of affection for Ferragut who was finding him more and more charming in spite of his slightly glacial attitude.

He suddenly noticed that it was not as a Russian count that he was speaking since, with brief and exact questions, he was making Ferragut reply just as though he were undergoing an examination.

These signs of interest shown by the great traveler in the little *mare nostrum,* and especially in the details of its western bowl which he wished to know most minutely, pleased Ferragut greatly.

He might ask him whatever he wished. Ferragut knew mile for mile all its shores,—Spanish, French, and Italian, the surface and also its depths.

Perhaps because he was staying in Naples, Kaledine insisted upon learning especially about that part of the Mediterranean enclosed between Sardinia, southern Italy, and Sicily,—the part which the ancients had called the Tyrrhenian Sea. . . . Did the captain happen to know those little frequented and almost forgotten islands opposite Sicily?

"I know all about all of them," replied the sailor boastfully. And without realizing exactly whether it was curiosity on the part of the listener, or whether he was being submitted to an interesting examination, he talked on and on.

He was well acquainted with the archipelago of the Lipari Islands with their mines of sulphur and pumice-stone,—a group of volcanic peaks which rise up from the depths of the Mediterranean. In these the ancients had placed Æolus, lord of the winds; in these was Stromboli, vomiting forth enormous balls of lava which exploded with the roar of thunder. Its volcanic slag fell again into the chimneys of the crater or rolled down the mountain slopes, falling into the waves.

More to the west, isolated and solitary in a sea free from shoals, was Ustica,—an abrupt and volcanic island that the Phœnicians had colonized and which had served as a refuge for Saracen pilots. Its population was scant and poor. There was nothing to see on it, apart from certain fossil shells interesting to men of science.

But the count showed himself wonderfully interested in this extinct and lonely crater in the midst of a sea frequented only by fishing smacks.

Ferragut had also seen, although far off, at the entrance of the harbor of Trapani, the archipelago of the

Ægadian Islands where are the great fishing grounds of the tunny. Once he had disembarked in the island of Pantellaria, situated halfway between Sicily and Africa. It was a very high, volcanic cone that came up in the midst of the strait and had at its base alkaline lakes, sulphurous fumes, thermal waters, and prehistoric constructions of great stone blocks similar to those in Sardinia and the Balearic Islands. Boats bound for Tunis and Tripoli used to carry cargoes of raisins, the only export from this ancient Phœnician colony.

Between Pantellaria and Sicily the ocean floor was considerably elevated, having on its back an aquatic layer that in some points was only twelve yards thick. It was the great shoal called the Aventura, a volcanic swelling, a double submerged island, the submarine pedestal of Sicily.

The ledge of Aventura also appeared to interest the count greatly.

"You certainly know the sea well," he said in an approving tone.

Ferragut was about to go on talking when the two ladies entered with a tray which contained the tea service and various plates of cakes. The captain saw nothing strange in their lack of servants. The doctor and her friend were to him a pair of women of extraordinary customs, and so he thought all their acts were logical and natural. Freya served the tea with modest grace as though she were the daughter of the house.

They passed the rest of the afternoon conversing on distant voyages. Nobody alluded to the war, nor to Italy's problem at that moment as to whether she should maintain or break her neutrality. They appeared to be living in an inaccessible place thousands of leagues from all human bustle.

The two women were treating the count with the

well-bred familiarity of persons in the same rank of life, but at times the sailor fancied that he noted that they were afraid of him.

At the end of the afternoon this personage arose and Ferragut did the same, understanding that he was expected to bring his visit to an end. The count offered to accompany him. While he was bidding the doctor good-by, thanking her with extreme courtesy for having introduced him to the captain, Ferragut felt that Freya was clasping his hand in a meaning way.

"Until to-night," she murmured lightly, hardly moving her lips. "I shall see you later. . . . Expect me."

Oh, what happiness! . . . The eyes, the smile, the pressure of her hand were telling him much more than that.

Never did he take such an agreeable stroll as when walking beside Kaledine through the streets of Chiaja toward the shore. What was that man saying? . . . Insignificant things in order to avoid silence, but to him they appeared to be observations of most profound wisdom. His voice sounded musical and affectionate. Everything about them seemed equally agreeable,—the people who were passing through the streets, the Neapolitan sounds at nightfall, the dark seas, the entire life.

They bade each other good-by before the door of the hotel. The count, in spite of his offers of friendship, went away without mentioning his address.

"It doesn't matter," thought Ferragut. "We shall meet again in the doctor's house."

He passed the rest of his watch agitated alternately by hope and impatience. He did not wish to eat; emotion had paralyzed his appetite. . . . And yet, once seated at the table, he ate more than ever with a mechanical and distraught avidity.

He needed to stroll around, to talk with somebody, in order that time might fly by with greater rapidity, beguiling his uneasy wait. She would not return to the hotel until very late. . . . And he therefore retired to his room earlier than usual, believing with illogical superstition that by so doing Freya might arrive earlier.

His first movement upon finding himself alone in his room, was one of pride. He looked up at the ceiling, pitying the enamored sailor that a week before had been dwelling on the floor above. Poor man! How they must have made fun of him! . . . Ulysses admired himself as though he were an entirely new personality, happy and triumphant, completely separated from that other creature by dolorous periods of humiliations and failures that he did not wish to recall.

The long, long hours in which he waited with such anxiety! . . . He strolled about smoking, lighting one cigar with the remnant of the preceding one. Then he opened the window, wishing to get rid of the perfume of strong tobacco. She only liked Oriental cigarettes. . . . And as the acrid odor of the strong, succulent Havana cigar persisted in the room, he searched in his dressing-case and sprinkled around the contents of various perfumed essences which he had long ago forgotten.

A sudden uneasiness disturbed his waiting. Perhaps she who was going to come did not know which was his room. He was not sure that he had given her the directions with sufficient clearness. It was possible that she might make a mistake. . . . He began to believe that really she had made a mistake.

Fear and impatience made him open his door, taking his stand in the corridor in order to look down toward Freya's closed room. Every time that footsteps sounded on the stairway or the grating of the elevator creaked, the bearded sailor trembled with a childish uneasiness.

He wanted to hide himself and yet at the same time he wanted to look to see if she was the one who was coming.

The guests occupying the same floor kept seeing him withdraw into his room in the most inexplicable attitudes. Sometimes he would remain firmly in the corridor as though, worn out with useless calling, he were looking for the domestics; and at other times they surprised him with his head poking out of the half-open door or hastily withdrawing it. An old Italian count, passing by, gave him a smile of intelligence and comradeship. . . . He was in the secret! The man was undoubtedly waiting for one of the maids of the hotel.

He ended by settling himself in his room, but leaving his door ajar. The rectangle of bright light that it marked on the floor and wall opposite would guide Freya, showing her the way. . . .

But he was not able to keep up this signal very long. Scantily clad dames in kimonos and gentlemen in pyjamas were slipping discreetly down the passage way in soft, slipper-clad silence, all going in the same direction, and casting wrathful glances toward the lighted doorway.

Finally he had to close the door. He opened a book, but it was impossible to read two paragraphs consecutively. His watch said twelve o'clock.

"She will not come! . . . She will not come!" he cried in desperation.

A new idea revived his drooping spirits. It was ridiculous that so discreet a person as Freya should venture to come to his room while there was a light under the door. Love needed obscurity and mystery. And besides, this visible hope might attract the notice of some curious person.

He snapped off the electric light and in the darkness

found his bed, throwing himself down with an exaggerated noise, in order that nobody might doubt that he had retired for the night. The darkness reanimated his hope.

"She's going to come. . . . She will come at any moment."

Again he arose cautiously, noiselessly, going on tiptoe. He must overcome any possible difficulty at the entrance. He put the door slightly ajar so as to avoid the swinging noise of the door-fastening. A chair in the frame of the doorway easily held it unlatched.

He got up several times more, arranging things to his satisfaction and then threw himself upon the bed, disposed to keep his watch all night, if it was necessary. He did not wish to sleep. No, he ought not to drowse. . . . And half an hour later he was slumbering profoundly without knowing at what moment he had slid down the soft slopes of sleep.

Suddenly he awoke as if some one had hit his head with a club. His ears were buzzing. . . . It was the rude impression of one who sleeps without wishing to and feels himself shaken by reviving restlessness. Some moments passed without his taking in the situation. Then he suddenly recalled it all. . . . Alone! She had not come! . . . He did not know whether minutes or hours had passed by.

Something besides his uneasiness had brought him back to life. He suspected that in the dark silence some real thing was approaching. A little mouse appeared to be moving down the corridor. The shoes placed outside one of the doors were moved with a slight creaking. Ferragut had the vague impression of air that is displaced by the slow advance of a body.

The door trembled. The chair was pushed back, little by little, very gently pushed. In the darkness he descried a moving shadow, dark and dense. He made a movement.

"Shhhh-h!" sighed a ghostly voice, a voice from the other world. "It is I."

Instinctively he raised his right hand to the wall and turned on the light.

Under the electric light it was she,—a different Freya from any that he had ever seen, with her wealth of hair falling in golden serpents over her shoulders covered with an Asiatic tunic that enveloped her like a cloud.

It was not the Japanese kimono, vulgarized by commerce. It was made in one piece of Hindustanic cloth, embroidered with fantastic flowers and capriciously draped. Through its fine texture could be perceived the flesh as though it were a wrapping of multicolored air.

She uttered a protest. Then, imitating Ulysses' gesture, she reached her hand toward the wall . . . and all was darkness.

Upon awakening, he felt the sunlight on his face. The window, whose curtains he had forgotten to draw, was blue,—blue sky above and the blue of the sea in its lower panes.

He looked around him. . . . Nobody! For a moment he believed he must have been dreaming, but the sweet perfume of her hair still scented the pillow. The reality of awakening was as joyous for Ulysses, as sweet as had been the night hours in the mystery of the darkness. He had never felt so strong and so happy.

In the window sounded a baritone voice singing one of the songs of Naples,—"Oh, sweet land, sweet gulf! . . ." That certainly was the most beautiful spot in the world. Proud and satisfied with his fate, he would have liked to embrace the waves, the islands, the city, Vesuvius.

A bell jangled impatiently in the corridor. Captain
Ferragut was hungry. He surveyed with the glance of
an ogre the *café au lait,* the abundant bread, and the
small pat of butter that the waiter brought him. A very
small portion for him! . . . And while he was attacking
all this with avidity, the door opened and Freya, rosy
and fresh from a recent bath and clad like a man, entered the room.

The Hindu tunic had been replaced with masculine
pyjamas of violet silk. The pantaloons had the edges
turned up over a pair of white Turkish slippers into
which were tucked her bare feet. Over her heart there
was embroidered a design whose letters Ulysses was not
able to decipher. Above this device the point of her
handkerchief was sticking out of the pocket. Her opulent hair, twisted on top of her head and the voluptuous
curves that the silk was taking in certain parts of her
masculine attire were the only things that announced the
woman.

The captain forgot his breakfast, enthusiastic over
this novelty. She was a second Freya,—a page, an
adorable, freakish novelty. . . . But she repelled his
caresses, obliging him to seat himself.

She had entered with a questioning expression in her
eyes. She was feeling the disquietude of every woman
on her second amorous interview. She was trying to
guess his impressions, to convince herself of his gratitude, to be certain that the fascinations of the first hours
had not been dissipated during her absence.

While the sailor was again attacking his breakfast with
the familiarity of a lover who has achieved his ends and
no longer needs to hide and poetize his grosser necessities, she seated herself on an old *chaise longue,* lighting a
cigarette.

She cuddled into this seat, her crossed legs forming an

angle within the circle of one of her arms. Then she
leaned her head on her knees, and in this position
smoked a long time, with her glance fixed on the sea.
He guessed that she was about to say something interesting, something that was puckering her mental interior,
struggling to come out.

Finally she spoke with deliberation, without taking her
eyes off the gulf. From time to time she would stop
this contemplation in order to fasten her eyes on Ulysses,
measuring the effect of her words. He stopped occupying himself definitely with the breakfast tray, foreseeing
that something very important was coming.

"You have sworn that you will do for me whatever I
ask you to do. . . . You do not wish to lose me forever."

Ulysses protested. Lose her? . . . He could not live
without her.

"I know your former life; you have told me all about
it. . . . You know nothing about me and you ought to
know about me—now that I am really yours."

The sailor nodded his head; nothing could be more
just.

"I have deceived you, Ulysses. I am not Italian."

Ferragut smiled. If that was all the deception con-
sisted of! . . . From the day in which they had spoken
together for the first time going to Pæstum, he had
guessed that what she had told him about her nationality
was false.

"My mother was an Italian. I swear it. . . . But my
father was not. . . ."

She stopped a moment. The sailor listened to her
with interest, with his back turned to the table.

"I am a German woman and . . ."

CHAPTER VII

THE SIN OF ULYSSES

EVERY morning on awaking at the first streak of dawn, Toni felt a sensation of surprise and discouragement.

"Still in Naples!" he would say, looking through the port-hole of his cabin.

Then he would count over the days. Ten had passed by since the *Mare Nostrum,* entirely repaired, had anchored in the commercial harbor.

"Twenty-four hours more," the mate would add mentally.

And he would again take up his monotonous life, strolling over the empty and silent deck of the vessel, without knowing what to do, looking despondently at the other steamers which were moving their freighting antennæ, swallowing up boxes and bundles and beginning to send out through their chimneys the smoke announcing departure.

He suffered great remorse in calculating what the boat might have gained were it now under way. The advantage was all for the captain, but he could not avoid despairing over the money lost.

The necessity of communicating his impressions to somebody, of protesting in chorus against this lamentable inertia, used to impel him toward Caragol's dominions. In spite of their difference in rank, the first officer always treated the cook with affectionate familiarity.

"An abyss is separating us!" Toni would say gravely.

This "abyss" was a metaphor extracted from his reading of radical papers and alluded to the old man's fervid and simple beliefs. But their common affection for the captain, all being from the same land, and the employment of the Valencian dialect as the language of intimacy, made the two seek each other's company instinctively. For Toni, Caragol was the most congenial spirit aboard . . . after himself.

As soon as he stopped at the door of the galley, supporting his elbow in the doorway and obstructing the sunlight with his body, the old cook would reach out for his bottle of brandy, preparing a "refresco" or a "caliente" in honor of his visitor.

They would drink slowly, interrupting their relish of the liquor to lament together the immovability of the *Mare Nostrum*. They would count up the cost as though the boat were theirs. While it was being repaired, they had been able to tolerate the captain's conduct.

"The English always pay," Toni would say. "But now nobody is paying and the ship isn't earning anything, and we are spending every day. . . . About how much are we spending?"

And he and the cook would again calculate in detail the cost of keeping up the steamer, becoming terrified on reaching the total. One day without moving was costing more than the two men could earn in a month.

"This can't go on!" Toni would protest.

His indignation took him ashore several times in search of the captain. He was afraid to speak to him, considering it a lack of discipline to meddle in the management of the boat, so he invented the most absurd pretext in order to run afoul of Ferragut.

He looked with antipathy at the porter of the *albergo* because he always told him that the captain had just gone out. This individual with the air of a procurer must be greatly to blame for the immovability of the steamer; his heart told him so.

Because he couldn't come to blows with the man, and because he could not stand seeing him laugh deceitfully while watching him wait hour after hour in the vestibule, he took up his station in the street, spying on Ferragut's entrances and exits.

The three times that he did succeed in speaking with the captain, the result was always the same. The captain was as greatly delighted to see him as if he were an apparition from the past with whom he could communicate the joy of his overflowing happiness.

He would listen to his mate, congratulating himself that all was going so well on the ship, and when Toni, in stuttering tones, would venture to ask the date of departure, Ulysses would hide his uncertainty under a tone of prudence. He was awaiting a most valuable cargo; the longer they waited for it, the more money they were going to gain. . . . But his words were not convincing to Toni. He remembered the captain's protests fifteen days before over the lack of good cargo in Naples, and his desire to leave without loss of time.

Upon returning aboard, the mate would at once hunt Caragol, and both would comment on the changes in their chief. Toni had found him an entirely different man, with beard shaved, wearing his best clothes, and displaying in the arrangement of his person a most minute nicety, a decided wish to please. The rude pilot had even come to believe that he had detected, while talking to him, a certain feminine perfume like that of their blonde visitor.

This news was the most unbelievable of all for Caragol.

"Captain Ferragut perfumed! . . . The captain scented! . . . The wretch!" And he threw up his arms, his blind eyes seeking the brandy bottles and the oil flasks, in order to make them witnesses of his indignation.

The two men were entirely agreed as to the cause of their despair. She was to blame for it all; she who was going to hold the boat spellbound in this port until she knew when, with the irresistible power of a witch.

"Ah, these females! . . . The devil always follows after petticoats like a lap-dog. . . . They are the ruination of our life."

And the wrathful chastity of the cook continued hurling against womankind insults and curses equal to those of the first fathers of the church.

One morning the men washing down the deck sent a cry passing from stem to stern,—"The captain!" They saw him approaching in a launch, and the word was passed along through staterooms and corridors, giving new force to their arms, and lighting up their sluggish countenances. The mate came up on deck and Caragol stuck his head out through the door of his kitchen.

At the very first glance, Toni foresaw that something important was about to happen. The captain had a lively, happy air. At the same time, he saw in the exaggerated amiability of his smile a desire to conciliate them, to bring sweetly before them something which he considered of doubtful acceptation.

"Now you'll be satisfied," said Ferragut, giving his hand, "we are going to weigh anchor soon."

They entered the saloon. Ulysses looked around his boat with a certain strangeness as though returning to it after a long voyage. It looked different to him; certain details rose up before his eyes that had never attracted his attention before.

He recapitulated in a lightning cerebral flash all that had occurred in less than two weeks. For the first time he realized the great change in his life since Freya had come to the steamer in search of him.

He saw himself in his room in the hotel opposite her, dressed like a man, and looking out over the gulf while smoking.

"I am a German woman, and . . ."

Her mysterious life, even its most incomprehensible details, was soon to be explained.

She was a German woman in the service of her country. Modern war had aroused the nations *en masse;* it was not as in other centuries, a clash of diminutive, professional minorities that have to fight as a business. All vigorous men were now going to the battlefield, and the others were working in industrial centers which had been converted into workshops of war. And this general activity was also taking in the women who were devoting their labor to factories and hospitals, or their intelligence on the other side of the frontiers, to the service of their country.

Ferragut, surprised by this outright revelation, remained silent, but finally ventured to formulate his thought.

"According to that, you are a spy?" . . .

She heard the word with contempt. That was an antiquated term which had lost its primitive significance. Spies were those who in other times,—when only the professional soldiers took part in war,—had mixed themselves in the operations voluntarily or for money, surprising the preparations of the enemy. Nowadays, with the mobilization of the nations *en masse,* the old official spy—a contemptible and villainous creature, daring death for money—had practically disappeared. Nowadays there only existed patriots—anxious to work for their country, some with weapons in their hands, others availing themselves of their astuteness, or exploiting the qualities of their sex.

Ulysses was greatly disconcerted by this theory.

"Then the doctor? . . . he again questioned, guessing what the imposing dame must be.

Freya responded with an expression of enthusiasm and respect. Her friend was an illustrious patriot, a very learned woman, who was placing all her faculties at the service of her country. She adored her. She was her protector; she had rescued her in the most difficult moment of her existence.

"And the count?" Ferragut continued asking.

Here the woman made a gesture of reserve.

"He also is a great patriot, but do not let us talk about him."

In her words there were both respect and fear. He suspected that she did not wish to have anything to do with this haughty personage.

A long silence. Freya, as if fearing the effects of the captain's meditations, suddenly cut them short with her headlong chatter.

The doctor and she had come from Rome to take refuge in Naples, fleeing from the intrigues and mutterings of the capital. The Italians were squabbling among themselves; some were partisans of the war, others of neutrality; none of them wished to aid Germany, their former ally.

"We, who have protected them so much!" she exclaimed. "False and ungrateful race! . . ."

Her gestures and her words recalled to Ulysses' mind the image of the doctor, execrating the Italian country from a little window of the coach, the first day that they had talked together.

The two women were in Naples, whiling away their

tedious waiting with trips to neighboring places of interest, when they met the sailor.

"I have a very pleasant recollection of you," continued Freya. "I guessed from the very first instant that our friendship was going to terminate as it has terminated."

She read a question in his glance.

"I know what you are going to say to me. You wonder that I have made you wait so long, that I should have made you suffer so with my caprices. . . . It was because while I was loving you, at the same time I wished to separate myself from you. You represented an attraction and a hindrance. I feared to mix you up in my affairs. . . . Besides, I need to be free in order to dedicate myself wholly to the fulfillment of my mission."

There was another long pause. Freya's eyes were fixed on those of her lover with scrutinizing tenacity. She wished to sound the depths of his thoughts, to study the ripeness of her preparation—before risking the decisive blow. Her examination was satisfactory.

"And now that you know me," she said with painful slowness, "begone! . . . You cannot love me. I am a spy, just as you say,—a contemptible being. . . . I know that you will not be able to continue loving me after what I have revealed to you. Take yourself away in your boat, like the heroes of the legends; we shall not see each other more. All our intercourse will have been a beautiful dream. . . . Leave me alone. I am ignorant of what my own fate may be, but what is more important to me is your tranquillity."

Her eyes filled with tears. She threw herself face downward on the divan, hiding her face in her arms, while a sobbing outburst set all the adorable curves of her back a-tremble.

Touched by her grief, Ulysses at the same time admired Freya's shrewdness in divining all his thoughts. The voice of good counsel,—that prudent voice that always spoke in one-half of his brain whenever the captain found himself in difficult situations,—had begun to cry out, scandalized at the first revelations made by this woman:

"Flee, Ferragut! . . . Flee! You are in a bad fix. Do not agree to any relations with such people. What have you to do with the country of this adventuress? Why should you encounter dangers for a cause that is of no importance to you? What you wanted of her, you already have gotten. Be an egoist, my son!"

But the voice in his other mental hemisphere, that boasting and idiotic voice which always impelled him to embark on vessels bound to be shipwrecked, to be reckless of danger for the mere pleasure of putting his vigor to the proof, also gave him counsel. It was a villainous thing to abandon a woman. Only a coward would do such a thing. . . . And this German woman appeared to love him so much! . . .

And with his ardent, meridional exuberance, he embraced her and lifted her up, patting the loosened ringlets on her forehead, petting her like a sick child, and drinking in her tears with interminable kisses.

No; he would not abandon her. . . . He was more disposed to defend her from all her enemies. He did not know who her enemies were, but if she needed a man,—there he was. . . .

In vain his inner monitor reviled him while he was making such offers; he was compromising himself blindly; perhaps this adventure was going to be the most terrible in his history. . . . But in order to quiet his scruples, the other voice kept crying, "You are a gentleman; and a gentleman does not desert a lady, through fear, a

few hours after having won her affection. Forward,
Captain!"

An excuse of cowardly selfishness arose in his
thoughts, fabricated from one single piece. He was a
Spaniard, a neutral, in no way involved in the conflict of
the Central Powers. His second had often spoken to him
of solidarity of race, of Latin nations, of the necessity of
putting an end to militarism, of going to war in order
that there might be no more wars. . . . Mere vaporings
of a credulous reader! He was neither English nor
French. Neither was he German; but the woman he
loved was, and he was not going to give her up for any
antagonisms in which he was not concerned.

Freya must not weep. Her lover affirmed repeatedly
that he wished to live forever at her side, that he was
not thinking of abandoning her because of what she had
said: and he even pledged his word of honor that he
would aid her in everything that she might consider possible and worthy of him.

Thus Captain Ulysses Ferragut impetuously decided
his destiny.

When his beloved again took him to the doctor's home,
he was received by her just as though he really belonged
to the family. She no longer had to hide her nationality. Freya simply called her *Frau Doktor* and she, with
the glib enthusiasm of the professor, finally succeeded
in converting the sailor, explaining to him the right and
reason of her country's entrance into war with half of
Europe.

Poor Germany had to defend herself. The Kaiser
was a man of peace in spite of the fact that for many
years he had been methodically preparing a military force
capable of crushing all humanity. All the other nations
had driven him to it; they had all been the first in aggression. The insolent French, long before the war, had

been sending clouds of aeroplanes over German cities, bombarding them.

Ferragut blinked with surprise. This was news to him. It must have occurred while he was on the high seas. The verbose positiveness of the doctor did not permit any doubt whatever. . . . Besides, that lady ought to know better than those who lived on the ocean.

Then had arisen the English provocation. . . . Like a traitor of melodrama, the British government had been preparing the war for a long time, not wishing to show its hand until the last moment; and Germany, lover of peace, had had to defend herself from this enemy, the worst one of all.

"God will punish England!" affirmed the doctor, looking at Ulysses.

And he not wishing to defraud her of her expectations, gallantly nodded his head. . . . For all he cared, God might punish England.

But in expressing himself in such a way, he felt himself agitated by a new duality. The English had been good comrades; he remembered agreeably his voyages as an official aboard the British boats. At the same time, their increasing power, invisible to the men on shore, monstrous for those who were living on the sea, had been producing in him a certain irritation. He was accustomed to find them either as dominators of all the seas, or else solidly installed on all the strategic and commercial coasts.

The doctor, as though guessing the necessity of arousing his hatred of the great enemy, appealed to his historical memories: Gibraltar, stolen by the English; the piracies of Drake; the galleons of America seized with methodical regularity by the British fleets; the landings on the coast of Spain that in other centuries had perturbed the life of the peninsula. England at the beginning of her greatness in the reign of Elizabeth, was the size of Belgium; if she had made herself one of the great powers, it was at the cost of the Spaniards and then of Holland, even dominating the entire world. And the doctor spoke in English and with so much vehemence about England's evil deeds against Spain that the impressionable sailor ended by saying spontaneously:

"May God punish her!"

But just here reappeared the Mediterranean navigator, the complicated and contradictory Ulysses. He suddenly remembered the repairs on his vessel that must be paid for by England.

"May God punish them . . . but may He wait a little bit!" he murmured in his thoughts.

The imposing professor became greatly exasperated when speaking of the land in which she was living.

"Mandolin players! Bandits!" she always cried when referring to the Italians.

How much they owed to Germany! The Emperor Wilhelm had been a father to them. All the world knew that! . . . And yet when the war was breaking out, they were going to refuse to follow their old friends. Now German diplomacy must busy itself, not to keep them at her side, but to prevent their going with the adversary. Every day she was receiving news from Rome. She had hoped that Italy might keep herself neutral, but who could trust the word of such people? . . . And she repeated her wrathful insults.

The sailor immediately adapted himself to this home, as though it were his own. On the few occasions that Freya separated herself from him, he used to go in search of her in the salon of the imposing dame who was now assuming toward Ulysses the air of a good-natured mother-in-law.

In various visits he met the count. This taciturn

personage would offer his hand instinctively though keeping a certain distance between them. Ulysses now knew his real nationality, and he knew that he knew it. But the two kept up the fiction of Count Kaledine, Russian diplomat, and this man exacted respect from every one in the doctor's dwelling. Ferragut, devoted to his amorous selfishness, was not permitting himself any investigation, adjusting himself to the hints dropped by the two women.

He had never known such happiness. He was experiencing the great sensuousness of one who finds himself seated at table in a well-warmed dining-room and sees through the window the tempestuous sea tossing a bark that is struggling against the waves.

The newsboys were crying through the streets terrible battles in the center of Europe; cities were burning under bombardment; every twenty-four hours thousands upon thousands of human beings were dying. . . . And he was not reading anything, not wishing to know anything. He was continuing his existence as though he were living in a paradisiacal felicity. Sometimes, while waiting for Freya, his memory would gloat over her wonderful physical charm, the refinements and fresh sensations which his passion was enjoying; at other times, the actual embrace with its ecstasy blotted out and suppressed all unpleasant possibilities.

Something, nevertheless, suddenly jerked him from his amorous egoism, something that was overshadowing his visage, furrowing his forehead with wrinkles of preoccupation, and making him go aboard his vessel.

When seated in the large cabin of his ship opposite his mate, he leaned his elbows on the table and commenced to chew on a great cigar that had just gone out.

"We're going to start very soon," he repeated with

visible abstraction. "You will be glad, Toni; I believe that you will be delighted."

Toni remained impassive. He was waiting for something more. The captain in starting on a voyage had
always told him the port of destiny and the special nature of the cargo. Therefore, noting that Ferragut did
not want to add anything more, he ventured to ask:

"Is it to Barcelona that we are going?"

Ulysses hesitated, looking toward the door, as though
fearing to be overheard. Then he leaned over toward
Toni.

The voyage was going to be one without any danger,
but one which must be shrouded in mystery.

"I am counting on you, because you know all my
affairs, because I consider you as one of my family."

The pilot did not appear to be touched with this sample
of confidence. He still remained impassive, though
within him all the uneasiness that had been agitating him
in former days was reawakening.

The captain continued talking. These were war times
and it was necessary to take advantage of them. For
those two it would not be any novelty to transport cargoes of military material. Once he had carried from
Europe arms and munitions for a revolution in South
America. Toni had recounted to him his adventures in
the Gulf of California, in command of a little schooner
which had served as a transport to the insurrectionists
of the southern provinces in the revolt against the Mexi-
can government.

But the mate, while nodding his head affirmatively, was
at the same time looking at him with questioning eyes.
What were they going to transport on this trip? . . .

"Toni, it is not a matter of artillery nor of guns.
Neither is it an affair of munitions. . . . It is a short

and well-paid job that will make us go very little out of our way on our return to Barcelona."

He stopped himself in his confidences, feeling a curious hesitation and finally he added, lowering his voice:

"The Germans are paying for it! . . . We are going to supply their Mediterranean submarines with petrol."

Contrary to all Ferragut's expectations, his second did not make any gesture of surprise. He remained as impassive as if this news were actually incomprehensible to him. Then he smiled lightly, shrugging his shoulders as though he had heard something absurd. . . . The Germans, perhaps, had submarines in the Mediterranean? It was likely, was it, that one of these navigating machines would be able to make the long crossing from the North Sea to the Strait of Gibraltar? . . .

He knew all about the great atrocities that the submarines were causing in the vicinity of England, but in a greatly reduced zone in the limited radius of action of which they were capable. The Mediterranean, fortunately for the merchant vessels, was quite beyond the range of their treacherous lying-in-wait.

Ferragut interrupted with his meridional vehemence. Beside himself with passion, he was already beginning to express himself as though the doctor were speaking through his mouth.

"You are referring to the submarines, Toni, to the little submarines that were in existence at the beginning of the war—little grasshoppers of fragile steel that moved with great difficulty when on a level with the water and might be overwhelmed at the slightest shock. . . . But to-day there is something more: there is a submersible that is like a submarine protected by a ship's hull which is able to go hidden between the two waters and, at the same time, can navigate over the surface better than a torpedo-boat. . . . You have no idea what these

Germans are capable of! They are a great nation, the finest in the world! . . ."

And with impulsive exaggeration, he insisted in proclaiming German greatness and its inventive spirit as though he had some share in this mechanical and destructive glory.

Then he added confidentially, placing his hand on Toni's arm:

"I'm going to tell it only to you: you are the only person who knows the secret, aside from those who have told it to me. . . . The German submersibles are going to enter the Mediterranean. We are going to meet them in order to renew their supplies of oil and combustibles."

He became silent, looking fixedly at his subordinate, and smiling in order to conquer his scruples.

For two seconds he did not know what to expect. Toni was remaining pensive with downcast eyes. Then, little by little, he drew himself erect, abandoned his seat, and said simply:

"No!"

Ulysses also left his revolving chair with the impulsiveness of surprise. "No? . . . And why not?"

He was the captain and they all ought to obey him. For that reason he was responsible for the boat, for the life of its crew, for the fate of the cargo. Besides, he was the proprietor; no one exceeded him in command; his power was unlimited. Through friendly affection and custom, he had consulted his mate, making him share in his secrets and here Toni, with an ingratitude never seen before, was daring to rebel. . . . What did this mean? . . .

But the mate, instead of giving any explanation, merely confined himself to answering, each time more obstinately and wrathfully:

"No! . . . No!"

"But why not?" insisted Ferragut, waxing impatient and in a voice trembling with anger.

Toni, without losing energy in his negatives, was hesitating,—confused, bewildered, scratching his beard, and lowering his eyes in order to reflect better.

He did not know just how to explain himself. He envied his captain's facility in finding just the right word. The simplest of his ideas suffered terribly before coming anxiously from his mouth. . . . But, finally, little by little, between his stutterings, he managed to express his hatred of those monsters of modern industry which were dishonoring the sea with their crimes.

Each time that he had read in the newspapers of their exploits in the North Sea a wave had passed over the conscience of this simple, frank and upright man. They were accustomed to attack treacherously hidden in the water, disguising their long and murderous eyes like the visual antennæ of the monsters of the deep. This aggression without danger appeared to revive in his soul the outraged souls of a hundred Mediterranean ancestors, cruel and piratical perhaps, but who, nevertheless, had sought the enemy face to face with naked breast, battle-axe in hand, and the barbed harpoon for boarding ship as their only means of struggle.

"If they would torpedo only the armed vessels!" he added. "War is a form of savagery, and it is necessary to shut the eyes to its treacherous blows, accepting them as glorious achievements. . . . But there is something more than that: you know it well. They sink merchant vessels, and passenger ships carrying women, carrying little children. . . ."

His weather-beaten cheeks assumed the color of a baked brick. His eyes flashed with a bluish splendor. He was feeling the same wrath that he had experienced when reading the accounts of the first torpedoing of the great transatlantic steamer on the coast of England.

He was seeing the defenseless and peaceable throng crowding to the boats that were capsizing; the women throwing themselves into the sea with children in their arms; all the deadly confusion of a catastrophe. . . . Then the submarine arising to contemplate its work; the Germans grouped on the decks of dripping steel, laughing and joking, satisfied with the rapid result of their labors; and for a distance of many miles the sea was filled with black bulks dragged slowly along by the waves—men floating on their backs, immovable, with their glassy eyes fixed on the sky; children with their fair hair clinging like masks to their livid face; corpses of mothers pressing to their bosom with cold rigidity little corpses of babies, assassinated before they could even know what life might mean.

When reading the account of these crimes, Toni had naturally thought of his own wife and children, imagining what their condition might have been on that steamer, experiencing the same fate as its innocent passengers. This imagination had made him feel so intense a wrath that he even mistrusted his own self-control on the day that he should again encounter German sailors in any port. . . . And Ferragut, an honorable man, a good captain whose praises every one was sounding, could he possibly aid in transplanting such horrors as these to the Mediterranean? . . .

Poor Toni! . . . He did not know how to express himself properly, but the very possibility that his beloved sea might witness such crimes gave new vehemence to his indignation. The soul of Doctor Ferragut appeared to be reviving in this rude Mediterranean sailor. He had never seen the white Amphitrite, but he trembled for her with a religious fervor, without even knowing her. Was

the luminous blue from which had arisen the early gods
to be dishonored by the oily spot that would disclose
assassination *en masse!* . . . Were the rosy strands from
whose foam Venus had sprung to receive clusters of
corpses, impelled by the waves! . . . Were the sea-gull
wings of the fishing-boats to flee panic-stricken before
those gray sharks of steel! . . . Were his family and
neighbors to be terrified, on awakening, by this floating
cemetery washed to their doors during the night! . . .

He was thinking all this, he was seeing it; but not
succeeding in expressing it, so he limited himself to insisting upon his protest:

"No! . . . I won't tolerate it in our sea!"

Ferragut, in spite of his impetuous character, now
adopted a conciliatory tone like that of a father who
wishes to convince his scowling and stubborn son.

The German submersibles would confine themselves,
in the Mediterranean, to military actions only. There
was no danger of their attacking defenseless barks
as in the northern seas. Their drastic exploits there had
been imposed by circumstances, by the sincere desire of
terminating the war as quickly as possible, by giving
terrifying and unheard-of blows.

"I assure you that in our sea there will be nothing of
that sort. People who ought to know have told me so.
. . . If that had not been the case, I should not have
promised to give them aid."

He affirmed this several times in good faith, with absolute confidence in the people who had given him their
promise.

"They will sink, if they can, the ships of the Allies
that are in the Dardanelles. But what does that matter
to us? . . . That is war! When we were carrying cannons and guns to the revolutionists in South America

we did not trouble ourselves about the use which they might make of them, did we?"

Toni persisted in his negative.

"It is not the same thing. . . . I don't know how to express myself, but it is not the same. There, cannon can be answered by cannon. He who strikes also receives blows. . . . But to aid the submarines is a very different thing. They attack, hidden, without danger. . . . And I, for my part, do not like treachery."

Finally his mate's insistence exasperated Ferragut, exhausting his enforced good nature.

"We will say no more about it," he said haughtily. "I am the captain and I command as I see fit. . . . I have given my promise, and I am not going to break it just to please you. . . . We have finished."

Toni staggered as though he had just received a blow on the breast. His eyes shone again, becoming moist. After a long period of reflection, he held out his shaggy right hand to the captain.

"Good-by, Ulysses! . . ."

He could not obey, and a sailor who takes disrespectful exception to the orders of his chief must leave the ship. In no other boat could he ever live as in the *Mare Nostrum*. Perhaps he might not get another job, perhaps the other captains might not like him, considering him to have grown too habituated to excessive familiarity. But, if it should be necessary, he would again become the skipper of a little coast-trader. . . . Good-by! He would not sleep on board that night.

Ferragut was very indignant, even yelling angrily:

"But, don't be such a barbarian! . . . What a stubborn fool you are! . . . What do these exaggerated scruples amount to? . . ."

Then he smiled malignly and said in a low tone, "You

know already what we know, and I know very well that in your youth you carried contraband."

Toni drew himself up haughtily. Now it was he who was indignant.

"I have carried contraband, yes. And what is there astonishing about that? . . . Your grandparents did the same thing. There is not a single honorable sailor on our sea who has not committed this little offense. . . . Who is the worse for that? . . ."

The only one who could complain was the State, a vague personality whose whereabouts and place nobody knew and who daily experienced a million of similar violations. In the custom-houses Toni had seen the richest tourists eluding the vigilance of the employees in order to evade an insignificant payment. Every one down in his heart was a smuggler. . . . Besides, thanks to these fraudulent navigators, the poor were able to smoke better and more cheaply. Whom were they assassinating with their business? . . . How did Ferragut dare to compare these evasions of the law which never did anybody any harm with the job of aiding submarine pirates in continuing their crimes? . . .

The captain, disarmed by this simple logic, now appealed to his powers of persuasion.

"Toni, at least you will do it for me. Do it for my sake. We shall continue friends as we have always been. On some other occasion I'll sacrifice myself. Think. . . . I have given my word of honor."

And the mate, although much touched by his pleadings, replied dolefully:

"I cannot. . . . I cannot!"

He was anxious to say something more to round out his thought, and added:

"I'm a *Republican.* . . ."

This profession of faith he brought forward as an

insurmountable barrier, striking himself at the same time on the breast, in order to prove the hardness of the obstacle.

Ulysses felt tempted to laugh, as he had always done, at Toni's political affirmations. But the situation was not one for joking, and he continued talking in the hope of convincing him.

He had always loved liberty and been on the side opposed to despotism! . . . England was the great tyrant of the sea; she had provoked the war in order to strengthen her jurisdiction and if she should achieve the victory, her haughtiness would have no limit. Poor Germany had done nothing more than defend herself. . . . Ferragut repeated all that he had heard in the doctor's home, winding up in a tone of reproach:

"And are you on the side of the English, Toni? You, a man of advanced ideas? . . ."

The pilot scratched his beard with an expression of perplexity, searching for the elusive words. He knew what he ought to say. He had read it in the writings of gentlemen who knew quite as much as his captain; besides, he had thought a great deal about this matter in his solitary pacing on the bridge.

"I am where I ought to be. I am with France. . . ."

He expressed this thought sluggishly, with stutterings and half-formed words. France was the country of the great Revolution, and for that reason he considered it as something to which he belonged, uniting its faith with that of his own person.

"And I do not need to say more. As to England . . ."

Here he made a pause like one who rests and gathers all his forces together for a difficult leap.

"There always has to be one nation on top," he continued. "We hardly amount to anything at present and, according to what I have read, Spain was once mistress of the entire world for a century and a half. Once we were everywhere; now we are in the soup. Then came France's turn. Now it is England's. . . . It doesn't bother me that one nation places itself above the rest. The thing that interests me is what that nation represents,—the fashion it will set."

Ferragut was concentrating his attention in order to comprehend what Toni wished to say.

"If England triumphs," the pilot continued, *"Liberty* will be the fashion. What does their haughtiness amount to with me, if there always has to be one dominating nation? . . . The nations will surely copy the victor. . . . England, so they say, is really a republic that prefers to pay for the luxury of a king for its grand ceremonials. With her, peace would be inevitable, the government managed by the people, the disappearance of the great armies, the true civilization. If Germany triumphs, we shall live as though we were in barracks. Militarism will govern everything. We shall bring up our children, not that they may enjoy life, but that they may become soldiers and go forth to kill from their very youth. Might as the only Right, that is the German method,—a return to barbarous times under the mask of civilization."

He was silent an instant, as though mentally recapitulating all that he had said in order to convince himself that he had not left any forgotten idea in the corners of his cranium. Again he struck himself on the breast. Yes, he was where he ought to be, and it was impossible for him to obey his captain.

"I am a Republican! . . . I am a *Republican!"* he repeated energetically, as though having said that, there was nothing more to add.

Ferragut, not knowing how to answer this simple and solid enthusiasm, gave way to his temper.

"Get out, you brute! . . . I don't want to see you again, ungrateful wretch! I shall do the thing alone; I don't need you. It is enough for me to take my boat where it pleases me and to follow out my own pleasure. Be off with all the old lies with which you have crammed your cranium. . . . You blockhead!"

His wrath made him fall into his armchair, swinging his back toward the mate, hiding his head in his hands, in order to make him understand that with this scornful silence everything between them had come to an end.

Toni's eyes, growing constantly more distended and glassy, finally released a tear. . . . To separate thus, after a fraternal life in which the months were like years! . . .

He advanced timidly in order to take possession of one of Ferragut's soft, inert, inexpressive hands. Its cold contact made him hesitate. He felt inclined to yield. . . . But immediately he blotted out this weakness with a firm, crisp tone:

"Good-by, Ulysses! . . ."

The captain did not answer, letting him go away without the slightest word of farewell. The mate was already near the door when he stopped to say to him with a sad and affectionate expression:

"Do not fear that I shall say anything about this to anybody. . . . Everything remains between us two. I will make up some excuse in order that those aboard will not be surprised at my going."

He hesitated as though he were afraid to appear importunate, but he added:

"I advise you not to undertake that trip. I know how our men feel about these matters; you can't rely upon them. Even Uncle Caragol, who only concerns himself with his galley, will criticize you. . . . Perhaps they will obey you because you are the captain, but when they go ashore, you will not be the master of their silence. . . . Believe me; do not attempt it. You are going to disgrace yourself. You well know for what cause. . . . Good-by, Ulysses!"

When the captain raised his head the pilot had already disappeared and solitude, with its deadly burden, soon weighed upon his thoughts. He felt afraid to carry out his plans without Toni's aid. It appeared to him that the chain of authority which united him to his men had been broken. The mate was carrying away a part of the prestige that Ferragut exercised over the crew. How could he explain his disappearance on the eve of an illegal voyage which exacted such great secrecy? How could he rely upon the silence of everybody? . . . He remained pensive a long time, then suddenly leaping up from his armchair, he went out on deck, shouting to the seamen:

"Where is Don Antonio? Go find him. Call him for me."

"*Don Antoni!* . . . *Don Antoni!* . . ." replied a string of voices from poop to prow, while Uncle Caragol's head poked itself out of the door of his dominions.

"*Don Antoni*" appeared through the hatchway. He had been going all over the boat, after taking leave of his captain. Ferragut received him with averted face, avoiding his glance, and with a complex and contradictory gesture. He felt angry at being vanquished and the shame of weakness yet, allied to these sensations, was the instinctive gratitude which one experiences upon being freed from an unwise step by a violent hand which mistreats and saves.

"You are to remain, Toni!" he said in a dull voice. "There is nothing to say. I will redeem my word as best I can. . . . To-morrow you shall know certainly what we are going to do."

The solar face of Caragol was beaming beatifically
without seeing anything, without hearing anything. He
had suspected something serious in the captain's arrival,
his long interview alone with the mate, and the departure
of the latter passing silent and scowling before the door
of his galley. Now the same presentiment advised him
that a reconciliation between the two men whose figures
he could only distinguish confusedly, must have taken
place. Blessed be the Christ of the Grao! . . . And
upon learning that the captain would remain aboard until
afternoon, he set himself to the confection of one of his
masterly rice-dishes in order to solemnize the return of
peace.

A little before sunset Ulysses again found himself with
his mistress in the hotel. He had returned to land, nervous and uneasy. His uneasiness made him fear this interview while at the same time he wished it.

"Out with it! I am not a child to feel such fears,"
he said to himself upon entering his room and finding
Freya awaiting him.

He spoke to her with the brusqueness of one who
wishes to conclude everything quickly. . . . "I could not
undertake the service that the doctor asked. I take back
my word. The mate on board would not consent to
it."

Her wrath burst forth without any finesse, with the
frankness of intimancy. She always hated Toni. "Hideous old faun! . . ." From the very first moment she
had suspected that he would prove an enemy.

"But you are master of your own boat," she continued. "You can do what you want to, and you don't
need his permission to sail."

When Ulysses furthermore said that he was not sure
of his crew either, and that the voyage was impossible,
the woman again became furious at him. She appeared

to have grown suddenly ten years older. To the sailor
she seemed to have another face, of an ashy pallor, with
furrowed brows, eyes filled with angry tears, and a light
foam in the corners of her mouth.

"Braggart. . . . Fraud. . . . Southerner! Meridional!"

Ulysses tried to calm her. It might be possible to find
another boat. He would try to help them find another.
He was going to send the *Mare Nostrum* to await him
in Barcelona, and he himself would stay in Naples, just
as long as she wished him to.

"Buffoon! . . . And I believed in you! And I yielded
myself to you, believing you to be a hero, believing your
offer of sacrifice to be the truth! . . ."

She marched off, furious, giving the door a spiteful
slam.

"She is going to see the doctor," thought Ferragut.
"It is all over."

He regretted the loss of this woman, even after having seen her in her tragic and fleeting ugliness. At the
same time, the injurious word, the cutting insults with
which she had accompanied her departure caused sharp
pain. He already was tired and sick of hearing himself
called "meridional," as though it were a stigma.

Yet he rather relished his enforced happiness, the
sensation of false liberty which every enamored person
feels after a quarrelsome break. "Now to live again!
. . ." He wished to return at once to the ship, but feared
a revival of the memories evoked by silence. It would
be better to remain in Naples, to go to the theater, to
trust to the luck of some chance encounter just as when
he used to come ashore for a few hours. The next
morning he would leave the hotel, with all his baggage,
and before sunset he would be sailing the open sea.

He ate outside of the *albergo*, and he passed the night
elbowing women in cabarets where an insipid variety

show served as a pretext to disguise the baser object. The recollection of Freya, fresh-looking and gay, kept rising between him and those painted mouths every time that they smiled upon him, trying to attract his attention.

At one o'clock in the morning he went up the hotel stairway, surprised at seeing a ray of light underneath the door of his room. He entered. . . . She was awaiting him—reading, tranquil and smiling. Her face, refreshed and retouched with juvenile color, did not show the slightest trace of the morning's spasmodic outbreak. She was clad in pyjamas.

Seeing Ulysses enter, she arose with outstretched arms.

"Tell me that you are not still angry with me! . . . Tell me that you will forgive me! . . . I was very naughty toward you this afternoon, I admit it."

She was embracing him, rubbing her mouth against his neck with a feline purr. Before the captain could respond she continued with a childish voice:

"My shark! My sea-wolf!—who has made me wait all these hours! . . . Swear to me that you have not been unfaithful! . . . I can perceive at once the trace of another woman."

Sniffing his beard and face, her mouth approached the sailor's.

"No, you have not been unfaithful. . . . I still find my own perfume. . . . Oh, Ulysses! My hero! . . ."

She kissed him with that absorbing kiss, which appeared to take all the life from him, obscuring his thoughts and annulling his will-power, making him tremble from head to foot. All was forgotten,—offenses, slights, plans of departure. . . . And, as usual, he fell, conquered by that vampire caress.

In the darkness he heard Freya's gentle voice. She

was recapitulating what they had not said, but what the two were thinking of at the same time.

"The doctor believes that you ought to remain. Let your boat go with its hideous old faun, who is nothing but a drawback. You are to remain here, on land. . . . You will be able to do us a great favor. . . . You know you will; you will remain? . . . What happiness!"

Ferragut's destiny was to obey this idolized and dominating voice. . . . And the following morning Toni saw him approaching the vessel with an air of command which admitted no opposition. The *Mare Nostrum* must set forth at once for Barcelona. He would entrust the command to his mate. He would join it just as soon as he could finish certain affairs that were detaining him in Naples.

Toni opened his eyes with a gesture of surprise. He wished to respond, but stood with his mouth open, not venturing to speak a single word. . . . This was his captain, and he was not going to permit any objections to his orders.

"Very well," he said finally. "I only ask you that you return as soon as possible to take up your command. . . . Do not forget what we are losing while the boat is tied up."

A few days after the departure of the steamer Ulysses radically changed his method of living.

Freya no longer wished to continue lodging in the hotel. Attacked by a sudden modesty, the curiosity and smiles of the tourists and servants were annoying her. Besides, she wished to enjoy complete liberty in her love affairs. Her friend, who was like a mother to her, would facilitate her desire. The two would live in her house.

Ferragut was greatly surprised to discover the extreme size of the apartment occupied by the doctor. Beyond her salon there was an endless number of rooms, somewhat dismantled and without furniture, a labyrinth of partitioned walls and passageways, in which the captain was always getting lost, and having to appeal to Freya for aid; all the doors of the stair-landings that appeared unrelated to the green screen of the office were so many other exits from the same dwelling.

The lovers were lodged in the extreme end, as though living in a separate house. One of the doors was for them only. They occupied a grand salon, rich in moldings and gildings and poor in furniture. Three armchairs, an old divan, a table littered with papers, toilet articles and eatables, and a rather narrow couch in one of the corners, were all the conveniences of this new establishment.

In the street it was hot, and yet they were shivering with cold in this magnificent room into which the sun's rays had never penetrated. Ulysses attempted to make a fire on a hearth of colored marble, big as a monument, but he had to desist half-suffocated by the smoke. In order to reach the doctor's apartment they had to pass through a row of numberless connecting rooms, long since abandoned.

They lived as newly-wed people, in an amorous solitude, commenting with childish hilarity on the defects of their quarters and the thousand little inconveniences of material existence. Freya would prepare breakfast on a small alcohol stove, defending herself from her lover, who believed himself more skilled than she in culinary affairs. A sailor knows something of everything.

The mere suggestion of hunting a servant for their most common needs irritated the German maiden.

"Never! . . . Perhaps she might be a spy!"

And the word "spy" on her lips took on an expression of immense scorn.

The doctor was absent on frequent trips and Karl

the employee in the study, was the one who received visitors. Sometimes he would pass through the row of deserted rooms in order to ask some information of Freya, and she would follow him out, deserting her lover for a few moments.

Left to himself, Ulysses would suddenly realize the dual nature of his personality. Then the man he was before that meeting in Pompeii would assert himself, and he would see his vessel and his home in Barcelona.

"What have you got yourself into?" he would ask himself remorsefully. "How is all this affair ever going to turn out? . . ."

But at the sound of her footsteps in the next room, on perceiving the atmospheric wave produced by the displacement of her adorable body, this second person would fold itself back and a dark curtain would fall over his memory, leaving visible only the actual reality.

With the beatific smile of an opium-smoker, he would accept the impetuous caress of her lips, the entwining of her arms, strangling him like marble boas.

"Ulysses, my master! . . . The moments that separate me from you weigh upon me like centuries!"

He, on the other hand, had lost all notion of time. The days were all confused in his mind, and he had to keep asking in order to realize their passing. After a week passed in the doctor's home, he would sometimes suppose that the sweet sequestration had been but forty-eight hours long, at others that nearly a month had flitted by.

They went out very little. The mornings slipped away insensibly between the late awakening and preparations for a breakfast made by themselves. If it was necessary to go after some eatable forgotten the day before, it was she who took charge of the expedition, wishing to keep him from all contact with outside life.

The afternoons were afternoons of the harem, passed upon the divan or stretched on the floor. In a low voice she would croon Oriental songs, incomprehensible and mysterious. Suddenly she would spring up impetuously like a spring that is unwound, like a serpent that uncoils itself, and would begin to dance, almost without moving her feet, waving her lithe limbs. . . . And he would smile with stupefied infatuation, extending a right hand toward an Arabian tabaret, covered with bottles.

Freya took even greater care of the supply of liquor than of things to eat. The sailor was half-drunk, but with a drunkenness wisely tempered that never went beyond the rose-colored period. But he was so happy! . . .

They dined outside the house. Sometimes their excursions were at midday and they would go to the restaurants of Posilipo or Vomero, the very places that he had known when he was a hopeless suppliant, and which saw him now with her hanging on his arm, with a proud air of possession. If nightfall surprised them, they would hastily betake themselves to a café in the interior of the city, a beer-garden whose proprietor always spoke to Freya in German in a low voice.

Whenever the doctor was in Naples she would seat herself at their table, with the air of a good mother who is receiving her daughter and son-in-law. Her scrutinizing glasses appeared to be searching Ferragut's very soul as though doubtful of his fidelity. Then she would become more affectionate in the course of these banquets composed of cold meats with a great abundance of drinks, in the German style. For her, love was the most beautiful thing in existence, and she could not look upon these two enamored ones without a mist of emotion blurring the crystals of her second eyes.

"Ah, Captain! . . . How much she loves you! . .

Do not disappoint her; obey her in every respect. . . .
She adores you."

Frequently she returned from her trips in evident bad
humor. Ulysses surmised that she had been in Rome.
At other times she would appear very gay, with an
ironic and tedious gayety. "The mandolin-strummers appear to be coming to their senses. Germany is constantly
receiving more support from their ranks. In Rome the
'German propaganda' is distributed among millions."

One night emotion overcame her rugged sensibilities.
She had brought back from her trip a portrait which
she pressed lovingly against her vast bosom before showing it.

"Look at it," she said to the two. "It is the hero
whose name brings tears of enthusiasm to all Germans.
. . What an honor for our family!"

Pride made her hasty, snatching the photograph from
Freya's hand in order to pass it on to Ulysses. He saw
a naval official rather mature, surrounded by a numerous
family. Two children with long blonde hair were seated
on his knees. Five youngsters, chubby and tow-headed,
appeared at his feet with crossed legs, lined up in the
order of their ages. Near his shoulder extended a double
line of brawny young girls with coronal braids imitating
the coiffures of empresses and grand duchesses. . . . Behind these, proudly erect, was his virtuous and prolific
companion, aged by too continuous maternity.

Ferragut contemplated this patriotic warrior very de-
liberately. He had the face of a kindly person with
clear eyes and grayish, pointed beard. He almost inspired
a tender compassion by his overwhelming duties as a
father.

Meanwhile the doctor's voice was chanting the glories
of her relative.

"A hero! . . . Our gracious Kaiser has decorated him

with the Iron Cross. They have given him honorary
citizenship in various capitals. . . . May God punish
England !"

And she extolled this patriarch's unheard-of exploit
He was the commandant of the submarine that had torpedoed one of the greatest English transatlantic steamers
Out of the twelve hundred passengers from New York
more than eight hundred were drowned. . . . Women
and children had gone down in the general destruction.

Freya, more quick-witted than the doctor, read Ulysses' thoughts in his eyes. . . . He was now surveying
with astonishment the photograph of this official surrounded with his biblical progeny, like a good-natured
burgher. And a man who appeared so complacent had
committed such butchery without encountering any danger whatever !—hidden in the water with his eye glued
to the periscope, he had coldly ordered the sending of
a torpedo against this floating and defenseless city ? . .

"Such is war," said Freya.

"Of course it is war !" retorted the doctor as if offended at the propitiatory tone of her friend. "And it
is our right also. They blockade us, and they wish our
women and children to die of hunger, and so we kill
theirs."

The captain felt obliged to protest, in spite of the
hidden nudges and gestures of his mistress. The doctor
had many times told him that, thanks to her organization, Germany could never know hunger, and that she
could exist years and years on the consumption of her
own product.

"That is so," replied the dame, "but war has to make
itself ferocious, implacable, in order that it may not
last so long. It is our human duty to terrify the

nemy with a cruelty beyond what they are able to
magine."

The sailor slept badly that night, evidently greatly
roubled. Freya guessed the presence of something
eyond the influence of her caresses. The follow-
ng day his pensive reserve continued and she, well
nowing the cause, tried to dissipate it with her
words. . . .

The torpedoing of defenseless steamers was only made
n the coast of England. They had to cut short, cost
what it might, the source of supplies for that hated
sland.

"In the Mediterranean nothing of that kind will ever
occur. I can assure you of that. . . . The submarines
will attack battleships only."

And, as if fearing a reappearance of Ulysses' scru-
les, she redoubled her seductions on their afternoons
f voluptuous imprisonment. She was constantly de-
ising new fascinations, that her lover might never be
urfeited. He, on his part, came to believe that he was
iving with several women at the same time, like an
Oriental personage. Freya upon multiplying her charms,
ad to do no more than to swing around on herself,
howing a new facet of her past existence.

The sentiment of jealousy, the bitterness of not hav-
ng been the first and only one, rejuvenated the sailor's
passion, alleviating the tedium of satiety, yet at the same
ime giving to her caresses an acrid, desperate and at-
ractive relish due to his enforced fraternity with un-
nown predecessors.

Desisting from her enchantments, she came and went
hrough the salon, sure of her beauty, proud of her firm
nd superb physique, which had not yielded in the slight-
st degree to the passing of the years. A couple of
olored shawls served as her transparent clothing.

Waving them as rainbow shafts around her marble-whit body, she used to interpret the priestess dances to th terrible Siva that she had learned in Java.

Suddenly the chill of the room would begin biting i awaking her from her tropical dream. With a fina bound, she sought refuge in his arms.

"Oh, my beloved Argonaut! . . . My shark!"

She threw herself on the sailor's breast, stroking hi beard, and pushing him so as to edge in on the divas which was too narrow for the two.

She guessed at once the cause of his furrowed brow the listlessness with which he responded to her caresses the gloomy fire that was smouldering in his eyes. Th exotic dance had made him recall her past and in orde to regain her sway over him, subjecting him in swee passivity, she sprang up from the divan, running abou the room.

"What shall I give to my bad little man, in order t make him smile a bit? . . . What shall I do in order t make him forget his wrong ideas? . . ."

Perfumes were her pet fad. As she herself used t say, it was possible for her to do without eating bu never without the richest and most expensive essences In that scantily furnished room, like the interior of a army and navy supply store, the cut glass flasks wit gold and nickel stoppers, protruded among the clothin and papers, and stood up in the corners denouncing th forgetfulness of their enchanting breath.

"Take it! Take it!"

And she sprinkled the precious perfumes as thoug they were water on Ferragut's hair, over his curlec beard, advising the sailor to close his eyes in order no to be blinded by this crazy baptism.

Anointed and fragrant as an Asiatic despot, the strong Ulysses would sometimes revolt against this effeminate

ess. At others, he would accept it with the delight of
new pleasure.

Suddenly a window-shutter would seem to swing open
n his imagination, and, passing by this luminous square,
e would see the melancholy Cinta, his son Esteban,
he bridge of his vessel and Toni at the helm.

"Forget!" cried the voice of his evil counselor, blot-
ing out the vision. "Enjoy the present! . . . There is
lenty of time to go in search of them."

And again he would sink himself in his refined and
rtificial luxurious state with the selfishness of the
atrap who, after ordering various cruelties, locks him-
elf in his harem.

The very finest linens, scattered by chance, enveloped
is body or served as cushions. They were her lin-
erie, stray petals of her beauty, that still kept the
warmth and perfume of her body. If Ferragut needed
any object belonging to him, he had to hunt for it
hrough sheaves of skirts, silk petticoats, white negligees,
erfumes and portraits, all scattered over the furniture
or tossed in the corners. When Freya, tired of dancing
n the center of the salon, was not curling herself up
n his arms she took delight in opening a box of san-
dalwood. In this she used to keep all her jewels, taking
hem out again and again with a nervous restless-
ess, as though she feared they might have evaporated
n their enclosure. Her lover had to listen to the gravest
explanations accompanying the display of her treasures.

"Kiss it," she said, offering him the string of pearls
almost always on her neck.

These grains of moonlight splendor were to her little
living beings, little creatures that she needed in contact
with her skin. She was impregnated with the essence of
all that she wore; she drank their life.

"They have slept upon me so many nights," she would

murmur, contemplating them amorously. "This ligh
amber tone I have given them with the warmth of m
body."

They were no longer a piece of jewelry, they formed
a part of her organism. They might grow pale and
die if they were to pass many days forgotten in the depth
of her casket.

After that she kept on ransacking the perfumed jewel
box for all the gems that were her great pride,—ear
rings and finger-rings of great price, mixed with othe
exotic jewels of bizarre form and slight value, picked
up on her voyages.

"Look carefully at this," she said gravely to Ferragut, while she rubbed against her bare arm an enormous
diamond in one of her rings.

Warmed by the friction, the precious stone became
converted into a magnet. A bit of paper placed a few
inches away was attracted to it with an irresistible fluttering.

She then rubbed one of the barbaric imitation-jewels
of thick cut glass, and the scrap of paper remained motionless without the slightest evidence of attraction.

Satisfied with these experiments, she replaced her
treasures in the casket and set herself to beguiling the
passing monotony, again devoting herself to Ulysses.

These long imprisonments in an atmosphere charged
with perfumes, Oriental tobaccos, and feminine seduction were gradually disordering Ferragut's mind. Besides this, he was drinking heavily in order to give new
vigor to his organism which was beginning to break
down under the excesses of his voluptuous seclusion. At
the slightest sign of weariness, Freya would fall upon
him with her dominating lips. If she freed herself from
his embraces, it was to offer him a glass full of the
strongest liquor.

When the spell of intoxication overcame him, weighing down his eyes, he always recalled the same dream. In his maudlin siestas, satiated and happy, there would always reappear another Freya who was not Freya, but Doña Constanza, the Empress of Byzantium. He could see her dressed as a peasant girl, just as she was portrayed in the picture in the church of Valencia, and at the same time completely undressed, like the other houri, who was dancing in the salon.

This double image, which disappeared and reappeared capriciously with the arbitrariness of dreams, was always telling him the same thing. Freya was Doña Constanza perpetuated across the centuries, taking on a new form. She was born of the union of a German and an Italian, just like this other one. . . . But the chaste empress was now smiling in her nudeness, satisfied with being simply Freya. Marital infidelity, persecution and poverty had been the result of her first existence when she was tranquil and virtuous.

"Now I know the truth," Doña Constanza would say with a sweetly immodest smile. "Only love exists; all the rest is illusion. Kiss me, Ferragut! . . . I have returned to life in order to recompense you. You gave me the first of your childish affection; you longed for me before you became a man."

And her kiss was like that of the spy—an absorbing kiss throughout his entire person, making him awake. . . . Upon opening his eyes he saw Freya with her mouth close to his.

"Arise, my sea-wolf! . . . It is already night. We are going to dine."

Outside the house, Ulysses would breathe in the twilight breeze and look at the first stars that were beginning to sparkle above the roofs. He felt the fresh delight and trembling limbs of the odalisque coming out of retreat.

The dinner finished, they would stroll through the darkest street or the promenades along the shore, avoiding the people. One night they stopped in the gardens of the *Villa Nazionale,* near the bench that had witnessed their struggle when returning from Posilipo.

"You wished to kill me, you little rascal! . . . You threatened me with your revolver, my bandit! . . ."

Ulysses protested. What a way to remember things! But she refuted his correction with a bold and lying authority.

"It was you! . . . It *was* you! I say so, and that is enough. You must become accustomed to accepting whatever I may affirm."

In the beer garden, where they used to dine almost every night—an imitation medieval saloon, with paneled beams made by machinery, plaster walls imitating oak, and neo-Gothic crystals—the proprietor used to exhibit as a great curiosity a jar of grotesque little figures among the porcelain steins that adorned the brackets of the pedestals.

Ferragut recognized it immediately; it was an ancient Peruvian jar.

"Yes, it is a *huaca,*" she said. "I have been in that, too. . . . We were engaged in manufacturing antiques."

Freya misunderstood the gesture that her lover made. She thought that he was astonished at the audacity of this manufacture of souvenirs. "Germany is great; nothing can resist the adaptive powers of her industries. . . ."

And her eyes burned with a proud light as she enumerated these exploits of false historical resurrection. They had filled museums and private collections with Egyptian and Phœnician statuettes recently reproduced.

Then, on German soil, they had manufactured Peruvian antiquities in order to sell them to the tourists who visit the ancient realm of the Incas. Some of the inhabitants received wages for disinterring these things opportunely with a great deal of publicity. Now the fad of the moment was the black art, and collectors were hunting horrible wooden idols carved by tribes in the interior of Africa.

But what had really impressed Ferragut was the plural which she had employed in speaking of such industries. Who had fabricated these Peruvian antiquities? . . . Was it her husband, the sage? . . .

"No," replied Freya tranquilly. "It was another one, —an artist from Munich. He had hardly any talent for painting, but great intelligence in business matters. We returned from Peru with the mummy of an Inca which we exhibited in almost all the museums of Europe without finding a purchaser. Bad business! We had to keep the Inca in our room in the hotel, and . . ."

Ferragut was not interested in the wanderings of the poor Indian monarch, snatched from the repose of his tomb. . . . One more! Each of Freya's confidences evoked a new predecessor from the haze of her past.

Coming out of the beer-garden, the captain stalked along with a gloomy aspect. She, on the other hand, was laughing at her memories surveying across the years, with a flattering optimism, this far-away adventure of her Bohemian days, and growing very merry on recalling the remains of the Inca on his passage from hotel to hotel.

Suddenly Ulysses' wrath blazed forth. . . . The Dutch officer, the natural history sage, the singer who killed himself in one shot and now the fabricator of antiquities. . . . How many more men had there been in her existence? How many were there still to be told of? Why had she not brought them all out at once? . . .

Freya was astounded at his abrupt violence. The sailor's wrath was terrifying. Then she laughed, leaning heavily on his arm, and putting her face close to his.

"You are jealous! . . . My shark is jealous! Go on talking. You don't know how much I like to hear you. Complain away! . . . Beat me! . . . It's the first time that I've seen a jealous man. Ah, you Southerners! . . . Meridionals! . . . With good reason the women adore you."

And she was telling the truth. She was experiencing a new sensation before this manly wrath, provoked by amorous indignation. Ulysses appeared to her a very different man from all the others she had known in her former life,—cold, compliant and selfish.

"My Ferragut! . . . My Mediterranean hero! How I love you! Come . . . come. . . . I must reward you!"

They were in a central street, near the corner of a sloping little alley with stairs. She pushed him toward it, and at the first step in the narrow and dark passageway embraced him, turning her back on the movement and light in the great street, in order to kiss him with that kiss which always made the captain's knees tremble.

Although his temper was soothed, he continued complaining during the rest of the stroll. How many had preceded him? . . . He must know. He wished to know, no matter how horrible the knowledge might be. It was the delight of the jealous who persist in scratching open the wound.

"I want to know you," he repeated. "I ought to know you, since you belong to me. I have the right! . . ."

This right recalled with childish obstinacy made Freya smile dolorously. Long centuries of experience appeared to peep out from the melancholy curl of her lips. In her gleamed the wisdom of the woman, more cautious and foresighted than that of the man, since love was her only preoccupation.

"Why do you wish to know?" she asked discouragingly. "How much further could you go on that? . . . Would you perchance be any happier when you did know? . . ."

She was silent for some steps and then said as though disclosing a secret:

"In order to love, it is not necessary for us to know one another. Quite the contrary. A little bit of mystery keeps up the illusion and dispells monotony. . . . He who wishes to know is never happy."

She continued talking. Truth perhaps was a good thing in other phases of existence, but it was fatal to love. It was too strong, too crude. Love was like certain women, beautiful as goddesses under a discreet and artificial light, but horrible as monsters under the burning splendors of the sun.

"Believe me; put away these bugbears of the past. Is not the present enough for you? . . . Are you not happy?"

And, trying to convince him that he was, she redoubled her exertions, chaining Ulysses in bonds which were sweet yet weighed heavily upon him. Strongly convinced of his vileness, he nevertheless adored and detested this woman, with her tireless sensuality. . . . And it was impossible to separate himself from her! . . .

Anxious to find some excuse, he recalled the image of his cook philosophizing in his culinary dominion. Whenever he had wished to call down the greatest of evils upon an enemy, the astute fellow had always uttered this anathema:

"May God send you a female to your taste! . . ."

Ferragut had found the "female to his taste" and was

forever slave of his destiny. It would follow him through every form of debasement which she might desire, and each time would leave him with less energy to protest, accepting the most disgraceful situations in exchange for love. . . . And it would always be so! And he who but a few months before used to consider himself a hard and overbearing man, would end by pleading and weeping if she should go away! . . . Ah, misery! . . .

In hours of tranquillity, when satiety made them converse placidly like two friends of the same sex, Ulysses would avoid allusions to the past, questioning her only about her actual life. These questions were chiefly concerned with the doctor's mysterious work; he wished to know with the interest that the slightest actions of a beloved person always inspire, the part that Freya was playing in them. Did he not belong now to the same association since he was obeying its orders? . . .

The responses were very incomplete. She had limited herself to obeying the doctor, who knew everything. . . . Then she hesitated and corrected herself. No, her friend could not know everything, because above her were the count and other personages who used to come from time to time to visit her like passing tourists. And the chain of agents, from the lowest to the highest, were lost in mysterious heights that made Freya turn pale, imposing on her eyes and voice an expression of superstitious respect.

She was free to speak only of her work, and she did this very cautiously, relating the measures she had employed, but without mentioning her co-workers nor stating what her final aim was to be. The most of the time she had been moved about without knowing toward what her efforts were converging, like a whirling wheel which knows only its immediate environments and is ignorant of the machinery as a whole and the class of production to which it contributes.

Ulysses marveled at the grotesque and dubious proceedings employed by the agents of the spy system.

"But that is like the paper novels! They are ridiculous and worn-out measures that any one can learn from books and melodramas."

Freya assented. For that very reason they were employing them. The surest way of bewildering the enemy was to avail themselves of obvious methods; thus the modern world, so intelligent and subtle, would refuse to believe in them. By simply telling the truth, Bismarck had deceived all European diplomacy, for the very reason that nobody was expecting the truth from his lips.

German espionage was comporting itself like the personages in a political novel, and people consequently could not seem to believe in it,—although it was taking place right under their eyes,—just because its methods appeared too exaggerated and antiquated.

"Therefore," she continued, "every time that France uncovers a part of our maneuvers, the opinion of the world which believes only in ingenious and difficult things ridicules it, considering it attacked with a delirium of persecution."

Women for some time past had been deeply involved in the service of espionage. There were many as wise as the doctor, as elegant as Freya, and many venerable ones with famous names, winning the confidence that illustrious dowagers inspire. They were very numerous, but they did not know each other. Sometimes they met out in the world and were suspicious of each other, but each continued on her special mission, pushed in different directions by an omnipotent and hidden force.

She showed him some portraits that were taken a few

years before. Ulysses was slow to recognize her as a
slim Japanese young girl, clad in a dark kimono.

"It is I when I was over there. It was to our interest
to know the real force of that nation of little men with
rat-like eyes."

In another portrait she appeared in short skirt, riding
boots, a man's shirt, and a felt cowboy hat.

"That was from the Transvaal."

She had gone to South Africa in company with other
German women of the "service" in order to sound the
state of mind of the Boers under English domination.

"I've been everywhere," she affirmed proudly.

"In Paris, too?" questioned the sailor.

She hesitated before answering, but finally nodded her
head. . . . She had been in Paris many times. The outbreak of the war had found her living in the Grand
Hotel. Fortunately, two days before the rupture of hostilities, she had received news enabling her to avoid
being made prisoner in a concentration camp. . . . And
she did not wish to say more. She was verbose and
frank in the relation of her far-distant experiences, but
the memory of the more recent ones enshrouded her in a
restless and frightened reserve.

To change the course of conversation, she spoke of
the dangers that had threatened her on her journeys.

"We have to be very courageous. . . . The doctor, just
as you see her, is a heroine. . . . You laugh, but if you
should know her arsenal, perhaps it might strike fear
to your heart. She is a scientist."

The grave lady had an invincible repugnance for vulgar weapons, and Freya referred freely to a portable
medicine case full of anesthetics and poisons.

"Besides this she carries on her person a little bag
full of certain powders of her own invention,—tobacco,
red pepper. . . . Perfect little devils! Whoever gets

them in the eyes is blinded for life. It is as though she were throwing flames."

She herself was less complicated in her measures of defense. She had her revolver, a species of firearms which she managed to keep hidden just as certain insects hide their sting, without knowing certainly when it might be necessary to draw it forth. And if she could not avail herself of that, she always relied on her hatpin.

"Just look at it! . . . With what gusto I could pierce the heart of many a person! . . ."

And she showed him a kind of hidden poniard, a keen, triangular stiletto of genuine steel, capped by a large glass pearl that served as its hilt.

"Among what kind of people are you living!" murmured the practical voice in Ferragut's interior. "What have you mixed yourself up with, my son!" But his tendency to discount danger, not to live like other people, made him find a deep enchantment in this novel-like existence.

The doctor no longer went on excursions, but her visitors were increasing in number. Sometimes, when Ulysses was starting toward her room, Freya would stop him.

"Don't go. . . . They're having a consultation."

Upon opening the door of the landing that corresponded to his quarters he saw, on various occasions, the green screened door of the office closing behind many men, all of them of Teutonic aspect, travelers who had just disembarked in Naples with a certain precipitation, neighbors from the city who used to receive orders from the doctor.

She appeared much more preoccupied than usual. Her eyes would pass over Freya and the sailor as though she did not see them.

"Bad news from Rome," Ferragut's companion told him. "Those accursed mandolin-strummers are getting away from us."

Ulysses began to feel a certain boredom in these monotonously voluptuous days. His senses were becoming blunted with so many indulgences mechanically repeated. Besides, a monstrous debilitation was making him think in self-defense of the tranquil life of the hearth. He timidly began calculating the time of his seclusion. How long had he been living with her? . . . His confused and crowded memory besought her aid.

"Fifteen days," replied Freya.

Again he persisted in his calculations, and she affirmed that only three weeks had passed by since his steamer had left Naples.

"I shall have to go," said Ulysses hesitatingly. "They will be expecting me in Barcelona; I have no news. . . . What will become of my vessel? . . ."

She who generally listened to these inquiries with a distraught air, not wishing to understand his timid insinuations, responded one afternoon unequivocally:

"The time is approaching when you are going to fulfill your word of honor in regard to sacrificing yourself for me. Soon you will be able to go to Barcelona, and I—I shall join you there. If I am not able to go, we shall meet again. . . . The world is very small."

Her thought did not go beyond this sacrifice exacted of Ferragut. After that, who could tell where she would stop? . . .

Two afternoons later, the doctor and the count summoned the sailor. The lady's voice, always so good-natured and protecting, now assumed a slight accent of command.

"Everything is all ready, Captain." As she had not been able to avail herself of his steamer, she had prepared another boat for him. He was merely to follow the instructions of the count who would show him the bark of which he was going to take command.

The two men went away together. It was the first time that Ulysses had gone out in the street without Freya, and in spite of his enamored enthusiasm, he felt an agreeable sensation of freedom.

They went down to the shore and in the little harbor of the *Castello dell' Ovo* passed over the plank that served as a bridge between the dock and a little schooner with a greenish hull. Ferragut, who had taken in its exterior with a single glance, ran his eye over its deck. . . . "Eighty tons." Then he examined the apparatus and the auxiliary machinery,—a petroleum motor which permitted it to make seven miles an hour whenever the sails did not find a breeze.

He had seen on the poop the name of the boat and its destination, guessing at once the class of navigation to which it was dedicated. It was a Sicilian schooner from Trapani, built for fishing. An artistic calker had sculptured a wooden cray-fish climbing over the rudder. From the two sides of the prow dangled a double row of cray-fish carved with the innocent prolixity of medieval imagination.

Coming out of the hatchway, Ferragut saw half of the hold full of boxes. He recognized this cargo; each one of these boxes contained two cans of gasoline.

"Very well," he said to the count, who had remained silent behind him, following him in all his evolutions. "Where is the crew? . . ."

Kaledine pointed out to him three old sailors huddled on the prow and a ragged boy. They were veterans of the Mediterranean, silent and self-centered, accustomed to obey orders mechanically, without troubling themselves as to where they were going, nor who was commanding them.

"Are there no more?" Ferragut asked.

The count assured him that other men would come to reënforce the crew at the moment of its departure. This would be just as soon as the loading was finished. They had to take certain precautions in order not to attract attention.

"In any case, you will be ready to embark quickly, Captain. Perhaps you may be advised with only a couple of hours' notice."

Talking it over with Freya at night, Ulysses was astonished at the promptness with which the doctor had found a boat, the discretion with which she had had it loaded,—with all the details of this business that had been developing so easily and mysteriously right in the very mouth of a great harbor without any one's taking any notice of it.

His companion affirmed proudly that Germany well understood how to conduct such affairs. It was not the doctor only who was working such miracles. All the German merchants of Naples and Sicily had been giving aid. . . . And convinced that the captain might be sent for at any moment, she arranged his baggage, packing the little suit-case that always accompanied him on short trips.

The next day at twilight the count came in search of him. All was ready; the boat was awaiting its captain.

The doctor bade Ulysses farewell with a certain solemnity. They were in the salon, and in a low voice she gave an order to Freya, who went out, returning immediately with a tall, thin bottle. It was mellow Rhine wine, the gift of a merchant of Naples, that the doctor was saving for an extraordinary occasion. She filled four glasses, and, raising hers, looked around her uncertainly.

"Where is the North? . . ."

The count pointed it out silently. Then the lady continued raising her glass, with solemn slowness, as though offering a religious libation to the mysterious power hidden in the North, far, far away. Kaledine imitated her with the same fervid manner.

Ulysses was going to raise the glass to his lips, wishing to hide a ripple of laughter provoked by the imposing lady's gravity.

"Do like the others," murmured Freya in his ear.

And the two quietly drank to his health with their eyes turned toward the North.

"Good luck to you, Captain!" said the doctor. "You will return promptly and with all happiness, since you are working for such a just cause. We shall never forget your services."

Freya wished to accompany him, even to the boat. The count began a protest, but stopped on seeing the good-natured gesture of the sentimental lady.

"They love each other so much! . . . Something must be conceded to love. . . ."

The three went down the sloping streets of Chiaja to the shore of S. Lucia. In spite of his preoccupation, Ferragut could not but look attentively at the count's appearance. He was now dressed in blue, with a yachtsman's black cap, as though prepared to take part in a regatta. He had undoubtedly adopted this attire in order to make the farewell more solemn.

In the gardens of the *Villa Nazionale* Kaledine stopped, giving an order to Freya. He could not permit her to go any further. She would attract attention in the little harbor *dell' Ovo* frequented only by fishermen. As the tone of his order was sharp and imperious, she obeyed without protest, as though accustomed to such superiority.

"Good-bye! . . . Good-bye."

Forgetting the presence of the haughty witness, she embraced Ulysses ardently; then she burst out weeping with a nervous sobbing. It seemed to him that she had never been so sincere as in that moment. And he had to make a great effort to disentangle himself from her embrace.

"Good-bye! . . . Good-bye! . . ."

Then he followed the count without daring to turn his head, suspecting that her eyes were still upon him.

On the shores of S. Lucia, he saw in the distance his old hotel with its illuminated windows. The porter was preceding a young man who was just descending from a carriage, carrying a suit-case. Ferragut was instantly reminded of his son Esteban. The young tourist bore a certain resemblance to him. . . . And Ferragut continued on, smiling rather bitterly at this inopportune recollection.

On entering the schooner he encountered Karl, the doctor's factotum, who had brought his little baggage and had just installed it in his cabin. "He could retire." . . . Then he looked over the crew. In addition to the three old Sicilians he now saw seven husky young fellows, blonde and stout, with rolled-up sleeves. They were talking Italian, but the captain had no doubt as to their real nationality.

As some of them were already beginning to weigh anchor, Ferragut looked at the count as though inviting him to depart. The boat was gradually detaching itself from the dock. They were going to draw in the gang-plank which had served as a bridge.

"I'm going, too," said Kaledine. "This trip interests me."

Ulysses, who was disposed not to be surprised at anything in this extraordinary voyage, merely exclaimed courteously, "So much the better!" He was no longer concerned with him, and devoted all his efforts to conducting the boat out of the little harbor, directing its course through the gulf. The glass windows on the shore of S. Lucia trembled with the vibration of the motor of the decrepit steamer—an old and scandalous piece of machinery imitating the paddling of a tired dog. Meanwhile the sails were unfurled and swelling under the first gusts of the wind.

The trip lasted three days. The first night, the captain enjoyed the selfish delights of resting alone. He was living among men. . . . And he appreciated the satisfaction chastity offered with all the enchantments of novelty.

The second night, in the narrow and noisome cabin of the skipper, he felt wakeful because of the memories that were again springing up. Oh, Freya! . . . When would he ever see her again?

The count and he conversed little, but passed long hours together, seated at the side of the wheel looking out on the sea. They were more friendly than on land, although they exchanged very few words. The common life lessened the haughtiness of the pretended diplomat and enabled the captain to discover new merits in his personality. The freedom with which he was going through the boat, and certain technical words employed against his will, left no doubt in Ferragut's mind regarding his true profession.

"You are in the navy," he said suddenly.

And the count assented, judging dissimulation useless. Yes, he was a naval officer.

"Then what am I doing here? Why have you given the command to me? . . ." So Ferragut was thinking.

without discovering why this man should seek his assistance when he could direct a boat himself, without any outside aid.

Undoubtedly he was a naval officer, and all the blonde sailors that were working like automatons must also have come from some fleet. Discipline was making them respect Ferragut's orders, but the captain suspected that for them he was merely a proxy, the true chief on board being the count.

The schooner passed within sight of the Liparian archipelago; then, twisting its course toward the west, followed the coast of Sicily, from Cape Gallo to the Cape of Vito. From there it turned its prow to the southeast, heading toward the Ægadian Islands.

It had to wait in the waters where the Mediterranean was beginning to narrow between Tunis and Sicily, where the volcanic peak of the Pantellarian Island rises up in the middle of the immense strait.

Brief indications from the count were sufficient to make the course followed by Ferragut in accordance with his desire. He finally could not hide his admiration for the Spaniard's mastery of navigation.

"You know your sea well," said the count.

The captain shrugged his shoulders, smiling. It truly was his. He could call it *"mare nostrum"* just as the Romans and their former rulers had done.

As though divining the subsea depths by a simple glance, he kept his boat within the limits of the extensive ledge of the Aventura. He was navigating slowly with only a few sails, crossing and recrossing the same water.

Kaledine, after two days had passed by, began to grow uneasy. Several times it sounded to Ferragut as though he were muttering the name of Gibraltar. The passage from the Atlantic to the Mediterranean was the greatest danger for those that he was expecting.

From the deck of the schooner he was able to see only a short distance, and the count clambered up the rigging in order that his eyes might take in a more extensive sweep.

One morning up aloft he called something to the captain, pointing out a speck on the horizon. He must steer in that very direction. What he was seeking was over there.

Ferragut obeyed him, and half an hour later there appeared, one after the other, two long, low boats, moving with great velocity. They were like destroyers, but without mastheads, without smokestacks, skimming along almost on a level with the water, painted in a gray that made them seem a short distance away of the same color as the sea. They came around on both sides of the sailboat as though they were going to crush it with the meeting of their hulls. Various metallic cables came up from their decks and were thrown over the bitts of the schooner, fastening it to them, and forming the three vessels into a solid mass that, united, followed the slow undulation of the sea.

Ulysses examined curiously his two companions in this improvised float. Were these the famous submarines? . . . He saw on their steel decks round and protruding hatchways like chimneys through which groups of heads were sticking out. The officers and crews were dressed like fishermen from the northern coast with waterproof suits of one piece and oilskin hats. Many of them were swinging their tarpaulins over their heads, and the count replied to them by waving his cap. The blonde sailors of the schooner shouted in reply to the acclamations of their comrades on the submersibles, *"Deutchsland über alles! . . ."*

But this enthusiasm, equivalent to a song of triumph in the midst of the solitude of the sea, lasted but a very

short time.   Whistles sounded, men ran over the steel
decks and Ferragut saw his vessel invaded by two files
of seamen.   In a moment the hatchways were opened;
there sounded the crash of breaking pieces of wood, and
the cases of petrol began to be carried off on both
sides.   The water all around the sailboat was filled with
broken cases that were gently floating away.

The count on the poop deck was listening to an officer
dressed in waterproof garments.

He was recounting their passage through the Strait of
Gibraltar, completely submerged, seeing through the
periscope the English torpedo-chasers on patrol.

"Nothing, Commandant," continued the officer.   "Not
even the slightest incident. . . . A magnificent voyage!"

"May God punish England!" said the count now
called Commandant.

"May God punish her!" replied the official as though
he were saying "Amen."

Ferragut saw himself forgotten, ignored, by all the
men aboard the schooner.   Some of the sailors even
pushed him to one side in the haste of their work.   He
was the mere master of a sailing vessel who counted
for nothing in this hierarchy of warlike men.

He now began to understand why they had given
him the command of the little vessel.   The count was
in possession of the situation.   Ferragut saw him
approaching as though he had suddenly recollected him,
stretching out his right hand with the affability of a
comrade.

"Many thanks, Captain.   This service is of the kind
that is not easily forgotten.   Perhaps we shall never see
each other again. . . . But if at any time you need
me, you may know who I am."

And, as though presenting him to another person, he
gave his name and titles ceremoniously:—Archibald von

Kramer, Naval Lieutenant of the Imperial Navy. . . .
His diplomatic rôle had not been entirely false. . . . He
had served as Naval Attaché in various embassies.

He then gave instructions for the return trip. Ferragut was to wait opposite Palermo where a boat would
come out after him and take him ashore. Everything
had been foreseen. . . . He must deliver the command to
the true owner of the schooner, a timorous man who had
made them pay very high for the hire of the boat without
venturing to jeopardize his own person. In the cabin
were the customary papers for clearing the vessel.

"Salute the ladies in my name. Tell them that they
will soon have news of us. We are going to make ourselves lords of the Mediterranean."

The unloading of combustibles still continued. Ferragut saw von Kramer slipping through the openings
of one of the submarines. Then he thought he recognized
on the submersible two of the sailors of the crew of
the schooner who, after being received with shouts and
embraces by their comrades, disappeared through a tubu-
lar hatchway.

The unloading lasted until mid-afternoon. Ulysses
had not imagined that the little boat could carry so many
cases. When the hold was empty, the last German
sailors disappeared and with them the cables that had
lashed them to the sailboat. An officer shouted to him
that he could get under way.

The two submersibles with their cargo of oil and gasoline were nearer the level of the sea than on their arrival
and now began to disappear in the distance.

Finding himself alone in the stern of the schooner,
the Spaniard felt a sudden disquietude.

"What have you done! . . . What have you done!"
clamored a voice in his brain.

But contemplating the three old men and the boy

who had remained as the only crew, he forgot his remorse. He would have to bestir himself greatly in
order to supply the lack of men. For two nights and a
day he scarcely rested, managing almost at the same
time both helm and motor, since he did not dare to
let out all his sails with this scarcity of sailors.

When he found himself opposite the port of Palermo,
just as it was beginning to extinguish its night lights,
Ferragut was able to sleep for the first time, leaving the
watch of the boat in charge of one of the seamen,
who maintained it with sails furled. In the middle of the
morning he was awakened by some voices shouting
from the sea:

"Where is the captain?"

He saw a skiff and various men leaping aboard the
schooner. It was the owner who had come to claim
his boat in order to bring it into port in the customary
legal form. The skiff was commissioned to take Ulysses
ashore with his little suitcase. He was accompanied
by a red-faced, fat gentleman who appeared to have
great authority over the skipper.

"I suppose you are already informed of what is
happening," he said to Ferragut while the two oarsmen
made the skiff glide over the waves. "Those bandits!
. . . Those mandolin-players! . . ."

Ulysses, without knowing why, made an affirmative
gesture. This indignant burgher was a German, one of
those that were useful to the doctor. . . . It was enough
just to listen to him.

A half hour later Ferragut leaped on the dock without any one's opposing his disembarking, as though the
protection of his obese companion had made all the
guards drowsy. The good gentleman showed, notwith-
standing, a fervent desire to separate himself from his
charge—to hurry away, attending to his own affairs.

He smiled upon learning that Ulysses wished to go immediately to Naples. "You do well. . . . The train leaves in two hours." And putting him in a vacant hack, he disappeared with precipitation.

Finding himself alone, the captain almost believed that he had dreamed of those two preceding days.

He was again seeing Palermo after an absence of long years: and he experienced the joy of an exiled Sicilian on meeting the various carts of the countryside, drawn by broken-down horses with plumes, whose badly-painted wagon bodies represented scenes from "Jerusalem Delivered." He recalled the names of the principal roads,— the roads of the old Spanish viceroys. In one square he saw the statue of four kings of Spain. . . . But all these souvenirs only inspired in him a fleeting interest. What he particularly noticed was the extraordinary movement in the streets, the people grouping themselves together in order to listen to the reading of the daily papers. Many windows displayed the national flag, interlaced with those of France, England, and Belgium.

Upon arriving at the station he learned the truth,—was informed of the event to which the merchant had alluded while they were in the skiff. It was war! . . . Italy had broken her relations the day before with the Central Powers.

Ulysses felt very uneasy on remembering what he had done out on the Mediterranean. He feared that the popular groups, thronging past him and giving cheers behind their flags, were going to guess his exploit and fall upon him. It was necessary to get away from this patriotic enthusiasm, and he breathed more freely when he found himself in one of the coaches of a train. . . . Besides, he was going to see Freya. And it was enough for him merely to evoke her image to make all his remorse vanish.

The short journey proved long and difficult. The necessities of war had made themselves felt from the very
first moment, absorbing all means of communication.
The train would remain immovable for hours together
in order to give the right of way to other trains loaded
with men and military materials. . . . In all the stations
were soldiers in campaign uniform, banners and cheer-
ing crowds.

When Ferragut arrived at Naples, fatigued by a journey of forty-eight hours, it seemed to him that the
coachman was going too slowly toward the old palace of
Chiaja.

Upon crossing the vestibule with his little suit-case, the
portress,—a fat old crone with dusty, frizzled hair whom
he had sometimes caught a glimpse of in the depths of
her hall cavern,—stopped his passage.

"The ladies are no longer living in the house. . . . The
ladies have suddenly left with Karl, their employee."
And she explained the rest of their flight with a hostile
and malignant smile.

Ferragut saw that he must not insist. The slovenly
old wife was furious over the flight of the German
ladies, and was examining the sailor as a probable spy
fit for patriotic denunciation. Nevertheless, through
professional honor, she told him that the blonde *signora,*
the younger and more attractive one, had thought of him
on going away, leaving his baggage in the porter's room.

Ulysses hastened to disappear. He would soon send
some one to collect those valises. And taking another
carriage, he betook himself to the *albergo* of S. Lucia.
. . . What an unexpected blow!

The porter made a gesture of surprise and astonishment upon seeing him enter. Before Ferragut could inquire for Freya, with the vague hope that she might have
taken refuge in the hotel, this man gave him some news.

"Captain, your son has been here waiting for you."

The captain stuttered in dismay, "What son? . . ."

The man with the embroidered keys brought the register, showing him one line, "Esteban Ferragut, Barcelona." Ulysses recognized his son's handwriting, and at the same time his heart was oppressed with indefinable anguish.

Surprise made him speechless, and the porter took advantage of his silence to continue speaking. He was such a charming and intelligent lad! . . . Some mornings he had accompanied him in order to point out to him the best things in the city. He had inquired among the consignees of the *Mare Nostrum,* hunting everywhere for news of his father. Finally convinced that the captain must already be returning to Barcelona, he also had gone the day before.

"If you had only come twelve hours sooner, you would have found him still here."

The porter knew nothing more. Occupied in doing errands for some South American ladies, he had been unable to say good-bye to the young man when he left the hotel, undecided whether to make the trip in an English steamer to Marseilles or to go by railroad to Genoa, where he would find boats direct to Barcelona.

Ferragut wished to know when he had arrived. And the porter, rolling his eyes, gave himself up to long mental calculation. . . . Finally he reached a date and the sailor, in his turn, concentrated his powers of recollection.

He struck himself on the forehead with his clenched hand. It must have been his son then, that youth whom he had seen entering the *albergo* the very day that he was going to take charge of the schooner, to carry combustibles to the German submarines!

CHAPTER VIII

THE YOUNG TELEMACHUS

WHENEVER the *Mare Nostrum* returned to Barcelona, Esteban Ferragut had always felt as dazzled as though a gorgeous stained glass window had opened upon his obscure and monotonous life as the son of the family.

He now no longer wandered along the harbor admiring from afar the great transatlantic liners in front of the monument of Christopher Columbus, nor the cargo steamers that were lined up along the commercial docks. An important boat was going to be his absolute property for some weeks, while its captain and officers were passing the time on land with their families. Toni, the mate, was the only one who slept aboard. Many of the seamen had begged permission to live in the city, and so the steamer had been entrusted to the guardianship of Uncle Caragol with half a dozen men for the daily cleaning. The little Ferragut used to play that he was the captain of the *Mare Nostrum* and would pace the bridge, pretending that a great tempest was coming up, and examine the nautical instrument with the gravity of an expert. Sometimes he used to race through all the habitable parts of the boat, climbing down to the holds that, wide open, were being ventilated, waiting for their cargo; and finally he would clamber into the ship's gig, untying it from the landing in order to row in it for a few hours, with even more satisfaction than in the light skiffs of the Regatta Club.

His visits always ended in the kitchen, invited there by Uncle Caragol, who was accustomed to treat him with fraternal familiarity. If the youthful oarsman was perspiring greatly. . . . "A refresquet?" And the *chef* would prepare his sweet mixture that made men, after one gulp, fall into the haziness of intoxication.

Esteban esteemed highly the "refrescos" of the cook. His imagination, excited by the frequent reading of novels of travel, had made him conceive a type of heroic, gallant, dashing sailor—a regular swash-buckler capable of swallowing by the pitcherful the most rousing drinks without moving an eyelid. He wanted to be that kind; every good sailor ought to drink.

Although on land he was not acquainted with other liquors than those innocent and over-sweet ones kept by his mother for family fiestas, once he trod the deck of a vessel he felt the necessity for alcoholic liquids so as to make it evident that he was entirely a man. "There wasn't in the whole world a drink that could do *him* any harm. . . ." And after a second "refresco" from Uncle Caragol, he became submersed in a placid nirvana, seeing everything rose-colored and considerably enlarged,—the sea, the nearby boats, the docks, and Montjuich in the background.

The cook, looking at him affectionately with his bleared eyes, believed that he must have bounded back a dozen years and be still in Valencia, talking with that other Ferragut boy who was running away from the university in order to row in the harbor. He almost came to believe that he had lived twice.

He always listened patiently to the lad's complaints, interrupting him with solemn counsels. This fifteen-year-old Ferragut appeared discontented with life. He was a man and he had to live with women—his mother and two nieces, who were always making laces,—just as in other times his mother had been the lace-making companion of her mother-in-law, Doña Cristina. He wanted to be a seaman and they were obliging him to study the uninteresting courses leading to a bachelor's degree. It was scarcely likely, was it, that a captain would have to know Latin? . . . He wanted to bring his student life to an end so as to become a pilot and continue practicing on the bridge, beside his father. Perhaps at thirty years of age, he might achieve the command of the *Mare Nostrum* or some similar boat.

Meanwhile the lure of the sea dragged him far from the classroom, prompting him to visit Uncle Caragol at the very hour that his professors were calling the roll and noting the students' absence.

The old man and his protégé used to betake themselves in the galley with the uneasy conscience of the guilty. Steps and voices on deck always changed their topic of conversation. "Hide yourself!" and Esteban would dodge under the table or hide in the provision-closet while the cook sallied forth with a seraphic countenance to meet the recent arrival.

Sometimes it was Toni, and the boy would then dare to come out, relying on his silence; for Toni liked him, too, and approved of his aversion to books.

If it was the captain who was coming to the boat for a few moments, Caragol would talk with him, obstructing the door with his bulk at the same time that he was smiling maliciously.

For Esteban the two most wonderful things in all the world were the sea and his father. All those romantic heroes that had come from the pages of novels to take their place in his imagination had the face and ways of Captain Ferragut.

From babyhood he had seen his mother weeping occasionally in resigned sadness. Years later, recognizing

with the precocity of a little-watched boy the relations
that exist between men and women, he suspected that all
these tears must be caused by the flirtations and infidelities of the distant sailor.

He adored his mother with the passion of an only and
spoiled child, but he admired the captain no less, excus-
ing every fault that he might commit. His father was
the bravest and handsomest man in all the world.

And when rummaging one day through the drawers
in his father's stateroom, he chanced upon various photographs having the names of women from foreign countries, the lad's admiration was greater still. Everybody
must have been madly in love with the captain of the
Mare Nostrum. *Ay!* No matter what he might do when
he became a man, he could never hope to equal this triumphant creature who had given him existence. . . .

When the boat, on its return from Naples, arrived
at Barcelona without its owner, Ferragut's son did not
feel any surprise.

Toni, who was always a man of few words, was very
lavish with them on the present occasion. Captain Ferragut had remained behind because of important business, but he would not be long in returning. His second
was looking for him at any moment. Perhaps he would
make the trip by land, in order to arrive sooner.

Esteban was astounded to see that his mother did
not accept this absence as an insignificant event. The
good lady appeared greatly troubled and her eyes filled
with tears. Her feminine instinct made her suspect
something ominous in her husband's delay.

In the afternoon, when her old lover, the professor,
visited her as usual, the two talked slowly with guarded
words but with eyes of understanding and long intervals of silence.

When Don Pedro reached the height of his glorious career, the possession of a professorship in the institute of Barcelona, he used to visit Cinta every afternoon passing an hour and a half in her parlor with chronometric exactitude. Never did the slightest impure thought agitate the professor. The past had fallen into oblivion . . . But he needed to see daily the captain's wife weaving laces with her two little nieces, as he had seen Ferragut's widow years before.

He informed them of the most important events in Barcelona and in the entire world; they would comment together on the future of Esteban, and the former suitor used to listen rapturously to her sweet voice, conceding great importance to the details of domestic economy or descriptions of religious fiestas, solely because it was she who was recounting them.

Many times they would remain in a long silence. Don Pedro represented patience, even temper, and silent respect, in that tranquil and immaculate house which lost its monastic calm only when its head presented himself there for a few days between voyages.

Cinta had accustomed herself to the professor's visits. At half-past three by the clock his footsteps could always be heard in the passageway.

If any afternoon he did not come, the sweet Penelope was greatly disappointed.

"I wonder what can be the matter with Don Pedro?" she would ask her nieces uneasily.

She oftentimes asked this question of her son; but Esteban, without exactly hating the visitor, appreciated him very slightly.

Don Pedro belonged to that group of gentlemen at the Institute whom the government paid to annoy youth with their explanations and their examinations. He still remembered the two years that he had passed in his course, as in the torture chamber, enduring the torments of Latin. Besides that, the professor was a timid man who was always afraid of catching cold, and who never dared to venture into the street on cloudy days without an umbrella. Let people talk to him about courageous men!

"I don't know," he would reply to his mother. "Perhaps he's gone to bed with seven kerchiefs on his head."

When Don Pedro returned, the house recovered its normality of a quiet and well-regulated clock. Doña Cinta, after many consultations, had come to believe his collaboration indispensable. The professor mildly supplemented the authority of the traveling husband, and took it upon himself to represent the head of the family in all outside matters. . . . Many times Ferragut's wife would be awaiting him with impatience in order to ask his mature counsel, and he would emit his opinion in a slow voice after long reflection.

Esteban found it intolerable that this gentleman, who was no more than a distant relative of his grandmother, should meddle in the affairs of the house, pretending to oversee him as though he were his father. But it irritated him still more to see him in a good humor and trying to be funny. It made him furious to hear his mother called "Penelope" and himself "the young Telemachus." . . . "Stupid, tedious old bore!"

The young Telemachus was not slow to wrath nor vengeance. From babyhood he had interrupted his play in order to "work" in the reception room near to the hatrack by the door. And the poor professor on his departure would find his hat crown dented in or its nap roughened up, or he would sally home innocently carrying spitballs on the skirts of his overcoat.

Now the boy contented himself with simply ignoring the existence of the family friend, passing in front of

him without recognizing him and only greeting him when
his mother ordered him to do so.

The day in which he brought the news of the return
of the ship without its captain, Don Pedro made a longer
visit than usual. Cinto shed two tears upon the lace
but had to stop weeping, vanquished by the good sense
of her counselor.

"Why weep and get your mind overwrought with so
many suppositions without foundation? . . . What you
ought to do, my daughter, is to call in this Toni who is
mate of the vessel; he must know all about it. . . . Perhaps he may tell you the truth."

Esteban was told to hunt him up the following day,
and he quickly noticed Toni's extreme disquietude upon
learning that Doña Cinta wished to talk with him. The
mate left the boat in lugubrious silence as though he were
being taken away to mortal torment: then he began to
hum loudly, an indication that he was in deep thought.

The young Telemachus was not able to be present at
the interview but he hung around the closed door and
succeeded in hearing a few loud words which slipped
through the cracks. His mother was speaking with
greater frequency. Toni was reiterating in a dull voice
the same excuse:—"I don't know. The captain will
come at any moment. . . ." But when the mate found
himself outside the house, his wrath broke out against
himself, against his cursed character that did not know
how to lie, against all women bad and good. He believed
he had said too much. That lady had the skill of a judge
in getting words out of him.

That night, at the supper hour, the mother scarcely
opened her mouth. Her fingers communicated a nervous
trembling to the plates and forks, and she looked at her
son with tragic commiseration as though she foresaw
terrible troubles about to burst upon his head. She

opposed a desperate silence to Esteban's questions and
finally exclaimed:

"Your father is deserting us! . . . Your father has
forgotten us! . . ."

And she left the dining-room to hide her overflowing
tears.

The boy slept rather restlessly, but he slept. The
admiration which he always felt for his father and a
certain solidarity with the strong examples of his sex
made him take little account of these complaints. Matters
for women! His mother just didn't know how to be
the wife of an extraordinary man like Captain Ferragut.
He who was really a man, in spite of his few years,
was going to intervene in this affair in order to show
up the truth.

When Toni, from the deck of the vessel, saw the lad
coming along the wharf the following morning, he was
greatly tempted to hide himself. . . . "If Doña Cinta
should call me again in order to question me! . . ." But
he calmed himself with the thought that the boy was
probably coming of his own free will to pass a few hours
on the *Mare Nostrum*. Even so, he wished to avoid his
presence as though he feared some slip in talking with
him, and so pretended that he had work in the hold.
Then he left the boat going to visit a friend on a steamer
some distance off.

Esteban entered the galley, calling gayly to Uncle
Caragol. He wasn't the same, either. His humid and
reddish eyes were looking at the child with an extraordinary tenderness. Suddenly he stopped his talk with
an expression of uneasiness on his face. He looked
uncertainly around him, as though fearing that a precipice
might open at his feet.

Never forgetful of the respect due to every visitor
in his dominion, he prepared two "refrescos." He was

going to treat Esteban for the first time on this return trip. On former days, incredible as it may seem, he had not thought of making even one of his delicious beverages. The return from Naples to Barcelona had been a sad one: the vessel had a funereal air without its master.

For all these reasons, Caragol's hand lavishly measured out the rum until the liquid took on a tobacco tone.

They drank . . . The young Telemachus began to talk about his father when the glasses were only half empty, and the cook waved both hands in the air, giving a grunt which signified that he had no wish to bother about the captain's absence.

"Your father will return, Esteban," he added. "He will return but I don't know when. Certainly later than Toni says."

And not wishing to say more, he gulped down the rest of the glass, devoting himself hastily to the confection of the second "refresco" in order to make up for lost time.

Little by little he slipped away from the prudent barrier that was hedging in his verbosity and spoke with his old time abandon; but his flow of words did not exactly convey news.

Caragol preached morality to Ferragut's son,—morality from his standpoint, interrupted by frequent caresses of the glass.

"Esteban, my son, respect your father greatly. Imitate him as a seaman. Be good and just toward the men that you command. . . . But avoid the females!"

The women! . . . There was no better theme for his piously drunken eloquence. The world inspired his pity. It was all governed by the infernal attraction exercised by the female of the species. The men were working, struggling, and trying to grow rich and celebrated, all in order to possess one of these creatures.

"Believe me, my son, and do not imitate your father in this respect."

The old man had said too much to back out now and he had to go on, letting out the rest of it, bit by bit. Thus Esteban learned that the captain was enamored with a lady in Naples and that he had remained there pretending business matters, but in reality dominated by this woman's influence.

"Is she pretty?" asked the boy eagerly.

"Very pretty," replied Caragol. "And such odors! . . . And such a swishing of fine clothes! . . ."

Telemachus thrilled with contradictory sensations of pride and envy. He admired his father once more, but this admiration only lasted a few seconds. A new idea was taking possession of him while the cook continued:

"He will not come now. I know what these elegant females are, reeking with perfume. They are true demons that dig their nails in when they clutch, and it is necessary to cut off their hands in order to loosen them. . . . And the boat as useless now as though it were aground, while the others are filling themselves with gold! . . . Believe me, my son, this is the only truth in the world."

And he concluded by gulping in one draft all that was left in the second glass.

Meanwhile the boy was forming in his mind an idea prompted by his pleasant intoxication. What if he should go to Naples in order to bring his father back! . . .

At this moment everything seemed possible to him. The world was rose-colored as it always was when he looked at it, glass in hand, near to Uncle Caragol. All obstacles would turn out to be trifling: everything would

arrange itself with wonderful facility. Men were able
to progress by bounds.

But hours afterward when his thoughts were cleared
of their beatific visions, he felt a little fearful when
recollecting his absent parent. How would he receive
him upon his arrival? . . . What excuses could he give
his father for his presence in Naples? . . . He trembled,
recalling the image of his scowling brow and angry eyes.

On the following day a sudden self-confidence replaced
this uneasiness. He recalled the captain as he had seen
him many times on the deck of his vessel, telling of his
escapades when rowing in the harbor of Barcelona, or
commenting to friends on his son's strength and intelligence. The image of the paternal hero now came to his
mind with good-humored eyes and a smile passing like
a fresh breeze over his face.

He would tell him the whole truth. He would make
him understand that he had come to Naples just to take
him away with him, like a good comrade who comes to
another's rescue in time of danger. Perhaps he might be
irritated and give him a blow, but he would eventually
accede to his proposition.

Ferragut's character was reborn in him with all the
force of decisive argument. And if the voyage should
prove absurd and dangerous? . . . All the better! So
much the better! That was enough to make him
undertake it. He was a man and should know no fear.

During the next two weeks he prepared his flight. He
had never taken a long journey. Only once he had
accompanied his father on a flying business trip to
Marseilles. It was high time that he should go out in
the world like the man that he was, acquainted with
almost all the cities of the earth,—through his readings.

The money question did not worry him any. Doña
Cinta had it in abundance and it was easy to find her

bunch of keys. An old and slow-going steamer, commanded by one of his father's friends, had just entered port and the following day would weigh anchor for Italy.

This sailor accepted the son of his old comrade without any traveling papers. He would arrange all irregularities with his friends in Genoa. Between captains they ought to exchange such services, and Ulysses Ferragut, who was awaiting his son in Naples (so Esteban told him), would not wish to waste time just because of some ridiculous, red tape formality.

Telemachus with a thousand pesetas in his pocket, extracted from a work box which his mother used as a cash box, embarked the following day. A little suit-case, taken from his home with deliberate and skillful precaution, formed his entire baggage.

From Genoa he went to Rome, and from there to Naples, with the foolhardiness of the innocent, employing Spanish and Catalan words to reinforce his scanty Italian vocabulary acquired at the opera. The only positive information that guided him on his quest of adventure was the name of the *albergo* on the shore of S. Lucia which Caragol had given him as his father's residence.

He sought him vainly for many days and visited in Naples the consignees who thought that the captain had returned to his country some time ago.

Not finding him, he began to be afraid. He ought to be back in Barcelona by this time and what he had begun as an heroic voyage was going to turn into a runaway, a boyish escapade. He thought of his mother who was perhaps weeping hours at a time, reading and rereading the letter that he had left for her explaining the object of his flight. Besides, Italy's intervention in the war,— an event which every one had been expecting but had supposed to be still a long way off,—had suddenly become

an actual fact.   What was there left for him to do in this
country? . . . And one morning he had disappeared.

Since the hotel porter could not tell him anything more,
the father, after his first impression of surprise had
passed, thought it would be a good plan to visit the firm
of consignees.   Perhaps there they might give him some
news.

The war was the only thing of interest in that office.
But Ferragut, owner of a ship and a former client, was
guided by the director to the employees who had received Esteban.

They did not know much about it.   They recalled
vaguely a young Spaniard who said that he was the
captain's son and was making inquiries about him.   His
last visit had been two days before.   He was then hesitating between returning to his country by rail or
embarking in one of the three steamers that were in
port ready to sail for Marseilles.

"I believe that he has gone by railroad," said one of
the clerks.

Another of the office force supported his companion's
supposition with a positive affirmation in order to attract
the attention of his chief.   He was sure of his departure
by land.   He himself had helped him to calculate what
the trip to Barcelona would cost him.

Ferragut did not wish to know more.   He must get
away as soon as possible.   This inexplicable voyage of
his son filled him with remorse and immeasurable alarm.
He wondered what could have occurred in his home. . . .

The director of the offices pointed out to him a
French steamer from Suez that was sailing that very
afternoon to Marseilles, and took upon himself all the
arrangements concerning his passage and recommendation to the captain.   There only remained four hours
before the boat's departure, and Ulysses, after collecting

his valises and sending them aboard, took a last stroll through all the places where he had lived with Freya. Adieu, gardens of the *Villa Nazionale* and white Aquarium! . . . Farewell, *albergo!* . . .

His son's mysterious presence in Naples had intensified his disgust at the German girl's flight. He thought sadly of lost love, but at the same time he thought with dolorous suspense of what might greet him when reëntering his home.

A little before sunset the French steamer weighed anchor. It had been many years since Ulysses had sailed as a simple passenger. Entirely out of his element, he wandered over the decks and among the crowds of tourists. Force of habit drew him to the bridge, talking with the captain and the officers, who from his very first words recognized his professional genius.

Realizing that he was no more than an intruder in this place, and annoyed at finding himself on a bridge from which he could not give a single order, he descended to the lower decks, examining the groups of passengers. They were mostly French, coming from Indo-China. On prow and poop there were quartered four companies of Asiatic sharpshooters,—little, yellowish, with oblique eyes and voices like the miauling of cats. They were going to the war. Their officers lived in the staterooms in the center of the ship, taking with them their families who had acquired a foreign aspect during their long residence in the colonies.

Ulysses saw ladies clad in white stretched out on their steamer chairs, having themselves fanned by their little Chinese pages; he saw bronzed and weather-beaten soldiers who appeared disgusted yet galvanized by the war that was snatching them from their Asiatic siesta, and children,—many children—delighted to go to France, the country of their dreams, forgetting in their

happiness that their fathers were probably going to their
death.

The passage could not have been smoother. The
Mediterranean was like a silver plain in the moonlight.
From the invisible coast came warm puffs of garden
perfumes. The groups on deck reminded one another,
with selfish satisfaction, of the great dangers that threatened the people embarking in the North Sea, harassed by
German submarines. Fortunately the Mediterranean
was free from such calamity. The English had so well
guarded the port of Gibraltar that it was all a tranquil
lake dominated by the Allies.

Before going to bed, the captain entered a room on the
upper deck where was installed the wireless telegraph
outfit. The hissing as of frying oil that the apparatus
was sending out attracted him. The operator, a young
Englishman, took off his nickel band with two ear-
phones. Greatly bored by his isolation, he was trying to
distract himself by conversing with the operators on the
other vessels that came within the radius of his apparatus.
They kept in constant communication like a group of
comrades making the same trip and conversing placidly
together.

From time to time the operator, advised by the sparking
of his induction coils, would put on the diadem with ear
pieces in order to listen to his far-away comrades.

"It is the man on the *Californian* bidding me good-
night," he said after one of these calls. "He is going to
bed. There's no news."

And the young man eulogized Mediterranean navigation. At the outbreak of the war, he had been on another
vessel going from London to New York and he recalled
the unquiet nights, the days of anxious vigilance, searching the sea and the atmosphere, fearing from one moment
to another the appearance of a periscope upon the waters,

or the electric warning of a steamer torpedoed by the submarine. On this sea, one could live as tranquilly as in times of peace.

Ferragut suspected that the poor operator was very anxious to enjoy the delights of such tranquillity. His companion in service was snoring in a nearby cabin and he was anxious to imitate him, putting his head down on the table of the apparatus. . . . "Until to-morrow!"

The captain also fell asleep as soon as he had stretched himself out on the narrow ledge in his stateroom. His sleep was all in one piece, gloomy and complete, without sudden surprises or visions. Just as he was feeling that only a few moments had passed by, he was violently awakened as though some one had given him a shove. In the dim light he could make out only the round glass of the port hole, tenuously blue and veiled by the humidity of the maritime dew, like a tearful eye.

Day was breaking and something extraordinary had just occurred on the boat. Ferragut was accustomed to sleep with the lightness of a captain who needs to awaken opportunely. A mysterious perception of danger had cut short his repose. He distinguished over his head the patter of quick runnings the whole length of the deck; he heard voices. While dressing as quickly as possible he realized that the rudder was working violently, and that the vessel was changing its course.

Coming up on deck, one glance was sufficient to convince him that the ship was not running any danger. Everything about it presented a normal aspect. The sea, still dark, was gently lapping the sides of the vessel which continued going forward with regular motion. The decks were cleared of passengers. They were all sleeping in their staterooms. Only on the bridge he saw a group of persons:—the captain and all the officers, some of them dressed very lightly as though they had been roused from slumber.

Passing by the wireless office, he obtained an explanation of the matter. The youth of the night before was near the door and his companion was now wearing the head phone and tapping the keys of the apparatus, listening and replying to invisible boats.

An half hour before, just as the English operator was going off guard and giving place to his just awakened companion, a signal had kept him in his seat. The *Californian* was sending out by wireless the danger call, the S. O. S., that is only employed when a ship needs help. Then in the space of a few seconds a mysterious voice had spread its tragic story over hundreds of miles. A submersible had just appeared a short distance from the *Californian* and had fired several shells at it. The English boat was trying to escape, relying on its superior speed. Then the submarine had fired a torpedo. . . .

All this had occurred in twenty minutes. Suddenly the echoes of the distant tragedy were extinguished as the communication was cut off. A prolonged, intense, sibilant buzzing in the apparatus, and—nothing! . . . Absolute silence.

The operator now on duty responded with negative movements to his companion's inquiring glances. He could hear nothing but the dialogue between the boats that had received the same warning. They too were alarmed by the sudden silence, and were changing their course going, like the French steamer, toward the place where the *Californian* had met the submersible.

"Can it be that they are already in the Mediterranean!" the operator exclaimed with astonishment on finishing his report. "How could the submarines possibly get 'way down here? . . ."

Ferragut did not dare to go up on the bridge. He was

afraid that the glances of those men of the sea might fasten themselves accusingly upon him. He believed that they could read his thoughts.

A passenger ship had just been sunk at a relatively short distance from the boat on which he was traveling. Perhaps von Kramer was the author of the crime. With good reason he had charged Ulysses to tell his compatriots that they would soon hear of his exploits. And Ferragut had aided in the preparation of this maritime barbarity! . . .

"What have you done? What have you done?" wrathfully demanded his mental voice of good counsel.

An hour afterward he felt ashamed to remain on deck. In spite of the captain's orders, the news had got out and was circulating among the staterooms. Entire families were rushing up on deck, frightened out of the calmness usually reigning on the boat, arranging their clothes with precipitation, and struggling to adjust to their bodies the life-preservers which they were trying on for the first time. The children were howling, terrified by the alarm of their parents. Some nervous women were shedding tears without any apparent cause. The boat was going toward the place where the other one had been torpedoed, and that was enough to make the alarmists imagine that the enemy would remain absolutely motionless in the same place, awaiting their arrival in order to repeat their attack.

Hundreds of eyes were fixed on the sea, scrutinizing the surface of the waves, believing every object which they saw,—bits of wood, seaweed or crates floating on the surface of the water,—to be the top of a periscope.

The officials of the battalion of snipers had gone to prow and poop in order to maintain discipline among their men. But the Asiatics, scornful of death, had not abandoned their serene apathy. Some merely looked out over the sea with a childish curiosity, anxious to become acquainted with this new diabolical toy, invented by the superior races. On the decks reserved for first class passengers astonishment was as great as the uneasiness.

"Submarines in the Mediterranean! . . . But is it possible? . . ."

Those last to awake appeared very incredulous and could only be convinced of what had occurred when they heard the news from the boat's crew.

Ferragut wandered around like a soul in torment. Remorse made him hide himself in his stateroom. These people with their complaints and their comments were causing him great annoyance. Soon he found that he could not remain in this isolation. He needed to see and to know,—like a criminal who returns to the place where he has committed his crime.

At midday they began to see on the horizon various little clouds. They were the ships hastening from all sides, attracted by this unexpected attack.

The French boat that was sailing ahead of them suddenly moderated its speed. They had come into the zone of the shipwreck. In the lookouts were sailors exploring the sea and shouting the orders that guided the steamer's course. During these evolutions, there began to slip past the vessel's sides the remains of the tragic event.

The two rows of heads lined up on the different decks saw life preservers floating by empty, a boat with its keel in the air, and bits of wood belonging to a raft evidently constructed in great haste and never finished.

Suddenly a howl from a thousand voices, followed by a funereal silence. . . . The body of a woman lying on some planks passed by. One of her legs was thrust into a gray silk stocking, her head was hanging on the opposite side, spreading its blonde locks over the water like a bunch of gilded seaweed.

Her firm and juvenile bust was visible through the opening of a drenched nightgown which was outlining her body with unavoidable immodesty. She had been surprised by the shipwreck at the very moment that she had been trying to dress; perhaps terror had made her throw herself into the sea. Death had twisted her face with a horrible contraction, exposing the teeth. One side of her face was swollen from some blow.

Looking over the shoulders of two ladies who were trembling and leaning against the deck-railing, Ferragut caught a glimpse of this corpse. In his turn the vigorous sailor trembled like a woman, and his eyes filmed with mistiness. He simply could not look at it! . . . And again he went down into his stateroom to hide himself.

An Italian torpedo-destroyer was maneuvering among the remains of the shipwreck, as though seeking the footprints of the author of the crime. The steamers stopped their circular course of exploration to lower the lifeboats into the water and collect the corpses and bodies of the living near to death.

The captain in his desperate imprisonment heard new shrieks announcing an extraordinary event. Again the cruel necessity of knowing what it could be dragged him from his stateroom!

A boat full of people had been found by the steamer. The other ships were also meeting little by little the rest of the life boats occupied by the survivors of the catastrophe. The general rescue was going to be a very short piece of work.

The most agile of the shipwrecked people. on reaching the deck, found themselves surrounded by sympathetic groups lamenting their misfortune and at the same time offering them hot drinks. Others, after staggering a few steps as though intoxicated, collapsed on the benches. Some had to be hoisted from the bottom of the boat and carried in a chair to the ship's hospital.

Various British soldiers, serene and phlegmatic, upon climbing on deck asked for a pipe and began to smoke vigorously. Other shipwrecked people, lightly clad, simply rolled themselves up in shawls, beginning the account of the catastrophe as minutely and serenely as though they were in a parlor. A period of ten hours in the crowded narrowness of the boat, drifting at random in the hope of aid, had not broken down their energy.

The women showed greater desperation. Ferragut saw in the center of a group of ladies a young English girl, blond, slender, elegant, who was sobbing and stammering explanations. She had found herself in a launch, separated from her parents, without knowing how. Perhaps they were dead by this time. Her slight hope was that they might have sought refuge in some other boat and been picked up by any one of the steamers that had happened to see them.

A desperate grief, noisy, meridional, silenced with its moanings the noise of conversation. There had just climbed aboard a poor Italian woman carrying a baby in her arms.

"*Figlia mia! . . . Mia figlia! . . .*" she was wailing with disheveled hair and eyes swollen by weeping.

In the moment of the shipwreck she had lost a little girl, eight years old, and upon finding herself in the French steamer, she went instinctively toward the prow in search of the same spot which she had occupied on the other ship, as though expecting to find her daughter there. Her agonized voice penetrated down the stairway: "*Figlia mia! . . . Mia figlia!*"

Ulysses could not stand it. That voice hurt him, as though its piercing cry were clawing at his brain.

He approached a group in the center of which was a young barefooted lad in trousers and shirt open at the breast who was talking and talking, wrapping himself from time to time in a shawl that some one had placed upon his shoulders.

He was describing in a mixture of French and Italian the loss of the *Californian*.

He had been awakened by hearing the first shot fired by the submersible against his steamer. The chase had lasted half an hour.

The most audacious and curious were on the decks and believed their salvation already sure as they saw their ship leaving its enemy behind. Suddenly a black line had cut the sea, something like a long thorn with splinters of foam which was advancing at a dizzying speed, in bold relief against the water. . . . Then came a blow on the hull of the vessel which had made it shudder from stem to stern, not a single plate nor screw escaping tremendous dislocation. . . . Then a volcanic explosion, a gigantic hatchet of smoke and flames, a yellowish cloud in which were flying dark objects:— fragments of metal and of wood, human bodies blown to bits. . . . The eyes of the narrator gleamed with an insane light as he recalled the tragic sight.

"A friend of mine, a boy from my own country," he continued, sighing, "had just left me in order to see the submersible better and he put himself exactly in the path of the explosion. . . . He disappeared as suddenly as if he had been blotted out. I saw him and I did not see him. . . . He exploded in a thousand bits, as though he had had a bomb within his body."

And the shipwrecked man, obsessed by this recollection, could hardly attach any importance to the scenes following,—the struggle of the crowds to gain the boats, the efforts of the officers to maintain order, the death of many that, crazy with desperation, had thrown themselves into the sea, the tragic waiting huddled in barks that were with great difficulty lowered to the water, fearing a second shipwreck as soon as they touched the waves.

The steamer had disappeared in a few moments,—its prow sinking in the waters and then its smokestacks taking on a vertical position almost like the leaning tower of Pisa, and its rudders turning crazily as the shuddering ship went down.

The narrator began to be left alone. Other shipwrecked folk, telling their doleful tales at the same time, were now attracting the curious.

Ferragut looked at this young man. His physical type and his accent made him surmise that he was a compatriot.

"You are Spanish?"

The shipwrecked man replied affirmatively.

"A Catalan?" continued Ulysses in the Catalan idiom.

A fresh oratorical vehemence galvanized the shipwrecked boy. "The gentleman is a Catalan also?" . . . And smiling upon Ferragut as though he were a celestial apparition, he again began the story of his misfortunes.

He was a commercial traveler from Barcelona, and in Naples he had taken the sea route because it had seemed to him the more rapid one, avoiding the railroads congested by Italian mobilization.

"Were there other Spaniards traveling on your boat?" Ulysses continued inquiring.

"Only one: my friend, that boy of whom I was just speaking. The explosion of the torpedo blew him into bits. I saw him. . . ."

The captain felt his remorse constantly increasing. A compatriot, a poor young fellow, had perished through his fault! . . .

The salesman also seemed to be suffering a twinge of

conscience. He was holding himself responsible for his companion's death. He had only met him in Naples a few days before, but they were united by the close brotherhood of young compatriots who had run across each other far from their country.

They had both been born in Barcelona. The poor lad, almost a child, had wanted to return by land and he had carried him off with him at the last hour, urging upon him the advantages of a trip by sea. Whoever would have imagined that the German submarines were in the Mediterranean! The traveling man persisted in his remorse. He could not forget that half-grown lad who, in order to make the voyage in his company, had gone to meet his death.

"I met him in Naples, hunting everywhere for his father."

"Ah! . . ."

Ulysses uttered this exclamation with his neck violently outstreched, as though he were trying to loosen his skull from the rest of his body. His eyes were protruding from their sockets.

"The father," continued the youth, "commands a ship. . . . He is Captain Ulysses Ferragut."

An outcry. . . . The people ran. . . . A man had just fallen heavily, his body rebounding on the deck.

CHAPTER IX

THE ENCOUNTER AT MARSEILLES

Toni, who abominated railway journeys on account of his torpid immovability, now had to abandon the *Mare Nostrum* and suffer the torture of remaining twelve hours crowded in with strange persons.

Ferragut was sick in a hotel in the harbor of Marseilles. They had taken him off of a French boat coming from Naples, crushed with silent melancholia. He wished to die. During the trip they had to keep sharp watch so that he could not repeat his attempts at suicide. Several times he had tried to throw himself into the water.

Toni learned of it from the captain of a Spanish vessel that had just arrived from Marseilles exactly one day after the newspapers of Barcelona had announced the death of Esteban Ferragut in the torpedoing of the *Californian*. The commercial traveler was still relating everywhere his version of the event, concluding it now with his melodramatic meeting with the father, the latter's fatal fall on receiving the news, and desperation upon recovering consciousness.

The first mate had hastened to present himself at his captain's home. All the Blanes were there, surrounding Cinta and trying to console her.

"My son! . . . My son! . . ." the mother was groaning, writhing on the sofa.

And the family chorus drowned her laments, overwhelming her with a flood of fantastic consolations and recommendations of resignation. She ought to think of

328

the father: she was not alone in the world as she was affirming: besides her own family, she had her husband.

Toni entered just at that moment.

"His father!" she cried in desperation. "His father! . . ."

And she fastened her eyes on the mate as though trying to speak to him with them. Toni knew better than anyone what that father was, and for what reason he had remained in Naples. It was his fault that the boy had undertaken the crazy journey at whose end death was awaiting him. . . . The devout Cinta looked upon this misfortune as a chastisement from God, always complicated and mysterious in His designs. Divinity, in order to make the father expiate his crimes, had killed the son without thinking of the mother upon whom the blow rebounded.

Toni went away. He could not endure the glances and the allusions made by Doña Cinta. And as though this emotion were not enough, he received the news a few hours later of his captain's wretched condition,— news which obliged him to make the trip to Marseilles immediately.

On entering the quarters of the hotel frequented by the officials of merchant vessels, he found Ferragut seated near a balcony from which could be seen the entire harbor.

He was limp and flabby, with eyes sunken and faded, beard unkempt, and a manifest disregard of his personal appearance.

"Toni! . . . Toni!"

He embraced his mate, moistening his neck with tears. For the first time he began to weep and this appeared to give him a certain relief. The presence of his faithful officer brought him back to life. Forgotten memories of business journeys crowded in his mind. Toni resuscitated all his past energies. It was as though the *Mare Nostrum* had come in search of him.

He felt shame and remorse. This man knew his secret: he was the only one to whom he had spoken of supplying the German submarines.

"My poor Esteban! . . . My son!"

He did not hesitate to admit the fatal relationship between the death of his son and that illegal trip whose memory was weighing him down like a monstrous crime. But Toni was discreet. He lamented the death of Esteban like a misfortune in which the father had not had any part.

"I also have lost sons . . . And I know that nothing is gained by giving up to despair. . . . Cheer up!"

He never said a word of all that had happened before the tragic event. Had not Ferragut known his mate so well, he might have believed that he had entirely forgotten it. Not the slightest gesture, not a gleam in his eyes, revealed the awakening of that malign recollection. His only anxiety was that the captain should soon regain his health. . . .

Reanimated by the presence and words of this prudent companion, Ulysses recovered his strength and a few days after, abandoned the room in which he had believed he was going to die, turning his steps toward Barcelona.

He entered his home with a foreboding that almost made him tremble. The sweet Cinta, considered until then with the protecting superiority of the Orientals who do not recognize a soul in woman, now inspired him with a certain fear. What would she say on seeing him? . . .

She said nothing of what he had feared. She permitted herself to be embraced, and drooping her head, burst into desperate weeping, as though the presence of her husband brought into higher relief the image of her son whom she would never see again. Then she dried her tears, and paler and sadder than ever, continued her habitual life.

Ferragut saw her as serene as a school-mistress, with her two little nieces seated at her feet, keeping on with her eternal lace-work. She forgot it only in order to attend to the care of her husband, occupying herself with the very slightest details of his existence. That was her duty. From childhood, she had known what are the obligations of the wife of the captain of a ship when he stops at home for a few days, like a bird of passage. But back of such attentions, Ulysses divined the presence of an immovable obstacle. It was something enormous and transparent that had interposed itself between the two. They saw each other but without being able to touch each other. They were separated by a distance, as hard and luminous as a diamond, that made every attempt at drawing nearer together useless.

Cinta never smiled. Her eyes were dry, trying not to weep while her husband was near her, but giving herself up freely to grief when she was alone. Her duty was to make his existence bearable, hiding her thoughts.

But this prudence of a good house-mistress was trampling under foot their conjugal life of former times. One day Ferragut, with a return of his old affection, and desiring to illuminate Cinta's twilight existence with a pale ray of sunlight, ventured to caress her as in the early days of their marriage. She drew herself up, modest and offended, as though she had just received an insult. She escaped from his arms with the energy of one who is repelling an outrage.

Ulysses looked upon a new woman, intensely pale, of an almost olive countenance, the nose curved with wrath and a flash of madness in her eyes. All that she was guarding in the depths of her thoughts came forth, boiling over, expelled in a hoarse voice charged with tears.

"No, no! . . . We shall live together, because you are my husband and God commands that it shall be so; but I no longer love you: I cannot love you. . . . The wrong that you have done me! . . . I who loved you so much! . . . However much you may hunt in your voyages and in your wicked adventures, you will never find a woman that loves you as your wife has loved you."

Her past of modest and submissive affection, of supine and tolerant fidelity, now issued from her mouth in one interminable complaint.

"From our home my thoughts have followed you in all your voyages, although I knew your forgetfulness and your infidelity. All the papers found in your pockets, and photographs lost among your books, the allusions of your comrades, your smiles of pride, the satisfied air with which you many times returned, the series of new manners and additional care of your person that you did not have when you left, told me all. . . . I also suspected in your bold caresses the hidden presence of other women who lived far away on the other side of the world."

She stopped her turbulent language for a few moments, letting the blush which her memories evoked fade away.

"I loathed it all," she continued. "I know the men of the sea; I am a sailor's daughter. Many times I saw my mother weeping and pitied her simplicity. There is no use weeping for what men do in distant lands. It is always bitter enough for a woman who loves her husband, but it has no bad consequences and must be pardoned. . . . But now. . . . *Now!* . . ."

The wife became irritated on recalling his recent infidelities. . . . Her rivals were not the public women of the great ports, nor the tourists who could give only a few days of love, like an alms which they tossed without stopping their progress. Now he had become enamored with the enthusiasm of a husky boy with an elegant and handsome dame, with a foreign woman who had made him forget his business, abandon his ship, and remain away, as though renouncing his family forever. . . . And poor Esteban, orphaned by his father's forgetfulness, had gone in search of him, with the adventurous impetuosity inherited from his ancestors: and death, a horrible death, had come to meet him on the road.

Something more than the grief of the outraged wife vibrated in Cinta's laments. It was the rivalry with that woman of Naples, whom she believed a great lady with all the attractions of wealth and high birth. She envied her superior weapons of seduction; she raged at her own modesty and humility as a home-keeping woman.

"I was resolved to ignore it all," she continued. "I had one consolation,—my son. What did it matter to me what you did? . . . You were far off, and my son was living at my side. . . . And now I shall never see him again! . . . My fate is to live eternally alone. You know very well that I shall not be a mother again,—that I cannot give you another son. . . . And it was you, you! who have robbed me of the only thing that I had! . . ."

Her imagination invented the most improbable reasons for explaining to herself this unjust loss.

"God wished to punish you for your bad life and has therefore killed Esteban, and is slowly killing me. . . . When I learned of his death I wished to throw myself off the balcony. I am still living because I am a Christian, but what an existence awaits me! What a life for you if you are really a father! . . . Think that your son might still be existing if you had not remained in Naples."

Ferragut was a pitiful object. He hung his head without strength to repeat the confused and lying protests with which he had received his wife's first words.

"If she knew all the truth!" the voice of remorse kept saying in his brain.

He was thinking with horror of what Cinta could say if she knew the magnitude of his sin. Fortunately she was ignorant of the fact that he had been of assistance to the assassins of their son. . . . And the conviction that she never would know it made him admit her words with silent humility,—the humility of the criminal who hears himself accused of an offense by a judge ignorant of a still greater offense.

Cinta finished speaking in a discouraged and gloomy tone. She was exhausted. Her wrath faded out, consumed by its own violence. Her sobs cut short her words. Her husband would never again be the same man to her; the body of their son was always interposing between the two.

"I shall never be able to love you. . . . What have you done, Ulysses? What have you done that I should have such a horror of you? . . . When I am alone I weep: my sadness is great, but I admit my sorrow with resignation, as a thing inevitable. . . . As soon as I hear your footsteps, the truth springs forth. I realize that my son has died because of you, that he would still be living had he not gone in search of you, trying to make you realize that you were a father and what you owe to us. . . . And when I think of that I hate you, I *hate you!* . . . You have murdered my son! My only consolation is in the belief that if you have any conscience you will suffer even more than I."

Ferragut came out from this horrible scene with the conviction that he would have to go away. That home was no longer his, neither was his wife his. The reminder of death filled everything, intervening between him and Cinta, pushing him away, forcing him again on the sea. His vessel was the only refuge for the rest of his life, and he must resort to it like the great criminals of other centuries who had taken refuge in the isolation of monasteries.

He needed to vent his wrath on somebody, to find some responsible person whom he might blame for his misfortunes. Cinta had revealed herself to him as an entirely new being. He would never have suspected such energy of character, such passionate vehemence, in his sweet, obedient, little wife. She must have some counselor who was encouraging her complaints and making her speak badly of her husband.

And he fixed upon Don Pedro, the professor, because there was still deep within him a certain dislike of the man since the days of his courtship. Besides, it offended him to see him in his home with a certain air of a noble personage whose virtue served as foil for the sins and shortcomings of the master of the house.

The professor evidently considered Ferragut on a level with all the famous Don Juans,—liberal and care-free when in far-away homes, punctilious and suspiciously correct in his own.

"That old blatherskite!" said Ulysses to himself, "is in love with Cinta. It is a platonic passion : with him, it couldn't be anything else. But it annoys me greatly. . . . I'm going to say a few things to him."

Don Pedro, who was continuing his daily visits in order to console the mother, speaking of poor Esteban as though he were his own son, and casting servile smiles upon the captain, found himself intercepted by him one afternoon, on the landing of the stairway.

The sailor aged suddenly while talking, and his features were accented with a vigorous ugliness. At that moment he looked exactly like his uncle, the *Triton*..

With a threatening voice, he recalled a classic passage well known to the professor. His namesake, old Ulysses, upon returning to his palace, had found Penelope surrounded with suitors and had ended by hanging them on tenterhooks.

"Wasn't that the way of it, Professor? . . . I do not find here more than one suitor, but this Ulysses swears to you that he will hang him in the same way if he finds him again in his home."

Don Pedro fled. He had always found the rude heroes of the Odyssey very interesting, but in verse and on paper. In reality they now seemed to him most dangerous brutes, and he wrote a letter to Cinta telling her that he would suspend his visits until her husband should have returned to sea.

This insult increased the wife's distant bearing. She resented it as an offense against herself. After having made her lose her son, Ulysses was terrifying her only friend.

The captain felt obliged to go. By staying in that hostile atmosphere, which was only sharpening his remorse, he would pile one error upon another. Nothing but action could make him forget.

One day he announced to Toni that in a few hours he was going to weigh anchor. He had offered his services to the allied navies in order to carry food to the fleet in the Dardanelles. The *Mare Nostrum* would transport eatables, arms, munitions, aeroplanes.

Toni attempted objection. It would be easy to find trips equally productive and much less dangerous; they might go to America. . . .

"And my revenge?" interrupted Ferragut. "I am going to dedicate the rest of my life to doing all the evil that I can to the assassins of my son. The Allies need boats, I'm going to give them mine and my person."

Knowing what was troubling his mate, he added,

"Besides, they pay well. These trips are very remunerative. . . . They will give me whatever I ask."

For the first time in his existence on board the *Mare Nostrum,* the mate made a scornful gesture regarding the value of the cargo.

"I almost forgot," continued Ulysses, smiling in spite of his sadness. "This trip flatters your ideals. . . . We are going to work for the Republic."

They went to England and, taking on their cargo, set forth for the Dardanelles. Ferragut wished to sail alone without the protection of the destroyers that were escorting the convoys.

He knew the Mediterranean well. Besides, he was from a neutral country and the Spanish flag was flying from the poop of his vessel. This abuse of his flag did not produce the slightest remorse, nor did it appear as disloyal to him. The German corsairs were coming closer to their prey, displaying neutral flags, in order to deceive. The submarines were remaining hidden behind pacific sailing ships in order to rise up suddenly near defenseless vessels. The most felonious proceedings of the ancient pirates had been resuscitated by the German fleet.

He was not afraid of the submarines. He trusted in the speed of the *Mare Nostrum* and in his lucky star.

"And if any of them should cross our path," he said to his second, "just let them go before the prow!"

He wished this so that he could send his vessel upon the submersible at full speed, daring it to come on.

The Mediterranean was no longer the same sea that it had been months before when the captains knew all its secrets; he could no longer live on it as confidently as in the house of a friend.

He stayed in his stateroom only to sleep. He and Toni

spent long hours on the bridge talking without seeing
each other, with their eyes turned on the sea, scanning
the heaving blue surface. All the crew, excepting those
that were resting, felt the necessity of keeping the same
watch.

In the daytime the slightest discovery would send the
alarm from prow to poop. All the refuse of the sea, that
weeks before had splashed unnoticed near the sides
of the vessel, now provoked cries of attention, and many
arms were outstretched, pointing it out. Bits of sticks,
empty preserve cans sparkling in the sunlight, bunches
of seaweed, a sea gull with outspread wings letting
itself rock on the waves; everything made them think of
the periscopes of the submarine coming up to the water's
level.

At night time the vigilance was even greater. To the
danger of submersibles must also be added that
of collision. The warships and the allied transports
were traveling with few lights or completely dark. The
sentinels on the bridge were no longer scanning the
surface of the sea with its pale phosphorescence. Their
gaze explored the horizon, fearing that before the prow
there might suddenly surge up an enormous, swift, black
form, vomited forth by the darkness.

If at any time the captain tarried in his stateroom,
instantly that fatal memory came to his mind.

"Esteban! . . . My son! . . ."

And his eyes were full of tears.

Remorse and wrath made him plan tremendous vengeance. He was convinced that it would be impossible
to carry it through, but it was a momentary consolation
to his meridional character predisposed to the most bloody
revenge.

One day, running over some forgotten papers in a
suit-case, he came across Freya's portrait. Upon seeing

her audacious smile and her calm eyes fixed upon him, he felt within him a shameful reversion. He admired the beauty of this apparition, a thrill passing over his body as their past intercourse recurred to him. . . . And at the same time that other Ferragut existing within him thrilled with the murderous violence of the Oriental who considers death as the only means of vengeance. She was to blame for it all. "Ah! . . . *Tal!*"

He tore up the photograph, but then he put the fragments together again and finally placed them among his papers.

His wrath was changing its objective. Freya really was not the principal person guilty of Esteban's death. He was thinking of that other one, of the pretended diplomat, of that von Kramer who perhaps had directed the torpedo which had blown his son to atoms. . . . Would he not raise the devil if he could meet him sometime? . . . What happiness if these two should find themselves face to face!

Finally he avoided the solitude of a stateroom that tormented him with desires of impotent revenge. Near Toni on deck or on the bridge he felt better. . . . And with a humble condescension, such as his mate had never known before, he would talk and talk, enjoying the attention of his simple-hearted listener, just as though he were telling marvelous stories to a circle of children.

In the Strait of Gibraltar he explained to him the great currents sent by the ocean into the Mediterranean, at certain times aiding the screw-propeller in the propulsion of the vessel.

Without this Atlantic current the *mare nostrum,* which lost through atmospheric evaporation much more water than the rains and rivers could bring to it, would become dry in a few centuries. It had been calculated that it might disappear in about four hundred and seventy years, leaving as evidence of its former existence a stratum of salt fifty-two meters thick.

In its deep bosom were born great and numerous springs of fresh water, on the coast of Asia Minor, in Morea, Dalmatia and southern Italy; it received besides a considerable contribution from the Black Sea, which on returning to the Mediterranean accumulated from the rains and the discharge of its rivers, more water than it lost by evaporation, sending it across the Bosporous and the Dardenelles in the form of a superficial current. But all these tributaries, enormous as they were, sank into insignificance when compared with the renovation of the oceanic currents.

The waters of the Atlantic poured into the Mediterranean so riotously that neither contrary winds nor reflex motion could stop them. Sailboats sometimes had to wait entire months for a strong breeze that would enable them to conquer the impetuous mouth of the strait.

"I know that very well," said Toni. "Once going to Cuba we were in sight of Gibraltar more than fifty days, going backwards and forwards until a favorable wind enabled us to overcome the current and go out into the great sea."

"Just such a current," added Ferragut, "was one of the causes that hastened the decadence of the Mediterranean navies in the sixteenth century. They had to go to the recently discovered Indies, and the Catalan or the Genoese ships would remain here in the strait weeks and weeks, struggling with the wind and the contrary current while the Galicians, the Basques, the French and the English who had left their ports at the same time were already nearing America. . . . Fortunately, navigation by steam has now equalized all that."

Toni was silently admiring his captain. What he must have learned in those books that filled the stateroom! . . .

It was in the Mediterranean that men had first entrusted themselves to the waves. Civilization emanated from India, but the Asiatic peoples were not able to master the art of navigation in their few seas whose coasts were very far apart and where the monsoons of the Indian Ocean blew six months together in one direction and six months in another.

Not until he reached the Mediterranean by overland migration did the white man wish to become a sailor. This sea that, compared with others, is a simple lake sown with archipelagoes, offered a good school. To whatever wind he might set his sails, he would be sure to reach some hospitable shore. The fresh and irregular breezes revolved with the sun at certain times of the year. The hurricane whirled across its bowl, but never stopped. There were no tides. Its harbors and waterways were never dry. Its coasts and islands were often so close together that you could see from one to the other; its lands, beloved of heaven, were recipients of the sun's sweetest smiles.

Ferragut recalled the men who had plowed this sea in centuries so remote that history makes no mention of them. The only traces of their existence now extant were the *nuraghs* of Sardinia and the *talayots* of the Balearic Islands,—gigantic tables formed with blocks, barbaric altars of enormous rocks which recalled the Celtic obelisks and sepulchral monuments of the Breton coast. These obscure people had passed from isle to isle, from the extreme of the Mediterranean to the strait which is its door.

The captain could imagine their rude craft made from trunks of trees roughly planed, propelled by one oar, or rather by the stroke of a stick, with no other aid than single rudimentary sail spread to the fresh breeze. The navy of the first Europeans had been like that

of the savages of the oceanic islands whose flotilla
of tree trunks are still actually going from archipelag
to archipelago.

Thus they had dared to sally forth from the coast
to lose sight of land, to venture forth into the blu
desert, advised of the existence of islands by the vaporou
knobs of the mountains which were outlined on the hori
zon at sunset. Every advance of this hesitating marin
over the Mediterranean had represented greater expendi
ture of audacity and energy than the discovery of Amer
ica or the first voyage around the world. . . . Thes
primitive sailors did not go forth alone to their adven
tures on the sea; they were nations *en masse,* they car
ried with them families and animals. Once installed o
an island, the tribes sent forth fragments of their ow
life, going to colonize other nearby lands across th
waves.

Ulysses and his mate thought much about the grea
catastrophes ignored by history—the tempest surprising
the sailing exodus, entire fleets of rough rafts swal
lowed up by the abyss in a few moments, families dying
clinging to their domestic animals,—whenever they at
tempted a new advance of their rudimentary civiliza
tion.

In order to form some idea of what these little em
barkations were, Ferragut would recall the fleets o
Homeric form, created many centuries afterwards. The
winds used to impose a religious terror on those war
riors of the sea, reunited in order to fall upon Troy
Their ships remained chained an entire year in the har
bor of Aulis and, through fear of the hostility of the
wind and in order to placate the divinity of the Mediter
ranean, they sacrificed the life of a virgin.

All was danger and mystery in the kingdom of the
waves. The abysses roared, the rocks moaned; on the

ledges were singing sirens who, with their music, attracted ships in order to dash them to pieces. There was not an island without its particular god, without its monster and cyclops, or its magician contriving artifices.

Before domesticating the elements, mankind had attributed to them their most superstitious fears.

A material factor had powerfully influenced the dangers of Mediterranean life. The sand, moved by the caprice of the current, was constantly ruining the villages or raising them to peaks of unexpected prosperity. Cities celebrated in history were to-day no more than streets of ruins at the foot of a hillock crowned with the remains of a Phœnician, Roman, Byzantine or Saracen castle, or with a fortress contemporary with the Crusades. In other centuries these had been famous ports; before their walls had taken place naval battles; now from their ruined acropolis one could scarcely see the Mediterranean except as a light blue belt at the end of a low and marshy plain. The accumulating sand had driven the sea back miles. . . . On the other hand, inland cities had come to be places of embarkation because of the continual perforation of the waves that were forcing their way in.

The wickedness of mankind had imitated the destructive work of nature. When a maritime republic conquered a rival republic, the first thing that it thought of was to obstruct its harbor with sand and stones in order to divert the course of its waters so as to convert it into an inland city, thereby ruining its fleets and its traffic. The Genoese, triumphant over Pisa, stopped up its harbor with the sands of the Arno; and the city of the first conquerors of Mallorca, of the navigators to the Holy Land, of the Knights of St. Stephen, guardians of the Mediterranean, came to be Pisa the Dead,—a settlement that knew the sea only by hearsay.

"Sand," continued Ferragut, "has changed the commercial routes and historic destinies of the Mediterranean."

Of the many deeds which had stretched along the scenes of the *mare nostrum*, the most famous in the captain's opinion was the unheard-of epic of Roger de Flor which he had known from childhood through the stories told him .by the poet Labarta, by the *Triton*, and by that poor secretary who was always dreaming of the great past of the Catalan marine.

All the world was now talking about the blockade of the Dardanelles. The boats that furrowed the Mediterranean, merchant vessels as well as battleships, were furthering the great military operation that was developing opposite Gallipoli. The name of the long, narrow maritime pass which separates Europe and Asia was in every mouth. To-day the eyes of mankind were converged on this point just as, in remote centuries, they had been fixed on the war of Troy.

"We also have been there," said Ferragut with pride. "The Dardanelles have been frequented for many years by the Catalans and the Aragonese. Gallipoli was one of our cities governed by the Valencian, Ramon Muntaner."

And he began the story of the Almogavars in the Orient, that romantic Odyssey across the ancient Asiatic provinces of the Roman Empire that ended only with the founding of the Spanish duchy of Athens and Neopatria in the city of Pericles and Minerva. The chronicles of the Oriental Middle Ages, the books of Byzantine chivalry, the fantastic tales of the Arab do not contain more improbable and dramatic adventures than the warlike enterprises of these Argonauts coming from the valleys of the Pyrenees, from the banks of the Ebro, and from the Moorish gardens of Valencia.

"Eighty years," said Ferragut, terminating his account

of the glorious adventures of Roger de Flor around Gallipoli, "the Spanish duchy of Athens and Neopatria flourished. Eighty years the Catalans governed these lands."

And he pointed out on the horizon the place where the red haze of distant promontories and mountains outlined the Grecian land.

Such a duchy was in reality a republic. Athens and Thebes were administered in accordance with the laws of Aragon and its code was "The book of Usages and Customs of the City of Barcelona." The Catalan tongue ruled as the official language in the country of Demosthenes, and the rude Almogavars married with the highest ladies of the country.

The Parthenon was still intact as in the glorious times of ancient Athens. The august monument of Minerva converted into a Christian church, had not undergone any other modification than that of seeing a new goddess on its altars, *La Virgen Santisima*.

And in this thousand-year-old temple of sovereign beauty the *Te Deum* was sung for eighty years in honor of the Aragonese dukes, and the clergy preached in the Catalan tongue.

The republic of adventurers did not bother with constructing nor creating. There does not remain on the Grecian land any trace of their dominion,—edifices, seals, nor coins. Only a few noble families, especially in the islands, took the Catalan patronym.

"Although they yet remember us confusedly, they do remember us," said Ferragut. "'May the vengeance of the Catalans overtake you' was for many centuries the worst of curses in Greece."

Thus terminated the most glorious and bloody of the Mediterranean adventures of the Middle Ages,—the clash of western crudeness, almost savage but frank and

noble, against the refined malice and decadent civilization of the Greeks,—childish and old at the same time,—
which survived in Byzantium.

Ferragut felt a pleasure in these relations of imperial splendor, palaces of gold, epic encounters and
furious frays, while his ship was navigating through the
black night and bounding over the dark sea accompanied
by the throbbing of machinery and the noisy thrum of
the screw, at times out of the water during the furious
rocking from prow to poop.

They were in the worst place in the Mediterranean
where the winds coming from the narrow passage of the
Adriatic, from the steppes of Asia Minor, from the
African deserts and from the gap of Gibraltar tempestu-
ously mingled their atmospheric currents. The waters
boxed in among the numerous islands of the Grecian
archipelago were writhing in opposite directions, enraged
and clashing against the ledges on the coast with a retro-
grading violence that converted them into a furious
surge.

The captain, hooded like a friar and bowed before
the wind that was striving to snatch him from the bridge,
kept talking and talking to his mate, standing immovable
near him and also covered with a waterproof coat that
was spouting moisture from every fold. The rain was
streaking with light, cobwebby lines the slaty darkness,
of the night. The two sailors felt as though icy nettles
were falling upon face and hands across the darkness.

Twice they anchored near the island of Tenedos, seeing the movable archipelago of ironclads enveloped
in floating veils of smoke. There came to their ears, like
incessant thunderings, the echo of the cannons that were
roaring at the entrance of the Dardanelles.

From afar off they perceived the sensation caused by

the loss of some English and French ships. The current of the Black Sea was the best armor for the defenders of this aquatic defile against the attacks of the fleets. They had only to throw into the strait a quantity of floating mines and the blue river which slipped by the Dardanelles would drag these toward the boats, destroying them with an infernal explosion. On the coast of Tenedos the Hellenic women with their floating hair were tossing flowers into the sea in memory of the victims, with a theatrical grief similar to that of the heroines of ancient Troy whose ramparts were buried in the hills opposite.

The third trip in mid-winter was a very hard one, and at the end of a rainy night, when the faint streaks of dawn were beginning to dissipate the sluggish shadows, the *Mare Nostrum* arrived at the roadstead of Salonica.

Only once had Ferragut been in this port, many years before, when it still belonged to the Turks. At first he saw only some lowlands on which twinkled the last gleams from the lighthouses. Then he recognized the roadstead, a vast aquatic extension with a frame of sandy bars and pools reflecting the uncertain life of daybreak. The recently awakened sea-gulls were flying in groups over the immense marine bowl. At the mouth of the Vardar the fresh-water fowls were starting up with noisy cries, or standing on the edge of the bank immovable upon their long legs.

Opposite the prow, a city was rising up out of the albuminous waves of fog. In a bit of the clear, blue sky appeared various minarets, their peaks sparkling with the fires of Aurora. As the vessel advanced, the morning clouds vanished, and Salonica became entirely visible from the cluster of huts at her wharves to the ancient castle topping the heights, a fortress of ruddy towers, low and strong.

Near the water's edge, the entire length of the harbor, were the European constructions, commercial houses with gold-lettered signs, hotels, banks, moving-picture shows, concert halls, and a massive tower with another smaller one upon it,—the so-called White Tower, a remnant of the Byzantine fortifications.

In this European conglomerate were dark gaps, open passageways, the mouths of sloping streets climbing to the hillock above, crossing the Grecian, Mohammedan and Jewish quarters until they reached a table-land covered with lofty edifices between dark points of cypress.

The religious diversity of the Oriental Mediterranean made Salonica bristle with cupolas and towers. The Greek temple threw into prominence the gilded bulbs of its roof; the Catholic church made the cross glisten from the peak of its bell-tower; the synagogue of geometrical forms overflowed in a succession of terraces; the Mohammedan minaret formed a colonnade, white, sharp and slender. Modern life had added factory chimneys and the arms of steam-cranes which gave an anachronistic effect to this decoration of an Oriental harbor. Around the city and its acropolis was the plain which lost itself in the horizon,—a plain that Ferragut, on a former voyage, had seen desolate and monotonous, with few houses and sparsely cultivated, with no other vegetation except that in the little oases of the Mohammedan cemetery. This desert extended to Greece and Servia or to the borders of Bulgaria and Turkey.

Now the brownish-gray steppes coming out from the fleecy fog of daybreak were palpitating with new life. Thousands and thousands of men were encamped around the city, occupying new villages made of canvas, rectangular streets of tents, cities of wooden cabins, and constructions as big as churches whose canvas walls were trembling under the violent squalls of wind.

Through his glasses, Ulysses could see warlike hosts occupied with the business of caring for strings of riderless horses that were going to watering places, parks of artillery with their cannon upraised like the tubes of a telescope, enormous birds with yellow wings that were trying to skip along the earth's surface with a noisy bumping, gradually reappearing in space with their waxy wings glistening in the first shafts of sunlight.

All the allied army of the Orient returning from the bloody and mistaken adventure of the Dardanelles or proceeding from Marseilles and Gibraltar were massing themselves around Salonica.

The *Mare Nostrum* anchored at the wharves filled with boxes and bales. War had given a much greater activity to this port than in times of peace. Steamers of all the allied and neutral flags were unloading eatables and military materials.

They were coming from every continent, from every ocean, drawn thither by the tremendous necessities of a modern army. They were unloading harvests from entire provinces, unending herds of oxen and horses, tons upon tons of steel, prepared for deadly work, and human crowds lacking only a tail of women and children to be like the great martial exoduses of history. Then taking on board the residuum of war, arms needing repair, wounded men, they would begin their return trip.

These cargoes quietly transported through the darkness in spite of bad times and the submarine threats, were preparing the ultimate victory. Many of these steamers were formerly luxurious vessels, but now commandeered by military necessity, were dirty and greasy and used as cargo boats. Lined up, drowsing along the docks, ready to begin their work, were new hospital ships, the more fortunate transatlantic liners that still retained a certain trace of their former condition, quite clean with a red cross painted on their sides and another on their smokestacks.

Some of the transports had reached Salonica most miraculously. Their crews would relate with the fatalistic serenity of men of the sea how the torpedo had passed at a short distance from their hulls. A damaged steamer lay on its side, with only the keel submerged, all its red exterior exposed to the air; on its water-line there had opened a breach, angular in outline. Upon looking from the deck into the depths of its hold filled with water, there might be seen a great gash in its side like the mouth of a luminous cavern.

Ferragut, while his boat was discharging its cargo under Toni's supervision, passed his days ashore, visiting the city.

From the very first moment he was attracted by the narrow lanes of the Turkish quarters—their white houses with protruding balconies covered with latticed blinds like cages painted red; the little mosques with their patios of cypresses and fountains of melancholy tinkling; the tombs of Mohammedan dervishes in kiosks which block the streets under the pale reflection of a lamp; the women veiled with their black *firadjes;* and the old men who, silent and thoughtful under their scarlet caps, pass along swaying to the staggering of the ass on which they are mounted.

The great Roman way between Rome and Byzantium, the ancient road of the blue flagstones, passed through a street of modern Salonica. Still a part of its pavement remained and appeared gloriously obstructed by an arch of triumph near whose weatherbeaten stone base were working barefooted bootblacks wearing the scarlet fez.

An endless variety of uniforms filed through the

streets, and this diversity in attire as well as the ethnical difference in the men who wore it was very noticeable. The soldiers of France and the British Isles touched elbows with the foreign troops. The allied governments had sent out a call to the professional combatants and volunteers of their colonies. The black sharpshooters from the center of Africa showed their smiling teeth of marble to the bronze giants with huge white turbans who had come from India. The hunters from the glacial plains of Canada were fraternizing with the volunteers from Australia and New Zealand.

The cataclysm of the world war had dragged mankind from the antipodes to this drowsy little corner of Greece where were again repeated the invasions of remote centuries which had made ancient Thessalonica bow to the conquest of Bulgarians, Byzantians, Saracens, and Turks.

The crews of the battleships in the roadstead had just added to this medley of uniforms the monotonous note of their midnight blue, almost like that of all the navies of the world. . . . And to the military amalgamation was also added the picturesque variety of civil dress,—the hybrid character of the neighborhood of Salonica, composed of various races and religions that were mingled together without confusing their individuality. Files of black tunics and hats with brimless crowns passed through the streets, near the Catholic priests or the rabbis with their long, loose gowns. In the outskirts might be seen men almost naked, with no other clothing than a sheep-skin tunic, guiding flocks of pigs, just like the shepherds in the Odyssey. Dervishes, with their aspect of dementia, chanted motionless in a crossway, enveloped in clouds of flies, awaiting the aid of the good believers.

A great part of the population was composed of Israelitish descendants of the Jews expelled from Spain and Portugal. The oldest and most conservative were clad just like their remote ancestors with large kaftans striped with striking colors. The women, when not imitating the European fashions, usually wore a picturesque garment that recalled the Spanish apparel of the Middle Ages. Here they were not mere brokers or traders as in the rest of the world. The necessities of the city dominated by them had made them pick up all the professions, becoming artisans, fishermen, boatmen, porters and stevedores of the harbor. They still kept the Castilian tongue as the language of the hearth like an original flag whose waving reunited their scattered souls,—a Castilian in the making, soft and without consistency like one newly-born.

"Are you a Spaniard?" they said brokenly to Captain Ferragut. "My ancestors were born there. It is a beautiful land."

But they did not wish to return to it. The country of their grandsires inspired a certain amount of terror in them, and they feared that upon seeing them return, the present-day Spaniards would banish the bullfights and reëstablish the Inquisition, organizing an *auto de fé* every Sunday.

Hearing them speak his language, the captain recalled a certain date—1492. In the very year that Christopher Columbus had made his first voyage, discovering the Indies, the Jews were expelled from the Spanish peninsula, and Nebrija brought out the first Castilian grammar. These Spaniards had left their native land months before their idiom had been codified for the first time.

A sailor of Genoa, an old friend of Ulysses, took him to one of the harbor cafés, where the merchant captains used to gather together. These were the only ones wearing civilian clothes among the crowds of land and sea officers who crowded the divans, obstructed the tables, and grouped themselves before the doorway.

These Mediterranean vagabonds who oftentimes could not converse together because of the diversity of their native idiom, instinctively sought each other out, keeping near together in a fraternal silence. Their passive heroism was in many instances more admirable than that of the men of war, who were able to return blow for blow. All the officers of the different fleets, seated near them, had at their disposition cannon, ram, torpedo, great speed and aerial telegraphy. These valorous muleteers of the sea defied the enemy in defenseless boats without wireless and without cannons. Sometimes when searching all the men of the crew, not a single revolver would be found among them, and yet these brave fellows were daring the greatest adventures with professional fatalism, and trusting to luck.

In the social groups of the café the captains would sometimes relate their encounters on the sea, the unexpected appearance of a submarine, the torpedo missing aim a few yards away, the flight at full speed while being shelled by their pursuers. They would flame up for an instant upon recalling their danger, and then relapse into indifference and fatalism.

"If I've got to die by drowning," they would always conclude, "it would be useless for me to try to avoid it."

And they would hasten their departure in order to return a month later transporting a regular fortune in their vessel, completely alone, preferring free and wary navigation to the journey in convoy, slipping along from island to island and from coast to coast in order to outwit the submersibles.

They were far more concerned about the state of their ships, that for more than a year had not been cleaned, than about the dangers of navigation. The captains of the great liners lamented their luxurious staterooms converted into dormitories for the troops, their polished decks that had been turned into stables, their dining-room where they used to sit among people in dress suits and low-neck gowns, which had now to be sprayed with every class of disinfectant in order to repel the invasion of vermin, and the animal odors of so many men and beasts crowded together.

The decline of the ships appeared to be reflected in the bearing of their captains, more careless than before, worse dressed, with the military slovenliness of the trench-fighter, and with calloused hands as badly cared for as those of a stevedore.

Among the naval men also there were some who had completely neglected their appearance. These were the commanders of "chaluteros," little ocean fishing steamers armed with a quickfirer, which had come into the Mediterranean to pursue the submersible. They wore oilskins and tarpaulins, just like the North Sea fishermen, smacking of fuel and tempestuous water. They would pass weeks and weeks on the sea whatever the weather, sleeping in the bottom of the hold that smelled offensively of rancid fish, keeping on patrol no matter how the tempest might roar, bounding from wave to wave like a cork from a bottle, in order to repeat the exploits of the ancient corsairs.

Ferragut had a relative in the army which was assembling at Salonica making ready for the inland march. As he did not wish to go away without seeing the lad he passed several mornings making investigations in the offices of the general staff.

This relative was his nephew, a son of Blanes, the manufacturer of knit goods, who had fled from Barcelona at the outbreak of the war with other boys devoted to singing *Los Segadores* and perturbing the tranquillity of the "Consul of Spain" sent by Madrid. The son of the pacific Catalan citizen had enlisted in the battalion of the Foreign Legion made up to a great extent of Spaniards and Spanish-Americans.

Blanes had asked the captain to see his son. He was sad yet at the same time proud of this romantic adventure blossoming out so unexpectedly in the utilitarian and monotonous existence of the family. A boy that had such a great future in his father's factory! . . . And then he had related to Ulysses with shaking voice and moist eyes the achievements of his son,—wounded in Champagne, two citations and the *Croix de Guerre*. Who would ever have imagined that he could be such a hero! . . . Now his battalion was in Salonica after having fought in the Dardanelles.

"See if you can't bring him back with you," repeated Blanes. "Tell him that his mother is going to die of grief. . . . You can do so much!"

But all that Captain Ferragut could do was to obtain a permit and an old automobile with which to visit the encampment of the legionaries.

The arid plain around Salonica was crossed by numerous roads. The trains of artillery, the rosaries of automobiles, were rolling over recently opened roads that the rain had converted into mire. The mud was the worst calamity that could befall this plain, so extremely dusty in dry weather.

Ferragut passed two long hours, going from encampment to encampment, before reaching his destination. His vehicle frequently had to stop in order to make way for interminable files of trucks. At other times machine-guns, big guns dragged by tractors, and provision cars with pyramids of sacks and boxes, blocked their road.

On all sides were thousands and thousands of soldiers

of different colors and races. The captain recalled the great invasions of history—Xerxes, Alexander, Genghis-Khan, all the leaders of men who had made their advance carrying villages *en masse* behind their horses, transforming the servants of the earth into fighters. There lacked only the soldierly women, the swarms of children, to complete exactly the resemblance to the martial exoduses of the past.

In half an hour more he was able to embrace his nephew, who was with two other volunteers, an Andulasian and a South American,—the three united by brotherhood of birth and by their continual familiarity with death.

Ferragut took them to the canteen of a trader established near the cantonment. The customers were seated under a sail-cloth awning before boxes that had contained munitions and were converted into office tables. This discomfort was surpassed by the prices. In no Palace Hotel would drink have cost such an extraordinary sum.

In a few moments the sailor felt a fraternal affection for these three youths to whom he gave the nickname of the "Three Musketeers," He wished to treat them to the very best which the canteen afforded, so the proprietor produced a bottle of champagne or rather ptisan from Rheims, presenting it as though it were an elixir fabricated of gold.

The amber liquid, bubbling in the glasses, seemed to bring the three youths back to their former existence. Boiled by the sun and the inclemency of the weather, habituated to the hard life of war, they had almost forgotten the softness and luxuriant conveniences of former years.

Ulysses examined them attentively. In the course of the campaign they had grown with youth's last rapid growth. Their arms were sticking out to an ungainly degree from the sleeves of their coats, already too short for them. The rude gymnastic exercise of the marches, with the management of the shovel, had broadened their wrists and calloused their hands.

The memory of his own son surged up in his memory. If only he could see him thus, made into a soldier like his cousin! See him enduring all the hardships of military existence . . . but living!

In order not to be too greatly moved, he drank and paid close attention to what the three youths were saying. Blanes, the legionary, as romantic as the son of a merchant bent upon adventure should be, was talking of the daring deeds of the troops of the Orient with all the enthusiasm of his twenty-two years. There wasn't time to throw themselves upon the Bulgarians with bayonets and arrive at Adrianopolis. As a Catalan, this war in Macedonia was touching him very close.

"We are going to avenge Roger de Flor," he said gravely.

And his uncle wanted to weep and to laugh before this simple faith comparable only to the retrospective memory of the poet Labarta and that village secretary who was always lamenting the remote defeat of Ponza.

Blanes explained like a knight-errant the impulse that had called him to the war. He wanted to fight for the liberty of all oppressed nations, for the resurrection of all forgotten nationalities,—Poles, Czechs, Jugo-Slavs. . . . And very simply, as though he were saying something indisputable, he included Catalunia among the people who were weeping tears of blood under the lashes of the tyrant. Thereupon his companion, the Andalusian, burst forth indignantly. They passed their time arguing furiously, exchanging insults and continually seeking each other's company as though they couldn't live apart.

The Andalusian was not battling for the liberty of this or that people. He had a longer range of vision. He was not near-sighted and egoistic like his friend, "the Catalan." He was giving his blood in order that the whole world might be free and that all monarchies should disappear.

"I am battling for France because it is the country of the great Revolution. Its former history makes no difference to me, for we still have kings of our own, but dating from the 14th of July, whatever France is, I consider mine and the property of all mankind."

He stopped a few seconds, searching for a more concrete affirmation.

"I am fighting, Captain, because of Danton and Hoche."

Ferragut in his imagination saw the white, disheveled hair of Michelet and the romantic foretop of Lamartine upon a double pedestal of volumes which used to contain the story-poem of the Revolution.

"And I am also fighting for France," concluded the lad triumphantly, "because it is the country of Victor Hugo."

Ulysses suspected that this twenty-year-old Republican was probably hiding in his knapsack a blank book full of original verses written in lead pencil.

The South American, accustomed to the disputes of his two companions, looked at his black fingernails with the melancholy desperation of a prophet contemplating his country in ruins. Blanes, the son of a middle-class citizen, used to admire him for his more distinguished family. The day of the mobilization he had gone to Paris in an automobile of fifty horse-power to enroll as a volunteer; he and his chauffeur had enlisted together. Then he had donated his luxurious vehicle to the cause.

He had wished to be a soldier because all the young fellows in his club were leaving for the war. Furthermore, he felt greatly flattered that his latest sweetheart, seeing him in uniform, should devote a few tears of admiration and astonishment to him. He had felt the necessity of producing a touching effect upon all the ladies that had danced the tango with him up to the week before. Besides that, the millions of his grandfather, "the Galician," held rather tight by his father, the Creole, were slipping through his hands.

"This experience is lasting too long, Captain."

In the beginning he had believed in a six months' war. The shells didn't trouble him much; for him the terrible things were the vermin, the impossibility of changing his clothing, and being deprived of his daily bath. If he could ever have supposed! . . .

And he summed up his enthusiasm with this affirmation:

"I am fighting for France because it is a *chic* country. Only in Paris do the women know how to dress. Those Germans, no matter how much they try, will always be very ordinary."

It was not necessary to add anything to this. All had been said.

The three recalled the hellish months suffered recently in the Dardanelles, in a space of three miles conquered by the bayonet. A rain of projectiles had fallen incessantly upon them. They had had to live underground like moles and, even so, the explosion of the great shells sometimes reached them.

In this tongue of land opposite Troy through which had slipped the remote history of humanity, their shovels, on opening the trenches, had stumbled upon the rarest finds. One day Blanes and his companions had excavated pitchers, statuettes, and plates centuries old. At other times, when opening trenches that had served as cemeteries for Turks, they had hacked into repulsive bits of pulp exhaling an insufferable odor. Self-defense had obliged the legionaries to live with their faces on a level with the corpses that were piled up in the vertical yard of removed earth.

"The dead are like the truffles in a pie," said the South American. "An entire day I had to remain with my nose touching the intestines of a Turk who had died two weeks before. . . . No, war is not *chic,* Captain, no matter how much they talk of heroism and sublime things in the newspapers and books."

Ulysses wished to see the three musketeers again before leaving Salonica, but the battalion had broken camp and was now situated several kilometers further inland, opposite the first Bulgarian lines. The enthusiastic Blanes had already fired his gun against the assassins of Roger de Flor.

In the middle of November the *Mare Nostrum* arrived at Marseilles. Its captain always felt a certain admiration upon doubling Cape Croisette, and noting the vast maritime curves opening out before the prow. In the center of it was an abrupt and bare hill, jutting into the sea, sustaining on its peak the basilica and square-sided tower of *Notre-Dame-de-la-Garde.*

Marseilles was the metropolis of the Mediterranean, the terminal for all the navigators of the *mare nostrum.* In its bay with choppy waves were various yellowish islands fringed with foam and upon one of these the strong towers of the romantic *Château d'If.*

All the crew, from Ferragut down to the lowest seaman, used to look upon this city somewhat as their own when they saw, appearing in the background of the bay, its forests of masts and its conglomeration of gray edifices upon which sparkled the Byzantian domes of the

new cathedral. Around Marseilles there opened out a
semi-circle of dry and barren heights brightly colored
by the sun of Provence and spotted by white cottages
and hamlets, and the pleasure villas of the merchants
of the city. On beyond this semi-circle the horizon was
bounded by an amphitheater of rugged and gloomy mountains.

On former trips the sight of the gigantic gilded Virgin
which glistened like a shaft of fire on the top of *Notre-
Dame-de-la-Garde* shed an atmosphere of joy over the
bridge of the vessel.

"Marseilles, Toni," the captain used to say gayly. "I
invite you to a *bouillabaisse* at Pascal's."

And Toni's hairy countenance would break into a
greedy smile, seeing in anticipation the famous restaurant
of the port, its twilight shadows smelling of shell-fish
and spicy sauces, and upon the table the deep dish of
fish with its succulent broth tinged with saffron.

But now Ulysses had lost his vigorous joy in living.
He looked at the city with kindly but sad eyes. He
could see himself disembarking there that last time, sick,
without will-power, overwhelmed by the tragic disappearance of his son.

The *Mare Nostrum* approached the mouth of the old
harbor having at its right the batteries of the *Phare*. This
old port was the most interesting souvenir of ancient
Marseilles, penetrating like an aquatic knife into the
heart of its clustered homes. The city extended along
the wharves. It was an enormous stretch of water into
which all the streets flowed; but its area was now so
insufficient for the maritime traffic that eight new harbors were gradually covering the north shore of the bay.

An interminable jetty, a breakwater longer than the
city itself, was parallel to the coast, and in the space
between the shore and this obstacle which made the

waves foam and roar were eight roomy communicating harbors stretching from Joliette at the entrance to the one which, farthest away, is connected inland by the great subterranean canal, putting the city in communication with the Rhone.

Ferragut had seen anchored in this succession of harbors the navies of every land and even of every epoch. Near to the enormous transatlantic liners were some very ancient tartans and some Greek boats, heavy and of archaic form, which recalled the fleets described in the Iliad.

On the wharves swarmed all kinds of Mediterranean men,—Greeks from the continent and from the islands, Levantines from the coast of Asia, Spaniards, Italians, Algerians, Moroccans, Egyptians. Many had kept their original costume and to this varied picturesque garb was united a diversity of tongues, some of them mysterious and well-nigh extinct. As though infected by the oral confusion, the French themselves began to forget their native language, speaking the dialect of Marseilles, which preserves indelible traces of its Greek origin.

The *Mare Nostrum* crossed the outer port, the inner harbor of Joliette, and slipped slowly along past groups of pedestrians and carts that were waiting the closing of the steel drawbridge now opening before their prow. Then they cast anchor in the basin of Arenc near the docks.

When Ferragut could go ashore he noticed the great transformation which this port had undergone in war times.

The traffic of the times of peace with its infinite variety of wares no longer existed. On the wharves there were piled up only the monotonous and uniform loads of provisions and war material.

The legions of longshoremen had also disappeared.

They were all in the trenches. The sidewalks were now swept by women, and squads of Senegalese sharpshooters were unloading the cargoes,—shivering with cold in the sunny winter days, and bent double as though dying under the rain or the breeze of the Mistral. They were working with red caps pulled down over their ears, and at the slightest suspension of their labor would hasten to put their hands in the pockets of their coats. Sometimes when formed in vociferating groups around a case that four men could have moved in ordinary times, the passing of a woman or a vehicle would make them neglect their work, their diabolical faces filled with childish curiosity.

The unloaded cargoes piled up the same articles on the principal docks,—wheat, much wheat, sulphur and saltpeter for the composition of explosive material. On other piers were lined up, by the thousands, pairs of gray wheels, the support of cannons and trucks; boxes as big as dwellings that contained aeroplanes; huge pieces of steel that served as scaffolding for heavy artillery; great boxes of guns and cartridges; huge cases of preserved food and sanitary supplies,—all the provisioning of the army struggling in the extreme end of the Mediterranean.

Various squads of men, preceded and followed by bayonets, were marching with rhythmic tread from one port to another. They were German prisoners,— rosy and happy, in spite of their captivity, still wearing their uniforms of green cabbage color, with round caps on their shaved heads. They were going to work on the vessels, loading and unloading the material that was to serve for the extermination of their compatriots and friends.

The ships at the docks seemed to be increasing in size, for on arrival they had extended only a few yards above the wharf; but now that their cargo was piled up on land, they appeared like towering fortresses. Two-thirds of the hull, usually hidden in the water, were now in evidence, showing the bright red of their curved shell. Only the keel kept itself in the water. The upper third, that which remained visible above the line of flotation in ordinary times, was now a simple black cornice that capped the long purple walls. The masts and smoke-stacks diminished by this transformation appeared to belong to other smaller boats.

Each of these merchant and peaceful steamers carried a quickfirer at the stern in order to protect itself from the submarine corsairs. England and France had mobilized their tramp ships and were beginning to supply them with means of defense. Some of them had not been able to mount their cannon upon a fixed gun carriage, and so carried a field gun with its mouth sticking out between the wheels bolted to the deck.

The captain in all his strolls invariably felt attracted by the famous Cannebière, that engulfing roadway which sucks in the entire activity of Marseilles.

Some days a fresh and violent wind would eddy through, littering it with dust and papers, and the waiters of the cafés would have to furl the great awnings as though they were the sails of a vessel. The Mistral was approaching and every owner of an establishment was ordering this maneuver in order to withstand the icy hurricane that overturns tables, snatches away chairs, and carries off everything which is not secured with marine cables.

To Ferragut this famous avenue of Marseilles was a reminder of the antechamber of Salonica. The same types from the army of the East crowded its sidewalks, —English dressed in khaki, Canadians and Australians in hats with up-turned brims, tall, slender Hindoos

with coppery complexion and thick fan-shaped beards,
Senegalese sharpshooters of a glistening black, and An-
ammite marksmen with round yellow countenance and
eyes forming a triangle. There was a continual procession of dark trucks driven by soldiers, automobiles
full of officers, droves of mules coming from Spain that
were going to be shipped to the Orient, leaving behind
their quick-trotting hoofs a pungent and penetrating
smell of the stable.

The old harbor attracted Ferragut because of its antiquity which was almost as remote as that of the
first Mediterranean navigations. On passing before
the Palace of the Bourse he shot a glance at the statue
of the two great Marseillaise navigators,—Eutymenes
and Pytas,—the most remote ancestors of Mediterranean
navigators. One had explored the coast of Senegambia,
the other had gone further up to Ireland and the Orkney
Islands.

The ancient Greek colony had been, during long
centuries, supplanted by others,—Venice, Genoa and
Barcelona having held it in humble subjection. But
when those had fallen and its hour of prosperity returned, that prosperity was accompanied by all the advantages of the present day. Steam machinery had been
invented and boats were easily able to overcome the
obstacles of the Strait of Cadiz without being obliged to
wait weeks until the violence of the current sent by the
Atlantic should abate. Industrialism was born and inland factories sent forward, over the recently-installed
railroads, a downpour of products that the fleets were
transporting to all the Mediterranean towns. Finally,
upon the opening of the Isthmus of Suez, the city unfolded in a prodigious way, becoming a world port, putting itself in touch with the entire earth, multiplying its
harbors, which became gigantic marine sheepfolds where

vessels of every flag were gathered together in herds.

The old port, boxed in the city, changed its aspect according to the time and state of the atmosphere. On calm mornings it was a yellowish green and smelled slightly of stale water,—organic water, animal water. The oyster stands established on its wharfs appeared sprinkled with this water impregnated by shell fish.

On the days of a strong wind the waters turned a terrible dark green, forming choppy and continuous waves with a light yellowish foam. The boats would begin to dance, creaking and tugging at their hawsers. Between their hulls and the vertical surface of the wharfs would be formed mountains of restless rubbish eaten underneath by the fish and pecked above by the sea-gulls.

Ferragut saw the swift torpedo destroyers dancing at the slightest undulation upon their cables of twisted steel, and examined the improvised submarine-chasers, robust and short little steamers, constructed for fishing, that carried quickfirers on their prows. All these vessels were painted a metallic gray to make them indistinguishable from the color of the water, and were going in and out of the harbor like sentinels changing watch.

They mounted guard out on the high sea beyond the rocky and desert islands that closed the bay of Marseilles, accosting the incoming ships in order to recognize their nationality or running at full speed, with their wisps of horizontal smoke toward the point where they expected to surprise the periscope of the enemy hidden between two waters. There was no weather bad enough to terrify them or make them drowsy. In the wildest storms they kept the coast in view, leaping from wave to wave, and only when others came to relieve them would they return to the old port to rest a few hours at the entrance of the Cannebière.

The narrow passageways of the right bank attracted Ferragut. This was ancient Marseilles in which may still be seen some ruined palaces of the merchants and privateers of other centuries. On these narrow and filthy slopes lived the bedizened and dismal prostitutes of the entire maritime city.

In this district were huddled together the warriors of the French-African colonies, impelled by their ardor of race and by their desire to free themselves gluttonously from the restrictions of their Mahommedan country where the women live in jealous seclusion. On every corner were groups of Moroccan infantry, recently disembarked or convalescing from wounds, young soldiers with red caps and long cloaks of mustard yellow. The Zouaves of Algiers conversed with them in a Spanish spattered with Arabian and French. Negro youths who worked as stokers in the vessels, came up the steep, narrow streets with eyes sparkling restlessly as though contemplating wholesale rapine. Under the doorways disappeared grave Moorish horsemen, trailing long garments fastened at the head in a ball of whiteness, or garbed in purplish mantles, with sharp pointed hoods that gave them the aspect of bearded, crimson-clad monks.

The captain went through the upper end of these streets, stopping appreciatively to note the rude contrast which they made with their terminal vista. Almost all descended to the old harbor with a ditch of dirty water in the middle of the gutter that dribbled from stone to stone. They were dark as the tubes of a telescope, and at the end of these evil smelling ditches occupied by abandoned womanhood, there opened out a great space of light and blue color where could be seen little white sailboats, anchored at the foot of the hill, a sheet of sparkling water and the houses of the opposite wharf diminished by the distance. Through other gaps appeared the mountain of *Notre-Dame-de-la-Garde* with its sharp pointed Basilica topped by its gleaming statue, like an immovable, twisted tongue of flame. Sometimes a torpedo destroyer entering the old harbor could be seen slipping by the mouth of one of these passageways as shadowy as though passing before the glass of a telescope.

Feeling fatigued by the bad smells and vicious misery of the old district, the sailor returned to the center of the city, strolling among the trees and flower stands of the avenues. . . .

One evening while awaiting with others a street car in the Cannebière, he turned his head with a presentiment that some one was looking at his back.

Sure enough! He saw behind him on the edge of the sidewalk an elegantly-dressed, clean-shaven gentleman whose aspect was that of an Englishman careful of his personal appearance. The dapper man had stopped in surprise as though he might have just recognized Ferragut.

The two exchanged glances without awakening the slightest echo in the captain's memory. . . . He could not recall this man. He was almost sure of never having seen him before. His shaven face, his eyes of a metallic gray, his elegant pomposity did not enlighten the Spaniard's memory. Perhaps the unknown had made a mistake.

This must have been the case, judging by the rapidity with which he withdrew his glance from Ferragut and went hastily away.

The captain attached no importance to this encounter. He had already forgotten it when, taking the car but a few minutes later, it recurred to him in a new light. The face of the Englishman presented itself to his imagination with the distinct relief of reality. He could see it more clearly than in the dying splendor of the Cannebière. . . . He passed with indifference over his features; in reality he had seen them for the first time. But the eyes! . . . He knew those eyes perfectly. They had often exchanged glances with him. Where? . . . When? . . .

The memory of this man accompanied him as an obsession even to his ship without giving the slightest answer to his questioning. Then, finding himself on board with Toni and the third officer, he again forgot it.

Upon going ashore on the following days, his memory invariably experienced the same phenomena. The captain would be going through the city without any thought of that individual, but on entering the Cannebière the same remembrance, followed by an inexplicable anxiety, would again surge up in his mind.

"I wonder where my Englishman is now," he would think. "Where have I seen him before? . . . Because there is no doubt that we are acquainted with each other."

From that time on, he would look curiously at all the passersby and sometimes would hasten his step in order to examine more closely some one whose back resembled the haunting unknown. One afternoon he felt sure that he recognized him in a hired carriage whose horse was going at a lively trot through one of the avenues, but when he tried to follow it the vehicle had disappeared into a nearby street.

Some days passed by and the captain completely forgot the meeting. Other affairs more real and immediate were demanding his atttention. His boat was ready; they were going to send it to England in order to load it with munitions destined for the army of the Orient.

The morning of its departure he went ashore without any thought of going to the center of the city.

In one of the wharf streets there was a barber shop frequented by Spanish captains. The picturesque chatter of the barber, born in Cartagena, the gay, brilliant chromos on the walls representing bullfights, the newspapers from Madrid, forgotten on the divans, and a guitar in one corner made this shop a little bit of Spain for the rovers of the Mediterranean.

Before sailing, Ferragut wished to have his beard clipped by this verbose master. When, an hour later, he left the barber-shop, tearing himself away from the interminable farewells of the proprietor, he passed down a broad street, lonely and silent, between two rows of docks.

The steel-barred gates were closed and locked. The warehouses, empty and resounding as the naves of a cathedral, still exhaled the strong odors of the wares which they had kept in times of peace,—vanilla, cinnamon, rolls of leather, nitrates and phosphates for chemical fertilizers.

In all the long street he saw only one man, coming toward him with his back to the inner harbor. Between the two long walls of brick appeared in the background the wharf with its mountains of merchandise, its squadrons of black stevedores, wagons and carts. On beyond were the hulls of the ships sustaining their grove of masts and smokestacks and, at the extreme end, the yellow breakwater and the sky recently washed by the rain, with flocks of little clouds as white and placid as silky sheep.

The man who was returning from the dock and walking along with his eyes fixed on Ferragut suddenly stopped and, turning upon his tracks, returned again to the quay. . . . This movement awakened the captain's curiosity, sharpening his senses. Suddenly he had a presentiment that this pedestrian was his Englishman, though dressed differently and with less elegance. He could only see his rapidly disappearing back, but his instinct in this moment was superior to his eyes. . . . He did not need to look further. . . . It was the Englishman.

And without knowing why, he hastened his steps in order to catch up with him. Then he broke into a run, finding that he was alone in the street, and that the other one had disappeared around the corner.

When Ferragut reached the harbor he could see him hastening away with an elastic step which amounted almost to flight. Before him was a ridge of bundles piled up in uneven rows. He was going to lose sight of him; a minute later it would be impossible to find him.

The captain hesitated. "What motive have I for pursuing this unknown person? . . ." And just as he was formulating this question, the other one slowed down a little in order to turn his head and see if he were still being followed.

Suddenly a rapid phenomenal transformation took place in Ferragut. He had not recognized this man's glance when he had almost run into him on the sidewalk of the Cannebière, and now that there was between the two a distance of some fifty yards, now that the other was fleeing and showing only a fugitive profile, the captain identified him despite the fact that he could not distinguish him clearly at such a distance.

With a sharp click a curtain of his memory seemed to be dashed aside, letting in torrents of light. . . . It was the counterfeit Russian count, he was sure of that,—shaven and disguised, who undoubtedly was "operating" in Marseilles, directing new services, months after having prepared the entrance of the submersibles into the Mediterranean.

Surprise held Ferragut spellbound. With the same imaginative rapidity with which a drowning person giddily recalls all the scenes of his former life, the captain now beheld his infamous existence in Naples, his expedition in the schooner carrying supplies to the submarines and then the torpedo which had opened a breach in the *Californian*. . . . And this man, perhaps, was the one who had made his poor son fly through the air in countless pieces! . . .

He also saw his uncle, the *Triton*, just as when a little chap he used to listen to him in the harbor of Valencia. He recalled his story of a certain night of Egyptian orgy in a low café in Alexandria where he had had to "sting" a man with his dagger in order to force his way.

Instinct made him carry his hand to his belt. Nothing! . . . He cursed modern life and its uncertain securities, which permit men to go from one side of the world to the other confident, disarmed, without means of attack. In other ports he would have come ashore with a revolver in the pocket of his trousers. . . . But in Marseilles! He was not even carrying a penknife; he had only his fists. . . . At that moment he would have given his entire vessel, his life even, for an instrument that would enable him to kill . . . kill with one blow! . . .

The bloodthirsty vehemence of the Mediterranean was overwhelming him. To kill! . . . He did not know how he was going to do it, but he must kill.

The first thing was to prevent the escape of his enemy. He was going to fall upon him with his fists, with his teeth, staging a prehistoric struggle,—the animal fight before mankind had invented the club. Perhaps that other man was hiding firearms and might kill him; but

ie, in his superb vengeance, could see only the death of
the enemy, repelling all fear.

In order that his victim might not get out of his sight,
he ran toward him without any dissimulation whatever,
as though he might have been in the desert, at full
speed. The instinct of attack made him stoop, grasp a
piece of wood lying on the ground,—a kind of rustic
handspike,—and armed in this primitive fashion he continued his race.

All this had lasted but a few seconds. The other one,
perceiving the hostile pursuit, was also running frankly,
disappearing among the hills of packages.

The captain saw confusedly that some shadows were
leaping around him, preventing his progress. His eyes
that were seeing everything red finally managed to distinguish a few black faces and some white ones. . . .
They were the soldiers and civilian stevedores, alarmed
by the aspect of this man who was running like a lunatic.

He uttered a curse upon finding himself stopped.
With the instinct of the multitude, these people were only
concerned with the aggressor, letting the one who was
fleeing go free. Ferragut could not keep his wrath bot-
tled up on that account. He had to reveal his secret.

"He is a spy! . . . A *Boche* spy! . . ."

He said this in a dull, disjointed voice and never did
his word of command obtain such a noisy echo.

"A spy! . . ."

The cry made men rise up as though vomited forth by
the earth; from mouth to mouth it leaped, repeating itself
incessantly, penetrating through the docks and the boats,
vibrating even beyond the reach of the eye, permeating
everywhere with the confusion and rapidity of sound
waves. "A spy! . . ." Men came running with redoubled agility; the stevedores were abandoning their
loads in order to join the pursuit; people were leaping

from the steamers in order to unite in the human hunt.

The author of the noisy alarm, he who had given the cry, saw himself outdistanced and ignored by the pursuing streams of people which he had just called forth. Ferragut, always running, remained behind the negro sharpshooters, the stevedores, the harbor guard, the seamen that were hastening from all sides crowding in the alleyways between the boxes and bundles. . . . They were like the greyhounds that follow the windings of the forest, making the stag come out in the open field, like the ferrets that slip along through the subterranean valleys, obliging the hare to return to the light of day. The fugitive, surrounded in a labyrinth of passageways, colliding with enemies at every turn, came running out through the opposite end and continued his race the whole length of the wharf. The chase lasted but a few instants after coming out on ground free of obstacles. "A spy! . . ." The voice, more rapid than the legs, outdistanced him. The cries of the pursuers warned the people who were working afar off, without understanding the alarm.

Suddenly the fugitive was within a concave semi-circle of men who were awaiting him firmly, and a convex semi-circle following his footsteps in irregular pursuit. The two multitudes, closing their extremes, united and the spy was a prisoner.

Ferragut saw that he was intensely pale, panting, casting his eyes around him with the expression of an animal at bay, but still thinking of the possibility of defending himself.

His right hand was feeling around one of his pockets. Perhaps he was going to draw out a revolver in order to die, defending himself. A negro nearby raised a beam of wood which he was grasping as a club. The spy's hand, displaying a bit of paper between the fingers, was hastily raised toward his mouth; but the negro's blow, suspended in the air, fell upon his arm, making it hang inert. The spy bit his lips in order to keep back a roar of pain.

The paper had rolled upon the ground and several hands at once tried to pick it up. A petty officer smoothed it out before examining it. It was a piece of thin paper sketched with the outline of the Mediterranean. The entire sea was laid out in squares like a chess board and in the center of each of these squares there was a number. These squares were charted sections whose numbers made the submarines know, by wireless, where they were to lie in wait for the allied vessels and torpedo them.

Another officer explained rapidly to the people crowding close, the importance of the discovery. "Indeed he was a spy!" This affirmation awakened the joy of capture and that impulsive desire for vengeance that at certain times crazes a crowd.

The men from the boats were the most furious, for the very reason that they were constantly encountering the treacherous submarine traps. "Ah, the bandit! . . ." Many cudgelings fell upon him, making him stagger under their blows.

When the prisoner was protected by the breasts of various sub-officers, Ferragut could see him close by, with one temple spotted with blood and a cold and haughty expression in his eye. Then he realized that the prisoner had dyed his hair.

He had fled in order to save himself; he had shown himself humble and timorous upon being approached, believing that it would still be possible to lie out of it. But the paper that he had tried to hide in his mouth was now in the hands of the enemy. . . . It was useless to pretend longer! . . .

And he drew himself up proudly like every army man who considers his death certain. The officer of the military caste reappeared, looking haughtily at his unknown pursuers, imploring protection only from the kepis with its band of gold.

Upon discovering Ferragut, he surveyed him fixedly with a glacial and disdainful insolence. His lips also curled with an expression of contempt.

They said nothing, but the captain surmised his soundless words. They were insults. It was the insult of the man of the superior hierarchy to his faithless servant; the pride of the noble official who accuses himself for having trusted in the loyalty of a simple merchant marine.

"Traitor! . . . Traitor!" his insolent eyes and murmuring, voiceless lips seemed to be saying.

Ulysses became furious before this haughtiness, but his wrath was cold and self-contained on seeing the enemy deprived of defense.

He advanced toward the prisoner, like one of the many who were insulting him, shaking his fist at him. His glance sustained that of the German and he spoke to him in Spanish with a dull voice.

"My son. . . . My only son was blown to a thousand atoms by the torpedoing of the *Californian!*"

These words made the spy change expression. His lips separated, emitting a slight exclamation of surprise.

"Ah! . . ."

The arrogant light in his pupils faded away. Then he lowered his eyes and soon after hung his head. The vociferating crowd was shoving and carrying him along without taking into consideration the man who had given the alarm and begun the chase.

That very afternoon the *Mare Nostrum* sailed from Marseilles.

CHAPTER X

IN BARCELONA

FOUR months later Captain Ferragut was in Barcelona.

During the interval he had made three trips to Salonica, and on the second had to appear before a naval captain of the army of the Orient. The French officer was informed of his former expeditions for the victualing of the allied troops. He knew his name and looked upon him as does a judge interested in the accused. He had received from Marseilles a long telegram with reference to Ferragut. A spy submitted to military justice was accusing him of having carried supplies to the German submarines.

"How about that, Captain? . . ."

Ulysses hesitated, looking at the official's grave face, framed by a grey beard. This man inspired his confidence. He could respond negatively to such questions; it would be difficult for the German to prove his affirmation; but he preferred to tell the truth, with the simplicity of one who does not try to hide his faults, describing himself just as he had been,—blind with lust, dragged down by the amorous artifices of an adventuress.

"The women! . . . Ah, the women!" murmured the French chief with the melancholy smile of a magistrate who does not lose sight of human weaknesses and has participated in them.

Nevertheless Ferragut's transgression was of gravest

377

importance. He had aided in staging the submarine attack in the Mediterranean. . . . But when the Spanish captain related how he had been one of the first victims, how his son had died in the torpedoing of the *Californian,* the judge appeared touched, looking at him less severely.

Then Ferragut related his encounter with the spy in the harbor of Marseilles.

"I have sworn," he said finally, "to devote my ship and my life to causing all the harm possible to the murderers of my son. . . . That man is denouncing me in order to avenge himself. I realize that my headlong blindness dragged me to a crime that I shall never forget. I am sufficiently punished in the death of my son. . . . But that does not matter; let them sentence me, too."

The chief remained sunk in deep reflection, forehead in hand and elbow on the table. Ferragut recognized here military justice, expeditious, intuitive, passional, attentive to the sentiments that have scarcely any weight in other tribunals, judging by the action of conscience more than by the letter of the law, and capable of shooting a man with the same dispatch that he would employ in setting him at liberty.

When the eyes of the judge again fixed themselves upon him, they had an indulgent light. He had been guilty, not on account of money nor treason, but crazed by a woman. Who has not something like this in his own history? . . . "Ah, the women!" repeated the Frenchman, as though lamenting the most terrible form of enslavement. . . . But the victim had already suffered enough in the loss of his son. Besides, they owed to him the discovery and arrest of an important spy.

"Your hand, Captain," he concluded, holding out his own. "All that we have said will be just between ourselves. It is a sacred, confessional secret. I will ar-

range it with the Council of War. . . . You may continue lending your services to our cause."

And Ferragut was not annoyed further about the affair of Marseilles. Perhaps they were watching him
discreetly and keeping sight of him in order to convince
themselves of his entire innocence; but this suspected
vigilance never made itself felt nor occasioned him any
trouble.

On the third trip to Salonica the French captain saw
him once at a distance, greeting him with a grave smile
which showed that he no longer was thinking of him as
a possible spy.

Upon its return, the *Mare Nostrum* anchored at Barcelona to take on cloth for the army service, and other industrial articles of which the troops of the Orient
stood in need. Ferragut did not make this trip for mer-
cantile reasons. An affectionate interest was drawing
him there. . . . He needed to see Cinta, feeling that in
his soul the past was again coming to life.

The image of his wife, vivacious and attractive, as in
the early years of their marriage, kept rising before him.
It was not a resurrection of the old love; that would
have been impossible. . . . But his remorse made him
see her, idealized by distance, with all her qualities of a
sweet and modest woman.

He wished to reëstablish the cordial relations of other
times, to have all the past pardoned, so that she would
no longer look at him with hatred, believing him responsible for the death of her son.

In reality she was the only woman who had loved
him sincerely, as she was able to love, without violence
or passional exaggeration, and with the tranquillity
of a comrade. The other women no longer existed.
They were a troop of shadows that passed through his
memory like specters of visible shape but without color.

As for that last one, that Freya whom bad luck had put in his way— . . . How the captain hated her! How he wished to meet her and return a part of the harm she had done him! . . .

Upon seeing his wife, Ulysses imagined that no time had passed by. He found her just as at parting, with her two nieces seated at her feet, making interminable, complicated blonde lace upon the cylindrical pillows supported on their knees.

The only novelty of the captain's stay in this dwelling of monastic calm was that Don Pedro abstained from his visits. Cinta received her husband with a pallid smile. In that smile he suspected the work of time. She had continued thinking of her son every hour, but with a resignation that was drying her tears and permitting her to continue the deliberate mechanicalness of existence. Furthermore, she wished to remove the impression of the angry words, inspired by grief,—the remembrance of that scene of rebellion in which she had arisen like a wrathful accuser against the father. And Ferragut for some days believed that he was living just as in past years when he had not yet bought the *Mare Nostrum* and was planning to remain always ashore. Cinta was attentive to his wishes and obedient as a Christian wife ought to be. Her words and acts revealed a desire to forget, to make herself agreeable.

But something was lacking that had made the past so sweet. The cordiality of youth could not be resuscitated. The remembrance of the son was always intervening between the two, hardly ever leaving their thoughts. And so it would always be!

Since that house could no longer be a real home to him, he again began to await impatiently the hour of sailing. His destiny was to live henceforth on the ship, to pass the rest of his days upon the waves like the accursed captain of the Dutch legend, until the pallid virgin wrapped in black veils—Death—should come to rescue him.

While the steamer finished loading he strolled through the city visiting his cousins, the manufacturers, or remaining idly in the cafés. He looked with interest on the human current passing through the Ramblas in which were mingled the natives of the country and the picturesque and absurd medley brought in by the war.

The first thing that Ferragut noticed was the visible diminution of German refugees.

Months before he had met them everywhere, filling the hotels and monopolizing the cafés,—their green hats and open-neck shirts making them recognized immediately. The German women in showy and extravagant gowns, were everywhere kissing each other when meeting, and talking in shrieks. The German tongue, confounded with the Catalan and the Castilian, seemed to have become naturalized. On the roads and mountains could be seen rows of bare-throated boys with heads uncovered, staff in hand, and Alpine knapsack on the back, occupying their leisure with pleasure excursions that were at the same time, perhaps, a foresighted study.

These Germans had all come from South America,—especially from Brazil, Argentina, and Chile. From Barcelona they had, at the beginning of the war, tried to return to their own country but were now interned, unable to continue their voyage for fear of the French and English cruisers patrolling the Mediterranean.

At first no one had wished to take the trouble to settle down in this land, and they had all clustered together in sight of the sea with the hope of being the first to embark at the very moment that the road of navigation might open for them.

The war was going to be very short. . . . Exceedingly short! The Kaiser and his irresistible army would require but six months to impose their rule upon all Europe. The Germans enriched by commerce were lodged in the hotels. The poor who had been working in the new world as farmers or shop clerks were quartered in a slaughter house on the outskirts. Some, who were musicians, had acquired old instruments and, forming strolling street bands, were imploring alms for their roarings from village to village.

But the months were passing by, the war was being prolonged, and nobody could now discern the end. The number of those taking arms against the medieval imperialism of Berlin was constantly growing greater, and the German refugees, finally convinced that their wait was going to be a very long one, were scattering themselves through the interior of the state, hunting a more satisfying and less expensive existence. Those who had been living in luxurious hotels were establishing themselves in villas and chalets of the suburbs; the poor, tired of the rations of the slaughter-house, were exerting themselves to find jobs in the public works of the interior.

Many were still remaining in Barcelona, meeting together in certain beer gardens to read the home periodicals and talk mysteriously of the works of war.

Ferragut recognized them at once upon passing them in the Rambla. Some were dealers, traders established for a long time in the country, bragging of their Catalan connections with that lying facility of adaptability peculiar to their race. Others came from South America and were associated with those in Barcelona by the freemasonry of comradeship and patriotic interest. But they were all Germans, and that was enough to make the captain immediately recall his son, planning bloody vengeance. He sometimes wished to have in his arm all the blind forces of Nature in order to blot out his enemies with one blow. It annoyed him to see them established in his country, to have to pass them daily without protest and without aggression, respecting them because the laws demanded it.

He used to like to stroll among the flower stands of the Rambla, between the two walls of recently-cut flowers that were still guarding in their corollas the dews of daybreak. Each iron table was a pyramid formed of all the hues of the rainbow and all the fragrance that the earth can bring forth.

The fine weather was beginning. The trees of the Ramblas were covering themselves with leaves and in their shady branches were twittering thousands of birds with the deafening tenacity of the crickets.

The captain found special enjoyment in surveying the ladies in lace mantillas who were selecting bouquets in the refreshing atmosphere. No situation, however anguished it might be, ever left him insensible to feminine attractions.

One morning, passing slowly through the crowds, he noticed that a woman was following him. Several times she crossed his path, smiling at him, hunting a pretext for beginning conversation. Such insistence was not particularly gratifying to his pride; for she was a female of protruding bust and swaying hips, a cook with a basket on her arm, like many others who were passing through the Rambla in order to add a bunch of flowers to the daily purchase of eatables.

Finding that the sailor was not moved by her smiles nor the glances from her sharp eyes, she planted herself before him, speaking to him in Catalan.

"Excuse me, sir, but are you not a ship captain named Don Ulysses? . . ."

This started the conversation. The cook, convinced that it was he, continued talking with a mysterious smile. A most beautiful lady was desirous of seeing him. . . . And she gave him the address of a towered villa situated at the foot of Tibidabo in a recently constructed district. He could make his visit at three in the afternoon.

"Come, sir," she added with a look of sweet promise. "You will never regret the trip."

All questions were useless. The woman would say no more. The only thing that could be gathered from her evasive answers was that the person sending her had left her upon seeing the captain.

When the messenger had gone away he wished to follow her. But the fat old wife shook her head repeatedly. Her astuteness was quite accustomed to eluding pursuit, and without Ferragut's knowing exactly how, she slipped away, mingling with the groups near the Plaza of Catalunia.

"I shall not go," was the first thing that Ferragut said on finding himself alone.

He knew just what that invitation signified. He recalled an infinite number of former unconfessable friendships that he had had in Barcelona,—women that he had met in other times, between voyages, without any passion whatever, but through his vagabond curiosity, anxious for novelty. Perhaps some one of these had seen him in the Rambla, sending this intermediary in order to renew the old relations. The captain probably enjoyed the fame of a rich man now that everybody was commenting upon the amazingly good business transacted by the proprietors of ships.

"I shall not go," he again told himself energetically. He considered it useless to bother about this interview, to encounter the mercenary smile of a familiar but forgotten acquaintance.

But the insistence of the recollection and the very tenacity with which he kept repeating to himself his promise not to keep the tryst, made Ferragut begin to suspect that it might be just as well to go after all.

After luncheon his will-power weakened. He didn't know what to do with himself during the afternoon. His only distraction was to visit his cousins in their counting-houses, or to meander through the Rambla. Why not go? . . . Perhaps he might be mistaken, and the interview might prove an interesting one. At all events, he would have the chance of retiring after a brief conversation about the past. . . . His curiosity was becoming excited by the mystery.

And at three in the afternoon he took a street car that conducted him to the new districts springing up around the base of Tibidabo.

The commercial bourgeoisie had covered these lands with an architectural efflorescence, legitimate daughter of their dreams. Shopkeepers and manufacturers had wished to have here a pleasure house, traditionally called a *torre,* in order to rest on Sundays and at the same time make a show of their wealth with these Gothic, Arabic, Greek, and Persian creations. The most patriotic were relying on the inspiration of native architects who had invented a Catalan art with pointed arches, battlements, and ducal coronets. These medieval coronets, which were repeated even on the peaks of the chimney pots, were the everlasting decorative motif of an industrial city little given to dreams and lusting for lucre.

Ferragut advanced through the solitary street between two rows of freshly transplanted trees that were just sending forth their first growth. He looked at the façades of the *torres* made of blocks of cement imitating the stone of the old fortresses, or with tiles which represented fantastic landscapes, absurd flowers, bluish, glazed nymphs.

Upon getting out of the street car he made a resolution. He would look at the outside only of the house. Perhaps that would aid him in discovering the woman! Then he would just continue on his way.

But on reaching the *torre*, whose number he still kept in mind, and pausing a few seconds before its architecture of a feudal castle whose interior was probably like that of the beer gardens, he saw the door opening, and appearing in it the same woman that had talked with him in the flower Rambla.

"Come in, Captain."

And the captain was not able to resist the suggestive smile of the cook.

He found himself in a kind of hall similar to the façade, with a Gothic fireplace of alabaster imitating oak, great jars of porcelain, pipes the size of walking-sticks, and old armor adorning the walls. Various wood-cuts reproducing modern pictures of Munich alternated with these decorations. Opposite the fireplace William II was displaying one of his innumerable uniforms, resplendent in gold and a gaudy frame.

The house appeared uninhabited. Heavy soft curtains deadened every sound. The corpulent go-between had disappeared with the lightness of an immaterial being, as though swallowed up by the wall. While scowling at the portrait of the Kaiser, the sailor began to feel disquieted in this silence which appeared to him almost hostile. . . . And he was not carrying arms.

The smiling woman again presented herself with the same slippery smoothness.

"Come in, Don Ulysses."

She had opened a door, and Ferragut on advancing felt that this door was locked behind him.

The first thing that he could see was a window, broader than it was high, of colored glass. A Valkyrie was galloping across it, with lance in rest and floating locks, upon a black steed that was expelling fire through its nostrils. In the diffused light of the stained glass he could distinguish tapestries on the walls and a deep divan with flowered cushions.

A woman arose from the soft depths of this couch, rushing towards Ferragut with outstretched arms. Her impulse was so violent that it made her collide with the captain. Before the feminine embrace could close around him he saw a panting mouth, with avid teeth, eyes tearful with emotion, a smile that was a mixture of love and painful disquietude.

"You! . . . You!" he stuttered, springing back.

His legs trembled with a shudder of surprise. A cold wave ran down his back.

"Ulysses!" sighed the woman, trying again to fold him in her arms.

"You! . . . *You!*" again repeated the sailor in a dull voice.

It was Freya.

He did not know positively what mysterious force dictated his action. It was perhaps the voice of his good counselor, accustomed to speak in his brain in critical instants, which now asserted itself. . . . He saw instantaneously a ship that was exploding and his son blown to pieces.

"Ah . . . *tal!*"

He raised his robust arm with his fist clenched like a mace. The voice of prudence kept on giving him orders. "Hard! . . . No consideration! . . . This female is shifty." And he struck as though his enemy were a man, without hesitation, without pity, concentrating all his soul in his fist.

The hatred that he was feeling and the recollection of the aggressive resources of the German woman made him begin a second blow, fearing an attack from her and wishing to repel it before it could be made. . . . But he stopped with his arm raised.

"Ay de mí! . . ."

The woman had uttered a child-like wail, staggering, swaying upon her feet, with arms drooping, without any attempt at defense whatever. . . . She reeled from side to side as though she were drunk. Her knees doubled under her, and she fell with the limpness of a bundle of clothes, her head first striking against the cushions of the divan. The rest of her body remained like a rag on the rug.

There was a long silence, interrupted from time to time by groans of pain. Freya was moaning with closed eyes, without coming out of her inertia.

The sailor, scowling with a tragic ugliness, and transported with rage, remained immovable, looking grimly at the fallen creature. He was satisfied with his brutality; it had been an opportune relief; he could breathe better. At the same time he was beginning to feel ashamed of himself. "What have you done, you coward? . . ." For the first time in his existence he had struck a woman.

He raised his aching right hand to his eyes. One of his fingers was bleeding. Perhaps it had become hooked in her earrings, perhaps a pin at her breast had scratched it. He sucked the blood from the deep scratch, and then forgot the wound in order to gaze again at the body outstretched at his feet.

Little by little he was becoming accustomed to the diffused light of the room. He was already beginning to see objects clearly. His glance rested upon Freya with a look of mingled hatred and remorse.

Her head, sunk in the cushions, presented a pitiful profile. She appeared much older, as though her age had been doubled by her tears. The brutal blow had made her freshness and her marvelous youth flit away with doleful suddenness. Her half-opened eyes were encircled with temporary wrinkles. Her nose had taken on the livid sharpness of the dead; her great mass of hair, reddening under the blow, was disheveled in golden, undulating tangles. Something black was winding through it making streaks upon the silk of the cushion. It was the blood that was dribbling between the heraldic flowers of the embroidery,—blood flowing from the hidden forehead, being absorbed by the dryness of the soft material.

Upon making this discovery, Ferragut felt his shame increasing. He took one step over the extended body, seeking the door. Why was he staying there? . . . All that he had to do was already done; all that he could say was already said.

"Do not go, Ulysses," sighed a plaintive voice. "Listen to me! . . . It concerns your life."

The fear that he might get away made her pull herself together with dolorous groans and this movement accelerated the flow of blood. . . . The pillow continued drinking it in like a thirsty meadow.

An irresistible compassion like that which he might feel for any stranger abandoned in the midst of the street, made the sailor draw back, his eyes fixed on a tall crystal vase which stood upon the floor filled with flowers. With a bang he scattered over the carpet all the springtime bouquet, arranged a little while before by feminine hands with the feverishness of one who counts the minutes and lives on hope.

He moistened his handkerchief in the water of the vase and knelt down beside Freya, raising her head upon the cushion. She let the wound be washed with the abandon of a sick creature, fixing upon her aggressor a pair of imploring eyes, opening now for the first time.

When the blood ceased to flow, forming on the temple a red, coagulated spot, Ferragut tried to raise her up.

"No; leave me so," she murmured. "I prefer to be at your feet. I am your bondslave . . . your plaything. Beat me more if it will appease your wrath."

She wished to insist upon her humility, offering her lips with the timid kiss of a grateful slave.

"Ah, no! . . . No!"

To avoid this caress Ulysses stood up suddenly. He again felt intense hatred toward this woman, who little by little was appealing to his senses. Upon stopping the flow of blood his compassion had become extinguished.

She, guessing his thoughts, felt obliged to speak.

"Do with me what you will. . . . I shall not complain. You are the first man who has ever struck me. . . . And I have not defended myself! I shall not defend myself though you strike me again. . . . Had it been any one else, I would have replied blow for blow; but you! . . . I have done you so much wrong! . . ."

She was silent for a few moments, kneeling before him in a supplicating attitude with her body resting upon her heels. She reached out her arms while speaking with a monotonous and sorrowful voice, like the specters in the apparitions of the theater.

"I have hesitated a long time before seeing you," she continued. "I feared your wrath; I was sure that in the first moment you would let yourself be overpowered by your anger and I was terrified at the thought of the interview. . . . I have spied upon you ever since I knew that you were in Barcelona; I have waited near your home; many times I have seen you through the doorway of a café, and I have taken my pen to write to you. But I feared that you would not come, upon recognizing my handwriting, or that you would pay no attention to a letter in another hand. . . . This morning in the Rambla I could no longer contain myself. And so I sent that woman to you and I have passed some cruel hours fearing that you would not come. . . . At last I see you and your violence makes no difference to me. Thank you, thank you many times for having come!"

Ferragut remained motionless with distracted glance, as though he did not hear her voice.

"It was necessary to see you," she continued. "It concerns your very existence. You have set yourself in opposition to a tremendous power that can crush you. Your ruin is decided upon. You are one lone man and you have awakened the suspicion, without knowing it, of a world-wide organization. . . . The blow has not yet fallen upon you, but it is going to fall at any moment, perhaps this very day; I cannot find out all about it. . . . For this reason it was necessary to see you in order that you should put yourself on the defensive, in order that you should flee, if necessary."

The captain, smiling scornfully, shrugged his shoulders as he always did when people spoke to him of danger, and counseled prudence. Besides, he couldn't believe a single thing that woman said.

"It's a lie!" he said dully. "It's all a lie! . . .

"No, Ulysses: listen to me. You do not know the interest that you inspire in me. You are the only man that I have ever loved. . . . Do not smile at me in that way: your incredulity terrifies me. . . . Remorse is now united to my poor love. I have done you so much wrong! . . . I hate all men. I long to cause them all the harm that I can; but there exists one exception: you! . . . All my desires of happiness are for you. My

dreams of the future always have you as the central
personage. . . . Do you want me to remain indifferent
upon seeing you in danger? . . . No, I am not lying. . . .
Everything that I tell you this afternoon is the truth: I
shall never be able to lie to you. It distresses me so that
my artifices and my falsity should have brought trouble
upon you. . . . Strike me again, treat me as the worst of
women, but believe what I tell you; follow my counsel."

The sailor persisted disdainfully in his indifferent
attitude. His hands were trembling impatiently. He
was going away. He did not wish to hear any more. . . .
Had she hunted him out just to frighten him with
imaginary dangers? . . .

"What have you done, Ulysses? . . . What have you
done?" Freya kept saying desperately.

She knew all that had occurred in the port of
Marseilles, and she also knew well the infinite number of
agents that were working for the greater glory of
Germany. Von Kramer, from his prison, had made
known the name of his informant. She lamented the
captain's vehement frankness.

"I understand your hatred; you cannot forget the
torpedoing of the *Californian.* . . . But you should have
denounced von Kramer without letting him suspect from
whom the accusation came. . . . You have acted like a
madman; yours is an impulsive character that does not
fear the morrow."

Ulysses made a scornful gesture. He did not like
subterfuges and treachery. His way of doing was the
better one. The only thing that he lamented was that
that assassin of the sea might still be living, not having
been able to kill him with his own hands.

"Perhaps he may not be living still," she continued.
"The French Council of War has condemned him to
death. We do not know whether the sentence has been

carried out; but they are going to shoot him any moment, and every one in our circle knows that you are the true author of his misfortune."

She became terrified upon thinking of the accumulated hatred brought about by this deed, and upon the approaching vengeance. In Berlin the name of Ferragut was the object of special attention; in every nation of the earth, the civilian battalions of men and women engaged in working for Germany's triumph were repeating his name at this moment. The commanders of the submarines were passing along information regarding his ship and his person. He had dared to attack the greatest empire in the world. He, one lone man, a simple merchant captain, depriving the kaiser of one of his most valiant, valuable servants!

"What have you done, Ulysses? . . . What have you done?" she wailed again.

And Ferragut began to recognize in her voice a genuine interest in his person, a terrible fear of the dangers which she believed were threatening him.

"Here, in your very own country, their vengeance will overtake you. Flee! I don't know where you can go to get rid of them, but believe me. . . . Flee!"

The sailor came out of his scornful indifference. Anger was lending a hostile gleam to his glance. He was furious to think that those foreigners could pursue him in his own country; it was as though they were attacking him beside his own hearth. National pride augmented his wrath.

"Let them come," he said. "I'd like to see them this very day."

And he looked around, clenching his fists as though these innumerable and unknown enemies were about to come out from the walls.

"They are also beginning to consider me as an

enemy," continued the woman. "They do not say so, because it is a common thing with us to hide our thoughts; but I suspect the coldness that is surrounding me. . . . The doctor knows that I love you the same as before, in spite of the wrath that she feels against you. The others are talking of your 'treason' and I protest because I cannot stand such a lie. . . . Why are you a traitor? . . . You are not one of our clan. You are a father who longs to avenge himself. We are the real traitors:—I, who entangled you in the fatal adventure,— they, who pushed me toward you, in order to take advantage of your services."

Their life in Naples surged up in her memory and she felt it necessary to explain her acts.

"You have not been able to understand me. You are ignorant of the truth. . . . When I met you on the road to Pæstum, you were a souvenir of my past, a fragment of my youth, of the time in which I knew the doctor only vaguely, and was not yet compromised in the service of 'information.' . . . From the very beginning your love and enthusiasm made an impression upon me. You represented an interesting diversion with your Spanish gallantry, waiting for me outside the hotel in order to besiege me with your promises and vows. I was greatly bored during the enforced waiting at Naples. You also found yourself obliged to wait, and sought in me an agreeable recreation. . . . One day I came to understand that you truly were interesting me greatly, as no other man had ever interested me. . . . I suspected that I was going to fall in love with you."

"It's a lie! . . . It's a lie," murmured Ferragut spitefully.

"Say what you will, but that was the way of it. We love according to the place and the moment. If we had met on some other occasion, we might have seen each other for a few hours, no more, each following his own road without further consideration. We belong to different worlds. . . . But we were mobilized in the same country, oppressed by the tedium of waiting, and what had to be . . . was. I am telling you the entire truth: if you could know what it has cost me to avoid you! . . .

"In the mornings, on arising in the room in my hotel, my first motion was to look through the curtains in order to convince myself that you were waiting for me in the street. 'There is my devoted: there is my sweetheart!' Perhaps you had slept badly thinking about me, while I was feeling my soul reborn within me, the soul of a girl of twenty, enthusiastic and artless. . . . My first impulse was to come down and join you, going with you along the gulf shores like two lovers out of a novel. Then reflection would come to my rescue. My past would come tumbling into my mind like an old bell fallen from its tower. I had forgotten that past, and its recurrence deafened me with its overwhelming jangle vibrating with memories. 'Poor man! . . . Into what a world of compromises and entanglements I am going to involve him! . . . No! No!' And I fled from you with the cunning of a mischievous schoolgirl, coming out from the hotel when you had gone off for a few moments, at other times doubling a corner at the very instant that you turned your eyes away. . . . I only permitted myself to approach coldly and ironically when it was impossible to avoid meeting you. . . . And afterwards, in the doctor's house, I used to talk about you, every instant, laughing with her over these romantic gallantries."

Ferragut was listening gloomily, but with growing concentration. He foresaw the explanation of many hitherto incomprehensible acts. A curtain was going to be withdrawn from the past showing everything behind it in a new light.

"The doctor would laugh, but in spite of my jesting she would assure me just the same: 'You are in love with this man; this Don José interests you. Be careful, Carmen!' And the queer thing was that she did not take amiss my infatuation, especially when you consider that she was the enemy of every passion that could not be made directly subservient to our work. . . . She told the truth; I was in love. I recognized it the morning the overwhelming desire to go to the Aquarium took possession of me. I had passed many days without seeing you: I was living outside of the hotel in the doctor's house in order not to encounter my inamorato. And that morning I got up very sad, with one fixed thought: 'Poor captain! . . . Let us give him a little happiness.' I was sick that day. . . . Sick because of you! Now I understood it all. We saw each other in the Aquarium and it was I who kissed you at the same time that I was longing for the extermination of all men. . . . Of all men except you!"

She made a brief pause, raising her eyes toward him in order to take in the effect of her words.

"You remember our luncheon in the restaurant of Vomero; you remember how I begged you to go away, leaving me to my fate. I had a foreboding of the future. I foresaw that it was going to be fatal for you. How could I join a direct and frank life like yours to my existence as an adventuress, mixed up in so many unconfessable compromises? . . . But I was in love with you. I wished to save you by leaving you, and at the same time I was afraid of not seeing you again. The night that you irritated me with the fury of your desires and I stupidly defended myself, as though it were an outrage, concentrating on your person the hatred which all men inspire in me,—that night, alone in my bed, I wept. I wept at the thought that I had lost you forever and at the same time I felt satisfied with myself because thus I was freeing you from my baleful influence. . . . Then von Kramer came. We were in need of a boat and a man. The doctor spoke, proud of her penetration which had made her suspect in you an available asset. They gave me orders to go in search of you, to regain the mastery over your self-control. My first impulse was to refuse, thinking of your future. But the sacrifice was sweet; selfishness directs our actions . . . and I sought you! You know the rest."

She became silent, remaining in a pensive attitude, as though relishing this period of her recollection, the most pleasing of her existence.

"Upon going over to the steamer for you," she continued a few moments afterward, "I understood just what you represented in my life. What need I had of you! . . . The doctor was preoccupied with the Italian events. I was only counting the days, finding that they were passing by with more slowness than the others. One . . . two . . . three . . . 'My adored sailor, my amorous shark, is going to come. . . . He is going to come!' And what came suddenly, while we were still believing it far away, was the blow of the war, rudely separating us. The doctor was cursing the Italians, thinking of Germany; I was cursing them, thinking of you, finding myself obliged to follow my friend, preparing for flight in two hours, through fear of the mob. . . . My only satisfaction was in learning that we were coming to Spain. The doctor was promising herself to do great things here. . . . I was thinking that in no place would it be easier for me to find you again."

She had gained a little more bodily strength. Her hands were touching Ferragut's knees, longing to embrace them, yet not daring to do so, fearing that he

might repel her and overcome that tragic inertia which
permitted him to listen to her.

"When in Bilboa I learned of the torpedoing of the
Californian and of the death of your son. . . . I shall not
talk about that; I wept, I wept bitterly, hiding myself
from the doctor. From that time on I hated her. She
rejoiced in the event, passing indifferently over your
name. You no longer existed for her, because she was
no longer able to make use of you. . . . I wept for
you, for your son whom I did not know, and also for
myself, remembering my blame in the matter. Since that
day I have been another woman. . . . Then we came to
Barcelona and I have passed months and months awaiting
this moment."

Her former passion was reflected in her eyes. A
flicker of humble love lit up her bruised countenance.

"We established ourselves in this house which belongs
to a German electrician, a friend of the doctor's. Whenever she went away on a trip leaving me free, my steps
would invariably turn to the harbor. I was waiting to
see your ship. My eyes followed the seamen sympathetically, thinking that I could see in all of them
something of your person. . . . 'Some day he will come,'
I would say to myself. You know how selfish love is!
I gradually forgot the death of your son. . . . Besides, I
am not the one who is really guilty: there are others. I
have been deceived just as you have been. 'He is going
to come, and we shall be happy again!' . . . *Ay!* If
this room could speak . . . if this divan on which I have
dreamed so many times could talk! . . . I was always arranging some flowers in a vase, making believe that you
were going to come. I was always fixing myself up a little bit, imagining it was for you. . . . I was living in your
country, and it was natural that you should come.
Suddenly the paradise that I was imagining vanished into

smoke. We received the news, I don't know how, of the
imprisonment of von Kramer, and that you had been his
accuser. The doctor anathematized me, making me
responsible for everything. Through me she had known
you, and that was enough to make her include me in her
indignation. All our band began to plan for your death,
longing to have it accompanied with the most. atrocious
tortures. . . ."

Ferragut interrupted her. His brow was furrowed as
though dominated by a tenacious idea. . . . Perhaps he
was not listening to her.

"Where is the doctor?" . . .

The tone of the question was disquieting. He clenched
his fists, looking around him as though awaiting the
appearance of the imposing dame. His attitude was just
like that which had accompanied his attack on Freya.

"I don't know where she's traveling," said his companion. "She is probably in Madrid, in San Sebastian,
or in Cadiz. She goes off very frequently. She has
friends everywhere. . . . And I have ventured to ask
you here simply because I am alone."

And she described the life that she was leading in this
retreat. For the time being her former protector was
letting her remain in inaction, abstaining from giving her
any work whatever. She was doing everything herself,
avoiding all intermediaries. What had happened to von
Kramer had made her so jealous and suspicious that
when she needed aids, she admitted only her compatriots
living in Barcelona.

A ferocious and determined band, made up of refugees
from the South American republics, parasites from the
coast cities or vagabonds from the inland forests, had
grouped itself around her. At their head, as message-
bearer for the doctor, was Karl, the secretary that Ferra-

gut had seen in the great old house of the district of Chiaja.

This man, in spite of his oily aspect, had several bloody crimes in his life history. He was a worthy superintendent of the group of adventurers inflamed by patriotic enthusiasm who were forwarding supplies to the submarines in the Spanish Mediterranean. They all knew Captain Ferragut, because of the affair at Marseilles, and they were talking about his person with gloomy reticence.

"Through them I learned of your arrival," she continued. "They are spying upon you, waiting for a favorable moment. Who knows if they have not already followed you here? . . . Ulysses, flee; your life is seriously threatened."

The captain again shrugged his shoulders with an expression of disgust.

"Flee, I repeat it! . . . And if you can, if I arouse in you a little compassion, if you are not completely indifferent to me . . . take me with you! . . ."

Ferragut began to wonder if all this preamble was merely a prelude to this final request. The unexpected demand produced an impression of scandalized amazement. Was he to flee with her, with the one who had done him so much harm? . . . Again unite his life to hers, knowing her as he now knew her! . . .

The proposition was so absurd that the captain smiled sardonically.

"I am just as much in danger as you are," continued Freya with a despairing accent. "I do not know exactly what the danger is that threatens me, nor whence it may come. But I suspect it, I foresee it hanging over my head. . . . I am of absolutely no use to them now; I no longer have their confidence, and I know too many things. Since I possess too many secrets for them to give me up, leaving me in peace, they have agreed to suppress me; I am sure of that. I can read it in the eyes of the one who was my friend and protector. . . . You cannot abandon me, Ulysses. You will not desire my death."

Ferragut waxed indignant before these supplications, finally breaking his disdainful silence.

"Comedienne! . . . All a lie! . . . Inventions to entangle yourself with me, making me intervene again in the network of your life, compromising me again in your work of detestable surveillance! . . ."

He was now taking the right path. His desire for vengeance had placed him among Germany's adversaries. He was lamenting his former blindness and was satisfied with his new interests. He was making no secret of his conduct. He was serving the Allies.

"And that is the reason you are hunting me up; that is the reason that you have arranged this interview, probably at the instigation of your friend, the doctor. You wish to employ me for a second time as the secret instrument of your espionage. 'Captain Ferragut is such an enamored simpleton,' you have said to one another. 'We have nothing to do but to make an appeal to his chivalry. . . .' And you wish to live with me, perhaps to accompany me on my voyages, to follow my existence in order to reveal my secrets to your compatriots that I may again appear as a traitor. Ah, you hussy! . . ."

This supposed treason again aroused his homicidal wrath. He raised his arm and foot, and was about to strike and crush the kneeling woman. But her passive humiliation, her complete lack of resistance, stopped him.

"No, Ulysses . . . listen to me!"

She tried her utmost to prove her sincerity. She was afraid of her own people; she could see them now in a new light, and they filled her with horror. Her manner of looking at things had changed radically. Her remorse, on thinking of what she had done, was making her a martyr. Her conscience was beginning to feel the wholesome transformation of repentant women who were formerly great sinners. How could she wash her soul of her past crimes? . . . She had not even the consolation of that patriotic faith, bloody and ferocious though it was, which inflamed the doctor and her assistants.

She had been reflecting a great deal. For her there were no longer Germans, English, nor French; there only existed men; men with mothers, with wives, with daughters. And her woman's soul was horrified at the thought of the combats and the killings. She hated war. She had experienced her first remorse upon learning of the death of Ferragut's son.

"Take me with you," she urged. "If you do not take me out of my world I shall not know how to get away from it. . . . I am poor. In these last years, the doctor has supported me; I do not know any way of earning my living and I am accustomed to living well. Poverty inspires me with greater fear than death. You will be able to maintain me; I will accept of you whatever you wish to give me; I will be your handmaiden. On a boat they must need the care and well-ordered supervision of a woman. . . . Life locks its doors against me; I am alone."

The captain smiled with cruel irony.

"I divine what your smile means. I know what you wish to say to me. . . . I can see myself; you believe without doubt that such has been my former life. No, . . . *no!* You are mistaken. I have not been *that.* There has to be a special predisposition, a certain talent for feigning what I do not feel. . . . I have tried to sell myself, and I cannot, I cannot avail myself of that. I embitter the life of men when they do not interest me; I am their adversary. I hate them and they flee from me."

But the sailor prolonged his atrociously sinister smile.

"It's a lie," he said again, "all a lie. Make no further effort. . . . You will not convince me."

As though suddenly reanimated with new force, she rose to her feet:—her face on a level with Ferragut's eyes. He saw her left temple with the torn skin; the spot caused by the blow extended around one eye, reddened and swollen. On contemplating his barbarous handiwork, remorse again tormented him.

"Listen, Ulysses; you do not know my true existence. I have always lied to you; I have eluded all your investigations in our happy days. I wished to keep my former life a secret . . . to forget it. Now I must tell you the truth, the actual truth, just as though I were going to die. When you know it, you will be less cruel."

But her listener did not wish to hear it. He protested in advance with a ferocious incredulity.

"Lies! . . . new lies! I wonder when you will ever stop your inventions!"

"I am not a German woman," she continued without listening to him. "Neither is my name Freya Talberg. . . . It is my *nombre de guerre*, my name as an adventuress. Talberg was the professor who accompanied me to the Andes, and who was not my husband, either. . . . My true name is Beatrice. . . . My mother was an Italian, a Florentine; my father was from Trieste."

This revelation did not interest Ferragut.

"One fraud more!" he said. "Another novel! . . . Keep on making them up."

The woman was in despair. She raised her hands above her head, twisting the interlaced fingers. Fresh tears welled up in her eyes.

"*Ay!* How can I succeed in making you believe me? . . . What oath can I take to convince you that I am telling you the truth? . . ."

The captain's impassive air gave her to understand that all such extremes would be unavailing. There was no oath that could possibly convince him. Even though she should tell the truth, he would not believe her.

She went on with her story, not wishing to protest against this impassable wall.

"My father also was of Italian origin but was Austrian because of the place of his birth. . . . Furthermore, the Germanic empires always inspired him with a blind enthusiasm. He was among those who detest their native land, and see all the virtues in the northern people.

"Inventor of marvelous business schemes, financial promoter of colossal enterprises, he had passed his existence besieging the directors of the great banking establishments and having interviews in the lobbies of the government departments. Eternally on the eve of surprising combinations that were bound to bring him dozens of millions, he had always lived in luxurious poverty, going from hotel to hotel—always the best—with his wife and his only daughter.

"You know nothing about such a life, Ulysses; you come from a tranquil and well-to-do family. Your people have never known existence in the Palace Hotels, nor have you known difficulties in meeting the monthly account, managing to have it included with those of the former months with an unlimited credit."

As a child she had seen her mother weeping in their extravagant hotel apartment while the father was talking with the aspect of an inspired person, announcing that the next week he was going to clear a million dollars. The wife, convinced by the eloquence of her remarkable husband, would finally dry her tears, powder her face,

and adorn herself with her pearls and her blonde laces
of problematic value. Then she would descend to the
magnificent hall, filled with perfumes, with the hum of
conversation and the discreet wailings of the violins, in
order to take tea with her friends in the hotel,—formidable millionaires from the two hemispheres who vaguely
suspected the existence of an infirmity known as poverty,
but incapable of imagining that it might attack persons
of their own world.

Meanwhile the little girl used to play in the hotel
garden of the Palace Hotel with other children dressed
up and adorned like luxurious and fragile dolls, each one
worth many millions.

"From my childhood," continued Freya, "I had been a
companion of women who are now celebrated for their
riches in New York, Paris, and in London. I have been
on familiar terms with great heiresses that are to-day,
through their marriages, duchesses and even princesses
of the blood royal. Many of them have since passed by
me, without recognizing me, and I have said nothing,
knowing that the equality of childhood is no more than a
vague recollection. . . ."

Thus she had grown into womanhood. A few of her
father's casual bargains had permitted them to continue
this existence of brilliant and expensive poverty. The
promoter had considered such environment indispensable
for his future negotiations. Life in the most expensive
hotels, an automobile by the month, gowns designed by
the greatest modistes for his wife and daughter, summers at the most fashionable resorts, winter-skating in
Switzerland,—all these luxuries were for him but a kind
of uniform of respectability that kept him in the world
of the powerful, permitting him to enter everywhere.

"This existence molded me forever, and has influenced
the rest of my life. Dishonor, death, anything is to me

preferable to poverty. . . . I, who have no fear of danger, become a coward at the mere thought of that!"

The mother died, credulous and sensuous, worn out with expecting a solid fortune that never arrived. The daughter continued with her father, becoming the type of young woman who lives among men from hotel to hotel, always somewhat masculine in her attitude;—a half-way virgin who knows everything, is not frightened at anything, guards ferociously the integrity of her sex, calculating just what it may be worth, and adoring wealth as the most powerful divinity on earth.

Finding herself upon her father's death with no other fortune than her gowns and a few artistic gems of scant value, she had coldly decided upon her destiny.

"In our world there is no other virtue than that of money. The girls of the people surrender themselves less easily than a young woman accustomed to luxury having as her only fortune some knowledge of the piano, of dancing, and a few languages. . . . We yield our body as though fulfilling a material function, without shame and without regret. It is a simple matter of business. The only thing that matters is to preserve the former life with all its conveniences . . . not to come down."

She passed hastily over her recollection of this period of her existence. An old acquaintance of her father, an old trader of Vienna, had been the first. Then she felt romantic flutterings which even the coldest and most positive women do not escape. She believed that she had fallen in love with a Dutch officer, a blonde Apollo who used to skate with her in Saint Moritz. This had been her only husband. Finally she had become bored with the colonial drowsiness of Batavia and had returned to Europe, breaking off her marriage in order to renew her life in the great hotels, passing the winter season at the most luxurious resorts.

"*Ay,* money! . . . In no social plane was its power so evident as that in which she was accustomed to dwell. In the Palace Hotels she had met women of soldierly aspect and common hands, smoking at all hours, with their feet up and the white triangle of their petticoats stretched over the seat. They were like the prostitutes waiting at the doors of their huts. How were they ever permitted to live there! . . . Nevertheless, the men bowed before them like slaves, or followed as suppliants these creatures who talked with unction of the millions inherited from their fathers, of their formidable wealth of industrial origin which had enabled them to buy noble husbands and then give themselves up to their natural tastes as fast, coarse women.

"I never had any luck. . . . I am too haughty for that kind of thing. Men find me ill-humored, argumentative, and nervous. Perhaps I was born to be the mother of a family. . . . Who knows but what I might have been otherwise if I had lived in your country?"

Her announcement of her religious veneration for money took on an accent of hate. Poor and well-educated girls, if afraid of the misery of poverty, had no other recourse than prostitution. They lacked a dowry,—that indispensable requisite in many civilized families for honorable marriage and home-making.

Accursed poverty! . . . It had weighed upon her life like a fatality. The men who had appeared good at first afterwards became poisoned, turning into egoists and wretches. Doctor Talberg, on returning from America, had abandoned her in order to marry a young and rich woman, the daughter of a trader, a senator from Hamburg. Others had equally exploited her youth, taking their share of her gayety and beauty only to marry, later, women who had merely the attractiveness of a great fortune.

She had finally come to hate them all, desiring their extermination, exasperated at the very thought that she needed them to live and could never free herself from this slavery. Trying to be independent, she had taken up the stage.

"I have danced. I have sung; but my successes were always because I was a woman. Men followed after me, desiring the female, and ridiculing the actress. Besides—the life behind the scenes! . . . A white-slave market with a name on the play-bills. . . . What exploitation! . . ."

The desire of freeing herself from all this had led her to make friends with the doctor, accepting her propositions. It seemed to her more honorable to serve a great nation, to be a secret functionary, laboring in the shadow for its grandeur. Besides, at the beginning she was fascinated by the novelty of the work, the adventures on risky missions, the proud consideration that with her espionage she was weaving the web of the future, preparing the history of time to come.

Here also she had, from the very first, stumbled upon sexual slavery. Her beauty was an instrument for sounding the depths of consciences, a key for opening secrets; and this servitude had turned out worse than the former ones, on account of its being irremediable,—she had tried to divorce herself from her life of tantalizing tourist and theatrical woman; but whoever enters into the secret service can nevermore go from it. She learns too many things; slowly she gains a comprehension of important mysteries. The agent becomes a slave of her functions; she is confined within them as a prisoner and with every new act adds a new stone to the wall that is separating her from liberty.

"You know the rest of my life," she continued. "The obligation of obeying the doctor, of seducing men in order to snatch their secrets from them, made me hate them with a deadly aggressiveness. . . . But you came. You, who are so good and generous! You who sought me with the enthusiastic simplicity of a growing boy, making me turn back a page in my life, as though I were still only in my teens and being courted for the first time! . . . Besides, you are not a selfish person. You gave with noble enthusiasm. I believe that if we had known each other in our early youth you would never have deserted me in order to make yourself rich by marrying some one else. I resisted you at first, because I loved you and did not wish to do you harm. . . . Afterwards, the mandates of my superiors and my passion made me forget these scruples. . . . I gave myself up. I was the 'fatal woman,' as always; I brought you misfortune. . . . Ulysses! My love! . . . Let us forget; there is no use in remembering the past. I know your heart so well, and finding myself in danger, I appeal to it. Save me! Take me with you! . . ."

As she was standing opposite him, she had only to raise her hands in order to put them on his shoulders, starting the beginning of an embrace.

Ferragut remained insensible to the caress. His immobility repelled these pleadings. Freya had traveled much through the world, had gone through shameful adventures, and would know how to free herself by her own efforts without the necessity of complicating him again in her net. The story that she had just told was nothing to him but a web of misrepresentations.

"It is all false," he said in a heavy voice. "I do not believe you. I never shall believe you. . . . Each time that we meet you tell me a new tale. . . . Who are you? . . . When do you tell the truth,—all the truth at once? . . . You fraud!"

Insensible to his insults, she continued speaking

anxiously of her future, as though perceiving the mysterious dangers which were surrounding her.

"Where shall I go if you abandon me? . . . If I remain in Spain, I continue under the doctor's domination. I cannot return to the empires where my life has been passed; all the roads are closed and in those lands my slavery would be reborn. . . . Neither can I go to France or to England; I am afraid of my past. Any one of my former achievements would be enough to make them shoot me: I deserve nothing less. Besides, the vengeance of my own people fills me with terror. I know the methods of the 'service,' when they find it necessary to rid themselves of an inconvenient agent who is in the enemy's territory. The 'service' itself denounces him, voluntarily making a stupid move in order that some documents may go astray, sending a compromising card with a false address in order that it may fall into the hands of the authorities of the country. What shall I do if you do not aid me? . . . Where can I flee? . . ."

Ulysses decided to reply, moved to pity by her desperation. The world was large. She could go and live in the republics of America.

She did not accept the advice. She had had the same thought, but the uncertain future made her afraid.

"I am poor: I have scarcely enough to pay my traveling expenses. . . . The 'service' recompenses well at the start. Afterwards when it has us surely in its clutches because of our past, it gives us only what is necessary in order to live with a certain freedom. What can I ever do in those lands? . . . Must I pass the rest of my existence selling myself for bread? . . . I will not do it. I would rather die first!"

This desperate affirmation of her poverty made Ferragut smile sarcastically. He looked at the necklace of pearls everlastingly reposing on the admirable cushion

of her bosom, the great emeralds in her ears, the diamonds
that were sparkling coldly on her hands. She guessed
his thoughts and the idea of selling these jewels gave her
even greater apprehension than the terrors that the
future involved.

"You do not know what all this represents to me," she
added. "It is my uniform, my coat-of-arms, the safe-
conduct that enables me to sustain myself in the world
of my youth. The women who pass alone through this
world need jewels in order to free their pathway of
obstructions. The managers of a hotel become human
and smile before their brilliancy. She who possesses
them does not arouse suspicion however late she may be
in paying the weekly account. . . . The employees at the
frontier become exceedingly gallant: there is no passport
more powerful. The haughty ladies become more
cordial before their sparkle, at the tea hour in the halls
where one knows nobody. . . . What I have suffered in
order to acquire them! . . . I would be reduced to
hunger before I would sell them. With them, I am
somebody. A person may not have a coin in her pocket
and yet, with these glittering vouchers, may enter where
the richest assemble, living as one of them."

She would take no advice. She was like a hungry
warrior in an enemy's country asked to surrender arms
in exchange for gold. Once the necessity was satisfied,
he would become a prisoner,—would be vilified and on a
par with the miserable creatures who a few hours
before were receiving his blows. She would meet courageously all dangers and sufferings rather than lay aside
her helmet and shield, the symbols of her superior caste.
The gown more than a year old, shabby, patched shoes,
negligee with badly mended rents, did not distress her
in the most trying moments. The important thing was
to possess a stylish hat and to preserve a fur coat, a

necklace of pearls, emeralds, diamonds,—all the honorable and glorious coat-of-mail in which she wished to die.

Her glance appeared to pity the ignorance of the sailor in venturing to propose such absurdities to her.

"It is impossible, Ulysses. . . . Take me with you! On the sea is where I shall be safest. I am not afraid of the submarines. People imagine them as numerous and close together as the flagstones of a pavement, but only one vessel in a thousand is the victim of their attacks. . . . Besides, with you I fear nothing; if it is our destiny to perish on the sea, we shall die together."

She became insinuating and enticing, passing her hands over his shoulders, pulling down his neck with a passion that was equal to an embrace. While speaking, her mouth came near to that of the sailor, the lips arched, beginning the rounding of a caressing kiss.

"Would you live so badly with Freya? . . . Do you no longer remember our past? . . . Am I now another being?"

Ulysses was remembering only too well that past, and began to recognize that this memory was becoming too vivid. She, who was following with astute eyes the seductive memories whirling through his brain, guessed what they were by the contraction of his face. And smiling trumphantly, she placed her mouth against his. She was sure of her power. . . . And she reproduced the kiss of the Aquarium, that kiss which had so thrilled the sailor, making his whole body tremble.

But when she gave herself up with more abandon to this dominating ascendancy, she felt herself repelled, shot back by a brutal hand-thrust similar to the blow that had hurled her upon the cushions at the beginning of the interview.

Some one had interposed between the two, in spite of their close embrace.

The captain, who was beginning to lose consciousness of his acts, like a castaway, descending and descending through the enchanting domains of limitless pleasure, suddenly beheld the face of the dead Esteban with his glassy eyes fixed upon him. Further on he saw another image, sad and shadowy,—Cinta, who was weeping as though her tears were the only ones that should fall upon the mutilated body of their son.

"Ah, no! . . . *No!*"

He himself was surprised at his voice. It was the roar of a wounded beast, the dry howling of a desperate creature, writhing in torment.

Freya, staggering under the rude push, again tried to draw near to him, enlacing him again in her arms, in order to repeat her imperious kiss.

"My love! . . . My love! . . ."

She could not go on. That tremendous hand again repelled her, but so violently that her head struck against the cushions of the divan.

The door trembled with a rude shove that made its two leaves open at the same time, dragging out the bolt of the lock.

The woman, tenacious in her desires, rose up quickly without noticing the pain of her fall. Nimbleness only could serve her now that Ferragut was escaping after mechanically picking up his hat.

"Ulysses! . . . Ulysses! . . ."

Ulysses was already in the street,—and in the little hallway various objects of bric-a-brac that had obtruded themselves and confused the fugitive in his blind flight were still trembling and then falling and breaking on the floor with a crash.

Feeling on his forehead the sensation of the free air,

the dangers to which Freya had referred now surged up in his mind. He surveyed the street with a hostile glance. . . . Nobody! He longed to meet the enemy of whom that woman had been speaking, to find vent for that wrath which he was feeling even against himself. He was ashamed and furious at his passing weakness which had almost made him renew their former existence.

In the days following, he repeatedly recalled the band of refugees under the doctor's control. When meeting German-looking people on the street, he would glare at them menacingly. Was he perhaps one of those charged with killing him? . . . Then he would pass on, regretting his irritation, sure that they were tradesmen from South America, apothecaries or bank employees undecided whether to return to their home on the other side of the ocean, or to await in Barcelona the always-near triumph of their Emperor.

Finally the captain began to ridicule Freya's recommendations.

"Just her lies! . . . Inventions in order to engage my interest again and make me take her with me! Ah, the old fraud!"

One morning, as he was stepping out on the deck of his steamer, Toni approached him with a mysterious air, his face assuming an ashy pallor.

When they reached the saloon at the stern, the mate spoke in a low voice, looking around him.

The night before he had gone ashore in order to visit the theater. All of Toni's literary tastes and his emotions were concentrated in vaudeville. Men of talent had never invented anything better. From it he used to bring back the humming songs with which he beguiled his long watches on the bridge. Besides, it had a feminine chorus brilliantly clad and bare-legged, a prima donna rich in flesh and poor in clothes, a row of rosy and voluptuous ninepins that delighted the seamen's imagination without making him forget the obligations of fidelity.

At one o'clock in the morning, when returning to the boat along the solitary entrance pier, some one had tried to assassinate him. Hearing footsteps, he fancied that he had seen forms hiding behind a mountain of merchandise. Then there had sounded three reports, three revolver shots. A ball had whistled by one of his ears.

"And as I was not carrying any arms, I ran. Fortunately, I was near the ship, almost to the prow. I had only to take a few leaps to put myself aboard the vessel. . . . And they did not shoot any more."

Ferragut remained silent. He, too, had grown pale, but with surprise and anger. Then they were true, those reports of Freya's! . . . He could not pretend incredulity, nor show himself bold and indifferent to danger while Toni continued talking.

"Take care, Ulysses! . . . I have been thinking a great deal about this thing. Those shots were not meant for me. What enemies have I? Who would want to harm a poor mate who never sees anybody? . . . Look out for yourself! You know perhaps where they came from; you have dealings with many people."

The captain suspected that he was recalling the adventure of Naples and that disgraceful proposition guarded as a secret, relating it to this nocturnal attack. But neither his voice nor his eyes justified such suspicions. And Ferragut preferred not to seem to suspect what he was thinking about.

"Does any one else know what occurred, . . ."

Toni shrugged his shoulders. "Nobody. . . ." He had leaped on the steamer, pacifying the dog on board, that was howling furiously. The man on guard had

heard the shots, imagining that it was some sailors' fight.
"You have not reported this to the authorities?"

The mate became indignant on hearing this question,
with the independence of the Mediterranean who never
remembers authority in moments of danger and whose
only defense is his manual dexterity.—"You take me,
perhaps, for a police-informer? . . ."

He had wanted to do the manly thing, but henceforth
he would always go armed while he happened to be in
Barcelona. *Ay,* with this he might shoot if he were not
wounded! . . . And winking an eye, he showed his
captain what he called his "instrument."

The mate disliked firearms, crazy and noisy toys of
doubtful result. With an ancestral affection which
appeared to evoke the flashing battle-axes used by his
ancestors, he loved the blow in silence, the gleaming
weapon which was a prolongation of the hand.

With gentle stealthiness he drew from his belt an
English knife, acquired at the time that he was skipper
of a small boat,—a shining blade which reproduced the
faces of those looking at it, with the sharp point of a
stiletto and the edge of a razor.

Perhaps he would not be long in making use of his
"instrument." He recalled various individuals who a
few days ago were strolling slowly along the wharf
examining the vessel, and spying upon those going on and
off. If he could manage to see them again he would go
off the steamer just to say a couple of words to them.

"You are to do nothing at all," ordered Ferragut.
"I'll take charge of this little matter."

All day long he was troubled over this news. Strolling
about Barcelona, he looked with challenging eyes at all
passersby who appeared to be Germans. To the aggressiveness of his character was now added the indignation
of a proprietor who finds himself assaulted within his

home. Those three shots were for him; and he was a Spaniard: and the *boches* were daring to attack him on his own ground! What audacity! . . .

Several times he put his hand in the back part of his trousers, touching a long, metallic bulk. He was only awaiting the nightfall to carry out a certain idea that had clamped itself between his two eyebrows like a painful nail. Whilst he was not carrying it forward he could not be tranquil.

The voice of his good counselor protested: "Don't do anything idiotic, Ferragut; don't hunt the enemy, don't provoke him. Simply defend yourself, nothing more."

But that reckless courage which in times gone by had made him embark on vessels destined to shipwreck, and had pushed him toward danger for the mere pleasure of conquering it, was now crying louder than prudence.

"In my own country!" he kept saying continually. "To try to assassinate me when I am on my own land! . . . I'll just show them that I am a Spaniard. . . ."

He knew well that waterfront saloon mentioned by Freya. Two men in his crew had given him some fresh information. The customers of the bar were poor Germans accustomed to endless drinking. Some one was paying for them, and on certain days even permitted them to invite the skippers of the fishing boats and tramp vessels. A gramophone was continually playing there, grinding out shrill songs to which the guests responded in roaring chorus. When war news favorable to the German Empire was received, the songs and drinking would redouble until midnight and the shrill music-box would never stop for an instant. On the walls were portraits of William II and various chromos of his generals. The proprietor of the bar, a fat-legged German with square head, stiff hair and drooping mustache, used to answer to the nickname of *Hindenburg*.

The sailor grinned at the mere thought of putting that *Hindenburg* underneath his own counter. . . . He'd just like to see this establishment where his name had been uttered so many times!

At nightfall, his feet took him toward the bar with an irresistible impulse which disdained all counsels of prudence.

The glass door resisted his nervous hands, perhaps because he handled the latch with too much force. And the captain finally opened it by giving a kick to its lower part, made of wood.

The panes almost flew out from the shock of this brutal blow. A magnificent entrance! . . . He saw much smoke, perforated by the red stars of three electric bulbs which had just been lit, and men around the various tables, facing him or with their backs turned. The gramophone was shrilling in a nasal tone like an old woman without teeth. Back of the counter appeared *Hindenburg,* his throat open, sleeves rolled up over arms as fat as legs.

"I am Captain Ulysses Ferragut."

The voice that said this had a power similar to that of the magic words of Oriental tales which held the life of an entire city in suspense, leaving persons and objects immovable in the very attitude in which the powerful conjurer surprised them.

There was the silence of astonishment. Those were beginning to turn their heads, attracted by the noise of the door, did not go on with the movement. Those in front remained with their eyes fixed on the one who was entering, eyes widened with surprise as if they could not believe what they saw. The gramophone was suddenly hushed. *Hindenburg,* who was washing out a glass, remained with motionless hands, without even taking the napkin from its crystal cavity.

Ferragut seated himself near an empty table with his back against the wall. A waiter, the only one in the establishment, hastened to find out what the gentleman wished. He was an Andalusian, small and sprightly, whose escapades had brought him to Barcelona. He usually served his customers with indifference, without taking any interest in their words and their hymns. He "didn't mix himself up in politics." Accustomed to the ways of gay and hot-blooded people, he suspected that this man had come to pick a quarrel, and hoped to soften him with his smiling and obsequious manner.

The sailor spoke to him aloud. He knew that in that low café his name was frequently used and that there were many there who desired to see him. He could give them the message that Captain Ferragut was there at their disposition.

"I shall do so," said the Andalusian.

And he went away to the counter, bringing him, in a little while, a bottle and a glass.

In vain Ulysses fixed his glance on those who were occupying the nearby tables. Some, turning their backs upon him, were absolutely rigid; others had their eyes cast down and were talking quietly with mysterious whispering.

Finally two or three exchanged glances with the captain. In their pupils was the snap of budding wrath. The first surprise having vanished, they seemed disposed to rise up and fall upon the recent arrival. But some one behind him appeared to be controlling them with murmured orders, and they finally obeyed him, lowering their eyes in submissive restraint.

Ulysses soon tired of this silence. He was beginning to find his attitude of animal-tamer rather ridiculous. He did not know whom to assail in a place where they avoided his glance and all contact with him. On the nearest table there was an illustrated newspaper, and he took possession of it, turning its leaves. It was printed in German, but he pretended to read it with great interest.

He had seated himself at the side, leaving free the hip on which his revolver was resting. His hand, feigning distraction, passed near the opening of his pocket, ready to take up arms in case of attack. In a little while he regretted this excessively swaggering posture. They were going to fall upon him, taking advantage of his reading. But pride made him remain motionless, that they might not suspect his uneasiness.

Then he laughed in an insolent way as though he were reading in the German illustration something that was provoking his jibes. As though this were not enough, he raised his eyes with aggressive curiosity in order to study the portraits adorning the wall.

Then he realized the great transformation which had just taken place in the bar. Almost all the customers had filed silently out during his reading. There remained only four blear-eyed drunkards who were guzzling with satisfaction, occupied with the contents of their glasses. *Hindenburg*, turning his mighty back upon his clientele, was reading an evening newspaper on the counter. The Andalusian, seated in the background, was looking at the captain, smiling. "There's an old sport for you! . . ." He was mentally chuckling over the fact that one of his countrymen had put to flight the brawling and brutal drinkers who gave him so much trouble on other evenings.

Ulysses consulted his watch: half-past seven. Already he had driven away all those people that Freya was so afraid of. What was left to do here? . . . He paid and went out.

Night had fallen. Under the light of the electric lamp

posts street cars and automobiles were passing toward
the interior of the city. Following the arcades of the
old edifices near the harbor, groups of workers from
the maritime establishments were filing by. Barcelona,
dazzling with splendor, was attracting the crowds. The
inner harbor, black and solitary, was filled with weak
little lights twinkling from the heights of the masts.

Ferragut stood undecided whether to go home to eat,
or to a restaurant in the Rambla. Then he suspected
that some of the fugitives from that dirty café were
near, intending to follow him. In vain he glanced
searchingly around: he could not recognize anybody in
the groups that were reading the papers or conversing
while waiting for the street car.

Suddenly he felt a desire to see Toni. Uncle Caragol
would improvise something to eat while the captain was
telling his mate all about his adventure at the bar.
Besides, it seemed to him a fitting finale to his escapade
to offer to any enemies that might be following him a
favorable occasion for attacking him on the deserted
wharf. The demon of false pride was whispering in his
ears: "Thus they will see that you are not afraid of
them."

And he marched resolutely toward the harbor, passing
over railroad tracks outlining the walls of long storehouses and winding in and out among mountains of merchandise. At first he met little groups going toward the
city, then pairs, then single individuals, finally nobody
—absolute solitude.

Further on, the darkness was cut by silhouettes of
ebony that sometimes were boats and at others, alleyways
of packages or hills of coal. The black water reflected
the red and green serpents from the lights on the boats.
A transatlantic liner was prolonging its loading operations by the light of its electric reflectors, standing forth

out of the darkness with the gayety of a Venetian fiesta.

From time to time a man of slow step would come within the circle of the street lamp, the muzzle of his gun gleaming. Others were lying in ambush among the mountains of cargo. They were custom-house men and guardians of the port.

Suddenly the captain felt an instinctive warning. They were following him. . . . He stopped in the shadows, close to a pile of crates and saw some men advancing in his direction, passing rapidly over the edge of the red spot made by the electric bulbs, so as not to be under the rain of light.

Although it was impossible for him to recognize them, he was positive, nevertheless, that they were the enemy seen at the bar.

His ship was far away, near the end of the dock most deserted at that hour. "You've done an idiotic thing," he said mentally.

He began to repent of his rashness, but it was now far too late to turn back. The city was further away than the steamer, and his enemies would fall upon him just as soon as they saw him going back. How many were there? . . . That was the only thing that troubled him.

"Go on! . . . *Go on!*" cried his pride.

He had drawn out his revolver and was carrying it in his right hand with the barrel to the front. In this solitude he could not count upon the conventions of civilized life. Night was swallowing him up with all the ambushed traps of a virgin forest while before his eyes was sparkling a great city, crowned with electric diamonds, throwing a halo of flame into the blackness of space.

Three times the Carabineers passed near him, but he did not wish to speak to them. "Forward! Only women had to ask assistance. . . ." Besides, perhaps he was under an hallucination: he really could not swear that they were in pursuit of him.

After a few steps, this doubt vanished. His senses, sharpened by danger, had the same perception as has the wild boar who scents the pack of hounds trying to cross his tracks. At his right, was the water. At his left, men were prowling behind the mountains of freight, wishing to cut him off; behind were coming still others to prevent his retreat.

He might run, advancing toward those who were trying to hem him in. But ought a man to run with a revolver in his hand? . . . Those who were coming behind would join in the pursuit. A human hunt was going to take place in the night, and he, Ferragut, would be the deer pursued by the low crowds from the bar. "Ah, no! . . ." The captain recalled von Kramer galloping miserably in full daylight along the wharves of Marseilles. . . . If they must kill him, let it not be in flight.

He continued his advance with a rapid step, seeing through his enemies' plans. They did not wish to show themselves in that part of the harbor obstructed by mountains of cases, fearing that he might hide himself there. They would await him near his ship in a safe, hidden spot by which he would undoubtedly have to pass.

"Forward!" he kept repeating to himself. "If I have to die, let it be within sight of the *Mare Nostrum!*" The steamer was near. He could recognize now its black silhouette fast to the wharf. At that moment the dog on board began to bark furiously, announcing the captain's presence and danger at the same time.

He abandoned the shelter of a hillock of coal, advancing over an open space. He concentrated all his will power upon gaining his vessel as quickly as possible.

A swift flame flashed out, followed by a report. They were already shooting at him. Other little lights began to twinkle from different sides of the dock, followed by reports of a gun. It was a sharp cross-fire; behind him they were firing, too. He felt various whistlings near his ears, and received a blow on the shoulder,—a sensation like that from a hot stone.

They were going to kill him. His enemies were too many for him. And, without knowing exactly what he was doing, yielding to instinct, he threw himself on the ground like a dying person.

Some few shots were still sounding. Then all was silent. Only on the nearby ship the dog was continuing its howling.

He saw a shadow advancing slowly toward him. It was a man, one of his enemies, coming out from the group in order to examine him at close range. He let him come close up to him, with his right hand grasping his revolver still intact.

Suddenly he raised his arm, striking the head that was bending over him. Two lightning streaks flashed from his hand, separated by a brief interval. The first flitting blaze of fire made him see a familiar face. . . . Was it really Karl, the doctor's factotum? . . . The second explosion aided his memory. Yes, it was Karl, with his features disfigured by a black gash in the temple. . . . The German pulled himself up with an agonizing shudder, then fell on his back, with his arms relaxed.

This vision was instantaneous. The captain must think only of himself now, and springing up with a bound, he ran and ran, bending himself double, in order to offer the enemy the least possible mark.

He dreaded a general discharge, a hail of bullets; but his pursuers hesitated a few moments, confused in the darkness and not knowing surely whether it was the captain who had fallen a second time.

Only upon seeing a man running toward the ship did they recognize their error, and renew their shots. Ferragut passed between the balls along the edge of the wharf, the whole length of the *Mare Nostrum*. His salvation was now but a matter of seconds provided that the crew had not drawn in the gangplank between the steamer and the shore.

Suddenly he found himself on the gangplank, at the same time seeing a man advancing toward him with something gleaming in one hand. It was the mate who had just come out with his knife drawn.

The captain feared that he might make a mistake.

"Toni, it is I," he said in a voice almost breathless because of the effort of his running.

Upon treading the deck of his vessel, he instantly recovered his tranquillity.

Already the shots had ceased and the silence was ominous. In the distance could be heard whistlings, cries of alarm, the noise of running. The Carabineers and guards were called and grouped together in order to charge in the dark, marching toward the spot where the shooting had sounded.

"Haul in the gangplank!" ordered Ferragut.

The mate aided three of the hands who had just come up to retire the gangplank hastily. Then he threatened the dog, to make it cease howling.

Ferragut, near the railing, scanned carefully the darkness of the quay. It seemed to him that he could see some men carrying another in their arms. A remnant of his wrath made him raise his right hand, still armed, aiming at the group. Then he lowered it again. . . . He remembered that officers would be coming to investigate the occurrence. It was better that they should find the boat absolutely silent.

Still panting, he entered the saloon under the poop and sat down.

As soon as he was within the circle of pale light that a hanging lamp spread upon the table Toni fixed his glance on his left shoulder.

"Blood! . . ."

"It's nothing. . . . Merely a scratch. The proof of it is that I can move my arm."

And he moved it, although with a certain difficulty, feeling the weight of an increasing swelling.

"By-and-by I'll tell you how it happened. . . . I don't believe they'll be anxious to repeat it."

Then he remained thoughtful for an instant.

"At any rate, it's best for us to get away from this port quickly. . . . Go and see our men. Not one of them is to speak about it! . . . Call Caragol."

Before Toni could go out, the shining countenance of the cook surged up out of the obscurity. He was on his way to the saloon, without being called, anxious to know what had occurred, and fearing to find Ferragut dying. Seeing the blood, his consternation expressed itself with maternal vehemence.

"Cristo del Grao! . . . My captain's going to die! . . ."

He wanted to run to the galley in search of cotton and bandages. He was something of a quack doctor and always kept things necessary for such cases.

Ulysses stopped him. He would accept his services, but he wished something more.

"I want to eat, Uncle Caragol," he said gayly. "I shall be content with whatever you have. . . . Fright has given me an appetite."

CHAPTER XI

WHEN Ferragut left Barcelona the wound in his shoulder was already nearly healed. The rotund negative given by the captain and his pilot to the questions of the Carabineers freed them from further annoyance. They "knew nothing,—had seen nothing." The captain received with feigned indifference the news that the dead body of a man had been found that very night,—a man who appeared to be a German, but without papers, without anything that assured his identification,—on a dock some distance from the berth occupied by the *Mare Nostrum*. The authorities had not considered it worth while to investigate further, classifying it as a simple struggle among refugees.

Provisioning the troops of the Orient obliged Ferragut, in the months following, to sail as part of a convoy. A cipher dispatch would sometimes summon him to Marseilles, at others to an Atlantic port,—Saint-Nazaire, Quiberon, or Brest.

Every few days ships of different class and nationality were arriving. There were those that displayed their aristocratic origin by the fine line of the prow, the slenderness of the smokestacks and the still white color of their upper decks: they were like the high-priced steeds that war had transformed into simple beasts of battle. Former mail-packets, swift racers of the waves, had descended to the humble service of transport boats. Others, black and dirty, with the pitchy plaster of hasty repara-

427

tion and a consumptive smokestack on an enormous hull, plowed along, coughing smoke, spitting ashes, panting with the jangle of old iron. The flags of the Allies and those of the neutral navies waved on the different ships. Reuniting, they formed a convoy in the broad bay. There were fifteen or twenty steamers, sometimes thirty, which had to navigate together, adjusting their different speeds to a common pace. The cargo boats, merchant steamers that made only a few knots an hour, exacted a desperate slowness of the rest of the convoy.

The *Mare Nostrum* had to sail at half speed, making its captain very impatient with these monotonous and dangerous peregrinations, extending over weeks and weeks.

Before setting out, Ferragut, like all the other captains, would receive sealed and stamped orders. These were from the Commodore of the convoy,—the commander of a torpedo destroyer, or a simple officer of the Naval Reserve in charge of a motor trawler armed with a quickfiring gun.

The steamers would begin belching smoke and hoisting anchors without knowing whither they were going. The official document was opened only at the moment of departure. Ulysses would break the seals and examine the paper, understanding with facility its formal language, written in a common cipher. The first thing that he would look out for was the port of destination, then, the order of formation. They were to sail in single file or in a double row, according to the number of vessels. The *Mare Nostrum,* represented by a certain number, was to navigate between two other numbers which were those of the nearest steamers. They were to keep between them a distance of about five hundred yards; it was important that they should not come any nearer in a moment of carelessness, nor prolong the line so that they would be out of sight of the watchful guardians.

At the end, the general instructions for all the voyages were repeated with a laconic brevity that would have made other men, not accustomed to look death in the face, turn pale. In case of a submarine attack, the transports that carried guns were to come out from the line and aid the patrol of armed vessels, attacking the enemy. The others were to continue their course tranquilly, without paying any attention to the attack. If the boat in front of them or the one following was torpedoed, they were not to stop to give it aid. The torpedo boats and "chaluteros" were charged with saving the wrecked ship if it were possible. The duty of the transport was always to go forward, blind and deaf, without getting out of line, without stopping, until it had delivered at the terminal port the fortune stowed in its holds.

This march in convoy imposed by the submarine war represented a leap backward in the life of the sea. It recalled to Ferragut's mind the sailing fleets of other centuries, escorted by navies in line, punctuating their course by incessant battles, and the remote voyages of the galleons of the Indies, setting forth from Seville in fleets when bound for the coast of the New World.

The double file of black hulks with plumes of smoke advanced very placidly in fair weather. When the day was gray, the sea choppy, the sky and the atmosphere foggy, they would scatter and leap about like a troop of dark and frightened lambs. The guardians of the convoy, three little boats that were going at full speed, were the vigilant mastiffs of this marine herd, preceding it in order to explore the horizon, remaining behind it, or marching beside it in order to keep the formation intact. Their lightness and their swiftness enabled them to make prodigious bounds over the waves. A girdle of smoke curled itself around their double smokestacks.

Their prows when not hidden were expelling cascades of foam, sometimes even showing the dripping forefoot of the keel.

At night time they would all travel with few lights, simple lanterns at the prow, as warning to the one just ahead, and another one at the stern, to point out the route to the ship following. These faint lights could scarcely be seen. Oftentimes the helmsman would suddenly have to turn his course and demand slackened speed behind, seeing the silhouette of the boat ahead looming up in the darkness. A few moments of carelessness and it would come in on the prow with a deadly ram. Upon slowing down, the captain always looked behind uneasily, fearing in turn to collide with his following ship.

They were all thinking about the invisible submarines. From time to time would sound the report of the guns; the convoy's escort was shooting and shooting, going from one side to the other with agile evolutions. The enemy had fled like wolves before the barking of watchdogs. On other occasions it would prove a false alarm, and the shells would wound the desert water with a lashing of steel.

There was an enemy more troublesome than the tempest, more terrible than the torpedoes, that disorganized the convoys. It was the fog, thick and pale as the white of an egg, enshrouding the vessels, making them navigate blindly in full daylight, filling space with the useless moaning of their sirens, not letting them see the water which sustained them nor the nearby boats that might emerge at any moment from the blank atmosphere, announcing their apparition with a collision and a tremendous, deadly crash. In this way the merchant fleets had to proceed entire days together and when, at the end, they found themselves free from this wet

blanket, breathing with satisfaction as though awaking
from a nightmare, another ashy and nebulous wall
would come advancing over the waters enveloping them
anew in its night. The most valorous and calm men
would swear upon seeing the endless bar of mist closing
off the horizon.

Such voyages were not at all to Ferragut's taste.
Marching in line like a soldier, and having to conform
to the speed of these miserable little boats irritated him
greatly, and it made him still more wrathful to find himself obliged to obey the Commodore of a convoy who
frequently was nobody but an old sailor of masterful
character.

Because of all this he announced to the maritime authorities, on one of his arrivals at Marseilles, his firm
intention of not sailing any more in this fashion. He
had had enough with four such expeditions which were
all well enough for timid captains incapable of leaving
a port unless they always had in sight an escort of
torpedo-boats, and whose crews at the slightest occurrence would try to lower the lifeboats and take refuge on
the coast. He believed that he would be more secure
going alone, trusting to his skill, with no other aid than
his profound knowledge of the routes of the Mediterranean.

His petition was granted. He was the owner of a
vessel and they were afraid of losing his coöperation
when means of transportation were growing so very
scarce. Besides, the *Mare Nostrum,* on account of its
high speed, deserved individual employment in extraordinary and rapid service.

He remained in Marseilles some weeks waiting for a
cargo of howitzers, and meandered as usual around the
Mediterranean capital. He passed the evenings on the
terrace of a café of the *Cannebière.* The recollection of

von Kramer always loomed up in his mind at such
times. "I wonder if they have shot him! . . ." He
wished to know, but his investigations did not meet with
much success. War Councils avoid publicity regarding
their acts of justice. A Marseilles merchant, a friend
of Ferragut, seemed to recall that some months before
a German spy, surprised in the harbor, had been executed. Three lines, no more, in the newspapers, gave
an account of his death. They said that he was an officer. . . . And his friend went on talking about the
war news while Ulysses was thinking that the executed
man could not have been any one else but von Kramer.

On that same afternoon he had an encounter. While
passing through the street of *Saint-Ferreol,* looking at
the show windows, the cries of several conductors of
cabs and automobiles who could not manage to drive their
vehicles through the narrow and crowded streets, attracted his attention. In one carriage he saw a blonde
lady with her back to him, accompanied by two officers
of the English navy. Immediately he thought of Freya.
. . . Her hat, her gown, everything about her personality, was so very distinctive. And yet, when the coach
had passed on without his being able to get a glimpse
of the face of the stranger, the image of the adventuress
persisted in his mind.

Finally he became very much irritated with himself,
because of this absurd resemblance suspected without any reason whatever. How could that English-
woman with the two officers be Freya? . . . How
could a German refugee in Barcelona manage to slip into
France where she was undoubtedly known by the military police? . . . And still more exasperating was his
suspicion that this resemblance might have awakened
a remnant of the old love which made him see Freya
in every blonde woman.

At nine o'clock the following morning, while the captain was in his stateroom dressing to go ashore, Toni opened the door.

His face was scowling and timid at the same time, as though he had some bad news to give.

"That creature is here," he said laconically.

Ferragut looked at him with a questioning expression: *"What* creature? . . ."

"Who else could it be? . . . The one from Naples! That blonde devil that brought us all so much trouble! . . . We'll see now if this witch is going to keep us immovable for I don't know how many weeks just as she did the other time."

He excused himself as though he had just failed in discipline. The boat was fastened to the wharf by a bridgeway and anybody could come aboard. The pilot was opposed to these dockings which left the passage free to the curious and the importunate. By the time he had finished announcing her arrival, the lady was already on deck near the staterooms. She remembered well the way to the saloon. She had wished to go straight in, but it had been Caragol who had stopped her, while Toni went to advise the captain.

"Cristo!" murmured Ulysses. *"Cristo! . . ."*

And his astonishment, his surprise, did not permit him to utter any other exclamation.

Then he burst out furiously. "Throw her overboard! . . . Let two men lay hold of her and put her back on the wharf, by main force, if necessary."

But Toni hesitated, not daring to comply with such commands. And the impetuous Ferragut rushed outside of his cabin to do himself what had been ordered.

When he reached the saloon some one entered at the same time from the deck. It was Caragol, who was trying to block the passage of a woman; but she, laughing and taking advantage of his purblind eyes, was slipping little by little in between his body and the wooden partition.

On seeing the captain, Freya ran toward him, throwing out her arms.

"You!" she cried in a merry voice. "I knew well enough that you were here, in spite of the fact that these men were assuring me to the contrary. . . . My heart told me so. . . . How do you do, Ulysses!"

Caragol turned his eyes toward the place where he supposed the mate must be, as though imploring his pardon. With females he never could carry out any order. . . . Toni, on his part, appeared in an agony of shame before this woman who was looking at him defiantly.

The two disappeared. Ferragut was not able to say exactly how they got away, but he was glad of it. He feared that the recent arrival might allude in their presence to the things of the past.

He remained contemplating her a long time. He had believed the day before that he had recognized her back, and now he was sure that he might have passed on with indifference had he seen her face. Was this really the same woman that the two English officials were accompanying? . . . She appeared much taller than the other one, with a slenderness that made her skin appear more clear, giving it a delicate transparency. The nose was finer and more prominent. The eyes were sparkling, hidden in bluish black circles.

These eyes began to look at the captain, humbly and pleadingly.

"You!" exclaimed Ulysses in wonder. "You! . . . What are you coming here for?" . . .

Freya replied with the timidity of a bondslave. Yes, it was she who had recognized him the day before, long before he had seen her, and at once had formed the plan of coming in search of him. He could beat her just as at their last meeting: she was ready to suffer everything . . . but with him!

"Save me, Ulysses! Take me with you! . . . I implore you even more anxiously than in Barcelona."

"What are you doing here? . . ."

She understood the captain's amazement on meeting her in a belligerent country, the disquietude he must naturally feel upon finding a spy on his vessel. She looked around in order to make sure that they were entirely alone and spoke in a low voice. The doctor had sent her to France in order that she should "operate" in its ports. Only to him could she reveal the secret.

Ulysses was more indignant than ever at this confidence.

"Clear out!" he said in a wrathful voice. "I don't want to know anything about you. . . . Your affairs do not interest me at all. I do not wish to know them. . . . Get out of here! What are you plaguing me for?"

But she did not appear disposed to comply with his orders. Instead of departing, she dropped wearily down on one of the divans of the stateroom.

"I have come," she said, "to beg you to save me. I ask it for the last time. . . . I'm going to die; I suspect that my end is very near if you will not hold out a helping hand; I foresee the vengeance of my own people. . . . Guard me, Ulysses! Do not make me go back ashore; I am afraid. . . . So safe I shall feel here at your side! . . ."

Fear, sure enough, was reflected in her eyes as she recalled the last months of her life in Barcelona.

"The doctor is my enemy. . . . She who protected me so in other times abandons me now like an old shoe that

it is necessary to get rid of. I am positive that her
superior officers have condemned me. . . ."

She shuddered on remembering the doctor's wrath
when on her return from one of her trips she learned
of the death of her faithful Karl. To her, Captain Ferragut was a species of invulnerable and victorious demon who was escaping all dangers and murdering the
servants of a good cause. First von Kramer; now Karl.
. . . As it was necessary for her to vent her wrath on
somebody, she had made Freya responsible for all her
misfortunes. Through her she had known the captain,
and had mixed him up in the affairs of the "service."

Thirst for vengeance made the imposing dame smile
with a ferocious expression. The Spanish sailor was
doomed by the Highest Command. Precise orders had
been given out against him. "As to his accomplices!
. . ." Freya was figuring undoubtedly among these accomplices for having dared to defend Ferragut, for
remembering the tragic event of his son, for having
refused to join the chorus desiring his extermination.

Weeks afterwards the doctor again became as smiling
and as amiable as in other times. "My dear girl, it is
agreed that you should take a trip to France. We need
there an agent who will keep us informed of the traffic
of the ports, of the goings and comings of the vessels
in order that our submersibles may know where to await
them. The naval officials are very gallant, and a beautiful woman will be able to gain their affection."

She had tried to disobey. To go to France! . . .
where her pre-war work was already known! . . . To
go back to danger when she had already become accustomed to the safe life of a neutral country! . . . But
her attempts at resistance were ineffectual. She lacked

sufficient will-power; the "service" had converted her into an automaton.

"And here I am, suspecting that probably I am going to my death, but fulfilling the commissions given to me, struggling to be accommodating and retard in this way the fulfillment of their vengeance. . . . I am like a condemned criminal who knows that he is going to die, and tries to make himself so necessary that his sentence will be delayed for a few months."

"How did you get into France?" he demanded, paying no attention to her doleful tones.

"Freya shrugged her shoulders. In her business a change of nationality was easily accomplished. At present she was passing for a citizen of a South American republic. The doctor had arranged all the papers necessary to enable her to cross the frontier.

"But here," she continued, "my accomplices have me more securely than as though I were in prison. They have given me the means of coming here and they only can arrange my departure. I am absolutely in their power. I wonder what they are going to do with me! . . ."

At certain times terror had suggested most desperate expedients to her. She had thought of denouncing herself, of appearing before the French authorities, telling them her story and acquainting them with the secrets which she possessed. But her past filled her with terror, so many were the evils which she had brought against this country. Perhaps they might pardon her life, taking into account her voluntary action in giving herself up. But the prison, the seclusion with shaved head, dressed in some coarse serge frock, condemned to silence, perhaps suffering hunger and cold, filled her with invincible repulsion. . . . No, death before that!

And so she was continuing her life as a spy, shutting

her eyes to the future, living only in the present, trying to keep from thinking, considering herself happy if she could see before her even a few days of security.

The meeting with Ferragut in the street of Marseilles had revived her drooping spirits, arousing new hope.

"Get me out of here; keep me with you. On your ship I could live as forgotten by the world as though I were dead. . . . And if my presence annoys you, take me far away from France, leave me in some distant country!"

She was anxious to evade isolation in the enemy's territory, obliged to obey her superiors like a caged beast who has to take jabs through the iron grating. Presentiment of her approaching death was making her tremble.

"I do not want to die, Ulysses! . . . I am not old enough yet to die. I adore my physical charm. I am my own best lover and I am terrified at the thought that I might be shot."

A phosphorescent light gleamed from her eyes and her teeth struck together with a chattering of terror.

"I do not want to die!" she repeated. "There are moments in which I suspect that they are following me and closing me in. . . . Perhaps they have recognized me and at this moment are waiting to surprise me in the very act. . . . Do help me; get me away from here; my death is certain. I have done so much harm! . . ."

She was silent a moment, as though calculating all the crimes of her former life.

"The doctor," she continued, "depends upon her consuming patriotic enthusiasm as the impetus to her work. I lack her faith. I am not a German woman, and being a spy is very repugnant to me. . . . I feel ashamed when I think of my actual life; every night I think over the

result of my abominable work; I calculate the use to
which they will put my warnings and my information;
I can see the torpedoed boats. . . . I wonder how many
human beings have perished through my fault! . . . I
have visions; my conscience torments me. Save me!
. . . I can do no more. I feel a horrible fear. I have
so much to expiate! . . ."

Little by little she had raised herself from the divan,
and, while begging Ferragut's protection, was going
toward him with outstretched arms; abject, and yet
at the same time caressing, through that desire of seduction that always predominated over all her acts.

"Leave me!" shouted the sailor. "Do not come near
me. . . . Do not touch me!"

He felt that same wrath that had made him so brutal
in their interview in Barcelona. He was greatly exasperated at the tenacity of this adventuress who, in addition
to the tragic influence she had already exercised upon
his life, was now trying to compromise him still further.

But a sentiment of cold compassion made him check
his anger and speak with a certain kindness.

If she needed money in order to make her escape, he
would give it to her without any haggling whatever.
She could name the sum. The captain was disposed to
satisfy all her desires except that of living with her.
He would give her a substantial amount in order to make
her fortune assured and never see her again.

Freya made a gesture of protest at the same time
that the sailor began repenting of his generosity.
. . . Why should he do such a favor to a woman
who reminded him of the death of his son? . . . What
was there in common between the two? . . . Their vile
love-affair in Naples had been sufficiently paid for with
his bereavement. . . . Let each one follow his own des-

tiny; they belonged to different worlds. . . . Was he
going to have to defend himself all his life long from
this insistent charmer? . . .

Moreover, he was not at all sure that even now she
was telling the truth. . . . Everything about her was
false. He did not even know with certainty her true
name and her past existence. . . .

"Clear out!" he roared in a threatening tone. "Leave
me in peace."

He raised his powerful hand against her, seeing that
she was going to refuse to obey. He was going to pick
her up roughly, carry her like a light bundle outside the
room, outside the boat, flinging her away as though she
were remorse.

But her physique, so opulent in its seductions, now
inspired him with an unconquerable repugnance; he was
afraid of its contact and wished to avoid its electric
surprises. . . . Besides, he wasn't going to maltreat her
at every meeting like a professional Apache who mixes
love and blows. He recalled with disgust his violence in
Barcelona.

And as Freya instead of going away sank back on
the divan, with a faintness that seemed to challenge his
wrath, it was he who fled in order to bring the interview to an end.

He rushed into his stateroom, locking the door with a
bang. This flight brought her out of her inertia. She
wished to follow him with the leap of a young panther,
but her hands collided with an obstacle that became impassable, while from within sounded the noise of keys
and bolts.

She pounded the door desperately, injuring her fists
with her fruitless efforts.

"Ulysses, open it! . . . Listen to me."

In vain she shrieked as though she were giving an

order, exasperated at finding that she was not obeyed. Her fury spent itself unavailingly against the solid immovability of the wood. Suddenly she began to cry, modifying her purpose upon finding herself as weak and defenseless as an abandoned creature. All her life appeared concentrated in her tears and in her pleading voice.

She passed her fingers over the door, groping over the moldings, slipping them over the varnished surface as though seeking at random a crevice, a hole, something that would permit her to get to the man that was on the other side.

Instinctively she fell upon her knees, putting her mouth to the keyhole.

"My lord, my master!" she murmured in the voice of a beggar. "Open the door. . . . Do not abandon me. Remember that I am going to my death if you do not save me."

Ferragut heard her, and, in order to evade her moaning, was getting as near as possible to the end of his stateroom. Then he unfastened the round window that opened on the deck, ordering a seaman to go after the mate.

"*Don Antoni! Don Antoni!*" various voices cried the whole length of the ship.

Toni appeared, putting his face in the circular opening only to receive the furious vituperation of his captain.

Why had they left him alone with that woman? . . . They must take her off the boat at once, even if it had to be done by main force. . . . He commanded it.

The mate went off with a confounded air, scratching his beard as though he had received an order very difficult to execute.

"Save me, my love!" the imploring whisper kept moaning. "Forget who I am. . . . Think only of the one

of Naples. . . . Of the one whom you knew at Pompeii.
. . . Remember our happiness alone together in the days
when you swore never to abandon me. . . . You are a
gentleman ! . . ."

Her voice ceased for a moment. Ferragut heard footsteps on the other side of the door. Toni was carrying
out his orders.

But in a few seconds the pleading again burst forth,
reconcentrated, tenacious, bent only upon carrying its
point, scorning the new obstacles about to interpose
between her and the captain.

"Do you hate me so? . . . Remember the bliss that I
gave you. You yourself swore to me that you had never
been so happy. I can revive that past. You do not
know of what things I am capable in order to make
your existence sweet. . . . And you wish to lose and to
ruin me ! . . ."

A clash against the door was heard, a struggle of
bodies that were pushing each other, the friction of a
scuffle against the wood.

Toni had entered followed by Caragol.

"Enough of that now, Señora," said the mate in a
grim voice in order to hide his emotion. "Can't you see
that the captain doesn't want to see you? . . . Don't you
understand that you are disturbing him? . . . Come,
now. . . . Get up !"

He tried to help her to stand up, separating her mouth
from the keyhole. But Freya repelled the vigorous sailor
with facility. He appeared to be lacking in force, without the courage to repeat his rough action. The beauty
of this woman made him afraid. He was still thrilled
by the contact of her firm body which he had just touched
during their short struggle. His drowsing virtue had
suffered the torments of a fruitless resurrection. "Ah

no! . . . Let somebody else take charge of putting her off."

"Ulysses, they're taking me away!" she cried, again putting her mouth to the keyhole. "And you, my love, will you permit it? . . . You who used to love me so? . . ."

After this desperate call, she remained silent for a few instants. The door maintained its immobility; behind it there seemed to be no living being.

"Farewell!" she continued in a low voice, her throat choked with sobs, "you will see me no more. . . . I am soon going to die; my heart tells me so. . . . To die because of you! . . . Perhaps some day you will weep on recalling that you might have saved me."

Some one had intervened to force Freya from her rebellious standstill. It was Caragol, solicited by the mate's imploring eyes.

His great hairy hands helped her to arise, without making her repeat the protest that had repelled Toni. Conquered and bursting into tears, she appeared to yield to the paternal aid and counsel of the cook.

"Up now, my good lady!" said Caragol. "A little more courage and don't cry any more. . . . There is some consolation for everything in this world."

In his bulky right hand he imprisoned her two, and, passing his other arm around her waist, he was guiding her little by little toward the exit from the salon.

"Trust in God," he added. "Why do you seek the captain who has his own wife ashore? . . . Other men who are free are still in existence, and you could make some arrangement with them without falling into mortal sin."

Freya was not listening to him. Near the door she again turned her head, beginning her return toward the captain's stateroom.

"Ulysses! . . . Ulysses!" she cried.

"Trust in God, Señora," said Caragol again, while he was pushing her along with his flabby abdomen and shaggy breast.

A charitable idea was taking possession of his thoughts. He had the remedy for the grief of this handsome woman whose desperation but made her more interesting.

"Come along, Señora. . . . Leave it to me, my child." Upon reaching the deck he continued driving her towards his dominions. Freya found herself seated in the galley, without knowing just exactly where she was. Through her tears she saw this obese old man of sacerdotal benevolence, going from side to side gathering bottles together and mixing liquids, stirring the spoon around in a glass with a joyous tinkling.

"Drink without fear. . . . There is no trouble that resists this medicine."

The cook offered her a glass and she, vanquished, drank and drank, making a wry face because of the alcoholic intensity of the liquid. She continued weeping at the same time that her mouth was relishing the heavy sweetness. Her tears were mingled with the beverage that was slipping between her lips.

A comfortable warmth began making itself felt in her stomach, drying up the moisture in her eyes and giving new color to her cheeks. Caragol was keeping up his chat, satisfied with the outcome of his handiwork, making signs to the glowering Toni,—who was passing and repassing before the door, with the vehement desire of seeing the intruder march away, and disappear forever.

"Don't cry any more, my daughter. . . . *Cristo del Grao!* The very idea! A lady as pretty as you, who can find sweethearts by the dozen, crying! . . . Believe me; find somebody else. This world is just full of men with nothing to do. . . . And always for every disappointment that you suffer, have recourse to my cordial. . . . I am going to give you the recipe."

He was about to note down on a bit of paper the proportions of brandy and sugar, when she arose, suddenly invigorated, looking around her in wonder. . . . But where was she? What had she to do with this good, kind, half-dressed man, who was talking to her as though he were her father? . . .

"Thanks! Many thanks!" she said on leaving the kitchen.

Then on deck she stopped, opening her gold-mesh bag, in order to take out the little glass and powder box. In the beveled edge of the oval glass she saw the faunlike countenance of Toni hovering behind her with glances of impatience.

"Tell Captain Ferragut that I shall never trouble him again. . . . All has ended. . . . Perhaps he may hear me spoken of some time, but he will never see me again."

And she left the boat without turning her head, with quickened step as though, fired by a sudden suggestion, she were hastening to put it into effect.

Toni ran also, but toward Ulysses' stateroom window.

"Has she gone yet?" asked the captain impatiently.

The mate nodded his head. She had promised not to return.

"Be it so!" said Ferragut.

Toni experienced the same desire. Would to God they might never again see this blonde who always brought them misfortune! . . .

In the days following, the captain rarely left his ship. He did not wish to run the risk of meeting her in the city streets for he was a little doubtful of the hardness of his character. He feared that upon seeing her again, weeping and pleading, he might yield to her beseeching.

Ulysses' uneasiness vanished as soon as the loading of the vessel was finished. This trip was going to be shorter than the others. The *Mare Nostrum* went to Corfu with war material for the Serbs who were reorganizing their battalions destined for Salonica.

On the return trip Ferragut was attacked by the enemy. One day at dawn just as he mounted the bridge to relieve Toni, the two spied at the same time the tangible form that they were always seeing in imagination. Within the circle of their glasses there framed itself the end of a stick, black and upright, that was cutting the waters rosy in the sunrise, leaving a wake of foam.

"Submarine!" shouted the captain.

Toni said nothing, but shoving aside the helmsman with a stroke of his paw, he grasped the wheel, making the boat swerve in another direction. The movement was opportune. Only a few seconds had passed by when there began to be seen upon the water a black back of dizzying speed headed directly for the steamer.

"Torpedo!" shouted the captain.

The anxious waiting lasted but a few seconds. The projectile, hidden in the water, passed some six yards from the stern, losing itself in space. Had it not been for Toni's rapid tacking, the boat would have been hit squarely in the side.

Through the speaking tube connecting with the engine-room the captain shouted energetic orders to put on full speed. Meanwhile the mate, clamped to the wheel, ready to die rather than leave it, was directing the boat in zigzags so as not to offer a fixed point to the submarine.

All the crew were watching from the rail the distant and insignificant upright periscope. The third officer had rushed out of his stateroom, almost naked, rubbing his sleepy eyes. Caragol was in the stern, his loose shirt-tail flapping away as he held one hand to his eyebrows like a visor.

"I see it! . . . I see it perfectly. . . . Ah, the bandit, the heretic!"

And he extended his threatening fist toward a point in the horizon exactly opposite to the one upon which the periscope was appearing.

Through the blue circle of the glasses Ferragut saw this tube climbing up and up, growing larger and larger. It was no longer a stick, it was a tower; and from beneath this tower was coming up on the sea a base of steel spouting cascades of smoke,—a gray whale-back that appeared little by little to be taking the form of a sailing vessel, long and sharp-pointed.

A flag was suddenly run up upon the submarine. Ulysses recognized it.

"They are going to shell us!" he yelled to Toni. "It's useless to keep up the zigzagging. The thing to do now is to outspeed them, to go forward in a straight line."

The mate, skillful helmsman that he was, obeyed the captain. The hull vibrated under the force of the engines taxed to their utmost. Their prow was cutting the waters with increasing noise. The submersible upon augmenting its volume by emersion appeared, nevertheless, to be falling behind on the horizon. Two streaks of foam began to spring up on both sides of its prow. It was running with all its possible surface speed; but the *Mare Nostrum* was also going at the utmost limit of its engines and the distance was widening between the two boats.

"They are shooting!" said Ferragut with the glasses to his eyes.

A column of water spouted near the prow. That was

the only thing that Caragol was able to see clearly and
he burst into applause with a childish joy. Then he
waved on high his palm-leaf hat. *"Viva el Santo
Cristo del Grao! . . ."*

Other projectiles were falling around the *Mare Nostrum,* spattering it with jets of foam. Suddenly it trembled from poop to prow. Its plates trembled with the
vibration of an explosion.

"That's nothing!" yelled the captain, bending himself
double over the bridge in order to see better the hull of
his ship. "A shell in the stern. Steady, Toni! . . ."

The mate, always grasping the wheel, kept turning his
head from time to time to measure the distance separating
them from the submarine. Every time that he saw an
aquatic column of spray, forced up by a projectile, he
would repeat the same counsel.

"Lie down, Ulysses! . . . They are going to fire at
the bridge!"

This was a recollection of his far-away youth when,
as a contrabandist, he used to stretch himself flat on
the deck of his bark, manipulating the wheel and the
sail under the fire of the custom-house officers on watch.
He feared for the life of his captain while he was standing, constantly offering himself to the shots of the enemy.

Ferragut was storming from side to side, cursing his
lack of means for returning the aggression. "This will
never happen another time! . . . They won't get another chance to amuse themselves chasing me!"

A second projectile opened another breach in the poop.
"If it only won't hit the engines!" the captain was thinking. After that the *Mare Nostrum* received no more
damage, the following shots merely raising up columns
of water in the steamer's wake. Every time now, these
white phantasms leaped up further and further away.

Although out of the range of the enemy's gun, it continued shooting and shooting uselessly. Finally the firing ceased and the submarine disappeared from the view of the glasses and completely submerged, tired of vain pursuit.

"That'll never happen again!" the captain kept repeating. "They'll never attack me another time with impunity!"

Then it occurred to him that this submarine had attack him knowing just who he was. On the side of his vessel were painted the colors of Spain. At the first shot from the gun, the third officer had hoisted the flag, but the shots did not cease on that account. They had wished to sink it "without leaving any trace." He believed that Freya, in her relations with the directors of the submarine campaign, must have advised them of his trip.

"Ah, . . . *tal!* If I meet her another time! . . ."

He had to remain several weeks in Marseilles while the damage to his steamer was being repaired.

As Toni lacked occupation during this enforced idleness, he accompanied him many times on his strolls. They liked to seat themselves on the terrace of a café in order to comment upon the picturesque differences in the cosmopolitan crowd.

"Look; people from our own country!" said the captain one evening.

And he pointed to three seamen drawn into the current of different uniforms and types of various races flowing familiarly around the tables of the café.

He had recognized them by their silk caps with visors, their blue jackets and their heavy obesity of Mediterranean sailors enjoying a certain prosperity. They must be skippers of small boats.

As though Ferragut's looks and gestures had mys-

teriously notified them, the three turned, fixing their
eyes on the captain. Then they began to discuss among
themselves with a vehemence which made it easy to
guess their words.

"It is he! . . ." "No, it isn't! . . ."

Those men knew him but couldn't believe that they
were really seeing him.

They went a little way off with marked indecision,
turning repeatedly to look at him once more. In a few
moments one of them, the oldest, returned, approaching
the table timidly.

"Excuse me, but aren't you Captain Ferragut? . . ."
He asked this question in Valencian, with his right hand
at his cap, ready to take it off.

Ulysses stopped his salutation and offered him a seat.
Yes, he was Ferragut. What did he want? . . .

The man refused to sit down. He wished to tell him
privately two special things. When the captain presented to him his mate as a man in whom they could
have complete confidence, he then sat down. The two
companions, breaking through the human current, were
standing on the edge of the sidewalk, turning their backs
to the café.

He was skipper of a small craft; Ferragut had not
been mistaken. He was speaking slowly, as though taken
up with his final revelation to which all that he was
saying was merely an introduction.

"The times are not so bad. . . . Money is to be
gained in the sea; more than ever. I am from Valencia.
. . . We have brought three boats from there with wine
and rice. A good trip, but it was necessary to navigate
close to the coast, following the curve of the gulf, without venturing to pass from cape to cape for fear of the
submarine. . . . I have met a submarine."

Ulysses suspected that these last words contained the

real motive which had made the man, overcoming his timidity, venture to address him.

"It was not on this trip nor on the one before," continued the man of the sea. "I met it two days before last Christmas. In the winter I devote myself to fishing. I am the owner of a pair of fishing smacks. . . . We were near the island Columbretas when suddenly we saw a submarine appear near us. The Germans did not do us any harm; the only vexatious thing was that we had to give them a part of our fish for what they wished to give us. Then they ordered me to come aboard the deck of a submarine in order to meet the commander. He was a young fellow who could talk Castilian as I have heard it spoken over there in the Americas when I was a youngster sailing on a brigantine."

The man stopped, rather reserved, as though doubtful whether to continue his story.

"And what did the German say?" asked Ferragut, in order to encourage him to continue.

"Upon learning that I was a Valencian, he asked me if I was acquainted with you. He asked me about your steamer, wanting to know if it generally sailed along the Spanish coast. I replied that I knew you by name, no more, and then he . . ."

The captain encouraged him with a smile on seeing that he was beginning to hesitate again.

"He spoke badly about me. Isn't that so? . . ."

"Yes, sir; very badly. He used ugly words. He said that he had an account to adjust with you and that he wished to be the first one to meet you. According to what he gave me to understand, the other submarines are hunting for you, too. . . . It is an order without doubt."

Ferragut and his mate exchanged a long look. Meanwhile the captain continued his explanations.

The two friends who were waiting a few steps off had seen the captain in Valencia and Barcelona many times. One of them had recognized him immediately; but the other was doubtful whether it might be he, and, as a matter of conscience, the old skipper had come back to give him this warning.

"We countrymen must help one another. . . . These are bad times!"

Seeing him standing, his two comrades now came up to Ferragut. "What would you like to drink?" He invited them to seat themselves at the table, but they were in a hurry. They were on their way to see the consignees of their boats.

"Now you know it, Captain," said the skipper on bidding him farewell. "These demons are after you in order to pay you up for something in the past. You know what for. . . . Be very careful!"

The rest of the evening Ferragut and Toni talked very little together. The two had exactly the same thought in their brain, but avoided putting it in shape because, as energetic men, they feared that some cowardly construction might be put upon such thoughts.

At nightfall when they returned to the steamer the pilot ventured to break the silence.

"Why do you not quit the sea? . . . You are rich. Besides, they'll give you whatever you ask for your ship. To-day boats are worth their weight in gold."

Ulysses shrugged his shoulders. He wasn't thinking of money. What good would that do him? . . . He wanted to pass the rest of his life on the sea, giving aid to the enemies of his enemies. He had a vengeance to fulfill. . . . Living on land, he would be abandoning this vengeance, though remembering his son with even greater intensity.

The mate was silent for a few moments.

"The enemies are so many," he then said in dismay. "We are so insignificant! . . . We only escaped by a few yards being sent to the bottom on our last trip. What has not happened yet will surely happen some day. . . . *They* have sworn to do away with you; and they are many . . . and they are at war. What could we do, we poor peaceable sailors? . . ."

Toni did not add anything further but his silent thoughts were divined by Ulysses.

He was thinking about his family over there in the *Marina,* enduring an existence of continual anxiety while he was aboard a vessel for which irresistible menace was lying in wait. He was thinking also of the wives and mothers of all the men of the crew who were suffering the same anguish. And Toni was asking himself for the first time whether Captain Ferragut had the right to drag them all to a sure death just because of his vengeful and crazy stubbornness.

"No; I have not the right," Ulysses told himself mentally.

But at the same time his mate, repentant of his former reflection, was affirming in a loud voice with heroic simplicity:

"If I counsel you to retire, it is for your own good; don't think it is because I am afraid. . . . I will follow you wherever you sail. I've got to die some time and it would be far better that it should be in the sea. The only thing that troubles me is worrying about my wife and children."

The captain continued walking in silence and, upon reaching his ship, spoke with brevity. "I was thinking of doing something that perhaps you would all like. Before next week your future will have been decided."

He passed the following day on land. Twice he returned with some gentlemen who examined the steamer minutely, going down into the engine room and the holds. Some of these visitors appeared to be experts in matters pertaining to the sea.

"He wants to sell the boat," said Toni to himself.

And the mate began to repent of his counsels. Abandon the *Mare Nostrum,* the best of all the ships on which he had ever sailed! . . . He accused himself of cowardice, believing that it was he who had impelled the captain to reach this decision. What were the two going to do on land when the steamer was the property of others? . . . Would he not have to sail on an inferior boat, running the same risks? . . . He decided to undo his work, and was about to counsel Ferragut again, declaring that his ideas were mere conjecture and that he must continue living as he was at present, when the captain gave the order for departure. The repairs were not yet entirely completed.

"We are going to Brest," said Ferragut laconically. "It's the last trip."

And the steamer put to sea without cargo as though going to fulfill a special mission.

"The last trip!" Toni admired his ship as though seeing it under a new light, discovering beauties hitherto unsuspected, lamenting like a lover the days that were running by so swiftly and the sad moment of separation that was approaching.

Never had the mate been so active in his vigilance. His seaman's superstition filled him with a certain terror. Just because it was the last voyage something horrible might occur to them. He paced the bridge for entire days, examining the sea, fearing the apparition of a periscope, varying the course in agreement with the captain, who was seeking less-frequented waters where the submarines could not expect to find any prey.

He breathed more freely upon entering one of the

three semi-circular sea-ledges which enclose the road-stead of Brest. When they were anchored in this bit of sea, foggy and insecure, surrounded with black mountains, Toni awaited with anxiety the result of the captain's excursions ashore.

During the entire course of the trip Ferragut had not been inclined to be confidential. The mate only knew that this voyage to Brest was the last. Who was going to be the new owner of the *Mare Nostrum?* . . .

One rainy evening, upon returning to the boat, Ulysses gave orders that they should hunt up the mate while he was shaking out his waterproof in the entry to the state-room.

The roadstead was dark with its foamy waves, choppy and thick, leaping like sheep. The men-of-war were sending out smoke from their triple chimneys ready to confront the bad weather with their steam engines.

The ship, anchored in the commercial port, was dancing restlessly, tugging at its hawsers, with a mournful croaking. All the nearby boats were tossing in the same way, just as though they were out on the high seas.

Toni entered the saloon, and one look at the captain's face made him suspect that the moment for knowing the truth had arrived. Avoiding his glance, Ulysses told him curtly, trying to evade by the conciseness of his language all signs of emotion.

He had sold the ship to the French:—a rapid and magnificent piece of business. . . . Whoever would have said when he bought the *Mare Nostrum* that some day they would give him such an enormous sum for it? . . . In no country could they find any vessels for sale. The invalids of the sea, rusting in the harbors as old iron, were now bringing fabulous prices. Boats, aground and forgotten on remote coasts, were placed afloat for enterprises that were gaining millions by this resurrection.

Others, submerged in tropical seas, had been brought up to the surface after a ten years' stay under the water, renewing their voyages. Every month a new shipyard sprang into existence, but the world war could never find enough vessels for the transportation of food and instruments of death.

Without any bargaining whatever, they had given Ferragut the price that he had exacted; fifteen hundred francs per ton,—four million and a half for the boat. And to this must be added the nearly two millions that it had gained in its voyages since the beginning of the war.

"I am rotten with money," concluded the captain.

And he said it sadly, remembering with a homesick longing the days of peace when he was wrestling with the problems of a badly paying business. But then his son was living. Of what avail was all this wealth that was assaulting him on all sides as though it were going to crush him with its weight? . . . His wife would be able to lavish money with full hands on works of charity; she would be able to give her nieces the dowry suitable for daughters of high-born personages. . . . Nothing more! Neither he nor she could for one moment resuscitate their past. These useless riches could only bring him a certain tranquillity in thinking of the future of his wife, who was his entire family. She was at liberty henceforth to dispose freely of her existence. Cinta, on his death, would fall heir to millions.

In order to evade the emotions of farewell, he spoke to Toni very authoritatively. A chart of the Atlantic was lying on the table and with his index finger he marked out the mate's course; this course was not across the sea, but far from it, following an inland route.

"To-morrow," he said, "the French are coming to take possession. You may leave whenever you please, but it will be convenient to have you go as soon as possible. . . ."

He explained his return trip to Toni, just as though he were giving him a lesson in geography. This sea-rover became timid and downhearted when they talked to him about railroad time-tables and changing trains.

"Here is Brest. . . . Follow this line to Bordeaux; from Bordeaux to the frontier. And once there, turn to Barcelona or go to Madrid, and from Madrid to Valencia."

The mate contemplated the map silently, scratching his beard. Then he raised his canine eyes slowly until he fixed them upon Ulysses.

"And you?" he asked.

"I remain here. The captain of the *Mare Nostrum* has sold himself with his vessel."

Toni made a distressed gesture. For a moment he almost believed that Ferragut wanted to get rid of him and was discontented with his services. But the captain hastened to explain further.

Because the *Mare Nostrum* belonged to a neutral country, it could not be sold to one of the belligerent nations while hostilities lasted. Because of this, he had transferred it in a way that would not make it necessary to change the flag. Although no longer its owner, he would stay on board as its captain, and the ship would continue to be Spanish the same as before.

"And why must I go away?" asked Toni in a tremulous tone, believing himself overlooked.

"We are going to sail armed," replied Ulysses energetically. "I have made the sale on that account more than for the money. We are going to carry a quickfirer at the stern, wireless installation, a crew of men from the naval reserves,—everything necessary to defend ourselves. We shall make our voyages without hunting for the enemy, carrying freight as before; but if the enemy comes out to attack us, it will find some one who will answer."

He was ready to die, if that was to be his fate, but attacking whoever attacked him.

"And may I not go, too?" persisted the pilot.

"No; back of you there is a family that needs you. You do not belong to a nation at war, nor have you anything to avenge. . . . I am the only one of the former crew that remains on board. All the rest of you are to go. The captain has a reason for exposing his life, and he does not wish to assume the responsibility of dragging all of you into his last adventure."

Toni understood that it would be useless to insist. His eyes became moist. . . . Was it possible that within a few hours they would be bidding each other a last good-by? . . . Should he never again see Ulysses and the ship on which he had spent the greater part of his past? . . .

In order to maintain his serenity, the captain tried to bring this interview promptly to an end.

"The first thing to-morrow morning," he said, "you will call the crew together. Adjust all the accounts. Each one must receive as an extra bonus a year's pay. I wish them to have pleasant memories of Captain Ferragut."

The mate attempted to oppose this generosity by a remnant of the keen interest that the business affairs of the boat had always inspired in him. But his superior officer would not let him continue.

"I am rotten with money, I tell you," he repeated as though uttering a complaint. "I have more than I need. . . . I can do foolish things with it if I wish to."

Then for the first time he looked his mate square in the face.

"As for you," he continued, "I have thought what you must do. . . . Here, take this!"

He gave him a sealed envelope and the pilot mechanically tried to open it.

"No, don't open it at present. You will find out what it contains when you are in Spain. Within it is enclosed the future of your own folks."

Toni looked with astonished eyes at the light scrap of paper which he held between his fingers.

"I know you," continued Ferragut. "You are going to protest at the quantity. What to me is insignificant, to you will appear excessive. . . . Do not open the envelope until you are in our country. In it you will find the name of the bank to which you must go. I wish you to be the richest man in your village that your sons may remember Captain Ferragut when he is dead."

The mate made a gesture of protest before this possible death, and at the same time rubbed his eyes as though he felt in them an intolerable itching.

Ulysses continued his instructions. He had rashly sold the home of his ancestors there in the *Marina*, the vineyards,—all his legacy from the *Triton*, when he had acquired the *Mare Nostrum*. It was his wish that Toni should redeem the property, installing himself in the ancient domicile of the Ferraguts.

He had money to spare for that and much more.

"I have no children and I like to feel that yours are occupying the house that was mine. . . . Perhaps when I get to be an old man—if they do not kill me, I will come to spend the summers with you. Courage now, Toni! . . . We shall yet go fishing together, as I used to go fishing with my uncle, the doctor."

But the mate did not regain his spirits on hearing these optimistic affirmations. His eyes were swollen with tears that sparkled in the corners of his eyes. He

was swearing between his teeth, protesting against the
coming separation. . . . Never to see him again, after
so many years of brotherly companionship! . . .
Cristo! . . .

The captain was afraid that he, too, might burst into
tears and again ordered his mate to present the accounts
of the crew.

An hour later Toni reëntered the saloon, carrying
in his hand the opened letter. He had not been able
to resist the temptation of forcing the secret, fearing that
Ferragut's generosity might prove excessive, and impossible to consider. He protested, handing to Ulysses
the check taken from the envelope.

"I could not accept it! . . . It's a crazy idea! . . ."

He had read with terror the amount made out to him in
the letter of credit, first in figures then in long hand.
Two hundred and fifty thousand pesetas! . . . fifty thousand dollars!

"That is not for me," he said again. "I do not deserve
it. . . . What could I ever do with so much money?"

The captain pretended to be irritated by his disobedience.

"You take that paper, you brute! . . . I was just
afraid that you were going to protest. . . . It's for your
children, and so that you can take a rest. Now we
won't talk any more about it or I shall get angry."

Then, in order to conquer Toni's scruples, he abandoned his violent tone, and said sadly:

"I have no heirs. . . . I don't know what to do with
my useless fortune."

And he repeated once more like a complaint against
destiny: "I am rotten with money! . . ."

The following morning, while Toni was in his cabin
adjusting the accounts of the crew, astonished by the

munificence of their paying-off, Uncle Caragol came into the saloon, asking to speak to Ferragut.

He had placed an old cape over his flapping and scanty clothing, more as a decoration for the visit than because the cold of Brittany was really making him suffer.

He removed from his shaved head his everlasting palm-leaf hat, fixing his bloodshot eyes on the captain who continued writing after replying to his greeting.

"What does this mean, this order that I've just received to prepare to leave the boat within a few hours? . . . It must be some kind of a joke of Toni's; he's an excellent fellow but an enemy to holy things and likes to tease me because of my piety. . . ."

Ferragut laid aside his pen, swinging around toward the cook whose fate had troubled him as much as the first mate's.

"Uncle Caragol, we are growing old and we must think about retiring. . . . I am going to give you a paper; you will guard it just as though it were a sacred picture, and when you present it in Valencia they will give you ten thousand dollars. Do you know how much ten thousand dollars are? . . ."

Bringing his mentality down to the level of this simple-minded man, he enjoyed tracing out for him a plan of living. He could invest his capital in whatever modest enterprise in the port of Valencia might appeal to his fancy; he could establish a restaurant which would soon become famous for its Olympian rice dishes. His nephews who were fishermen would receive him like a god. He could also be partner in a couple of barks, dedicated to fishing for the *bou*. There was awaiting him a happy and honorable old age; his former sailing companions were going to look upon him with envy. He could get up late in the morning; he could go to the cafés; as a rich devotee he could figure in all the religious processions of the Grau and of the Cabanal; he could have a place of honor in the holy processions. . . .

Heretofore, when Feragut was talking, Uncle Caragol had always mechanically interrupted him, saying: "That is so, my captain." For the first time he was not nodding his head nor smiling with his sun-like face. He was pale and gloomy. He shook his round head energetically and said laconically:

"No, my captain."

Before the glance of astonishment which Ulysses flashed upon him, he found it necessary to explain himself.

"What am I ever going to do ashore? . . . Who is expecting me there? . . . Or what business with my family would have any interest for me? . . ."

Ferragut seemed to be hearing an echo of his own thoughts. He, like the cook, would have nothing to do on land. . . . He was mortally bored when far from the sea, just as in those months when, still young, he had believed that he could create for himself a new profession in Barcelona. Besides, it was impossible to return to his home, taking up life again with his wife; it would be simply losing his last illusions. It would be better to view from afar all that remained of his former existence.

Caragol, meanwhile, was going on talking. His nephews would not remember the poor old cook and he had no reason to trouble himself about their fate, making them rich. He would prefer to remain just where he was, without money but happy.

"Let the others go!" he said with childish selfishness. "Let Toni go! . . . I'm going to stay. . . . I've got to stay. When the captain goes, then Uncle Caragol will go."

Ulysses enumerated the great dangers that the boat

was about to face. The German submarines were lying in wait for it with deadly determination; there would be combats . . . they would be torpedoed. . . .

The old man's smile showed contempt of all such dangers. He was certain that nothing bad could possibly happen to the *Mare Nostrum*. The furies of the sea were unavailing against it and still less could the wickedness of man injure it.

"I know what I'm talking about, Captain. . . . I am sure that we shall come out safe and sound from all dangers."

He thought of his miracle-working amulets, of his sacred pictures, of the supernatural protection that his pious prayers were bringing him. Furthermore, he was taking into consideration the Latin name of the ship which had always inspired him with religious respect. It belonged to the language used by the Church, to the idiom which brought about miracles and expelled the devil, making him run away aghast.

"The *Mare Nostrum* will not suffer any misfortune. If it should change its title . . . perhaps. But while it is called *Mare Nostrum*,—how *could* anything happen to it? . . ."

Smiling before this faith, Ferragut brought forth his last argument. The entire crew was going to be made up of Frenchmen; how could they ever understand each other if he were ignorant of their language? . . .

"I know it all," affirmed the old man superbly.

He had made himself understood with men in all the different ports of the world. He was counting on something more than mere language,—on his eyes, his hands, the expressive cunning of an exuberant and gesticulating meridional.

"I am just like *San Vicente Ferrer*," he added with pride.

His saint had spoken only the Valencian dialect, and yet had traveled throughout half Europe preaching to throngs of different tongues, making them weep with mystic emotion and repent of their sins.

While Ferragut retained the command, he was going to stay. If he didn't want him for a cook, he would be the cabin boy, washing up the pots and pans. The important thing for him was to continue treading the deck of the vessel.

The captain had to give in. This old fellow represented a remnant of his past. He could betake himself from time to time to the galley to talk over the far-away days in which they first met.

And Caragol retired, content with his success.

"As for those Frenchmen," he said before departing, "just leave them to me. They must be good people. . . . We'll just see what they say about my rice dishes."

In the course of the week the *Mare Nostrum* was de-organized and re-manned. Its former crew went marching away in groups. Toni was the last to leave, and Ulysses did not wish to see him, fearing to show his emotion. They'd surely write to each other.

A sympathetic curiosity impelled the cook toward the new marine force. He saluted the officers affably, regretting not to know their language sufficiently to begin a friendly conversation with them. The captain had accustomed him to such familiarity.

There were two mates that the mobilization had converted into auxiliary lieutenants of the navy. The first day they presented themselves on board arrayed in their uniform; then they returned in civilian clothes in order to habituate themselves to being simple merchant officers on a neutral steamer. The two knew, by hearsay, of Ferragut's former voyages and his services to the Allies, and they understood each other sympathetically without

the slightest national prejudice. Caragol achieved equal
success with the forty-five men who had taken possession
of the machinery and the messrooms in the forecastle.
They were dressed like seamen of the fleet, with a broad
blue collar and a cap topped by a red pompom. Some
displayed on the breast military medals and the recent
Croix de Guerre. From their canvas bags which served
them for valises, they unpacked their regulation suits,
worn when they were working on the freight steamers,
on the schooners plying to Newfoundland, or on the
simple coasting smacks.

The galley at certain hours was full of men listening
to the old cook. Some knew the Spanish tongue on
account of having sailed in brigs from Saint-Malo and
Saint-Nazaire, going to the ports of the Argentine, Chili
and Peru. Those who could not understand the old fellow's words, could guess at them from his gesticulations.
They were all laughing, finding him bizarre and interesting. And this general gayety induced Caragol to bring
forth liquid treasures that had been piling up in former
voyages under Ferragut's careless and generous admin-
istration.

The strong alcoholic wine of the coast of the Levant
began falling into the glasses like ink crowned with a circle of rubies. The old man poured it forth with a
prodigal hand. "Drink away, boys; in your land you
don't have anything like this. . . ." At other times he
would concoct his famous "refrescoes," smiling with the
satisfaction of an artist at seeing the sensuous grin that
began flashing across their countenances.

"When did you ever drink anything like that? What
would ever become of you all without your Uncle Caragol? . . ."

These Bretons, accustomed to the discipline and sobriety of other vessels, admired greatly the extraordi-

nary privileges of a cook who could display as much generosity as the captain himself. He frequently communicated to Ferragut his opinion regarding his new comrades. With good reason he had said that they would understand each other! . . . They were serious and religious men, and he preferred them to the former Mediterranean crews, blasphemers and incapable of resignation, who at the slightest vexation would rip out God's name, trying to affront him with their curses.

They were all muscular and well set-up with blue eyes and blonde mustaches, and were wearing hidden medallions. One of them had presented to the cook one of his religious charms which he had bought on a pilgrimage to *Ste. Anne d'Auray.* Caragol was wearing it upon his hairy chest, and experiencing a new-born faith in the miracles of this foreign image.

"To her sanctuary, Captain, the pilgrims go in thousands. Every day she performs a miracle. . . . There's a holy staircase there which the devout climb on their knees and many of these lads have mounted it. I should like . . ."

On some of their voyages to Brest he was hoping that Ferragut would permit him to go to Auray long enough to climb that same stairway on his knees, to see *Ste. Anne* and return aboard ship.

The vessel was no longer in a commercial harbor. It had gone to a military harbor,—a narrow river winding through the interior of the city, dividing it in two. A great drawbridge put in communication the two shores bordered with vast constructions and high chimneys, naval shops, warehouses, arsenals, and dry-docks for cleaning up the boats. Tug-boats were continually stirring up its green and miry waters. Steamers undergoing repairs were lined up the length of the breakwaters undergoing a continual pounding that made their plates resound. Lighters topped with hills of pit coal were going slowly to take their position along the flanks of the ships. Under the drawbridge launches were coming and going from the warships, leaving on the floating piers the crews celebrating their shore-leave with scandalous uproar.

The *Mare Nostrum* remained isolated while the workmen from the arsenal were installing on the poop rapid-fire guns and the wireless telegraph apparatus. No one could come aboard that did not belong to the crew.

The sailors' families were waiting for them on the wharf, and Caragol had occasion to become acquainted with many Breton women,—mothers, sisters, or fiancées of his new friends. He liked these women: they were dressed in black with full skirts, and white, stiff caps which brought to his mind the wimples of the nuns. . . . Some tall, stout girls with blue and candid eyes laughed at the Spaniard without understanding a single word. The old women with faces as dark and wrinkled as winter apples touched glasses with Caragol in the low cafés near the port. They all could do honor to a goblet in an opportune moment, and had great faith in the saints. The cook did not require anything more. . . . Most excellent and charming people!

Certain lads decorated with the *Croix de Guerre* used to relate their experiences to him. They were survivors of the battalion of marines who defended Dixmude. After the battle of the Marne they had been sent to intercept the enemy on the side of Flanders. There were not more than six thousand of them and, aided by a Belgian division, they had sustained the onrush of an entire army. Their resistance had lasted for weeks:—a combat of barricades in the street, of struggles the length of the canal with the bloodiness of the ancient piratical forays. The officers had shouted their orders with broken swords and bandaged heads. The men had fought on without thinking of their wounds, covered with blood, until they fell down dead.

Caragol, hitherto little interested in military affairs, became most enthusiastic when relating this heroic struggle to Ferragut, simply because his new friends had taken part in it.

"Many died, Captain. . . . Almost half of them. But the Germans couldn't make any headway. . . . Then, on learning that the marines had been no more than six thousand, the generals tore their hair. So great was their wrath! They had supposed that they were confronted by dozens of thousands. . . . It was just great to hear the lads relate what they did there."

Among these "lads" wounded in the war, who had passed to the naval reserve and were manning the *Mare Nostrum,* one was especially distinguished by the old man's partiality. He could talk to him in Spanish, because of his transatlantic voyages, and besides he had been born in Vannes.

If the youth ever approached the cook's dominions he was invariably met with a smile of invitation. "A refresco, Vicente?" The best seat was for him. Caragol had forgotten his name as not worth while. Since he came from Vannes, he could not have any other name but Vicente.

The first day that they chatted together, the marine, in love with his country, described to the cook the beauties of Morbihan,—a great interior sea surrounded with groves and with islands covered with pines. Among the venerable antiquities of the city was the Gothic cathedral with its many tombs, among them that of a Spanish saint, —St. Vicente Ferrer.

This gave a tug at Caragol's heart-strings. He had never before bothered to find out where the famous apostle of Valencia was entombed. . . . He recalled suddenly a strophe of the songs of praise that the devotees of his land used to sing before the altars of this saint. Sure enough he had gone to die in "Vannes, in Brittainy,"—a mere geographical name which until then had lacked any significance for him. . . . And so this lad was from Vannes? Nothing more was needed to make Caragol regard him with the respect due to one born in a miraculous country.

He made him describe many times the tomb of the saint, the only one in the transept of the cathedral, the moth-eaten tapestries that perpetuated his miracles, the silver bust which guarded his heart. . . . Furthermore, the principal portal of Vannes was called the gate of St. Vicente and recollections of the saint were still alive in their chronicles.

Caragol proposed to visit this city also when the ship should return to Brest. Brittainy must be very holy ground, the holiest in the world, since the miracle-working Valencian, after traversing so many nations, had wished to die there.

It, therefore, did not produce the slightest astonishment that this slip of a boy who had been picked up at Dixmude covered with wounds, was now showing himself sane and vigorous. . . . On board the *Mare Nostrum* he was the head gunner. He and two comrades had charge of the quickfirers. For Caragol there was not the slightest doubt as to the fate of every submarine that should venture to attack them; the "lad from Vannes" would send them to smithereens at the first shot. A picture post-card, a gift of the lad from Brittany, showing the tomb of the saint, occupied the position of honor in the galley. The old man used to pray before it as though it were a miracle-working print, and the *Cristo del Grao* was relegated to second place.

One morning Caragol went in search of the captain
and found him writing in his stateroom. He had just
come from making purchases in the shore market.
While passing through the *rue de Siam,* the most important road in Brest, where the theaters are, the moving-
picture shows, and the cafés, he had had an encounter.

"An unexpected meeting," he continued with a mysterious smile. "Who do you suppose it was with? . . ."

Ferragut shrugged his shoulders. And, noting his indifference, the old man could not keep the secret any
longer.

"The lady-bird!" he added. "That handsome, perfumed lady-bird that used to come to see you. . . . The
one from Naples. . . . The one from Barcelona. . . ."

The captain turned pale, first with surprise and then
with anger. Freya in Brest! . . . Her spy work was
reaching even here? . . .

Caragol went on with his story. He was returning to
the ship, and she, who was walking through the *rue de
Siam,* had recognized him, speaking to him affectionately.

"She asked to be remembered to you. . . . She has
been informed that no foreigner can come aboard. She
told me that she had tried to come to see you."

The cook began a search through his pockets, ex-
tricating a bit of wrinkled paper, a white sheet snatched
from an old letter.

"She also gave me this paper, written right there in the
street with a lead pencil. You will know what it says.
I did not wish to look at it."

Ferragut, on taking the paper, recognized immediately
her handwriting, although uneven, nervous and scrib-
bled with great precipitation. Six words, no more:—
"Farewell, I am going to die."

"Lies! Always lies!" said the voice of prudence in his brain.

He tore up the paper and passed the rest of the morning very much preoccupied. . . . It was his duty to defend himself against this espionage that had even established its base in a port of war. . . . Every boat anchored near the *Mare Nostrum* was menaced by Freya's power to give information. Who knew but what her mysterious communications would bring about their attack by a submarine on going out from the roadstead of Brest! . . .

His first impulse was to denounce her. Then he repented because of his absurd scruples of chivalry. . . . Besides, he would have to explain his past to the head officers at Brest who knew him very slightly. He was far from that naval captain at Salonica who had so well understood his passional errors.

He wished to watch her for himself, and in the evening he went ashore. He detested Brest as one of the dullest cities of the Atlantic. It was always raining there, and there was no diversion except the eternal promenade through the *rue de Siam,* or a bored stay in the cafés full of seamen and English and Portuguese land-officers.

He went through the public establishments night and day; he made investigations in the hotels; he hired carriages in order to visit the more picturesque suburbs. For four days he persisted in his inquiries without any result.

He began to doubt Uncle Caragol's veracity. Perhaps he had been drunk on returning to the ship, and had made up such an encounter. But the recollection of that paper written by her discounted such a supposition. . . . Freya was in Brest.

The cook explained it all simply enough when the captain besieged him with fresh questions.

"The lady-bird must just be passing through. Perhaps she flitted away that same evening. . . . That meeting was just a chance encounter."

Ferragut had to give up his investigations. The defensive work on the ship was about terminated and the holds contained their cargo of projectiles for the army of the Orient and various unmounted guns. He received his sailing orders, and one gray and rainy morning they lifted anchor and steamed out of the bay of Brest. The fog made even more difficult the passage between the reefs that obstruct this port. They passed before the lugubrious Bay of the Dead, ancient cemetery of sailboats, and continued their navigation toward the south in search of the strait in order to enter the Mediterranean.

Ferragut felt increased pride in examining the new aspect of the *Mare Nostrum*. The wireless telegraph was going to keep him in contact with the world. He was no longer a merchant captain, slave of destiny, trusting to good luck, and incapable of repelling an attack. The radiographic stations were watching for him the entire length of the coast, advising him of changes in his course that he might avoid the ambushed enemy. The apparatus was constantly hissing and sustaining invisible dialogues. Besides, mounted on the stern was a cannon covered with a canvas hood, ready to begin work.

The dreams of his childhood when he used to devour stories of corsairs and novels of maritime adventures seemed about to be realized. He was now entitled to call himself "Captain of Sea and War" like the ancient navigators. If a submarine should pass before him, he would attack it from the prow; if it should try to pursue him, he would respond with the cannon.

His adventurous humor actually made him anxious for one of these encounters. A maritime combat had not yet occurred in his life, and he wished to see how these modest and silent men who had made war on land and contemplated death at close range, would demean themselves.

It was not long before his desire was realized. One morning on the high seas near Lisbon, when he had just fallen asleep after a night on the bridge, the shouts and runnings of the crew awakened him.

A submarine had broken the surface about fifteen hundred yards astern and was coming toward the *Mare Nostrum*, evidently fearing that the merchant-boat would try to escape; but in order to oblige it to stop, its gun fired two shells which fell into the water.

The steamer moderated its pace but only to place itself in a more favorable position and to maneuver with more sea room, with its arms at the stern. At the first shot the submarine began to recede, keeping a more prudent distance, surprised to receive an answer to its aggression.

The combat lasted half an hour. The shots repeated themselves on both sides with the speed of rapid fire artillery. Ferragut was near the gun, admiring the calm coolness with which its servants manipulated it. One always had a projectile in his arms ready to give it to his companion who rapidly introduced it into the smoking chamber. The gunner was concentrating all his life in his eyes, and bending over the cannon, moved it carefully, seeking the sensitive part of that gray and prolonged body that was rising to the surface of the water as though it were a whale.

Suddenly a cloud of kindling wood flew near the steamer's prow. An enemy's projectile had just hit the edge of the roofs that covered the galley and mess rooms.

Caragol, who was standing in the door of his dominions, raised his hands to his hat. When the yellowish and evil-smelling cloud dissolved, they saw him still standing there, scratching the top of his head, bare and red.

"It's nothing!" he cried. "Just a bit of wood that drew a little of my blood. Fire away! . . . Fire!"

He was yelling directions, inflamed by the shooting. The drug-like smell of the smokeless powder, the dull thud of the detonations appeared to intoxicate him. He was leaping and wringing his hands with the ardor of a war-dancer.

The gunners redoubled their activity; the shots became continuous.

"There it is!" yelled Caragol. "They have hit it. . . . They have hit it!"

Of all those aboard, he was the one who could least appreciate the effects of the shots for he could scarcely discern the silhouette of the submersible. But in spite of that he continued bellowing with all the force of his faith.

"Now you've hit it! . . . Hurrah! Hurrah!"

And the strange thing was that the enemy instantly disappeared from the blue surface. The gunners still sent some shots against their periscope. Then there was left in the place which they had occupied only a white and glistening expanse.

The steamer went toward this enormous spot of oil whose undulations were twinkling with sunflower-like reflections.

The marines uttered shouts of enthusiasm. They were sure of having sent the submersible to the bottom. The officers were less optimistic. They had never seen one raise itself up vertically, tilting its stern high in the air before sinking. Perhaps it simply had been damaged and obliged to hide.

The loss of the submarine was a sure thing in Caragol's estimation, and he considered it entirely unnecessary to ask the name of the one who had blown it to
smithereens.

"It must have been that lad from Vannes. . . . He's
the only one who could have done it."

For him the other gunners simply did not exist. And,
inflamed by his enthusiasm, he wriggled out of the hands
of the two seamen who had begun to bandage his head
with a deftness learned in land combats.

Ferragut was entirely satisfied with this encounter.
Although he could not be absolutely certain of the destruction of the enemy, the fact that his boat had saved
itself would spread abroad the fact that the *Mare Nostrum* was entirely capable of self-defense.

His joy took him to Caragol's domains.

"Well done, old man! We're going to write to the
Ministry of Marine to give you the *Croix de Guerre.*"

The cook, taking his words in all seriousness, declined
the honor. If such recompense were to be given to any
one, let it be handed to "that lad from Vannes." Then he
added as though reflecting the captain's thoughts:

"I like to sail in this fashion. . . . Our steamer has
gotten its teeth, and now it will not have to run like a
frightened rabbit. . . . They'll have to let it go on its
way in peace because now it can bite."

The rest of the journey toward Salonica was without
incident. Telegraphy kept it in contact with the instructions arriving from the shore. Gibraltar advised it to
sail close to the African coast; Malta and Bizerta pointed
out that it could continue forward since the passage
between Tunis and Sicily was clear of enemies. From
distant Egypt tranquillizing messages came to meet them
while they were sailing among the Grecian Islands with
the prow toward Salonica.

On their return, they were to take freight to the harbor of Marseilles.

Ferragut did not have to bother about the boat while it was at anchor. The French officials were the ones who made arrangements with the harbor authorities. He merely had to be the justification for the flag, a captain of a neutral country, whose presence certified to the nationality of the vessel. Only on the sea did he recover command, every one becoming obedient to those on the bridge.

He wandered through Marseilles as at other times, passing the first hours of the evening on the terraces of the *Cannebière*.

An old Marseillaise, captain of a merchant steamer, used to chat with him before returning to his office. One afternoon, while Ferragut was absent-mindedly glancing at a certain Paris daily that his friend was carrying, his attention was suddenly attracted by a name printed at the head of a short article. Surprise made him turn pale while at the same time something contracted within his breast. Again he spelled out the name, fearing that he had been under an hallucination. Doubt was impossible : it was very clear,—*Freya Talberg*. He took the paper from his comrade's hand, disguising his impatience by an assumption of curiosity.

"What is the war news to-day? . . ."

And while the old sailor was giving him the news, he read feverishly the few lines grouped beneath that name.

He was bewildered. The heading told little to one ignorant of the preceding facts to which the periodical alluded. These lines were simply voicing a protest against the government for not having made the famous Freya Talberg pay the penalty to which she had been sentenced. The paragraph terminated with mention of the beauty and elegance of the delinquent as though to these qualities might be attributed the delay in punishment.

Ferragut put forth all his efforts to give his voice a tone of indifference.

"Who is this individual?" he said, pointing to the heading of the article.

His companion had some difficulty in recalling her. So many things were happening because of the war. . . .

"She is a *boche,* a spy, sentenced to death. . . . It appears that she did a great deal of work here and in other ports, sending word to the German submarines about the departure of our transports. . . . They arrested her in Paris two months ago when she was returning from Brest."

His friend said this with a certain indifference. These spies were so numerous! . . . The newspapers were constantly publishing notices of their shooting:—two lines, no more, as though treating of an ordinary casualty.

"This Freya Talberg," he continued, "has had enough said about her personality. It seems that she is a *chic* woman,—a species of lady from a novel. Many are protesting because she has not yet been executed. It is sad to have to kill one of her sex,—to kill a woman and especially a beautiful woman! . . . But nevertheless it is very necessary. . . . I believe that she is to be shot at any moment."

CHAPTER XII

AMPHITRITE! . . . AMPHITRITE!

THE *Mare Nostrum* made another trip from Marseilles to Salonica.

Before sailing, Ferragut hunted vainly through the Paris periodicals for fresh news of Freya. For some days past, the attention of the public had been so distracted by various other events that for the time being the spy was forgotten.

On arriving at Salonica, he made discreet inquiries among his military and marine friends in the harbor cafés. Hardly any one had ever heard the name of Freya Talberg. Those who had read it in the newspapers merely replied with indifference.

"I know who she is: she is a spy who was an actress,— a woman with a certain *chic*. I think that they've shot her. . . . I don't know certainly, but they ought to have shot her."

They had more important things to think about. A spy! . . . On all sides they were discovering the intrigues of German espionage. They had to shoot a great many. . . . And immediately they forgot this affair in order to speak of the difficulties of the war that were threatening them and their comrades-at-arms.

When Ferragut returned to Marseilles two months afterwards, he was still ignorant as to whether his former mistress was yet among the living.

The first evening that he met his old comrade, the captain, in the café of the *Cannebière,* he skillfully guided

the conversation around until he could bring out naturally the question in the back of his mind: "What was the
fate of that Freya Talberg that there was so much talk
about in the newspapers before I went to Salonica? . . ."

The Marseillaise had to make an effort to recall her.

"Ah, yes! . . . The *boche* spy," he said after a long
pause. "They shot her some weeks ago. The papers
said little of her death,—just a few lines. Such people
don't deserve any more. . . ."

Ferragut's friend had two sons in the army; a nephew
had died in the trenches, another, a mate aboard a transport, had just perished in a torpedo attack. The old man
was passing many nights without sleeping thinking of his
sons battling at the front. And this uneasiness gave a
hard and ferocious tone to his patriotic enthusiasm.

"It's a good thing she is dead. . . . She was a woman,
and shooting a woman is a painful thing. It is always
repugnant to be obliged to treat them like men. . . . But
according to what they tell me, this individual with her
spy-information brought about the torpedoing of sixteen vessels. . . . Ah, the wicked beast! . . ."

And he said no more, changing the subject. Every one
evinced the same revulsion on recalling the spy.

Ferragut eventually shared the same sentiments, his
brain having divested itself of the contradictory duality
which had attended all the critical moments of his existence. Remembering only her crimes, he hated Freya. As
a man of the sea, he recalled his nameless fellow-sailors
killed by torpedoes. This woman had indirectly prepared
the ground for many assassinations. . . . And at the same
time he recalled another image of her as the mistress who
knew so well how to keep him spellbound by her artifices
in the old palace of Naples, making that voluptuous
prison her best souvenir.

"Let's think no more about her," he said to himself

energetically. "She has died. . . . She does not exist."

But not even after her death did she leave him in peace. Remembrance of her soon came surging back, binding her to him with a tragic interest.

The very evening that he was talking with his friend in the café of the *Cannebière,* he went to the post office to get the mail which had been forwarded to him at Marseilles. They gave him a great package of letters and newspapers. By the handwriting on the envelopes, and the postmarks on the postals, he tried to make out who was writing to him:—one letter only from his wife, evidently but a single sheet, judging from its slender flexibility, three very bulky ones from Toni,—a species of diary in which he continued relating his purchases, his crops, his hope of seeing the captain,—all this mixed in with abundant news about the war, and the wretched condition of the people. There were, besides, various sheets from the banking establishments at Barcelona, rendering Ferragut an account of the investment of his capital.

At the foot of the staircase he completed his examination of the outside of his correspondence. It was just what was always awaiting him on his return from his voyages.

He was about to put the package in his pocket and continue on his way when his attention was attracted by a voluminous envelope in an unknown handwriting, registered in Paris. . . .

Curiosity made him open it immediately and he found in his hand a regular sheaf of loose leaves, a long account that far exceeded the limits of a letter. He looked at the engraved letter-head and then at the signature. The writer was a lawyer in Paris, and Ferragut suspected by the luxurious paper and address that he must be a celebrated *maître.* He even recalled having run across his name somewhere in the newspapers.

Then and there he began reading the first page, anxious to know why this distinguished personage had written to him. But he had scarcely run his eyes over some of the sheets before he stopped his reading. He had come across the name of Freya Talberg. This lawyer had been her defender before the Council of War.

Ferragut hastened to put the letter in a safe place, and curb his impatience. He felt that necessity for silent isolation and absolute solitude which a reader, anxious to delve into a new book, experiences. This bundle of papers doubtless contained for him the most interesting of stories.

Returning to his ship, the road seemed to him far longer than at other times. He longed to lock himself in his stateroom, away from all curiosity as though he were about to perform some mysterious rite.

Freya was not in existence. She had disappeared from the world in the infamous manner in which criminals disappear,—doubly condemned since even her memory was hateful to the people; and Ferragut within a few moments was going to resurrect her like a ghost, in the floating house that she had visited on two occasions. He now might know the last hours of her existence wrapped in disreputable mystery; he could violate the will of her judges who had condemned her to lose her life and after death to perish from every one's memory. With eager avidity he seated himself before his cabin table, arranging the contents of the envelope in order;—more than twelve sheets, written on both sides, and several newspaper clippings. In these clippings he saw portraits of Freya, a hard and blurred likeness which he could recognize only by her name underneath. He also beheld the portrait of her defender,—an old lawyer of fastidious aspect with white locks carefully combed, and sharp eyes.

From the very first lines, Ferragut suspected that the *maître* could neither write nor speak except in the most approved literary form. His letter was a moderated and correct account in which all emotion, however keen it might have been, was discreetly controlled so as not to disorganize the sweep of a majestic style.

He began by explaining that his professional duty had made him decide to defend this spy. She was in need of a lawyer; she was a foreigner; public opinion, influenced by the exaggerated accounts given by the newspapers of her beauty and her jewels, was ferociously inimical, demanding her immediate punishment. Nobody had wished to take charge of her defense. And for this very reason he had accepted it without fear of unpopularity.

Ferragut believed that this sacrifice might be attributed to the impulse of a gallant old beau, attracted to Freya because of her beauty. Besides, this criminal process represented a typical Parisian incident and might give a certain romantic notoriety to the one intervening in its developments.

A few paragraphs further on the sailor became convinced that the *maître* had fallen in love with his client. This woman even in her dying moments shed around her most amazing powers of seduction. The professional success anticipated by the lawyer disappeared on his first questioning. Defense of Freya would be impossible. When he questioned her regarding the events of her former life, she either wept for every answer, or else remained silent, immovable, with as unconcerned a glance as though the fate of some other woman were at stake.

The military judges did not need her confessions: they

knew, detail for detail, all her existence during the war
and in the last years of peace. Never had the police
agents abroad worked with such rapidity and success.
Mysterious and omnipotent good fortune had crowned
every investigation. They knew all of Freya's doings.
They had even received from a secret agent exact data
regarding her personality, the number by which she was
represented in the director's office at Berlin, the salary
that she was paid, as well as her reports during the past
month. Documents written by her personally, of an
irrefutable culpability, had poured in without any one's
knowing from what point they were sent or by whom.

Every time that the judge had placed before Freya's
eyes one of these proofs, she looked at her lawyer in
desperation.

"It is *they!*" she moaned. "They who desire my
death!"

Her defender was of the same opinion. The police
had learned of her presence in France by a letter that her
superiors in Barcelona had sent, stupidly disguised,
written with regard to a code whose mystery had been
discovered some time before by the French counter-spies.
To the *maître* it was only too evident that some mysterious power had wished to rid itself of this woman,
dispatching her to an enemy's country, intending to
send her to death.

Ulysses suspected in the defender a state of mind
similar to his own,—the same duality that had tormented
him in all his relations with Freya.

"I, sir," wrote the lawyer, "have suffered much. One
of my sons, an officer, died in the battle of the Aisne.
Others very close to me, nephews and pupils, died in
Verdun and with the expeditionary army of the
Orient. . . ."

As a Frenchman, he had felt an irresistible aversion

upon becoming convinced that Freya was a spy who had
done great harm to his country. . . . Then as a man, he
had commiserated her inconsequence, her contradictory
and frivolous character, amounting almost to a crime,
and her egoism as a beautiful woman and lover of
luxury that had made her willing to suffer moral vileness
in exchange for creature comfort.

Her story had attracted the lawyer with the palpitating
interest of a novel of adventure. Commiseration had finally developed the vehemence of a love affair. Besides,
the knowledge that the exploiters of this woman were the
ones that had denounced her, had aroused his knightly
enthusiasm in the defense of her indefensible cause.

Appearance before the Council of War had proved
painful and dramatic. Freya, who until then, had
seemed brutalized by the régime of the prison, roused
herself upon being confronted by a dozen grave and
uniformed men.

Her first moves were those of every handsome and
coquettish female. She knew perfectly well her physical
influence. These soldiers transformed into judges were
recalling those other flirts that she had seen at the teas
and grand balls at the hotels. . . . What Frenchman
can resist feminine attraction? . . .

She had smiled, she had replied to the first questions
with graceful modesty, fixing her wickedly guileless eyes
upon the officials seated behind the presidential table,
and on those other men in blue uniform, charged with
accusing her or reading the documents of her pros-
ecution.

But something cold and hostile existed in the atmosphere and paralyzed her smiles, leaving her words
without echo and making ineffectual the splendors of her
eyes. All foreheads were bowed under the weight of
severe thought: all the men in that instant appeared

thirty years older. They simply would not see such a
one as she was, however much effort she might make.
They had left their admiration and their desires on the
other side of the door.

Freya perceived that she had ceased to be a woman
and was no more than one accused. Another of her sex,
an irresistible rival, was now engrossing everything,
binding these men with a profound and austere love.
Instinct made her regard fixedly the white matron of
grave countenance whose vigorous bust appeared over
the head of the president. She was Patriotism, Justice,
the Republic, contemplating with her vague and hollow
eyes this female of flesh and blood who was beginning
to tremble upon realizing her situation.

"I do not want to die!" cried Freya, suddenly
abandoning her seductions and becoming a poor,
wretched creature crazed by fear. "I am innocent."

She lied with the absurd and barefaced illogicalness
of one finding herself in danger of death. It was necessary to re-read her first declarations, which she was now
denying, of presenting afresh the material proofs whose
existence she did not wish to admit, of making her entire
past file by supported by that irrefutable data of
anonymous origin.

"It is *they* who have done it all! . . . They have mis-
represented me! . . . Since they have brought about my
ruin, I am going to tell what I know."

In his account the lawyer passed lightly over what had
occurred in the Council of War. Professional secrecy
and patriotic interest prevented greater explicitness.
The session had lasted from morning till night, Freya
revealing to her judges all that she knew. . . . Then her
defender had spoken for five hours, trying to establish
a species of interchange in the application of the penalty.
The guilt of this woman was undeniable and the wicked-

ness that she had carried through was very great, but they should spare her life in exchange for her important confessions. . . . Besides, the inconsequence of her character should be taken into consideration . . . also, that vengeance of which the enemy had made her the victim. . . .

With Freya he had waited, until well on into the night, the decision of the tribunal. The defendant appeared animated by hope. She had become a woman again: she was talking placidly with him and smiling at the gendarmes and eulogizing the army. . . . "Frenchmen, gentlemen, were incapable of killing a woman. . . ."

The *maître* was not surprised at the sad and furrowed brows of the officers as they came out from their deliberations. They appeared discontented with their recent vote, and yet at the same time showed the serenity of a tranquil countenance. They were soldiers who had just fulfilled their full duty, suppressing every purely masculine instinct. The one deputed to read the sentence swelled his voice with a fictitious energy. . . . *"Death!* . . ." After a long enumeration of crimes Freya was condemned to be shot:—she had given information to the enemy that represented the loss of thousands of men and boats, torpedoed because of her reports, on which had perished defenseless families.

The spy nodded her head upon listening to her own acts, for the first time appreciating their enormity and recognizing the justice of their tremendous punishment. But at the same time she was relying upon a good-natured reprieve in exchange for all which she had revealed, upon a gallant clemency . . . because she was she.

As the fatal word sounded, she uttered a cry, became ashy pale, and leaned upon the lawyer for support.

"I do not want to die! . . . I ought not to die! . . .
I am innocent."

She continued shrieking her innocence, without giving
any other proof of it than the desperate instinct of self-
preservation. With the credulity of one who wishes to
save herself, she accepted all the problematical consolations of her defender. There remained the last recourse of appealing to the mercy of the President of the
Republic: perhaps he might pardon her. . . . And she
signed this appeal with sudden hope.

The lawyer managed to delay the fulfillment of the
sentence for two months, visiting many of his colleagues
who were political personages. The desire of saving the
life of his client was tormenting him as an obsession. He
had devoted all his activity and his personal influence to
this affair.

"In love! . . . In love, as you were!" said, with
scornful accent, the voice of Ferragut's prudent counselor.

The periodicals were protesting against this delay in
the execution of the sentence. The name of Freya
Talberg was beginning to be heard in conversation as an
argument against the weakness of the government. The
women were the most implacable.

One day, in the Palace of Justice, the *maître* became
convinced of this general animosity that was pushing the
defendant toward the day of execution. The woman
who had charge of the gowns, a verbose old wife, on a
familiar footing with the illustrious lawyers, had rudely
made known their opinions.

"I wonder when they're going to execute that spy! . . .
If she were a poor woman with children and needed to
earn their bread, they would have shot her long ago. . . .
But she is an elegant *cocotte* and with jewels. Perhaps
she has bewitched some of the cabinet ministers. We

are going to see her on the street now almost any day. . . . And my son who died at Verdun! . . ."

The prisoner, as though divining this public indignation, began to consider her death very near losing, little by little, that love of existence which had made her burst forth into lies and delirious protests. In vain the *maître* held out hopes of pardon.

"It is useless: I must die. . . . I ought to be shot. . . . I have done so much mischief. . . . It horrifies even me to remember all the crimes named in that sentence. . . . And there are still others that they don't know! . . . Solitude has made me see myself just as I am. What shame! . . . I ought to perish; I have ruined everything. . . . What is there left for me to do in the world? . . ."

"And it was then, my dear sir," continued the attorney, in his letter, "that she spoke to me of you, of the way in which you had known each other, of the harm which she had done you unconsciously."

Convinced of the uselessness of his efforts to save her life, the *maître* had solicited one last favor of the tribunal. Freya was very desirous that he should accompany her at the moment of her execution, as this would maintain her serenity. Those in the government had promised their colleague in the forum, to send opportune notice that he might be present at the fulfillment of the sentence.

It was at three o'clock in the morning and while he was in the deepest sleep that some messengers, sent by the prefecture of police, awakened him. The execution was to take place at daybreak: this was a decision reached at the last moment in order that the reporters might learn too late of the event.

An automobile took him with the messengers to the prison of St. Lazare, across silent and shadowy Paris.

Only a few hooded street lamps were cutting with their sickly light the darkness of the streets. In the prison they were joined by other functionaries and many chiefs and officers who represented military justice. The condemned woman was still sleeping in her cell, ignorant of what was about to occur.

Those charged with awakening her, gloomy and timid, were marching in line through the corridors of the jail, bumping into one another in their nervous precipitation.

The door was opened. Under the regulation light Freya was on her bed, with closed eyes. Upon opening them and finding herself surrounded by men, her face was convulsed with terror.

"Courage, Freya!" said the prison warden. "The appeal for pardon has been denied."

"Courage, my daughter," added the priest of the establishment, starting the beginning of a discourse.

Her terror, due to the rude surprise of awakening with the brain still paralyzed, lasted but a few seconds. Upon collecting her thoughts, serenity returned to her face.

"I must die?" she asked. "The hour has already come? . . . Very well, then: let them shoot me. Here I am."

Some of the men turned their heads, and so averted their glance. . . . She had to get out of the bed in the presence of the two watchmen. This precaution was so that she might not attempt to take her life. She even asked the lawyer to remain in the cell as though in this way she wished to lessen the annoyance of dressing herself before strangers.

Upon reaching this passage in his letter, Ferragut realized the pity and admiration of the *maître* who had seen her preparing the last toilet of her life.

"Adorable creature! So beautiful! . . . She was born

for love and luxury, yet was going to die, torn by bullets like a rude soldier. . . ."

The precautions adopted by her coquetry appeared to him admirable. She wanted to die as she had lived, placing on her person the best that she possessed. Therefore, suspecting the nearness of her execution, she had a few days before reclaimed the jewels and the gown that she was wearing when arrest prevented her returning to Brest.

Her defender described her "with a dress of pearl gray silk, bronze stockings and low shoes, a great-coat of furs, and a large hat with plumes. Besides, the necklace of pearls was on her bosom, emeralds in her ears and all her diamonds on her fingers."

A sad smile curled her lips upon trying to look at herself in the window panes, still black with the darkness of night, which served her as a mirror.

"I die in my uniform like a soldier," she said to her lawyer.

Then in the ante-chamber of the prison, under the crude artificial light, this plumed woman, covered with jewels, her clothing exhaling a subtle perfume, memory of happier days, turned without any embarrassment toward the men clad in black and in blue uniforms.

Two religious sisters who accompanied her appeared more moved than she. They were trying to exhort her and at the same time were struggling to keep back the tears. . . . The priest was no less touched. He had attended other criminals, but they were men. . . . To assist to a decent death a beautiful perfumed woman scintillating with precious stones, as though she were going to ride in an automobile to a fashionable tea! . . .

The week before she had been in doubt as to whether to receive a Calvinist pastor or a Catholic priest. In her cosmopolitan life of uncertain nationality she had never taken the time to decide about any religion for herself. Finally she had selected the latter on account of its being more simple intellectually, more liberal and approachable. . . .

Several times when the priest was trying to console her, she interrupted him as though she were the one charged with inspiring courage.

"To die is not so terrible as it appears when seen afar off! . . . I feel ashamed when I think of the fears that I have passed through, of the tears that I have shed. . . . It turns out to be much more simple than I had believed. . . . We all have to die!"

They read to her the sentence refusing the appeal for pardon. Then they offered her a pen that she might sign it.

A colonel told her that there were still a few moments at her disposition in which to write to her family, her friends, or to make her last will. . . .

"To whom shall I write?" said Freya. "I haven't a single friend in the world. . . ."

"Then it was," continued the lawyer, "that she took the pen as if a recollection had occurred to her, and traced some few lines. . . . Then she tore up the paper and came toward me. She was thinking of you, Captain: her last letter was for you and she left it unfinished, fearing that it might never reach your hands. Besides, she wasn't equal to writing; her pulse was nervous: she preferred to talk. . . . She asked me to send you a long, very long letter, telling about her last moments, and I had to swear to her that I would carry out her request."

From that time on the *maître* had seen things badly. Emotion was perturbing his sensibilities, but there yet lived in his mind Freya's last words on coming out of the jail.

"I am not a German," she said repeatedly to the men in uniform. "I am not German!"

For her the least important thing was to die. She was only worried for fear they might believe her of that odious nationality.

The attorney found himself in an automobile with many men whom he scarcely knew. Other vehicles were before and behind theirs. In one of them was Freya with the nuns and the priest.

A faint streak was whitening the sky, marking the points of the roofs. Below, in the deep blackness of the streets, the renewed life of daybreak was slowly beginning. The first laborers going to their work with their hands in their pockets, and the market women returning from market pushing their carts, turned their heads, following with interest this procession of swift vehicles almost all of them with men in the box seat beside the conductor. To the working-folk, this was perhaps a morning wedding. . . . Perhaps these were gay people coming from a nocturnal fiesta. . . . Several times the cortege slackened its speed, blocked by a row of heavy carts with mountains of garden-stuff.

The *maître,* in spite of his emotions, recognized the road that the automobile was following. In the *place de la Nation* he caught glimpses of the sculptured group, *le Triomphe de la Republique,* piercing the dripping mistiness of dawn; then the grating of the enclosure; then the long *cours de Vincennes* and its historic fortress.

They went still further on until they reached the field of execution.

Upon getting down from the automobile, he saw an extensive plain covered with grass on which were drawn up two companies of soldiers. Other vehicles had arrived before them. Freya detached herself from the group of persons descending from the automobile, leaving behind the nuns and the officers who were escorting her.

The light of daybreak, blue and cold as the reflection of steel, threw into relief the two masses of armed men who formed a narrow passageway. At the end of this impromptu lane there was a post planted in the ground and beyond that, a dark van drawn by two horses, and various men clad in black.

The woman's approach was signalized by a voice of command, and immediately sounded the drums and trumpets at the head of the two formations. There was a rattle of guns; the soldiers were presenting arms. The martial instruments delivered the triumphal salute due to the presence of the head of a state, a general, a flag-raising. . . . It was an homage to Justice, majestic and severe,—a hymn to Patriotism, implacable in defense.

Recalling the white woman with deep bosom and hollow eyes that she had seen over the head of the President of the Council, the spy for a moment recognized that all this was in her honor; but afterwards, she wished to believe that the triumphal reception was for herself. . . . She was marching between guns, accompanied by bugle-call and drum-beat, like a queen.

To her defender, she appeared taller than ever. She seemed to have grown a palm higher because of her intense, emotional uplift. Her theatrical soul was moved just as when she used to present herself on the boards to receive applause. All these men had arisen in the middle of the night and were there on her account: the horns and the drums were sounding in order to greet her. Discipline was keeping their countenances grave and cold but she had the certain consciousness that they were finding her beautiful, and that back of many immovable eyes, desire was asserting itself.

If there remained a shred of fear of losing her life, it

disappeared under the caress of this false glory. . . .
To die contemplated by so many valiant men who were
rendering her the greatest of honors! She felt the
necessity of being adorable, of falling into an artistic
pose as though she were on a stage.

She was passing between the two masses of men, head
erect, stepping firmly with the high-spirited tread of a
goddess-huntress, sometimes casting a glance on some
of the hundreds of eyes fixed upon her. The illusion of
her triumph made her advance as upright and serene as
though passing the troops in review.

"Good heavens! . . . What poise!" exclaimed a
young officer behind the lawyer, admiring Freya's
serenity.

Upon approaching the post, some one read a brief
document, a summary of the sentence,—three lines to
apprise her that justice was about to be fulfilled.

The only thing about this rapid notification that
annoyed her was the fear that the trumpets and drums
would cease. But they continued sounding and their
martial music was as conforting to her ears as a very
intoxicating wine slipping through her lips.

A platoon of corporals and soldiers (twelve rifles)
detached themselves from the double military mass. A
sub-officer with a blond beard, small, delicate, was commanding it with an unsheathed sword. Freya contemplated him a moment, finding him interesting, while the
young man avoided her glance.

With the gesture of a tragedy queen, she repelled the
white handkerchief that they were offering her to bandage
her eyes. She did not need it. The nuns took leave of
her forever. As soon as she was alone, two gendarmes
commenced to tie her with the back supported against
the post.

"They say," her defender continued writing, "that one

of her hands waved to me for the last time just before it was fastened down by the rope. . . . I saw nothing. I could not see! . . . It was too much for me! . . ."

The rest of the execution he knew only by hearsay. The trumpets and drums continued sounding. Freya, bound and intensely pale, smiled as though she were drunk. The early morning breeze waved the plumes of her hat.

When the twelve fusileers advanced placing themselves in a horizontal line eight yards distant, all of them aiming toward her heart, she appeared to wake up. She shrieked, her eyes abnormally dilated by the horror of the reality that so soon was to take place. Her cheeks were covered with tears. She tugged at the ligatures with the vigor of an epileptic.

"Pardon! . . . Pardon! I do not want to die!"

The sub-lieutenant raised his sword, and lowered it again rapidly. . . . A shot.

Freya collapsed, her body slipping the entire length of the post until it fell forward on the ground. The bullets had cut the cords that bound her.

As though it had acquired sudden life, her hat leaped from her head, flying off to fall about four yards further on. A corporal with a revolver in his right hand came forward from the shooting picket:—"the death-blow." He checked his step before the puddle of blood that was forming around the victim, pressing his lips together and averting his eyes. He then bent over her, raising with the end of the barrel the ringlets which had fallen over one of her ears. She was still breathing. . . . A shot in the temple. Her body contracted with a final shudder, then remained immovable with the rigidity of a corpse.

Voices were heard. The firing-squad re-formed in line, and to the rhythm of their instruments went filing past the body of the dead. From the funeral wagon two black-robed men drew out a bier of white wood.

Turning their backs upon their work, the double military mass marched toward the encampment. The ends of Justice had been served. Trumpets and drums were lost on the horizon but their sounds were still magnified by the fresh echoes of the coming morn. The corpse was despoiled of its jewels and then deposited in that poor coffin which looked so like a packing-box. The two nuns took with timidity the gems which the dead woman had given them for their works of charity. Then the lid was fastened down, shutting away forever the one who a few moments before was a woman of sumptuous charm upon whom men could not look unmoved. The four planks now guarded merely bloody rags, mutilated flesh, broken bones.

The vehicle went to the cemetery of Vincennes, to the corner in which the executed were buried. . . . Not a flower, not an inscription, not a cross. The lawyer himself could not be sure of finding her burial place if at any time it was necessary to seek it. . . . Such was the last scene in the career of this luxurious and pleasure-loving creature! . . . Thus had that body gone to dissolution in an unknown hole in the ground like any abandoned beast of burden! . . .

"She was good," said her defender, "and yet at the same time, she was a criminal. Her education was to blame. Poor woman! . . . They had brought her up to live in riches, and riches had always fled before her."

Then in his last lines the old *maître* said with melancholy, "She died thinking of you and a little of me. . . . We have been the last men of her existence."

This reading left Ulysses in a mournful state of stupefaction. Freya was no longer living! . . . He was no longer running the danger of seeing her appear on his ship at whatever port he might touch! . . .

The duality of his sentiments again surged up with violent contradiction.

"It was a good thing!" said the sailor, "how many men have died through her fault! . . . Her execution was inevitable. The sea must be cleared of such bandits."

And at the same time the remembrance of the delights of Naples, of that long imprisonment in a harem pervaded with unlimited sensuousness was reborn in his mind. He saw her in all the majesty of her marvelous body, just as when she was dancing or leaping from side to side of the old salon. And now this form, molded by nature in a moment of enthusiasm, was no longer in existence. . . . It was nothing but a mass of liquid flesh and pestilent pulp! . . .

He recalled her kiss, that kiss that had so electrified him, making him sink down and down through an ocean of ecstasy, like a castaway, content with his fate. . . . And he would never know her more! . . . And her mouth, with its perfume of cinnamon and incense, of Asiatic forests haunted with sensuousness and intrigue, was now . . . ! Ah, misery!

Suddenly he saw the profile of the dead woman with one eye turned toward him, graciously and malignly, just as the "eye of the morning" must have looked at its mistress while uncoiling her mysterious dances in her Asiatic dwelling.

Ulysses concentrated his attention on the Phantasm's pallid brow touched by the silky caress of her curls. There he had placed his best kisses, kisses of tenderness and gratitude. . . . But the smooth skin that had appeared made of petals of the camellia was growing dark before his eyes. It became a dark green and was oozing with blood. . . . Thus he had seen her that other

time. . . . And he recalled with remorse his blow in
Barcelona. . . . Then it opened, forming a deep hole,
angular in shape like a star. Now it was the mark of the
gunshot wound, the *coup de grâce* that brought the death-
agony of the executed girl to its end.

Poor Freya, implacable warrior, unnerved by the
battle of the sexes! . . . She had passed her existence
hating men yet needing them in order to live,—doing
them all the harm possible and receiving it from them in
sad reciprocity until finally she had perished at their
hands.

It could not end in any other way. A masculine hand
had opened the orifice through which was escaping the
last bubble of her existence. . . . And the horrified
captain, poring over her sad profile with its purpling
temple, thought that he never would be able to blot that
ghastly vision from his memory. The phantasm would
diminish, becoming invisible in order to deceive him, but
would surely come forth again in all his hours of pensive
solitude; it was going to embitter his nights on watch, to
follow him through the years like remorse.

Fortunately the exactions of real life kept repelling
these sad memories.

"It was a good thing she was shot!" affirmed authoritatively within him the energetic official accustomed to
command men. "What would you have done in forming
a part of the tribunal that condemned her? . . . Just
what the others did. Think of those who have died
through her deviltry! . . . Remember what Toni said!"

A letter from his former mate, received in the same
mail with the one from Freya's defender, spoke of the
abominations that submarine aggression was committing
in the Mediterranean.

News of some of the crimes was beginning to be
received from shipwrecked sailors who had succeeded in

reaching the coast after long hours of struggle, or when picked up by other boats. The most of the victims, however, would remain forever unknown in the mystery of the waves. Torpedoed boats had gone to the bottom with their crews and passengers, "without leaving any trace," and only months afterwards a part of the tragedy had become evident when the surge flung up on the coast numberless bodies impossible of identification, without even a recognizable human face.

Almost every week Toni contemplated some of these funereal gifts of the sea. At daybreak the fishermen used to find corpses tossed on the beach where the water swept the sand, resting there a few moments on the moist ground, only to be snatched back again by another and stronger wave. Finally their backs had become imbedded on land, holding them motionless—while, from their clothing and their flesh, swarms of little fishes came forth fleeing back to the sea in search of new pastures. The revenue guards had discovered among the rocks mutilated bodies in tragic positions, with glassy eyes protruding from their sockets.

Many of them were recognized as soldiers by the tatters that revealed an old uniform, or the metal identification tags on their wrists. The shore folks were always talking of a transport that had been torpedoed coming from Algiers. . . . And mixed with the men, they were constantly finding bodies of women so disfigured that it was almost impossible to judge of their age : mothers who had their arms arched as though putting forth their utmost efforts to guard the babe that had disappeared. Many whose virginal modesty had been violated by the sea, showed naked limbs swollen and greenish, with deep bites from flesh-eating fishes. The tide had even tossed ashore the headless body of a child a few years old.

It was more horrible, according to Toni, to contemplate this spectacle from land than when in a boat. Those on ships are not able to see the ultimate consequences of the torpedoings as vividly as do those who live on the shore, receiving as a gift of the waves this continual consignment of victims.

The pilot had ended his letter with his usual supplications:—"Why do you persist in following the sea? . . . You want a vengeance that is impossible. You are one man, and your enemies are millions. . . . You are going to die if you persist in disregarding them. You already know that they have been hunting you for a long time. And you will not always succeed in eluding their clutches. Remember what the people say, 'He who courts danger——!' Give up the sea; return to your wife or come to us. Such a rich life as you might lead ashore! . . ."

For a few hours Ferragut was of Toni's opinion. His reckless undertaking was bound to come to a bad end. His enemies knew him, were lying in wait for him, and were many arrayed against one who was living alone on his ship with a crew of men of a different nationality. Aside from the few who had always loved him, nobody would lament his death. He did not belong to any of the nations at war; he was a species of privateer bound not to begin an attack. He was even less,—an officer carrying supplies under the protection of a neutral flag. This flag was not deceiving anybody. His enemies knew the ship, seeking for it with more determination than if he were with the Allied fleets. Even in his own country, there were many people in sympathy with the German Empire who would celebrate joyously the disappearance of the *Mare Nostrum* and its captain.

Freya's death had depressed his spirits more than he had imagined possible. He had gloomy presentiments; perhaps his next journey might be his last.

"You are going to die!" cried an anguished voice in his brain. "You'll die very soon if you do not retire from the sea."

And to Ferragut the queerest thing about the warning was that this counselor had the voice of the one who had always egged him on to foolish adventures,—the one that had hurled him into danger for the mere pleasure of discounting it, the one that had made him follow Freya even after knowing her vile profession.

On the other hand the voice of prudence, always cautious and temperate, was now showing an heroic tranquillity, speaking like a man of peace who considers his obligations superior to his life.

"Be calm, Ferragut; you have sold your person with your boat, and they have given you millions for it. You must carry through what you have promised even though it may send you out of existence. . . . The *Mare Nostrum* cannot sail without a Spanish captain. If you abandon it, you will have to find another captain. You will run away through fear and put in your place a man who has to face death in order to maintain his family. Glorious achievement, that! . . . while you would be on land, rich and safe! . . . And what are you going to do on land, you coward?"

His egoism hardly knew how to reply to such a question. He recalled with antipathy his bourgeois existence over there in Barcelona, before buying the steamer. He was a man of action and could live only when occupied in risky enterprises.

He would be bored to death on land and at the same time would be considered belittled, degraded, like one who comes down to an inferior grade in a country of hierarchies. The captain of a romantic, adventurous life would be converted into a real estate proprietor, knowing no other struggles than those which he might sustain with his tenants. Perhaps, in order to avoid a commonplace existence, he might invest his capital in navigation, the only business that he knew well. He might become a ship-owner acquiring new vessels and, little by little, because of the necessity of keeping a sharp watch over them, would eventually renew his voyages. . . . Well, then, why should he abandon the *Mare Nostrum?*

Upon asking himself anxiously what his life had so far amounted to, he underwent a profound moral revolution.

All his former existence appeared to him like a desert. He had lived without knowing why nor wherefore, challenging countless dangers and adventures for the mere pleasure of coming out victorious. Neither did he know with certainty what he had wanted until then. If it was money, it had flowed into his hands in the last months with overwhelming abundance. . . . He had it to spare and it had not made him happy. As to professional glory, he could not desire anything greater than he already had. His name was celebrated all over the Spanish Mediterranean. Even the rudest and most ungovernable of sailors would admit his exceptional ability.

"Love remained! . . ." But Ferragut made a wry face when thinking of that. He had known it and did not wish to meet it again. The gentle love of a good companion, capable of surrounding the latter part of his existence with congenial comfort, he had just lost forever. The other, impassioned, fantastic, voluptuous, giving to life the crude interest of conflicts and contrasts, had left him with no desire of recommencing it.

Paternity, stronger and more enduring than love, might have filled the rest of his days had his son not died. . . . There only remained vengeance, the savage task of returning evil to those who had done him so much evil. But he was so powerless to struggle against all of them! . . . This final act appeared to be turning out so small and selfish in comparison with that other patriotic enthusiasm which was now dragging to sacrifice such great masses of men! . . .

While he was thinking it all over, a phrase which he had somewhere heard—formed perhaps from the residuum of old readings—began to chant in his brain: "A life without ideals is not worth the trouble of living."

Ferragut mutely assented. It was true: in order to live, an ideal is necessary. But where could he find it? . . .

Suddenly, in his mind's eye, he saw Toni,—just as when he used to try to express his confused thoughts. With all his credulity and simplicity, his captain now considered his humble mate his superior. In his own way Toni had his ideal: he was concerned with something besides his own selfishness. He wished for other men what he considered good for himself, and he defended his convictions with the mystical enthusiasm of all those historic personages who have tried to impose a belief;— with the faith of the warriors of the Cross and those of the Prophet, with the tenacity of the Inquisition and of the Jacobins.

He, a man of reason, had only known how to ridicule the generous and disinterested enthusiasms of other men, detecting at once their weak points and lack of adaptation to the reality of the moment. . . . What right had he to laugh at his mate who was a believer, dreaming, with the pure-mindedness of a child, of a free and happy humanity? . . . Aside from his stupid jeers, what could he oppose to that faith? . . .

Life began to appear to him under a new light, as something serious and mysterious that was exacting a bridge toll, a tribute of courage from all the beings who pass over it, leaving the cradle behind them and having the grave as a final resting-place.

It did not matter at all that their ideals might appear false. Where is the truth, the only and genuine truth? . . . Who is there that can demonstrate that he exists, and is not an illusion? . . .

The necessary thing was to believe in something, to have hope. The multitudes had never been touched by impulses of argument and criticism. They had only gone forward when some one had caused hopes and hallucinations to be born in their souls. Philosophers might vainly seek the truth by the light of logic, but the rest of mankind would always prefer the chimerical ideals that become transformed into powerful motives of action.

All religions were becoming beautifully less upon being subjected to cold examination. Yet, nevertheless, they were producing saints and martyrs, true super-men of morality. All revolutions had proved imperfect and ineffectual when submitted to scientific revision. Yet, nothwithstanding, they had brought forth the greatest individual heroes, the most astonishing collective movements of history.

"To believe! . . . To dream!" a mysterious voice kept chanting in his brain. "To have an ideal! . . ."

He did not fancy living, like the mummies of the great Pharaohs, in a luxurious tomb, anointed with perfume and surrounded with everything necessary for nourishment and sleep. To be born, to grow up, to reproduce oneself was not enough to form a history:—all the animals do the same. Man ought to add something more which he alone possesses,—the faculty of framing a future. . . . To dream! To the heritage of idealism left by our forebears should be added a new ideal, or the power of bringing it about.

Ferragut realized that in normal times, he would have

gone to his death just as he had lived, continuing a monotonous and uniform existence. Now the violent changes around him were resuscitating the dormant personalities which we all carry within us as souvenirs of our ancestors, revolving around a central and keen personality the only one that has existed until then.

The world was in a state of war. The men of Middle Europe were clashing with the other half on the battlefields. Both sides had a mystic ideal, affirming it with violence and slaughter just as the multitudes have always done when moved by religious or revolutionary certainty accepted as the only truth. . . .

But the sailor recognized a profound difference in the two masses struggling at the present day. One was placing its ideal in the past, wishing to rejuvenate the sovereignty of Force, the divinity of war, and adapt it to actual life. The other throng was preparing for the future, dreaming of a world of free democracy, of nations at peace, tolerant and without jealousy.

Upon adjusting himself to this new atmosphere, Ferragut began to feel within him ideas and aspirations that were, perhaps, an ancestral legacy. He fancied he could hear his uncle, the *Triton,* describing the impact of the men of the North upon the men of the South when trying to make themselves masters of the blue mantle of Amphitrite. He was a Mediterranean, but just because the country in which he had been born happened to be uninterested in the fate of the world, he was not going to remain indifferent.

He ought to continue just where he was. Whatever Toni had told him of Latinism and Mediterranean civilization, he now accepted as great truths. Perhaps they might not be exact when examined in the light of pure reason, but they were worth as much as the assurances of the others.

He was going to continue his life of navigation with
new enthusiasm. He had faith, the ideals, the illusions
that heroes are made of. While the war lasted he
would assist in his own way, acting as an auxiliary to
those who were fighting, transporting all that was
necessary to the struggle. He began to look with greater
respect upon the sailors obedient to his orders, simple
folk who had given their blood without fine phrases and
without arguments.

When peace should come he would not, therefore,
retire from the sea. There would still be much to be
done. Then would begin the commercial war, the sharp
rivalry to conquer the markets of the younger nations
of America. Audacious and enormous plans were outlining themselves in his brain. In this war he might
perhaps become a leader. He dreamed of the creation
of a fleet of steamers that might reach even to the coast
of the Pacific; he wished to contribute his means to the
victorious re-birth of the race which had discovered
the greater part of the planet.

His new faith made him more friendly with the ship's
cook, feeling the attraction of his invincible illusions.
From time to time he would amuse himself consulting
the old fellow as to the future fate of the steamer; he
wished to know if the submarines were causing him any
fear.

"There's nothing to worry about," affirmed Caragol.
"We have good protectors. Whoever presents himself
before us is lost."

And he showed his captain the religious engravings and
postal cards which he had tacked on the walls of the
galley.

One morning Ferragut received his sailing orders.
For the moment they were going to Gibraltar, to pick up
the cargo of a steamer that had not been able to continue

its voyage.   From the strait they might turn their course to Salonica once more.

The captain of the *Mare Nostrum* had never undertaken a journey with so much joy.   He believed that he was going to leave on land forever the recollection of that executed woman whose corpse he was seeing so many nights in his dreams.   From all the past, the only thing that he wished to transplant to his new existence was the image of his son.   Henceforth he was going to live, concentrating all his enthusiasm and ideals on the mission which he had imposed on himself.

He took the boat directly from Marseilles to the Cape of San Antonio far from the coast, keeping to the mid-Mediterranean, without passing the Gulf of Lyons.   One twilight evening the crew saw some bluish mountains in the hazy distance,—the island of Mallorca.   During the night the lighthouses of Ibiza and Formentera slipped past the dark horizon.   When the sun arose a vertical spot of rose color like a tongue of flame, appeared above the sea line.   It was the high mountain of Mongó, the Ferrarian promontory of the ancients.   At the foot of its abrupt steeps was the village of Ulysses' grandparents, the house in which he had passed the best part of his childhood.   Thus it must have looked in the distance to the Greeks of Massalia, exploring the desert Mediterranean in ships which were leaping the foam like wooden horses.

All the rest of the day, the *Mare Nostrum* sailed very close to the shore.   The captain knew this sea as though it were a lake on his own property.   He took the steamer through shallow depths, seeing the reefs so near to the surface that it appeared almost a miracle that the boat did not crash upon them.   Sometimes the space between the keel and the sunken rocks was hardly two yards wide.   Then the gilded water would take on a dark tone and the steamer would continue its advance over the greater depths.

Along the shore, the autumn sun was reddening the yellowing mountains, now dry and fragrant, covered with pasturage of strong odor which could be smelt at great distances. In all the windings of the coast,—little coves, beds of dry torrents or gorges between two peaks—were visible white groups of hamlets.

Ferragut contemplated carefully the native land of his grandparents. Toni must be there now: perhaps from the door of his dwelling he was seeing them pass by; perhaps he was recognizing the ship with surprise and emotion.

A French official, motionless near Ulysses on the bridge, was admiring the beauty of the day and the sea. Not a single cloud was in the sky. All was blue above and below, with no variation except where the bands of foam were combing themselves on the jutting points of the coast, and the restless gold of the sunlight was forming a broad roadway over the waters. A flock of dolphins frisked around the boat like a cortege of oceanic divinities.

"If the sea were always like this!" exclaimed the captain, "what delight to be a sailor!"

The crew could see the people on land running together and forming groups, attracted by the novelty of a steamer that was passing within reach of their voice. On each of the jutting points of the shore was a low and ruddy tower,—last vestige of the thousand-year war of the Mediterranean. Accustomed to the rugged shores of the ocean and its eternal surf, the Breton sailors were marveling at this easy navigation, almost touching the coast whose inhabitants looked like a swarm of bees. Had the boat been directed by another captain, so close a journey would have resulted most disastrously: but

Ferragut was laughing, throwing out gloomy hints to the officers who were on the bridge, merely to accentuate his professional confidence. He pointed out the rocks hidden in the deeps. Here an Italian liner that was going to Buenos Ayres had been lost. . . . A little further on, a swift four-masted sailboat had run aground, losing its cargo. . . . He could tell by the fraction of an inch the amount of water permissible between the treacherous rocks and the keel of his boat.

He usually sought the roughest waters by preference, but they were in the danger-zone of the Mediterranean where the German submarines were lying in wait for the French and English convoys navigating in the shelter of the Spanish coast. The obstacles of the submerged coast were for him now the best defense against invisible attacks.

Behind him, the Ferrarian promontory was growing more and more shadowy, becoming a mere blur on the horizon. By nightfall the *Mare Nostrum* was in front of Cape Palos and he had to sail in the outer waters in order to double it, leaving Cartagena in the distance. From there, he turned his course to the southwest, to the cape where the Mediterranean was beginning to grow narrow, forming the funnel of the strait. Soon they would pass before Almeria and Malaga, reaching Gibraltar the following day.

"Here is where the enemy is oftentimes waiting," said Ferragut to one of the officers. "If we have no bad luck before night, we shall have safely concluded our voyage."

The boat had withdrawn from the shore route, and it was no longer possible to distinguish the lower coast. Only from the prow could be seen the jutting hump of the cape, rising up like an island.

Caragol appeared with a tray on which were smoking two cups of coffee. He would not yield to any cabin-boy the honor of serving the captain when on the bridge.

"Well, what do you think of the trip?" asked Ferragut gayly, before drinking. "Shall we arrive in good condition? . . ."

The cook made as scornful a gesture as though the Germans could see him.

"Nothing will befall us; I am sure of that. . . . We have One who is watching over us, and . . ."

He was suddenly interrupted in his affirmations. The tray leaped from his hands and he went staggering about like a drunken man, even banging his abdomen against the balustrade of the bridge. *"Cristo del Grao! . . ."*

The cup that Ferragut was carrying to his mouth fell with a crash, and the French officer, seated on a bench, was almost thrown on his knees. The helmsman had to clutch the wheel with a jerk of surprise and terror.

The entire ship trembled from keel to masthead, from quarter-deck to forecastle, with a deadly shuddering as though invisible claws had just checked it at full speed.

The captain tried to account for this accident. "We must be aground," he said to himself, "a reef that I did not know, a shoal not marked on the charts. . . ."

But a second had not passed before something else was added to the first shock, refuting Ferragut's suppositions. The blue and luminous air was rent with the thud of a thunderclap. Near the prow, appeared a column of smoke, of expanding gases of yellowish and fulminating steam and, coming up through its center in the form of a fan, a spout of black objects, broken wood, bits of metallic plates and flaming ropes turning to ashes.

Ulysses was no longer in doubt. They must have just been struck by a torpedo. His anxious look scanned the waters.

"There! . . . There!" he said, pointing with his hand.

His keen seaman's eyes had just discovered the light outline of a periscope that nobody else was able to see.

He ran down from the bridge or rather he slid down the midship ladder, running toward the stern.

"There! . . . There!"

The three gunners were near the cannon, calm and phlegmatic, putting a hand to their eyes, in order to see better the almost invisible speck which the captain was pointing out.

None of them noticed the slant that the deck was slowly beginning to take. They thrust the first projectile into the breech of the cannon while the gunner made an effort to distinguish that small black cane hardly perceptible among the tossing waves.

Another shock as rude as the first one! Everything groaned with a dying shudder. The plates were trembling and falling apart, losing the cohesion that had made of them one single piece. The screws and rivets sprang out, moved by the general shaking-up. A second crater had opened in the middle of the ship, this time bearing in its fan-shaped explosion the limbs of human beings.

The captain saw that further resistance was useless. His feet warned him of the cataclysm that was developing beneath them—the liquid water-spout invading with a foamy bellowing the space between keel and deck, destroying the metal screens, knocking down the bulkheads, upsetting every object, dragging them forth with all the violence of an inundation, with the ramming force of a breaking dyke. The hold was rapidly becoming converted into a watery and leaden coffin fast going to the bottom.

The aft gun hurled its first shot. To Ferragut its report seemed mere irony. No one knew as he did the ship's desperate condition.

"To the life boats!" he shouted. "Every one to the boats!"

The steamer was tipping up in an alarming way as the men calmly obeyed his orders without losing their self-control.

A desperate vibration was jarring the deck. It was the engines that were sending out death-rattles at the same time that a torrent of steam as thick as ink was pouring from the smokestack. The firemen were coming up to the light with eyes swollen with the terror stamping their blackened faces. The inundation had begun to invade their dominions, breaking their steel compartments.

"To the boats! . . . Lower the life boats!"

The captain repeated his shouts of command, anxious to see the crew embark, without thinking for one moment of his own safety.

It never even occurred to him that his fate might be different from that of his ship. Besides, hidden in the sea, was the enemy who would soon break the surface to survey its handiwork. . . . Perhaps they might hunt for Captain Ferragut among the boatloads of survivors, wishing to bear him off as their triumphant booty. . . . No, he would far rather give up his life! . . .

The seamen had unfastened the life boats and were beginning to lower them, when something brutal suddenly occurred with the annihilating rapidity of a cataclysm of Nature.

There sounded a great explosion as though the world had gone to pieces, and Ferragut felt the floor vanishing from beneath his feet. He looked around him. The prow no longer existed; it had disappeared under the water, and a bellowing wave was rolling over the deck crushing everything beneath its roller of foam. On the other hand, the poop was climbing higher and higher, becoming almost vertical. It was soon a cliff, a mountain steep, on whose peak the white flagstaff was sticking up like a weather-vane.

In order not to fall he had to grasp a rope, a bit of wood, any fixed object. But the effort was useless. He felt himself dragged down, overturned, lashed about in a moaning and whirling darkness. A deadly chill paralyzed his limbs. His closed eyes saw a red heaven, a sky of blood with black stars. His ear drums were buzzing with a roaring *glu-glu,* while his body was turning somersaults through the darkness. His confused brain imagined that an infinitely deep hole had opened in the depths of the sea, that all the waters of the ocean were passing through it, forming a gigantic vortex, and that he was swirling in the center of this revolving tempest.

"I am going to die! . . . I am already dead!" said his thoughts.

And in spite of the fact that he was resigned to death, he moved his legs desperately, wishing to bring himself up to the yielding, treacherous surface. Instead of continuing to descend, he noticed that he was going up, and in a little while he was able to open his eyes and to breathe, judging from the atmospheric contact that he had reached the top.

He was not sure of the length of time he had passed in the abyss,—surely not more than a few minutes, since his breathing capacity as a swimmer could not exceed that limit. . . . He, therefore, experienced great astonishment upon discovering the tremendous changes which had taken place in so short a parenthesis.

He thought it was already night. Perhaps in the upper strata of the atmosphere were still shining the last rays of the sun, but at the water's level, there was no more than a twilight gray, like the dim glimmer of a cellar.

The almost even surface seen a few minutes before from the height of the bridge was now moved by broad swells that plunged him in momentary darkness. Each one of these appeared a hillock interposed before his eyes, leaving free only a few yards of space. When he was raised upon their crests he could take in with rapid vision the solitary sea that lacked the gallant mass of the ship, astir with dark objects. These objects were slipping inertly by or moving along, waving pairs of black antennæ. Perhaps they were imploring help, but the wet desert was absorbing the most furious cries, converting them into distant bleating.

Of the *Mare Nostrum* there was no longer visible either the mouth of the smokestack nor the point of a mast; the abyss had swallowed it all. . . . Ferragut began to doubt if his ship had ever really existed.

He swam toward a plank that came floating near, resting his arms upon it. He used to be able to remain entire hours in the sea, when naked and within sight of the coast, with the assurance of returning to *terra firma* whenever he might wish. . . . But now he had to keep himself up, completely dressed; his shoes were tugging at him with a constantly increasing force as though made of iron . . . and water on all sides! Not a boat on the horizon that could come to his aid! . . . The wireless operator, surprised by the swiftness of the catastrophe, had not been able to send out the S. O. S.

He also had to defend himself from the débris of the shipwreck. After having grasped the raft as his last means of salvation, he had to avoid the floating casks, rolling toward him on the swelling billows, which might send him to the bottom with one of their blows.

Suddenly there loomed up between two waves a species of blind monster that was agitating the waters furiously with the strokes of its swimming. Upon coming close to it, he saw that it was a man; as it drifted away, he recognized Uncle Caragol.

He was swimming like a drunken man with a super-human force which made half of his body come out of the water at each stroke. He was looking before him as though he could see, as if he had a fixed destination, without hesitating a moment, yet going further out to sea when he imagined that he was heading toward the coast.

"*Padre San Vicente!*" he moaned. "*Cristo del Grao! . . .*"

In vain the captain shouted. The cook could not hear him, and continued swimming on with all the force of his faith, repeating his pious invocations between his noisy snortings.

A cask climbed the crest of a wave, rolling down on the opposite side. The head of the blind swimmer came in its way. . . . A thudding crash. "*Padre San Vicente! . . .*" And Caragol disappeared with bleeding head and a mouth full of salt.

Ferragut did not wish to imitate that kind of swimming. The land was very far off for a man's arms; it would be impossible to reach it. Not a single one of the ship's boats had remained afloat. . . . His only hope, a remote and whimsical one, was that some vessel might discover the shipwrecked men and save them.

In a little while this hope was almost realized. From the crest of a wave he could see a black bark, long and low, without smokestack or mast, that was nosing slowly among the débris. He recognized a subma-rine. The dark silhouettes of several men were so plainly visible that he believed he heard them shout-ing,—

"Ferragut! . . . Where is Captain Ferragut? . . ."

"Ah, no! . . . Better to die!"

And he clung to his raft, hanging his head as though drowning. Then as night closed down upon him he heard still other shouts, but these were cries of help, cries of anguish, cries of death. The rescuers were searching for him only, leaving the others to their fate.

He lost all notion of time. An agonizing cold was paralyzing his entire frame. His stiffened and swollen hands were loosening from the raft and grasping it again only by a supreme effort of his will.

The other shipwrecked men had taken the precaution to put on their life preservers when the ship began to sink. Thanks to this apparatus, their death agony was going to be prolonged a few hours more. Perhaps if they could hold out until daybreak, they might be discovered by some boat! But he! . . .

Suddenly he remembered the *Triton*. . . . His uncle also had died in the sea; all the most vigorous members of the family had finally perished in its bosom. For centuries and centuries it had been the tomb of the Ferraguts; with good reason they had called it *"mare nostrum."*

He fancied that the currents might possibly have dragged his uncle's dead body from the other promontory to the place over which he was floating. Perhaps he might be now beneath his feet. . . . An irresistible force was pulling at them; his paralyzed hands loosened their hold on the wood.

"Uncle! . . . Uncle!"

In his thoughts he was shrieking to his relative with the timorous plaint of the little fellow taking his first swimming lesson. But his agonized hands again encountered the cold and weak support of the raft instead of that island of hard muscles crowned with a hairy and smiling face.

He continued his tenacious floating, struggling against

the drowsiness that was urging him to relax from his drifting support and let himself go to the bottom, to sleep . . . to sleep forever! His shoes and clothing were continuing to pull and tug with even greater force. They became an undulating shroud, growing heavier and heavier, surging and dragging down and down to the uttermost depths. His desperation made him raise his eyes and look at the stars. . . . So high! . . . Only to be able to grasp one of them, as his hands were now clutching the wood! . . .

At the same time he made instinctively a movement of repulsion. His head had sunk in the water without his being conscious of it. A bitter liquid was beginning to filter through his mouth. . . .

He made a mighty effort to keep himself in a vertical position, looking again at the sky, still black as ink, and all the stars as red as drops of blood.

Suddenly he felt a certain consciousness that he was not alone, and he closed his eyes. . . . Yes, somebody was near him. It was a woman! . . .

It was a woman white as the clouds, white as the sail, white as the foam. Her sea-green tresses were adorned with pearls and phosphorescent corals; her proud smile was that of a goddess, in keeping with the majesty of her diadem.

She stretched her pearly arms around him, pressing him close against her life-giving and eternally virginal bosom. A dense and greenish atmosphere was giving her whiteness a reflection like that of the light of the caves of the sea. . . .

Her pale mouth then pressed against the sailor's, making him feel as though all the light of this white apparition had liquefied and was passing into his body by means of her impelling kiss.

He could no longer see, he could no longer speak.

His eyes had closed, never to open again; a bitter river of salt was flowing down his throat.

Nevertheless he continued looking at her,—more luminous, pressed closer and closer,—with a sad expression of love in his glassy eyes. . . . And thus he went down and down the infinite levels of the abyss, inert, and without volition, while a voice within him was crying, as though just recognizing her:

"Amphitrite! . . . Amphitrite!"

THE END

3300